A CONVENIENT HUSBAND

Bride Train 4

Reece Butler

MENAGE EVERLASTING

Siren Publishing, Inc.
www.SirenPublishing.com

A SIREN PUBLISHING BOOK
IMPRINT: Ménage Everlasting

A CONVENIENT HUSBAND
Copyright © 2011 by Reece Butler

ISBN-10: 1-61926-105-7
ISBN-13: 978-1-61926-105-1

First Printing: October 2011

Cover design by Les Byerley
All art and logo copyright © 2011 by Siren Publishing, Inc.

Printed in the U.S.A.

PUBLISHER
Siren Publishing, Inc.
www.SirenPublishing.com

DEDICATION

As always, this is for the three men in my life: Paul, Andy, and David.

I'd also like to thank the wonderful people I met in Montana in June of 2011 while researching the realities of ranch life. Thank you for welcoming me into your homes and lives, and for patiently showing me how to ride, rope, brand, shovel, feed, irrigate, drive an ATV and tractor, and dance the two-step and jitterbug.

A CONVENIENT HUSBAND

Bride Train 4

REECE BUTLER
Copyright © 2011

Chapter One

Philadelphia train station, September, 1871

Benjamin Elliott raced toward the Bride Train about to pull out of the station. He grabbed a handrail, set his foot on the step and hauled himself up between the first and second carriages. He winced as the train's shrill whistle damn near deafened him. The engine puffed a couple of times, and then the wheels began to move.

Finally, he was on his way home. Not back to The MacDougal's ranch in Texas, but to Montana Territory and Tanner's Ford.

He stood between the carriages as the train picked up speed, leaving the crowded, noisy city behind. The track suddenly curved, carriages rattling as they followed the engine. A blast of smoke, thick with ash, hit him. Coughing, he pushed open the door to the second carriage and grabbed an empty seat. All the men looked up but quickly turned away.

"Sorry, boys, but I'm not one of the brides."

He set his carpetbag next to him on the seat. It contained necessities for the journey, including the book he'd gotten caught up in, making him almost miss the train. When the door behind him rattled open, every man turned to look once more. Ben turned as well, but it was only a railroad official in a black uniform.

"Don't none of you be coming through this door," said the official with a scowl. "The first carriage is for ladies only. Now, haul out your tickets."

"Where's the dining car, and when is it open?" asked a portly man in a well-cut black suit. Diamonds glittered from a couple of his fingers. Ben figured him for a banker or gambler. They were the same in his mind, both eager to take the earnings of honest folk.

"Diner will be open for breakfast in the morning. It's two carriages back."

Ben's stomach grumbled. Getting lost in his book meant he hadn't had time to eat supper before boarding. It wasn't the first time he'd missed a meal, and it sure wouldn't be the last. Going hungry for the night would make breakfast all the more enjoyable.

More enjoyable would be watching the brides-to-be walk through the carriage every time they wished to eat. Ben, along with every other man, would get a good look at the possibilities. He wasn't looking for a wife for himself, but for his twin brother, Ranger.

Few decent women could be found in the Texas wilderness where the younger Elliotts had lived with Finan MacDougal. The situation wasn't much better in Montana Territory, where the rest of the Elliotts lived.

Before Ben left Texas for Virginia to attend law school, he and Ranger had made a solemn vow. If Ranger found a ranch in Montana Territory near their brothers, Ben would bring Ranger a wife.

When their sister, Jessie, followed Ben to Virginia, she brought the news that Ranger had purchased a ranch. It was located in a valley west of Tanner's Ford, next to their older brothers' ranch.

Jessie also passed on Ranger's extensive requirements for a wife.

Ben always kept his promises. Ranger found the ranch, so it was up to him to provide the wife. Unfortunately, he'd neglected to start his search before leaving Virginia. When he heard a Bride Train was leaving from Philadelphia, he immediately booked a ticket.

Surely one of the ladies waving from the windows of the Bridal carriage would meet Ranger's requirements. Though he was a lawyer and part owner of a ranch, Ben knew no dew-eyed bride would want him. Ranger, with all his faults, could give a wife something Ben could never provide.

* * * *

"You can't leave for breakfast until the rest of the ladies are ready," insisted the railroad official. Puffing out his chest like a pigeon, he blocked the carriage door.

The sun was up and Florence Peabody was hungry. She'd not experienced an empty stomach in years. When she took over the running of his household, Father could no longer send her to bed without her supper for speaking back to him.

She'd given the basket of food, packed by the family's cook, to the children for supper the night before. They came first now, and she would gladly go without. She just wasn't used to doing so yet.

Her children were so slight she expected they'd gone without many meals in their short lives. That was one of the reasons she agreed to take them as her own. The most important reason was that their mother begged her to save them as she was dying, and there was no one else to care for them. Florence had put on the woman's wedding ring and changed her name from Miss Peabody, spinster, to Mrs. Peabody, widow.

Only after Emma and Johnny fell into an exhausted sleep did the reality of her situation hit her. Florence hadn't worried much about travelling on her own, as the Bride Train took care of its brides. But her status as widow and mother, rather than eager bride-to-be, might change things.

Her plan was to find a dear school friend who lived southwest of Virginia City, Montana Territory. However, Florence only knew Elizabeth's maiden name, as her brother said he misplaced the letter stating his sister's new name and location. It was his excuse for not sending the money due to her on her marriage.

But that worry could wait until they reached Virginia City. Right now she had more pressing issues, such as two hungry children. At five inches over five feet plus her sturdy shoes, she was taller than most women. She didn't tower over any man, but that didn't stop her from behaving as if she did.

"It will be hours before those simpering girls are primped enough to be seen in public," said Florence. She stared down her nose at the official as if he was a fishmonger trying to sell something three days old. "My children and I wish to eat now. Stand aside."

"I'm sorry, ma'am, I can't put you in harm's way. There may be some rough men in the next few carriages. All the brides must stay together."

"We're widows, not blushing virgins," groused Mary Douglas. A buxom woman with a strong get-out-of-my-way attitude, Mary had three children between six and ten. "Mrs. Peabody and I have five children between us. No man would dare bother us."

Florence squared her shoulders and stepped forward, crowding her bosom against polished silver buttons. The official harrumphed, but opened the door and stood aside.

"You go first, Mary," said Florence. "Your children are bigger and can move more quickly."

Mary sailed past, following her chattering children. Florence had never set foot on a train before, much less walked between rattling carriages. She'd have to step between them with the train swaying. Then she must get herself and both children across the gap and into the next carriage before one of them fell under the rails.

She straightened her trembling spine. Since accepting Emma and Johnny into her care the day before and becoming an instant widow, she'd done many new things. Not all of them were pleasant, but she was a Peabody. Never would she shy from a disagreeable, but necessary, task.

Florence took a calming breath and opened the sliding door. She shivered as the roar of the wheels blasted her. Pressing against the open door for balance, she encouraged five-year-old Emma through first. Johnny, almost four, followed. She slid the door to the second carriage open, pushed the children forward and scuttled through. Just as the door closed behind her, the train went into a curve. The sudden jerking tossed her sideways.

She flailed her arms, hitting someone in the process. That someone grabbed her around her waist and pulled. Instead of the filthy floor, she landed in his lap.

"You all right, ma'am?"

The deep voice resonated through her chest. She looked up and found herself gazing into laughing hazel eyes. The color, tinted with a hint of green, resembled her great-aunt's prized Italian marble table. Medium brown hair tumbled over her rescuer's forehead. Someone had broken his nose at least once. His chin, below full lips, had a few thin scars to suggest he'd landed face-first on something hard. None of the men who'd scorned her the last few years had been damaged that way. Of course, they all avoided labor which might cause them effort or injury.

"You'd better stay on my lap until you get your breath back," the voice murmured in her ear.

Warm air tickled the hair that had escaped from the braids circling her head. Strong arms, one around her back and the other on her thigh, warmed her almost as much as his thighs under her bottom. She should get up, but she'd never felt her body tingle before. Of course, she'd never had a man's body touch her. Was this tingling what her well-married sister had taunted her about?

He chuckled. "I don't mind holding you for a few hours, but your children look hungry."

"My children?" She blinked up at him.

"A small girl and smaller boy are looking at you as if you are their mother."

"Oh! Emma and Johnny!" She scrambled off his lap. She knelt on one knee in front of them. "Are you hurt?"

They shook their head as they stared at the man behind her.

"Is that your fancy man?" whispered Emma.

"My what?"

"*Maman* had a fancy man," her new daughter continued. "He was very nice."

"I don't know what you mean, Emma." She'd vaguely noted the man who caught her was well dressed, though a bit scruffy. Not what she'd call fancy.

"She wants to know if I'm your protector," said the man quietly.

"Well, I suppose you are, since you protected me from falling on the floor."

She heard him choke at her answer. Emma nudged Johnny. Both of them turned to the man. They smiled in a practiced way. Emma curtsied and Johnny bowed.

"Are you going to feed us breakfast?" asked Emma. "We're very hungry."

"Emma," said Florence, her face heating at the girl's impolite question, "this gentleman isn't going to—"

"Yes, he is," replied the man. He looked at all three of them. "I'm Mr. Elliott, and I would be pleased to feed you breakfast. I missed supper last night, and I'm mighty hungry. May I escort you to the dining car?"

"My name is Emma. Shall I kiss you now?"

Florence, too stunned to speak, turned until she could see both the children and Mr. Elliott. Though she smiled prettily, Emma's chin trembled. Her free hand was curled into a white fist. When the man smiled gently and shook his head, Emma's shoulders dropped, and she let out a breath. She gave Johnny an encouraging nudge. Mr. Elliott looked at her solemnly, then at Johnny.

"I'm not going to touch you, or your brother, unless I'm helping you, like I did your mother when she slipped. I'm not that kind of man. I will protect you and your mother, but without payment. You don't have to pretend you like me." He winked, adding a kind smile. "I won't get mad if you're hungry and out of sorts. Now, shall I escort you to breakfast?"

"I can't ask you to—"

"You didn't ask, madam. I am on my way home after being away for too many years. I would very much enjoy the company of a pleasant woman and her children." He placed a hand over his heart. "My six brothers, sister, and many cousins would be horrified to think anyone would believe I would harm a woman or child."

Florence tried to think as he helped her to her feet with a hand under her elbow. They were in public, it was daylight, and as a widow, she no longer had a reputation to protect. She nodded agreement. His answering smile changed his face, making him appear a bit rakish.

"I am Florence Peabody. Mrs. Peabody. These are my children, Emma and Johnny."

"Pleased to meet you, Mrs. Peabody. Shall we dine and get better acquainted?"

Chapter Two

Ben watched the flustered woman settle her two children into seats by the window. Emma had long, golden-red hair. Johnny had the same features, but his hair was blond. They patiently looked out the window. He noted it as unusual, at least from what he remembered as a hungry boy eager for food.

Florence turned and waved at a woman with three children sitting at the other end of the car. She took the chair across from him before he could seat her. His suit coat covered his reaction to the bundle of womanhood which fate had tossed in his lap. He had little experience with women, though his cock was eager for more. Unfortunately, that was not likely to happen.

Ranger, his older twin brother, had lots of experience with women. The few times a year they made it to the saloon closest to the Texas ranch, Ranger could always convince a woman or two to return with them. The ladies were never disappointed.

Growing up on wild and lonely ranches, Ben had to learn to read both people and the land. Watching the land showed who had passed by and what animals were around, both to eat and to keep clear of. The last few years of legal training and experience had honed his ability to read people. It had also created a need to find out the answers to puzzling things.

This woman puzzled him. The children referred to her as 'Mother,' yet spoke of another woman using the French, '*Maman*.' From what he could tell, that woman kept company with men for payment. Mrs. Peabody, however, seemed to know nothing of that world.

While she wore a wedding ring, he doubted a husband had put it on her finger. The way she played with that ring intrigued him. Had she gained weight and it was tight? Or had she only recently put it on?

She didn't know much about children, including those she claimed as hers. Perhaps they'd had a nurse, but he doubted it. The lady spoke well and held herself erect as had the women Aunt Jessamine Bonham encouraged him to associate with. One big difference was this woman didn't simper or primp.

The hair wrapped around her head was missing a few pins. She had not taken the time to fix it before going to breakfast. Her dress was wrinkled, not surprising if she'd spent the night sharing a hard seat with two children. His legs were so long his knees touched hers. He noted the faint flush which rose to her cheeks. It was not the response of a well-bedded widow.

"Are you a sheriff? Can you put bad men in jail?"

Ben looked at Johnny, beside him. "No, I'm not a sheriff. I'm a lawyer. We lawyers work with sheriffs to put bad men in jail. Do you know someone who needs to be locked up?"

Johnny nodded solemnly.

"He's not here," whispered Emma to him. "*Maman* said we would be safe on the train."

"*Maman?*" Johnny looked eagerly around. Emma pressed her lips together and shook her head. Johnny turned to the window, his chin quivering.

There was a lot going on here that Ben didn't yet understand, but he would. He lifted his hand, and the waiter appeared to pour coffee. Florence was so desperate that she'd already put in her cream and sugar. After a quick stir she brought the cup to her lips.

"Oh, yes," she said, closing her eyes. The wrinkles on her brow smoothed out.

"Four complete breakfasts, please," he ordered. "And milk for the children."

Florence set her cup down and pushed it aside. The wrinkles were back.

"Excuse me, but it's a bit presumptuous of you to order breakfast for us."

"Presumptuous?" Anger made her eyes sparkle. She pressed her shoulders back. His eyes focused on the breasts which must lie behind the navy serge. An experienced woman would have realized where his thoughts were, but not this one.

"I intensely dislike men who think they know what I want, and do not bother to enquire."

"Then please, order what you would like."

She nodded as if having won the argument and opened her mouth to speak.

"It's a full breakfast, or nothing," said the waiter in a bored tone.

She shut her mouth. "In that case, I would like three breakfasts."

She glared as if it was his fault. The waiter rolled his eyes at Ben and walked away. Florence turned to the window. Ben sipped his black coffee, watching her. A smile played around her lips as she watched the children pointing things out to each other. They passed a farm with horses running across a field, tails streaming behind.

"I want to ride a horse," declared Johnny. He turned to Ben. "Have you got a horse?"

Both children perked up when Ben nodded. "We ride horses to take care of our cattle."

"Is there lots of people there?" asked Emma.

He shook his head. "Our ranch is in a valley west of town. There's so much land you can ride all day and never see another person. Then you come home and your whole family's there. So you have quiet during the day, and company in the evening. What about you?" he said to Florence. "Are you meeting your husband out west?"

"I"—she swallowed and looked down—"I'm a widow."

"I'm sorry for your loss. Was it recent?"

She blinked at him for a second as pink flooded her cheeks. Either she'd had servants so didn't need to care for the children previously, or she was no widow. She turned her head, eyes flicking down, then to the side. He figured she was thinking something up.

"Johnny was just a baby. But life must go on."

He knew how to hedge an answer. He figured she spoke truth, but only part of it.

"You looking to find a husband? We passed through two carriages of men to get to the dining room. One of them might suit. Or will you get off the train, talk for twenty minutes, and then stand in front of the preacher?"

She stabbed him with a glare. "Absolutely not! We will travel to Montana Territory where I have a school friend. I will take my time and ensure any prospects would serve as a good husband and father. My children come first, Mr. Elliott. Only if they are satisfied with my choice, will I marry." She blinked. "Again."

Ben relaxed against the seat. Since they were both traveling to the end of the line, he'd have at least a week to find out more about her. So far, he liked her. Perhaps she could advise him as to which of the other women would best suit Ranger as a wife. It would give him a reason to spend time with her. After all, if neither of them was looking to marry, they could relax and enjoy the journey. He would enjoy a chance to engage wits with a pretty woman.

"Are you travelling to meet your wife?"

The sudden pink on Florence's cheeks suggested she'd not planned to blurt out the question. The color deepened when he winked. While legal discussions and debates were fascinating, talking with this woman was far more interesting. He wanted to enjoy her company for a few days. Though she said she wasn't looking for a husband, it was a topic he could devil her about.

"I don't have a wife." He leaned forward and winked. "Are you making me an offer, Mrs. Peabody?"

Chapter Three

"Mr. Elliott!"

Though Mrs. Peabody might think that icy glare would chastise him, the blush that followed encouraged him further.

"No? Then why don't you tell me what you're looking for in a husband." He issued the challenge, figuring she would rise to the bait. It took a couple of minutes of fussing, but she finally met his eyes.

"I wish to find a kind man who appreciates an intelligent woman who knows her own mind and expresses it. He will choose to have me by his side, not trailing behind. He will create rather than just talk, but will enjoy reading and discussion for its own sake. He will raise all our children with love and caring. He will show dignity and respect to us all. And he will always keep his promises."

From the way she pursed her lips and pushed out her chin, she expected him to balk. But he could understand what she meant. Neither his mother nor his sister accepted what Eastern society decreed was acceptable for women. It would frustrate him beyond measure to have a brain, yet be forced to pretend otherwise. Ma raised all six sons to treat women as equals if they deserved it. This woman deserved his respect.

He smiled to show his understanding and looked at her. *Really* looked at her.

Her nose and chin were strong for a woman, but they matched her character. A few freckles dotted her cheeks from the summer sun. That alone was unusual, and showed she did not follow the dictates of fashion. Her dress was sensible—plain, dark, and somewhat worn.

His eyes traveled down as far as the table, and then back up. He'd have to walk behind to escort her back to her carriage so he could see her backside again. It certainly felt full during the few moments she sat on his lap. Unfortunately, she quickly caught her breath after her near tumble and his rescue, and returned to her feet. She had a waist wider than his hands could span, and a good set of breasts. He'd had a wild idea to raise his hand and caress them while she sat on him, startled. He'd refrained, of course.

"And if you don't find such a man? What will you do?"

She gave a slight moue and ladylike shrug. "I will be content to live alone with my children, near my friend. Elizabeth lives southwest of Virginia City. I believe it is somewhat smaller than Philadelphia, but it will suit us very well." Though she faced him, she didn't look him in the eyes.

That was just as well, as her destination took him by surprise. His ranch was west of Tanner's Ford, a day's ride from gold-mad Bannack City. That was a bustling hellhole southwest of Virginia City, which was an even bigger den of golden depravity. It meant they would be traveling to the end of the line together. He missed twisting his sister's tail. Would Mrs. Peabody react the same as Jessie?

"Don't take too long looking, ma'am. Winter's coming, and you don't want to be stuck alone in a chilly hotel for months when you could be cozying up to a warm husband."

She gasped and huffed, looking around to see if anyone had heard. But her color was high and her nostrils flared. He leaned forward, forearms on the white tablecloth. He felt like Patrick, pulling another of his practical jokes. No, he was more like Ranger. The man loved flirting with a pretty woman just to see her blush. He'd never enjoyed speaking with the women Aunt Jessamine thought acceptable. Poking fun at the woman across from him was quite another matter. He loved the way she fought to appear proper when her body betrayed her with blushes.

"Things are different in the West, Mrs. Peabody. We don't have time to shilly-shally. We say what we mean, and then take action. I may not want a wife, but there are thousands of men out there who do." He looked toward her children, then back. "You wish to find a husband and father for these children. Many men would take them for their own, in order to have a wife to cook and clean. Of course, there are other, more enjoyable, benefits of marriage."

He winked, making her sputter. He figured it was more likely due to his comment about the benefits, rather than the daytime wifely duties. Yet another reason to suspect her widowhood.

"Mrs. Peabody, many couples take less time to make a decision about marriage than the few minutes we've had this morning. If they can tolerate each other, they marry for the convenience." He noticed her color also rose with her temper. When she pursed her lips, he waited for a blast.

"Marriage is a holy sacrament, binding until death."

She pursed her lips like the back end of a chicken. What would those lips look like snug around his cock?

"Mr. Elliott, I am looking for a suitable partner for myself and my children. I want more than a convenient husband!"

She busied herself with the children until her color faded. When she looked back at him, he saw a steely determination he recognized in himself as well as all six of his siblings.

"Are you looking for a wife, Mr. Elliott?" She asked the question sweetly, but he was sure her rapier wit waited to stab him. He shrugged.

"Perhaps I will marry at some point in the future. You see, I'm a lawyer, and must travel to establish my practice. Since I wish to become a judge, I will need to cultivate support. That requires even more travel." He smiled at her, raising his hands in a what-can-I-do gesture. "I expect to be gone weeks, perhaps months, every year. While two of my brothers are also partners on the Bitterroot Ranch, and I have family nearby, I would not wish to leave my wife alone in bed so many nights."

"I see. Are your brothers married?"

She asked the question politely, as if enquiring about the weather. She looked him in the eye this time. The crisp blue of a summer afternoon's wide-open sky caught him. He bet there was more intelligence lurking behind those eyes than in half the men in his law study group. No wonder she wanted to take the Bride Train west. Outgoing, educated women would be shunned by most of the fluffed-up dandies he'd seen since leaving Texas. With over a hundred single men for every free woman in Montana Territory, she would have her pick of husbands.

The part of him that yearned for children yanked at his heart. But even marrying a woman with children, which would solve half his problem, still didn't stop the issue of having to leave her in a cold bed for a good part of the year. She was far too regal and opinionated to suit his twin. Even leaving her alone with Ranger for a few days might send his brother to the barn in order to sleep. Worse, it may send her to Virginia City to escape Ranger's growls.

"I understand my oldest brother, Trace, married the other year. I haven't heard of anyone else marrying. But I promised my next oldest brother, Ranger, that I would bring a bride home for him." He leaned forward. "Perhaps you would be so kind as to help me on my quest?"

She pulled back, eyes wide, and gave him a hard stare.

"Mr. Elliott, that would be highly irregular!"

"So is the idea of taking a group of unmarriageable women and sending them all the way across the country in order to make the men populating wild western towns settle down. But we're on that very train, are we not?"

More than her cheeks flushed. He winced when he realized what he'd said.

"Pardon me, madam. I did not mean to imply you were unmarriageable. But the West can provide many opportunities for women with the strength of character to shun the ridiculous ways of Eastern society, in order to forge their own lives, their way."

She looked at him for a moment as her flush faded.

"A lawyer and a poet, Mr. Elliott?"

This time it was he who felt the rush of heat rising from his collar at her touch of sarcasm.

"Not a poet, Mrs. Peabody," he said quietly. "A man with a dream."

Chapter Four

Florence Peabody also had a dream.

She wanted a husband who wished her guidance and would keep her by his side, not three steps behind with her mouth shut. She wanted more children to love. Emma and Johnny were given to her by their mother at the railroad station. With no other way of feeding her children, their mother had resorted to working in a brothel. She was terribly sick and knew what would happen to a pretty child on her death. She took them to the train station and begged Florence to raise them as her own. Of course, Florence agreed. She put the woman's wedding ring on her finger and began calling herself Mrs. Peabody, widow and mother.

Florence didn't know exactly what happened between a man and woman to create children. However, from what her older sister implied, there could be a lot of pleasure in their creation.

Actually, Charity did not imply anything about the marriage bed. She rubbed the fact of it into Florence's face. She laughed that Florence, the large, ugly bookworm, was wanted by no man. Charity insisted she'd never know what it felt like for a man to hold her close and do wonderful things which, eventually, produced children to love. Considering she'd never been kissed by a male, even by her father, Florence had little to judge by.

She smiled at the way the man across from her openly laughed at something the children said. His baritone chuckle rippled down her spine. If she ever got to the point where she had to find a husband, someone like Mr. Elliott might be acceptable. He'd shocked her to the bone by accepting her list of needs in a husband. He was handsome, a rancher who was also a lawyer, with family living nearby. She'd never known the joy of belonging to a loving family.

She didn't need, or particularly want, a husband. But for a short while on this journey into the wilderness, she would like a friend. One who may cause her to lose her temper, but at least she and the children would not be alone.

"What is your brother looking for in a wife, Mr. Elliott?"

He turned to her, still laughing. A jolt hit her in the breastbone. The men she'd met never laughed with such open abandon. His smile changed to something which might be embarrassment.

"If you are helping me find a wife, could we not call ourselves by our given names? We are not so stuffy in the West. Please, call me Ben."

She felt another flush of heat rise up her chest. She never let a man fluster her. Perhaps it was the lack of sleep which made him affect her so. "I am Florence."

He took her hand from the table, sandwiching it between his palms. "Pleased to meet you, Florence. You have wonderful children."

He said her name in a way she'd never heard it before, with an intensity of feeling that made her feel special. His touch sent an unfamiliar heat tingling through her body, from her hand to her heart and from there, all over.

"Thank you." She pulled her hand back. He released it reluctantly, causing another river of heat to flood through her veins.

"Ranger wants a wife who I expect is your exact opposite."

Small lines around the corners appeared when his smile reached those eyes. She finally understood that the phrase "her heart fluttered" was not something invented for the penny dreadful books she hid from everyone.

Thankfully, the waiter interrupted, bringing full plates and refilling coffee cups. She took the next few minutes to get the children settled. Only then did she begin to appease her hunger.

"And what is my exact opposite, Mr.—I mean—Ben?" She kept her eyes on her plate to more easily hide any reaction to what he might say.

"I have his list memorized. With the children present, I will use the phrase, 'unmarried lady,' but the word I mean has two syllables, begins with a 'v,' and ends with an 'n.' As a widow, you would not meet that qualification."

Her coffee cup rattled in its saucer as she hastily set it back down. His chuckle made her think of dark brown velvet. Seemingly simple, but luxurious against the skin.

"While I went to school in the east for the last four or so years, Ranger continued to work on a relative's ranch in Texas. He is my height, but has more muscle. He's a natural leader, with a need to be in charge. Therefore, he wishes a wife who will obey him without question or complaint. Since he had no opportunity for an education, he does not want her to know more than the basics. She must be a hard worker, a good cook, and a good breeder."

Florence choked on her egg. She dabbed her lips. "How unfortunate for the poor woman," she murmured.

"But the most important thing, according to Ranger, is that she enjoy the process which culminates in children."

She stifled a gasp. A quick check proved Emma and Johnny were far more interested in their breakfast than a conversation between adults.

"Do you mean, um, marital relations?"

"Very much so. Did you enjoy the process to create your son and daughter?"

Ben's hazel eyes seemed to grow when he whispered the last sentence. Sea-green seeped into the cognac-brown. His nostrils flared, and his lips curved up in a sensuous smile. The tingle in her breasts spread down her belly and settled in her lap. No, below her lap, in the place where her legs joined. She shifted on the seat, but the feeling only increased. Ben winced and resettled his long legs.

"This is not a suitable conversation to be held in front of children," she replied.

"Not when we are sharing a breakfast table, after you landed in my lap?"

"Mr. Elliott! I was escorting my children to the dining car when the train swerved. I appreciate you catching me so I did not fall on the floor, but—"

"But you enjoyed sitting there until I reminded you that two children watched with extreme interest. And then Emma asked if I was your fancy man." He winked. "Something tells me you are not aware what that means."

She looked at his neat, sober clothing. "You are not what I'd call 'fancy.' However, if you wore a red waistcoat with your black suit, the phrase may fit."

His laugh mocked her ignorance. She did not like the feeling. She bit back a retort and attacked her plate instead of the smiling man.

"It means a man who pays a woman to attend to him. In every way." He waggled his eyebrows at her as if he was a dastardly villain on the stage. "One would wonder why your daughter would know the phrase, yet you do not?"

"If one was a gentleman, he would keep his wonderings to himself!"

He threw back his head and laughed once more. Emma and Johnny stared, mouths open, as if they'd never seen such a thing. When he smiled at them, they hesitantly returned it. He turned to Florence. His eyes bored deep into her soul. They raised questions, begging for answers she was not sure she was ready to provide, even to herself.

"I would be more than pleased to show you what I mean, Mrs. Peabody."

Chapter Five

Ben enjoyed baiting the delicious woman. She blushed and fidgeted with her too-snug wedding ring as if she wished to remove it. The children didn't resemble her in any way. She must have taken them on, and was doing the best she could. Perhaps they were distant relatives, orphans whose parents had died in the war.

He expected she was a virgin who decided to call herself a widow for safety. She was unaware that some men considered widows, since they'd already been breached, as fair game. After all, how could she prove she'd been attacked? It was a man's word against a weak woman's, who everyone knew was easily swayed.

Ben knew differently. His sister, Jessie, had a stronger will than many of his fellow law students. She also had a temper to match and the physical strength to run a ranch. She needed them to survive. The man who'd taken them in at his parents' death was a harsh taskmaster. Finan MacDougal honestly believed that the punishments he meted out were for the benefit of the Clan. That way, only the strong survived. Ben came from a long line of survivors. His relative lack of physical strength would not stop him from ranching with his brothers.

Though he had little sexual experience, he could tell Florence Peabody, Miss or Mrs., was feeling just as hot under the collar as he was. Her red face, the way she shifted in her seat, and the nipples jutting against her sensible dark serge dress, also suggested she could be a woman of passion. Not with him, however.

He had to find a wife, but not for himself. If he returned to Tanner's Ford without a wife for Ranger, he would have broken his word to his twin. Identical at birth, with Ranger emerging just before

Ben, they were closer than the other twins, Simon and Jack, who merely looked like brothers.

He'd never broken a promise. But this was more than a simple promise, it was their future. There were few women to choose from west of the Missouri, and Ranger was a difficult man. Their faces might be the same, but their attitudes were not. Ranger had been beaten hard, and Ben knew it would have continued after he left for Virginia. Right from birth, Ranger had fought to be first. He had to be the best, the strongest, the hardiest.

Those traits made for a great rancher, but Ranger would need a strong woman to put up with him. Not that he'd ever hurt a woman or child. None of them would tolerate such a thing.

Someday, Florence may have a man raise the passion in her. He'd better be good at his job, though. Ben expected she didn't tolerate shoddy performance in anything. Given a chance, Ranger could handle her, sending her screaming into one orgasm after another.

Ranger would also make her scream outside the bedroom, but it would be in anger and frustration. Ben wasn't a wild lover. He preferred slow, sensuous cuddling. But he'd be easier to get along with the rest of the time. Unfortunately, it would be a long time, if ever, before he had the luxury of a wife.

"Since we have finished our breakfast, Mr. Elliott, perhaps you could escort us back to the Bride carriage? Even better, perhaps Mary is ready to leave."

She turned around in her seat to look at the laughing woman with three children at the far end of the car. They were only halfway through their meal. Florence smiled at her friend, but when she faced Ben, she frowned.

"Unfortunately, we must rely on you."

"Does your anger with me mean you won't help me find Ranger a wife? There must be dozens of eager women in the Bridal carriage. Perhaps one would suit my brother?"

"I could ask the ladies for you," said Emma, piping up. She smiled eagerly at him from across the table. "You wish to have a pretty lady who can laugh and make you jolly?"

"*Maman* used to laugh," whispered Johnny. His chin quivered and his eyes glistened, but he kept the tears from falling.

Florence glared at Ben and then turned a gentle smile on the children. "We shall all help Mr. Elliott find someone to suit his brother."

"If one of the women is interested," said Ben, "please tell her that, should he not suit, there are hundreds of other men desiring a wife. And if the marriage doesn't work out, divorce is quick in Virginia City. Often a woman is married again the day after she divorces."

He winced at Florence's calculating look. He might as well tell her about that now as she would discover that information at the end of their journey. The men who met the Bride Trains in Virginia City also went after married women, until they were put straight.

Ben regretted telling Florence what Ranger had demanded in a wife. He should have sugarcoated it, which would make it easier for her to sell the idea. But he'd sworn to uphold truth and the law.

"Emma," he said, "my brother, Ranger, is looking for a wife who loves children and is a good cook. We live on a big ranch in a protected valley a couple of days ride from where you're going. Only good men live in our valley. We've got horses, lots and lots of cows, with pigs, chickens, and goats. Everyone works hard, and no one goes hungry."

The two children looked at each other. Considering how thin they were, he didn't doubt they'd gone hungry many a time. He knew what it was like to try to sleep with your backbone cozied up to your belly.

"My older brother, Trace, is married with a baby son. He and another two brothers live on the ranch next to us. The ranch across the valley belongs to three of our cousins. They have a baby girl. Our youngest brother, Patrick, also lives with us. And our sister lives in the valley, as well."

"We will help as best as we can," continued Florence. "But we may not be successful in finding a husband for Mr. Elliott's brother. Many ladies do not wish to travel so far. Also, they prefer to meet their husband before making such an important decision."

Emma looked at Florence, obviously thinking hard. After a moment she turned to Ben and gave him the widest, most inviting smile he'd ever had from a female. Not the sort a small child should know existed. He gulped when he saw her eyes were a beautiful shade of violet. If her mother had those eyes and that golden-red hair, no wonder she attracted a fancy man.

"We like you, don't we, Johnny?" He jumped as if someone kicked his leg. "Do you like us?"

Ben nodded when she waited for a response. Her smile widened.

"Please marry our mother. Then we could live in your valley and be safe from all the bad men."

Florence choked. Ben looked at the beautiful pleading faces. Emma's smile had slipped, desperation taking its place.

"Emma, marriage is a very serious decision. Mr. Elliott has said he does not wish to marry. He is looking for a wife without children, to suit his brother." Florence quietly stammered the words, her face and neck almost as red as Emma's hair.

Emma's eager face crumpled. "You don't want us. Nobody does." She dropped her head, wrapping her arms around her stomach. Johnny looked at his sister and began to cry, too quietly for Ben's liking.

Chapter Six

Somehow, Florence got herself and her two devastated children out of the dining car. Ben tried to explain that he did, indeed, care for them. Emma's shoulders shook, though she made no sound. That was what broke Florence's heart. They knew how to be quiet and invisible. Emma had asked for the only thing she knew could make her world safe, and it was not to be.

Ben didn't know that Emma's fear was based on reality. He said nothing to Florence as he followed her. The children clung to him, one in each arm, all the way to the Bridal carriage. They hid their tear-stained faced against his coat as they passed through cars full of staring men. Her face still flaming, she went first, to open the doors between the carriages.

Of course, she couldn't hide Ben's presence from the other brides. He was allowed just far enough in the carriage to set the children down safely then was pushed away by their self-appointed guard. Mary, very concerned, ushered her children in as he left.

The young women, furious about Florence and Mary seeing potential husbands before they staked a claim, finally left for breakfast, twittering and complaining. She and Mary settled their children for naps. After the excitement of the train, and the full breakfast, Mary's three didn't object. Emma and Johnny clung to each other on their wooden seat. Florence rubbed their backs until they fell into an exhausted sleep.

"Dear me, tell me what all that was all about," said Mary once Florence had settled herself. "Such a handsome gentleman!" She put her hand on her chest and fluttered it, rolling her eyes as if about to faint. "He's far too young for me, but the children seem to like him very much."

"Yes, they do. A bit too much." Florence didn't mention they had to pry Johnny's hands from Ben's neck before the man could leave.

"What happened in the dining car? All of a sudden you jumped up and rushed out, with your man carrying the children."

"He's not my man—that's what they're upset about." Florence kept her eyes low as she tried to smooth the wrinkles out of her dress. "They begged him to marry me, so they could have a home and be safe."

"And you said yes?"

"Mary! I met the man when I fell in his lap on the way to breakfast." Mary smiled even wider. "Mr. Benjamin Elliott does not wish to marry. He took the Bride Train because he gave a solemn promise to his older brother to bring home a bride. Since he's also traveling all the way to Virginia City, he asked me if I could see if any of the other women would do." She rubbed her temples in small circles. "Even if he wished to marry, he wouldn't want an outspoken, opinionated woman such as myself."

"I don't know about that," replied Mary. "I faced him all during breakfast and saw how he looked at you." She held up a warning finger. "You could do a lot worse. Does he have any prospects?"

"He's a lawyer. He and two brothers are partners in a ranch. A married brother and a set of cousins also have ranches in the same valley, and there's a sister."

Mary's eyebrows went higher with each comment. "You'd be crazy to refuse him. Just think of the life you would have. A decent home, family…"

"He's looking for a wife for his brother, not himself. Ranger wants a"—she lowered her voice, disgust dripping from every word—"a virgin who enjoys the marriage bed, who has little education but is a good cook and, worst of all, obeys orders well and doesn't talk back."

"Gracious!" Mary covered her mouth to try to quiet her laughs. "I just met you yesterday, but I'd say that was about opposite to you. Except for the first part." Her merry eyes danced. "I think you have the passion to enjoy the attentions of a husband."

"Mary!"

"Don't look so shocked. Why do you think I want another husband? I could get by on my own, but having a warm man to hold you in the night, after a wonderful round of lovemaking, looking forward to another in the morning..." She sighed and rolled her eyes. "Why else would a woman want to marry, other than the reward of good bedding?" She looked over at her children. "And the children that come from such loving."

"I don't know how much older Ranger is than Ben. Perhaps you would suit?"

Mary shook her head. "No ranches for me, thank you. I want to live where I'll see different people every day. I want a respectable husband with a job. If it's not something I can help him with, then I want to be able to run a small shop out of our home." She winked. "If he asked, would you take him as a husband?"

Florence flushed at Mary catching her own thoughts. "He's kind to the children, he's well educated, with good manners, and—"

"He makes your breasts and the place between your legs tingle?"

Florence gasped. "How did you know?"

"You, my friend, are ripe for a husband. Maybe we can get this Ben to change his mind about marriage."

"And put up with his older brother and the cow-like wife he wants?" Florence shook her head. "Don't most of these places have small homes? I wouldn't be able to get away from the swine who doesn't like educated women."

"Hmm, there is that," mused Mary. She yawned and quickly covered her mouth. "That's for later. I am going to take this quiet time to have a nap."

Florence felt the fatigue suddenly hit her. "So shall I."

"Since I'm planning on staying at least a few days on this train, I'll have time to tell you all the tricks about enjoying life as a wife. Different ways to use a bed, a table, the wall, and then there's—"

"Mary!"

Mary's quiet snicker was soon followed by soft snores. In spite of her fatigue, Florence couldn't sleep. What did she think of Mr. Benjamin Elliott?

He had good manners, spoke well, loved his family and knew how to behave around children. He treated them with far more respect than her father ever did his daughters. Even when she was an adult and discussing important issues with him, Father always had a condescending attitude, as if surprised she could read, much less reason.

Benjamin even listened to the children without interrupting.

Then there was the way her body reacted to him. She shifted on the hard bench. What would it be like to have such a man touch her? She slept, dreaming of a high mountain meadow full of flowers and one handsome man.

The slam of the carriage door opening startled her awake. She blinked, heart pounding, and pulled herself upright as the chattering brides returned. Emma and Johnny both jolted awake at the noise and rushed to her, eyes wide and bodies trembling. She soothed them, wondering how long it would take before they felt safe. The Elliotts were unacceptable, but once they were at her friend Elizabeth's home, she was sure her friend's husband would show Emma that not all men were bad. Perhaps spending time with Benjamin would start the process. She could meet him to discuss her progress in finding Ranger a husband.

Mary rolled her eyes when the carriage exploded into multiple discussions about the men the young women had seen. They debated whether any of them were worth cultivating, who should receive the cut direct, and which men might purchase a meal for them without them having to do anything but smile and listen.

Expecting to be bored for hours, if not days, Florence had packed a game of checkers in her bag. The children were delighted. She was surprised at how quickly they learned the rules. They played quietly, with none of the outbursts and enthusiasm of Mary's children.

For dinner they ate from the leftovers in the basket she'd brought from home. They'd eaten Cook's fried chicken the previous night, but apples, bread, and cheese filled them after the full breakfast.

By the time the train's chugging slowed, suggesting they'd be coming to a stop to load water and fuel, she was more than ready for a walk. From the window, Florence saw eager men, hats in their hands, waiting their turn to help a lady off the train, in hopes of walking with her for a few minutes.

Florence gave a ladylike snort when she saw a preacher, complete with bible, patiently waiting on the far side of the platform. Should any of the brides wish to marry, they could have a wedding service immediately. She turned away from the window and guided her children toward the door. She went last, figuring she'd have to help Emma down and try to stop Johnny from jumping.

"I'll catch you if you wish to jump," said a familiar voice at her feet.

Johnny laughed and leaped from the top step. Benjamin caught him under the arms and turned, twirling him around and around before setting his feet on the platform. She'd not seen Johnny laugh before. She would speak kindly to the man for providing that touch of joy for her son.

"Would you like a turn?"

He held his arms out to Emma. She waited for Florence's nod before doing the same. In the rush to get off, Florence hadn't put Emma's bonnet on. Her long hair trailed behind her head in the afternoon light like a beacon. Hearing the girl's delighted laugh, Florence decided she'd put up with Mr. Elliott whenever he wanted to walk with them. He set Emma down, holding on to her elbow until she found her feet. Florence turned to back down the stairs. She held on with one hand and lifted her skirts with the other.

"I don't suppose I could convince you to try?"

She looked at him over her shoulder. "That sounds like a challenge."

"It is." His eyes dared her to try.

"I'm too heavy for you."

"Nonsense." He slid his arms around her waist, locking his fingers under her breasts.

"I don't think—"

"Good. You think too much."

He lifted her feet off the ground and turned. She shrieked when he spun, laughing at the same time. She had to close her eyes to stop the jumbled flashes. Finally, he slowed and let her feet touch the ground. She stumbled, and he caught her, chest to chin.

"You're beautiful when you laugh," he said.

She tried to catch her breath, but his eyes drew her in. He slowly lowered his head. She knew he was going to kiss her, but she couldn't move away. Couldn't breathe.

He brushed his lips across her cheek, humming something. She opened her mouth to speak, and that's when he moved. His lips covered hers, pressing them open. He was gentle, yet forceful, claiming her yet holding her just tightly enough so she could escape if she wanted.

"May I have a hug?"

"Me, too!"

She heard the quiet voices as if from a distance. Ben gave her a last kiss on the forehead and stepped back. Florence opened her eyes to find the world no longer spun. She heard giggles and turned to the left.

Ben held a child in each arm, rocking from side to side as they hugged him. He met her glance. He blinked rapidly, his eyes bright as if from unshed tears. He ducked his head, resting brown hair on Emma's fiery head.

She stared at this large man, a virtual stranger, tenderly holding her children as if he loved them. Children he'd just met. But then, she loved them and had known them only a few hours longer. Johnny wiggled to be let down, so Ben set them both on their feet.

"Shall we stretch our legs?" he asked. She nodded.

"Are you going to pull on them?" asked Emma.

"Pull on what, sweetheart?" Ben crouched near Emma's worried face.

"My legs. You said you wanted to stretch them."

Florence watched Ben struggle not to laugh. He bit his lip as if thinking. "Sometimes people say things which don't make sense unless you understand it. By stretching our legs, I mean to walk in big steps. We can't do that on the train."

"Oh." She took his hand and smiled. "Let's go stretch."

Emma and Johnny held Ben's hands and took exaggerated long steps. He kept his speed to theirs. Florence held back a smile. Was his ability and ease with children due to having six siblings and many cousins? She only had one sister and knew nothing of caring for children.

She followed them off the platform and into the small town. The children pulled free of Ben's hands to follow Mary's brood. They almost danced in eagerness as they looked around. A man sat on a bench outside a shop eating ice cream. It was hot, and she could see the children's yearning looks. But she had no money for such things.

"Doughnuts!" cried Ben. He smiled widely, gesturing to a woman holding a number of sticks in the air. Each was loaded with thick, cake-like disks. "I haven't had good bear sign since I left Montana. How much for the stick?"

"Ten cents."

"Sold."

He hauled coins out of his pocket, trading them for a stick. He aimed it at her like a fencing foil. She plucked the first one off the top, frowning to show she didn't think he should spend so much money on a treat. He laughed and held it out to Emma and then Johnny. She made them wait until Ben had one in his hand before nodding for them to eat. She bit into the sweet cake, groaning at the luxury.

While they had more than enough money, her mother kept a very close eye on Florence's figure. She insisted that, if only she tried enough, Florence could be as petite as Charity, her older sister. But Charity took after their mother, both of them barely five feet tall and reed slender. Though five inches taller, Florence was only allowed as much food as Charity. Until she was old enough to get out on her own, she was forever hungry. The only reason she was allowed out unescorted was because her mother finally realized no man wanted her. She was too big, too loud, too opinionated, and too plain.

She savored each bite. It tasted like freedom. As she told Ben, she had enough money to live without having to marry, but she would have to be careful, and also have a business to help support herself. She hadn't thought beyond taking the Bride Train, finding a husband, and having some children to love.

"You've got a sugar frosting moustache."

"So do you. Let me help you get rid of it." He waggled his eyebrows suggestively. "I could lick the frosting off your lips."

She shuddered at the thought of a man doing so in public, but it was in delight, not disgust. "Thank you, but I have a handkerchief."

"Spoilsport." His eyes promised he'd attempt another kiss at some point.

Face flaming, she approached the children, leaving Ben to clean his own face. She knelt to wipe the sugar off Johnny. It took a few minutes before she'd cleaned both children's faces and hands.

"There's the girlie I'm after."

Emma cried out at the rough male voice and hid behind Florence. Johnny stepped in front of his sister. From their expressions, they knew, and feared, this man.

"Come here, Emma. Now," he demanded in a cold, cruel voice.

Florence rose to her feet, an arm around each child, and pushed them behind her. A bald, sour-looking man walked closer, sneering. Dust covered his clothing. She held herself tall and proud, hoping to intimidate him with her presence.

"Take another step, and I'll shoot you dead."

Chapter Seven

The man stopped at Ben's quiet words. Florence turned her head to the side. Ben had his coat tucked behind a set of pearl-handled pistols. He stood with legs wide, hands loose at his hips. If she hadn't seen him laughing, or felt his sensuous kiss, she would be terrified of his sinister stare.

Mary, her children peeking from behind her, stood about twenty feet behind the brute, watching. Florence shook her head to keep Mary from intruding.

"This isn't your business, mister. This is my girl. Come here, Emma. Don't make me have to come get you." The man gestured impatiently.

Florence felt the child's forehead rub back and forth against her leg in a clear, though silent, no. Ben suddenly had a pistol in each hand.

"The child is mine. I suggest you get out of my sight before I shoot you," said Ben calmly.

"What's going on here?"

A man a few years older than Ben strode toward them from the side. Florence sighed in relief when she saw the sheriff's badge glint in the sun. She pointed at the man demanding Emma.

"That beast is trying to steal my daughter," she said. She hated that her voice shook, showing fear.

"That's a lie," snared the man. "She stole Emma from my wife in the city. I most killed my horse riding here to get my little girl back. She's mine."

"No!" yelled Emma. "My father's dead!"

The sheriff looked from one man to the other. His guns were easily accessible, his hands within quick reach. Mary stepped closer as a crowd gathered at the raised voices.

"Emma and Johnny's father died years ago," said Ben quietly. He'd replaced his pistols and held his hands up and out. "I married their mother and adopted these children as my own."

"Who are you when you're not stuffing doughnuts in your mouth?" asked the sheriff. He sounded gruff, but not mean.

"Benjamin Elliott of Tanner's Ford, Montana Territory. This is my wife, Florence Elliott, and my children, Emma Elliott and Johnny Elliott. We're on our way home."

"It's a lie! You can't prove a damn thing!" yelled the brute.

"You got a marriage license to prove it?"

Ben shook his head at the sheriff's question. "Lost in a fire."

"He's lying through his teeth. That's my Emma, and I want her back."

The sheriff looked at Florence and tilted his head.

"This man your husband?"

She licked dry lips. Marriage was forever. If she agreed, Ben would be her husband. He'd made it clear he didn't want to marry, and his older brother would despise her. Yet he'd said she was his wife. She nodded her head. She'd do anything to keep Emma from this man, from the life the child's mother had warned her about. A short, horrid, brutal life.

"So you won't mind repeating your vows for the preacher? He's had a dry spell lately and could use the business."

Florence couldn't see Ben to get a hint of what he might be thinking. If she went through with a wedding, she'd be married to him forever. Evangeline Leduc had begged Florence to take her children to safety because she was too sick to protect them anymore. How could Florence say no, then or now?

"Of course I'll stand in front of the preacher again," she choked out. She turned to Ben. He moved his head just enough for her to see it as a nod of agreement. "I expect your brothers would prefer if we arrived with a license."

"She's lying, dammit!"

Florence knelt and hugged Emma and Johnny. She spoke loudly, so all could hear.

"Isn't it wonderful? We're going to have another wedding ceremony, and you can be part of it. Your poppa and I will promise that we love each other and that we'll take care of you forever and ever."

Emma and Johnny had seen enough in their short lives to understand her silent, pleading message.

"Afterward, we'll celebrate with a dish of ice cream," said Ben. "If my wife agrees?"

Florence stood up. "I expect ice cream would be much better than champagne on a hot afternoon." Her laugh sounded a bit hysterical to her own ears, but no one else knew her well enough to know.

"Let's get moving, folks," said the sheriff. "That train waits for no man." He gave Florence a piercing look. "Or woman."

* * * *

"Thanks for being a witness, Sheriff Barstow," said Ben.

He folded the marriage certificate and tucked it into the inner pocket of his brocade vest. It wasn't the wedding his bride had likely hoped for, but he now had a wife, along with a daughter and son. A family of his own. He smiled at Florence, sitting on a bench nearby with Mary and their children. Since Mary acted as Florence's witness, he insisted she and her children join them in enjoying dishes of ice cream. Emma and Johnny, already excited at having a father to protect them, were overwhelmed by the treat.

Sheriff Barstow had declined, though his eyes watched Mary and her children squealing with delight. His two deputies had escorted the protesting brute to jail before their hasty wedding.

"That wasn't much of a kiss you gave your bride," said the sheriff quietly. "Makes me think I might have been told some stories. Mind you, I didn't trust that sidewinder when he wanted such a pretty little girl and not her brother."

Ben met the sheriff head-on. "We both know this is the first time I married Florence. But it will stand. When I claim something, it's forever. She, and her children, are mine now."

Sheriff Barstow raised an eyebrow. "I saw you swinging those kids and buying doughnuts. You wanted the woman, and her young'uns. Now you got 'em. All he's got is a sore ass and a half-dead horse from racing all the way from Philadelphia."

"Even if I didn't fancy Florence, I wouldn't let filth like that touch an innocent child."

"There's not enough evidence for a hanging, but I expect he'll be roughed up a mite before he leaves town."

Ben nodded his appreciation. He'd love to put his boots to the man, but as a lawyer, he shouldn't do such things. It didn't stop him from thinking about it, though.

"Thank you, Sheriff Barstow. Anything happens, you can get hold of me through Sheriff Frank Chambers in Tanner's Ford. Pretty much anyone in Bannack City can point you toward the Elliott ranches."

"That's gold rush country." He leaned back his head and looked sharply at Ben.

"There's more gold to be had in cattle. It doesn't destroy the land, and you're less likely to be dry-gulched."

The sheriff nodded. "Maybe it's time to check out some new ground. Getting mighty crowded here." His gaze lingered on Mary, enthusiastically devouring her dish of ice cream.

Florence licked her spoon, and a jolt of lust shot through Ben. This woman belonged to him. He would be the one giving her satisfaction on long, cold nights.

"I won't forget your help," said Ben. "We'd welcome another man of integrity in town. I suggest you bring a wife of your own, though," he added. "Good ones are rare west of the Mississippi."

"I just might do that," he replied, still looking at Mary. "Any work for someone like me?"

"Sheriff Chambers is getting on in years, and his wife wants to spend all her time with their grandchildren back East. He might be interested in passing on his badge."

"I'll think about it." He winked at Ben. "Now how about giving your wife that kiss…"

A long blast of the train whistle had Florence and Emma shoving fingers in their ears. Johnny, acting like a typical boy for once, whooped.

"Saved by the whistle," said the sheriff with a gruff laugh. "You'd better get your family on the train."

Ben held his arms out to Johnny. The boy ran forward with a wide smile. Ben swooped him up and onto his shoulders. Johnny gasped and slapped his hands over Ben's eyes to hold on. Ben moved the boy's hands to under his chin. He carefully bent and picked up Emma in his right arm. He held out his left elbow to Florence. She smiled and tucked her hand into his elbow. She had to stretch her legs to meet his long stride. Mary rushed her children behind them. They were all laughing when they reached the steps of the bride's carriage. His leg complained at the added weight but he ignored it. He was lucky not to have lost it from the bad break. A bit of pain was a small price to pay for carrying his children.

"Married or not, no men in here," said the officious guard in front of the Bride carriage. "You can take them back with you, or—"

"No, let them stay where there are other children," said Ben. He set Emma's feet on the step and then lifted Johnny off his shoulders. When they were aboard, he set his hands around Florence's waist. "Later," he whispered. She set a foot on the step. He dropped his hands under her bottom and gave her a lift up. She whirled around, eyes wide and mouth gasping.

"I've got a wedding kiss waiting for you, wife."

"I've got something for you too, *husband!*" She brandished her fist at him for his impertinence in touching her posterior.

He laughed, more lighthearted than he could ever remember.

* * * *

"Thank you for being my witness," said Florence to Mary once they'd settled the excited children.

"I should thank your husband for treating my three to ice cream, Mrs. Elliott." She emphasized the name, laughing. "They cared far more about the sweet, cold treat than the wedding ceremony."

"It may have been short, but I intend to stand by my words."

"The way he looks at you, he plans to do the same." Mary nudged Florence. "That handsome sheriff caught my eye. I bet he knows what to do once he takes his boots off." Her eyes sparkled. "Mind you, there's a lot one can do with boots on, out of bed."

Though heat flared from her belly on up, Florence raised her chin and faced Mary.

"Since I'm a married woman now, there's no reason you can't explain a few things to me, is there? I prefer to have some idea of an activity before I become involved." She cleared her throat. "I always thought one needed a bed, but you mentioned a table, and wall…"

Mary leaned even closer. "A man bends his woman over the table with her legs wide, or puts her back against a wall so she can wrap her legs around his hips." She winked. "If a woman doesn't wear drawers, it's very easy to lift her skirts and do whatever makes one feel good."

Florence blinked, her mind racing. She imagined lying on her back on the kitchen table while her husband did…whatever it was.

"What is it that husbands do with their wives? If you don't mind me asking?"

Mary tilted her head and looked speculatively at Florence. "We've got some long evenings between here and the end of the line. I believe it's my duty to explain why, with a good man, a wife might be the one demanding her marital rights, rather than the other way around."

Florence's entire body tingled as they shared a slow smile.

* * * *

"I have something to say to you, Mr. Benjamin Elliott!"

Ben, waiting for Florence to finish in the privy, watched Mary bustle toward him. She had a look in her eye that reminded him of Ma just before he got a good talking to. At least Mary wouldn't be reinforcing her opinion with a willow switch.

"I'm listening, Mrs. Douglas. Shall we stretch our legs as we talk? It's so wonderful to be off that train for a few minutes."

She captured his arm with hers and stomped away. He had no choice but to follow.

"As you know, I'm a widow. Mr. Douglas, Bertrand, was a very good man." She peered up at him and tugged his arm. "He was equally good to me at night. Do you understand?"

"You're saying you enjoyed your marriage bed."

"Yes. I've been speaking with Mrs. Elliott about it. In detail."

Ben closed his eyes for a moment in a wince. It was good that a bride know something about her wedding night beforehand. However, knowing she'd received detailed descriptions of wonderful things, set high standards. Standards that he was not sure he could achieve.

"And how did my dear wife respond?"

Mary slowed her steps. He waited for her to speak. Finally, he tilted his head to look at her. He groaned at her wide, wicked smile and twinkling eyes.

"Let's just say she's eager to experience your charms."

"You expect me to thank you for that?"

She slowly shook her head, still grinning.

"No, but I expect Florence will thank you." She raised her eyebrows in a way that was nothing close to innocent. "You *will* make sure she is happy in bed, won't you, Mr. Elliott?"

He attempted to speak but swallowed wrong, and choked. She snickered as he coughed to clear his lungs, as if he was purposely taking his time before answering.

"To be blunt, Mrs. Douglas, I do not have a lot of experience in pleasuring a wife. My older brother is the one with that knowledge."

"Then, Mr. Elliott, I suggest you either ask him for suggestions, or take time to find out how to best pleasure your wife. I told Florence how nightly loving can make up for a lot in a husband. If you don't make her spark each evening, she will not be a happy bride. Do we understand each other?"

The privy door opened. Ben pulled away from Mary, though not without her shaking her finger at him. He hurried across the square toward Florence.

"You look serious, but Mary's laughing. What was that about?"

He took the easy way out.

"Did you notice how Mary and Sheriff Barstow were eyeing each other after the ceremony?"

Florence nodded. "Wouldn't it be wonderful if Mary could find a good man like that? She has certain things she wants from a husband. Oh!" She pressed her fingertips to her lips, her eyes wide.

"She didn't say anything to you about, um—"

"My husbandly duties? Yes."

A rush of pink stained Florence's cheeks. Ben felt a matching heat on his own. He cleared his throat. She raised an eyebrow at him.

"Is it true?"

"If you mean that a man who satisfies his wife in bed will have a much happier life, then yes. But, like every other skill, it takes time to learn."

"I expect we'll need lots, and lots, of practice. Won't we?"

Ben gulped at the eager glint in her eyes. "Perhaps we need another kiss."

"Yes, please!"

He looked around. There didn't seem to be anyone watching, so he placed his hands on her waist and pulled her snug against him. She wrapped her arms around him, under his suit coat. She wiggled her hips, rubbing herself against his cock. He groaned and leaned down to kiss her. She moaned and opened her mouth to him.

The shrill blast of the train whistle made them jump apart. He dropped his forehead on hers and groaned, one of exasperation rather than need.

"I can't wait until we get off this train."

"And I can't wait until we can touch each other's skin, and kiss more than each others' lips."

She pulled away and ran, laughing, toward the train.

Chapter Eight

When the train pulled into Virginia City a few days later, Ben was no closer to finding Ranger a wife. He'd agonized about breaking this vital promise, but found no solution. He hoped one of the brides would suit, but whatever Florence had said to the ladies had not gone over well. They almost lifted their skirts out of the way so he wouldn't touch the fabric and contaminate them whenever he walked past.

Just as well. If they were that prissy, Ranger would want nothing to do with them.

He sent a telegram to Trace the day after they married. FOUND WIFE. STOP. SEND NEVIN NOT RANGER TO V CITY. STOP. BEN. STOP.

Nevin MacDougal would keep his mouth closed. Elliotts and MacDougals were always there for each other, no questions asked. He, Ranger, and Nev were all the same age and, though it was years since they'd met, nothing would change their friendship.

Though they liked his loving, few women would want to marry a man like Ranger. When he wasn't flirting, he was big, strong, loud, opinionated, and scarred, inside and out. Florence would stand up to him, which was both a good thing and not. She would not be cowed, but might send his twin into a rage. The only good thing that came out of Ranger's rages was the woodpile. Lots of logs got split while his temper boiled.

But, could he leave Florence with Ranger and Patrick, for weeks? He hadn't seen Patrick since the boy was about seventeen. Who knows what The MacDougal and his brutal sons might have done to him. Ranger could only protect his siblings so much, no matter how hard he tried.

Though they were identical in appearance, his twin was always popular with the ladies who enjoyed a quick romp. He only had to wink a half-lidded eye, and the experienced women would flock around. No doubt about it, Ranger knew far more about satisfying a woman in bed.

Ben would do anything for Ranger. In addition, he wanted to prove to Florence that she could have a wonderful physical relationship. One that her dear friend Mary had convinced her was not only possible, but required. Could he keep the essence of his promise to Ranger, and give Florence a first night to savor, all at once?

He'd made a solemn promise to bring his twin a wife, and had not followed through. The only thing that might ease the sting was if Ranger agreed to bed his wife for him. The crazy idea had flickered through his brain every day since he married Florence.

He'd made a promise to Florence as well, before God, to honor and cherish her. Would she understand that the only reason he would even think to do this, was to enhance their marriage? That he was thinking of how to best please her?

He didn't want to deceive her, but it would be to make their future better. Just once, and then he'd explain why and beg her forgiveness. If Ranger provided the pleasure Ben knew he could, perhaps Florence would understand.

He was torn between his brother and his wife. How could he do what was best for all of them?

For now, he'd wait.

After all, they had so little time alone. The one time he'd been able to thoroughly kiss her, was when Mary offered to keep the children during a long stop. Of course, she'd given him a look stating what he was supposed to do. It didn't matter, as he wanted to kiss Florence senseless.

He'd pulled his wife behind a building and done just that. She'd gasped when he touched her bare breast. He suckled her nipple, and she almost came on the spot, not that she knew what was happening. He was fighting the urge to take her right against the wall when the train whistle brought him to his senses.

They barely made it back in time. Ben had put Florence on the steps as the train started up. He had to run alongside until he could board, both of them laughing. He ached for hours, both from the raging hard-on and the chafing from running with such a hard cock.

They didn't have another chance to do more than sweetly kiss. Of course, they couldn't consummate their wedding until they had a room to themselves, and that wasn't likely to happen until they reached the Bitterroot Ranch.

Ben's memory of Florence's demanding cries proved the newest Mrs. Elliott was a bundle of passion. The woman was ready to explode at any time, given enough fuel.

Ben loved her mind, her insistence on doing what was right, and, of course, her body. She was the woman for him. She had enough curves to make Ranger smile. Patrick would love her laugh.

He couldn't think past waking up in her arms the first morning on the ranch. He wasn't sure how the four of them would live together in a small home. That was another thing to figure out later. Ranger had bought the ranch and, along with Patrick, brought their cattle all the way from Texas. He was joining them, and must find a way for all of them to get along. If not, he would be the one leaving, along with Florence and their children.

Ben stood and stretched as the train whistled for Virginia City, slowing for the last time. They'd share a room at a decent hotel and go by stage to Bannack City in the morning. A day from there to Tanner's Ford, and home a few hours later.

* * * *

Florence stood on the balcony of the Virginia City hotel and looked around. Night was falling and, if anything, it made the city look even more dangerous. There was one main street and a few side streets, most of which seemed to be filled with noisy saloons, hotels, and gaming houses. Almost all were of wood. She was sure they were all bigger than her new home.

Ben had explained about sharing the ranch with his two brothers, Ranger and Patrick. The idea was startling at first, as she was used to Eastern homes which were large and comfortable. But as the train continued westward, the homes she glimpsed from the train became smaller and smaller. Of course, if there was only one home, she would share it. As the only woman, she'd prepare meals for them all, clean the home and their clothing, and take care of the children, garden, and, she was sure, many other things. She was strong, and would learn.

As Ben had never been to the Bitterroot Ranch, he couldn't tell her anything about it. Was their home a single room with thin curtains separating them from their children and his two brothers? It made her shudder, but her reaction mattered not. She would live as best she could. She'd accepted her children willingly and went into the marriage to protect them. Everything else was, as Ben the lawyer would say, moot.

She looked around for her missing husband. Supper was about to be delivered, and he hadn't returned. By twisting and looking underneath the balcony, she finally found him standing almost directly below her, hands at his sides, staring into the sunset.

Something dark crept from a pile of wooden crates behind him. It was a tall, dark-skinned man. Bare arms stuck out from a leather fringed vest. A black line of dark hair hung down his back. He was only a few feet away from Ben. He lifted his right hand up and over his shoulder. She saw his fingers curl around something poking up from under his vest.

He lifted his arm. The sun's setting rays reflected off a long knife. She screamed as he lunged, but only heard a squeak emerge. Ben whirled at the last moment and grabbed the hand holding the knife. He wrestled the attacker to the ground. They rolled into the shadows. She cursed the dusk, making it impossible for her to see.

Suddenly, one hauled the other to his feet. They clapped each other on the back, both laughing. They pushed and shoved until they were near a lamp. The attacker's white teeth, so different from his dark face, shone brilliantly in the light.

She snapped her open mouth shut, her heart still pounding. Furious at the fear she'd experienced, she curled her hands around the balcony railing and leaned over.

"Benjamin Elliott!" she hollered. "What are you doing? Supper is about to be served."

He waved back, grinning broadly.

"Give us a moment, sweetheart, and we'll be up to join you."

The other man gaped at her for a moment, grinned, and then slapped Ben on the back so hard he almost fell over. The man stood straight and executed a formal bow, complete with embellishments, as if they were at a cotillion. Both men broke into laughter and shoved each other.

She threw up her hands and went back into their room. Obviously, they were friends. Sneaking up on each other like little boys must be a male ritual she knew nothing about. She winced when she saw Emma's face tight in apprehension. Johnny seemed oblivious as he worked on the wooden block puzzle she'd given him.

"I'm sorry I frightened you, Emma," said Florence. "I was startled by Poppa's friend. They're coming up now."

Emma nodded. She turned her worried face from her mother to the door. She jumped at the loud knock, but it was their supper. The servants placed everything on the table and slipped out. She and the children washed their hands. Ben rapped on the door and let himself in. He'd attempted to brush dirt off his suit but he'd missed a few spots.

"Sweetheart, I'd like you to meet my good friend and cousin,

Nevin MacDougal. Nev, this is my wife, Florence. Emma, Johnny, say hello to your Uncle Nevin."

"I apologize for frightening you, Mrs. Elliott." He spoke with a hint of a soft accent. It was the only thing soft about him. "Sometimes we still act like the boys we used to be."

"Your name is Nevin MacDougal?" She looked at his dark skin, broad cheekbones, and hawk-like nose. A leather thong tied back his long, straight, black hair.

"I have my Highland Scot father's height and name. The rest comes from my mother's side. She is of the Bannock people, members of the Shoshone nation."

"Are you a red Indian?" asked Johnny. He stared, eyes wide.

Nevin held his arms out wide, like a pastor blessing his flock, and turned in a circle. It pulled his leather vest open. There was nothing but smooth, brown skin under the vest. She'd never seen a man's bare chest, much less the muscles that rippled as he moved. A fresh male scent flowed from him, and power radiated from his presence. He knelt beside Johnny and held his arm out to the boy.

"What do you think?"

Johnny pushed up his sleeve. He placed his thin, pale forearm on Nevin's thick, dark one. "You're not red, Uncle Nevin. Just browner than me."

"Maybe next summer, when you're working all day without a shirt on, your skin will be the same color as mine."

"I don't have to wear a shirt?" His grin was infectious.

"Not at my home, the MD Connected Ranch, but you have to follow the rules of the home you live in. Your mother may not agree."

"I do apologize, Mr. MacDougal, if we've given offense with Johnny's question," said Florence.

"None taken," he said jovially. He laughed and turned to Ben. "Ross and his wife, Amelia, were married by contract and met for the first time in a dark bedroom, by her choice. He said they had an, um," he winked at Florence, "an enjoyable night. When the morning sun came through the window, she was a mite surprised to find a dark arm around her...ah, shoulder." He broke out in a wide smile. "They're expecting a little one come spring. Ross hovers over her like a horse fly."

"Congratulations, old man!" Ben enthusiastically shook Nevin's hand. They stared into each other's eyes, squeezing hard, grinning and daring the other to let go first.

"Oh, for goodness's sakes!" Florence smacked Ben on the shoulder with the back of her hand. He grunted and let go, feigning how her blow had wounded him.

Nevin nodded to the children. "You work fast," he said to Ben.

"Emma and Johnny are Florence's children by her first husband."

"May I offer you something to eat or drink, Mr. MacDougal?" asked Florence before the man could ask any questions. "We were waiting for my husband to return before dining. There's plenty to share."

He looked at Ben and gave an eye twitch which could have been accidental but which Florence expected was a signal.

"I would be delighted, Mrs. Elliott."

"Florence," she replied.

"Then you must call me Nevin." He turned to Johnny. "I'd better take this off, or your ma might not let me sit at the table with you." He reached behind his back, fiddled with something, and then reached for the knife handle again. This time he removed the whole thing, knife and scabbard.

"Is that a sword?" asked Johnny with awe. Emma was as intrigued as her brother, leaning over to see.

"Something like it," replied Nevin. He looked at Emma, and then Johnny. "I want your word that you'll never, ever touch something like this. I keep my knives sharp because they are used to protect my family. You could get badly hurt from playing with them." He waited for their nods before slowly pulling the weapon from its leather scabbard.

"Oh, my godfathers," gasped Florence. "That blade must be ten inches long. Do you always carry it with you?"

"When I leave home, yes." He turned his eyes to Ben. "We know there are evil people in the world. But they will never, ever, touch my family."

"Are we your family?" asked Emma quietly. She had that frightened look again, just like before they married.

Nevin placed the knife on the floor. He knelt and held out his palms, one to each child. "Put your hands in mine." They did so, unafraid. He curled his hands to enfold theirs. "I swear that I will protect you, Emma, and you, Johnny, with my life. My family includes the children of my brothers. Ben is a brother to me, and you are under my protection, now and forever. So is your mama."

Florence couldn't move as she watched him meet Emma's eyes, staring at her until she nodded her belief in him. Emma inhaled, tears forming. She raggedly exhaled and then smiled. A smile of joy, such as a child should always have. Nevin kissed her hand and released it. He met Johnny's gaze the same. When the boy nodded, Nevin moved his hand until they solemnly shook, man-to-man.

"Well," said Florence, trying to lighten the mood before she burst into tears, "are there more of you at home?"

"My older brother, your Uncle Ross, looks almost like me," Nevin said to the children. He smiled. "But I'm much more handsome. Gillis is the oldest. He has a baby girl named Hope. Her mama, Amelia's older sister, was sick a long time, and she died after Hope was born."

"I'm so sorry for your loss," said Florence.

"Thanks. Gil was pretty shook up, but he's really looking forward to the new baby. You can tell he and I have different mothers, as he's got red hair all over. He's my Clan Chief. That means we have to do what he says, unless we can convince him otherwise."

"This isn't a feudal society, Mr. MacDougal," said Florence. "Surely you jest for the children's sake."

He looked up at her, power radiating from him even though he was kneeling.

"My grandfathers and their grandfathers, both here and in Scotland, held the power of life and death over their Clan and Tribe. My father, known as The MacDougal, believes he has the same power. The Chief speaks the law, and the people obey."

"What if they don't obey?" she asked, thinking of the times she stood up to her father.

"They are banished, or killed," he said quietly. "This is a hard land. Unless a man grows up strong, able to protect himself and his family, he is not worthy of being part of that family, be it Clan or Tribe." He raised an eyebrow at Ben. "Your book learning will protect us all from attack by those who use paper and words to lie and steal. Your brothers and cousins will protect your family from physical threats."

Ben scowled. "I managed to fight you off, didn't I?"

Nevin laughed, his seriousness gone as if it had never appeared. "You'd be dead if I'd wished it. I had to stomp my foot before you heard me behind you." He winked at Emma. "After I wash, may I escort you to the table, Miss Emma Elliott?"

She looked to Ben for confirmation, not Florence. Ben and Nevin washed up quickly. Emma smiled and rested her hand on her Uncle Nevin's arm as if she'd been doing so for years. It was not something Florence had taught her.

Nevin helped Emma into her seat and then looked pointedly at Florence. She realized she must sit before he would. Johnny stood behind his chair as well. She let Ben settle her into her seat at one end of the table. Johnny climbed into his chair, Nevin pulled up a hassock and Ben took the other end. They had the usual quick prayer and began passing food.

"Your sisters-in-law, Beth, Amelia, and Jessie, will be pleased to have another woman in the valley," said Nevin. He held the bowl of mashed potatoes for Emma before helping himself to a large scoop. "Are you a stubborn woman?" He looked at Florence.

"Nevin," warned Ben.

"I'll take that as a yes. The rest of the wives are, so you'll fit in," replied Nevin. "If so, you also know your own mind. So do they," he added, shaking his head and sighing like a martyr.

"I haven't met Beth or Amelia, but if they're anything like my *dear* sister, Jessie, Florence will be able to hold her own," said Ben. "No man can make Jessie do anything she doesn't want to," he explained to Florence. "She swears she'll never get hog-tied to a husband."

"She's Mrs. Kendrick Langford now."

"What?" sputtered Ben. He wiped potatoes off his chin. "How did that happen?"

Florence caught the lip twitch and wink Nevin sent her way. The man was enjoying twisting Ben's tail. It eased her mind to know her husband had family who cared about each other enough to joke this way. Perhaps the sisters-in-law Nevin spoke of would become the friends she'd never had. Only Elizabeth James had the mix of wit, education, and spark that allowed her to speak her mind and laugh about it.

"Jessie was caught in a compromising position with the ramrod of the Double Diamond. It's east of the MD Connected. You just missed the wedding."

Ben shook his head. "I can't believe Jessie agreed to take a husband."

"But, if she was caught doing," Florence looked at the young ears flanking her, "um, what she was doing, wouldn't she have to marry?"

"Nope," said Nevin. He helped himself to another biscuit and then offered the basket to Johnny. "She doesn't care what anyone thinks. Ranger set her up, and Ace, also known as Kenrick Langford, caught the bait. He said he'd marry, but she refused. But Ranger had her horse, Nightwind. He told her she could have her horse back if she married Ace. He's from England, the younger son of an earl. He won the ranch and a herd of cattle in an all-night poker game. His three aces beat two pair, and got him a nickname." He turned to Ben. "Ranger and Patrick brought the cattle up from Texas. Ace, with his partners Sin and Henry, are still learning how to ranch from Jessie, but they're coming along fine."

"When did this all happen?"

Nevin speared himself another pork chop before answering Ben. "If you came home last October as expected, you would have been here for everything." He turned to Florence. "When did the two of you get married?"

"Monday," she said.

"Oh, newlyweds," drawled Nevin. He pointedly looked around the room. Florence had set three pillows on the bed. Another one on the couch had a set of folded sheets lying on it. Nevin raised an eyebrow. "You must be looking forward to getting home."

Though she'd never been one to flush easily, since she set eyes on Ben, she'd been lighting up like a flame far too often. Nevin winked at her and turned to Emma.

"Did you know your cousin Bridie has the same color of hair as you?" said Nevin.

"She does?"

Nevin nodded. "Only, her eyes are green."

"*Maman* said mine are violet, like the flower. See?" Emma tilted her head at Nevin and opened her eyes wide.

"My, oh, my," said Nevin. "So they are."

Emma had no fear of the large, gentle man, who seemed fully at ease with the children. If she closed her eyes, Florence had a hard time believing the quiet gentleman with impeccable manners was the same savage who snuck up behind her husband as if to kill him.

"That was the best meal I've had since Beth gave me dinner," said Nevin. He crossed his knife and fork and patted his mouth with his napkin. Johnny imitated him.

"I thought your brother's wife was named Amelia?" said Florence.

Nevin's wide smile held a laugh. "Yes, but she's a terrible cook. Auntie, my mother's sister, lives with us. She does most of the cooking and takes care of Gillis' daughter, Hope. But she's been away hunting for the last few days. Yesterday I told Amelia I had an urgent matter to discuss with Trace, but really I wanted some of Beth's home cooking." He patted his flat stomach.

"You don't mind her not being able to cook well?" Florence asked.

Nevin shook his head slowly. "Not everyone can do everything well. Ross says Amelia's good at other things," he said. He winked at her, a lazy wink suggesting things a married couple should know about. She flushed again.

"Hmm, I didn't ask about your cooking skills before I married you," interrupted Ben.

"I assumed you would be doing the cooking," Florence replied calmly.

Ben sputtered as Nevin burst into laughter. "Oh, you'll fit right in with Beth, Amelia, and Jessie. And Auntie will be pleased to have more children." He turned to Johnny. "My nephew, Daniel Thomson MacDougal, is about ten years old. He'll be glad to have another boy around. The rest are all girls, except Trace's son, James, but he's a baby." He exchanged looks of disgust with the boy. "Maybe you'll be lucky and get a little brother soon."

"We need to talk," said Ben to Nevin between gritted teeth. His fingers clenched the corners of the table.

"Good. I've got a lot of boring news to give you, as well."

As soon as Florence stood up, the men followed. She'd never seen Ben so agitated. Instead of upsetting her, it made her feel good that he could relax enough to show his true self. Perhaps, in time, she could do the same.

"Take your time visiting," she said to Ben. "I won't wait up for you."

Nevin, still snickering, returned his knife to his back. Ben almost pushed him out of the door.

"You want to hear how the rest of us manage our wives?" she heard Nevin say as the door closed behind them.

"Don't bother teaching him how to 'manage' me," she muttered as she bolted the door behind them. "When I find her, Elizabeth will tell me how to manage you Montana men!"

Chapter Nine

"I can hardly wait until Florence and Beth meet." Nevin snickered as he led Ben down the hotel hallway.

"You might think otherwise when they put their heads together and tell Amelia things."

Nevin winced. "Didn't think of that."

"My wife is an educated woman. She's had letters printed in a number of newspapers. Not the sort of topic that would endear her to most of the townsmen. She doesn't consider herself worth less just because she's a woman."

"Good thing we like our wives to have spirit. But winter's coming and we can't spend the whole time in bed. Did Florence bring any books with her?"

Ben laughed at the eagerness on Nevin's face. "Remember those crates I said needed to be forwarded by wagon? Most of them contain my wife's books."

"That's the sort of wealth that has real value." Nevin turned the corner and started up the stairs, two at a time.

"I thought we were going out for a drink," said Ben. Though it made his leg ache, he followed quickly behind.

"We're staying in." Nevin turned left. These floorboards were rough on their boots, and the doors were closer together.

"Why?"

A slight creak of wood warned Ben that a door opened behind him. The arm around his neck and knife at his throat stopped him from reacting.

"This a good reason?" The deep voice was almost as familiar as his own.

"Ranger!" The knife didn't retreat, so Ben didn't move. Nevin leaned a shoulder against the wall in front of Ben. His smirk said, *See? You're too slow.*

"You said you brought a bride, but told me to stay away. Why?"

Ranger's pride was a double-edged sword. It kept him going when others would have broken under The MacDougal's harsh yoke. It also made him deeply suspicious of any slight or touch of pity. Ben hadn't seen his twin in over four years. A lot could happen to a man. Considering where he'd been living, Ben doubted it was good. The short, clipped words were the actions of a hardened, cynical man.

Hard, unmoving muscles choked him. The knife hadn't wavered. The body behind him might have been identical once, but Ranger's musculature was far greater than Ben's. If he wanted to beat Ben to a pulp using only his knuckles, he could. He was the brawn, Ben the brain. At the moment, brawn won. The knife moved back from his throat, just enough to allow him to talk.

"I couldn't find a wife to suit your requirements. Florence's not your type of woman, but I had to marry her to save my new daughter. I don't know what might have happened to you over the last few years. I thought you and Florence might not get along."

"You couldn't find the woman I wanted? What about the other brides? Wasn't that train chock full of them?"

"The other brides were light-brained or eager for gold. They all got off long before we reached the Territory. The only one left on the train when we arrived except Florence was her friend, an older widow. The others couldn't stand to live this far from 'civilization.' Give me time, and I'll find you a wife of your own. I don't break my promises."

"But I want a wife now." Ranger lowered his voice. "Why don't I just take yours?"

Ben tried to move his head. The sharp sting of the blade stopped him.

"Actually, brother, for a few moments I even considered you showing Florence about orgasms, as in just the first night."

Nevin raised his eyebrows at the news but said nothing.

"Keep talking," growled Ranger.

"I haven't had a chance to bed my wife yet."

"Why?"

"Do we have to do this in the hallway?"

"Yep."

Ben held back a gasp as Ranger tightened his hold, tilting his neck further back.

"I didn't bed her because we married during a quick stop just outside Philadelphia. Men are not allowed in the Bridal carriage, so I could only see her in the dining carriage, or when the train stopped."

"You feel guilty about not bringing me a wife, so you thought a pity fuck, taking your wife on your wedding night, would make up for it?"

"That's not it at all. I don't want Florence hurt. Yes, I feel guilty for not fulfilling my promise to you, but I made one to my wife as well. I want her to really enjoy sex. I knew you've got a way with women, and far more experience. I doubt she's ever had an orgasm. I thought if you made sure she had a few the first night, she'd be more likely to stay. But it was a stupid idea, unfair to both of you. I'll do the best I can with Florence, and find you a wife elsewhere. Forget I said anything."

The knife disappeared, and Ben was thrust through an open door. He stumbled over a stool and fell onto the bed. There wasn't much else in the small room. Ranger followed, and Nevin shut the door.

"He still limps," said Nevin. "Not much, but it was an effort for him to take the stairs so fast."

"Surprised he can walk at all," said Ranger, staring down at him. "Good thing Sunbird knows how to fix bones."

Ben's temper didn't rise often. In fact, rarely since he left Texas had he felt a need to get riled. But this was his twin. They knew each other well.

"How's your back?" he taunted in reply. "And I see you can finally string more than two words together at once."

"Back's so good I forgot all about it. And I can talk fine when I want. Since I left Texas, I've been wanting a lot more."

Nevin looked from one to the other, but they just stared at each other, unspeaking. He slid a throwing knife from his sleeve and began cleaning his fingernails.

"You don't look like twins anymore," said Nevin. He pointed the knife at Ranger. "Be easy for you to shave and trim your hair and look like Ben. But you've got muscles. You," he switched the knife point to Ben, "don't."

"I've always been bigger, stronger, and better looking than you, little brother," taunted Ranger.

Ben rolled to his feet. Because of the room's dimensions, it brought him almost nose to nose. He kept his voice low, his gaze steady.

"Maybe so, but I've been to places and seen things."

"Things that I don't give a damn about."

"So we're even. Right?"

Ranger nodded. He spit on his hand and held it out, palm up. Ben, keeping total eye contact, did the same and slapped his palm on top. They shook, hard.

"Damn, it's good to see you again," said Ranger, breaking out in a laugh. He pounded Ben on the back, wiping the spit on Ben's coat. Ben did the same, using Ranger's shirt.

"Nev said Jessie's married, but I can't believe it."

"Our little big sister has English aristocrats twisted around her little finger," said Ranger. He smiled smugly. "I'm very proud of my part in getting Jessie married off so well. I made her work for them for three weeks, dressed as a boy."

"You missed a good wedding," said Nevin. "She's well married, with three husbands to keep her in line."

"Three husbands? What the—"

Nevin held up his hands, interrupting. "Ben, you don't know about the way things are done in our valley." He let loose a wide grin. "Our wives share themselves with our brothers. It started when Trace married Beth. Trace, Simon, and Jack always shared everything, and long ago insisted they'd do the same with a wife. There's not enough women to go around, and our wives are demanding enough to appreciate more than one man. Trace has a son, but Beth's now carrying Simon's child, and Jack will have his turn. Amelia shares her bed with Ross, me, and Gillis. As I said at supper, she'll give Ross a wee one this spring."

Ben looked at Nevin, and then Ranger. "Wait a minute. Trace shares his wife with the twins? Even Jackass?"

Ranger nodded, nonchalant. He didn't have the issues with Jack that Ben did. Or rather, that Jack had with Ben. He turned to Nevin. "You think that woman who just fed you supper might be willing to share her bed with three men?"

"Florence reminds me of Beth," said Nevin. "They're from the same city and may even know each other. They're both full of starch on the outside but simmering, just off the boil, underneath." His lip twitched. He tilted his head to Ranger. "You should have heard her yell when I tackled Ben right under her balcony. I'd say there's a bit of passion lurking inside all those layers of petticoats. I think Florence Elliott can be persuaded to enjoy all three of you. She's a smart woman, and this sharing is the answer to a problem."

Ben dropped on the bed before his leg gave out. He hadn't yet wrapped his brain around the fact that Ranger wasn't furious for him breaking the most important promise he'd ever made.

No, his vow to Florence was his most sacred promise.

But if she was willing to share herself with his brothers, then both his promise to Ranger and his vow to care for Florence and their children, could be kept. He vowed to love, honor and cherish her, body, mind, and soul. It didn't stop others from also caring for her.

"If Florence agrees with this, she wouldn't be alone for weeks in a cold bed when I have to travel. He looked at Ranger. "Do you want children of your own?"

"We need children to pass the ranch to. Doesn't matter to me where they come from. You, me, Patrick. Hell, we can adopt a couple dozen for all I care."

Ranger shrugged nonchalantly but Ben saw the tiny tic at the corner of his eye. His twin wanted someone to love, who'd love him back. Ben's breath shuddered out. If Florence shared her bed, even now and then, with his brothers, no one needed to know he shot blanks. He'd never have to tell his secret.

Patrick, at twenty-one, likely wouldn't care what education Florence had, as long as she fed him well and gave herself to him in bed. Ranger, on the other hand, would go head to head with Florence on pretty much everything Ben had discussed with her over the last week. The two of them were so stubborn they'd choose opposite sides just to be ornery.

But how would he explain all this to Florence?

He realized Ranger and Nevin stared at him. If they'd asked a question, he'd missed it.

"What's that big brain of yours doing now?"

"I worried about leaving Florence alone when I traveled," said Ben to Ranger. "I knew you and Patrick would keep her safe, but she'd have an empty bed for weeks or months at a time."

"That's easy to fix. We'll get a bigger bed."

"But Florence is nothing like that list you sent. You might not get along."

Ranger gave Nevin a speaking glance. Nevin made an hourglass shape with both hands. He mimicked grasping her buttocks, then raised his hands and did the same for her breasts, grinning the whole time. Ranger nodded as if that's all he needed to know about a wife.

"You up to sharing your woman, little brother? Beth and Amelia didn't find out until after they married, but Jessie jumped in with both feet. They're all strong women. Yours can't be that different."

Ben stood and punched Ranger in the shoulder. He didn't move, though Ben felt the impact in his knuckles. "I'm the one who said I want her to come eagerly to bed each night. If she's agreeable, I'm all for it."

"I remember you did fine with the ladies those few times in Texas when we shared." He snickered. "That the only times you've been with a woman?"

"No, but this is too important. Even more so now." Ben pulled on his ear. "Look, if she was only my wife, there would be no issue. But if she's got to learn to enjoy all three of us, she needs to start with a few explosions. I think that'll make it more likely she'll want to stay."

"You think too much."

"So does Florence," groaned Ben.

"Then I'll bed her first. I can keep her from thinking. After all, I'm the prime stud in our stable."

Ben forced a laugh. "Prime stud? Never." He poked Ranger in the gut with his finger. It didn't sink in. "Florence says she's a widow, but she kisses like it's her first time. If she agrees, I'll go along with you being her first. But I study things and learn fast. We'll see who she prefers by Christmas. But she has to know it's you before you get too far the first night."

The near-identical men nodded at each other, challenge given and accepted.

"I doubt she's a widow," said Nevin "I also don't think she's their mother. Emma said *Maman*, and she didn't mean Florence." He frowned. "I want to find out who scared that little girl so deep." He looked at Ranger. "Emma had that look, so sure the world would keep attacking her. But her smile when I said they were under my protection? It was like I'd given her a prize beyond measure."

"We had to marry because someone tried to take Emma," said Ben. "He raced his horse for hours to get at that pretty little girl. I think Emma knew him, and what he was after. That she knows about such things makes it far worse."

"I knew you wouldn't marry unless a woman forced you into it," crowed Ranger. "Damn, I should have taken that bet."

"Florence and I haven't had any time alone," said Ben, ignoring him. "I expect she'll tell me everything as soon as she can."

"So," drawled Ranger, "If this works out, I'm either bedding an experienced widow who might have high expectations, or a scared virgin. Either way, I'll have to take my time."

"That a problem?" asked Ben, daring Ranger to complain.

"You know me." He smoothed the moustache he'd have to shave off to resemble Ben. "Always do the best job possible given the circumstances. My hard cock can gentle a soft woman just fine."

"I don't guarantee this'll happen, but if it does, she wakes up with me," warned Ben. "I want her in the morning."

Ranger lost ten years off his face when he beamed. "Little brother, I'll have her purring so hard she'll wake *you* up, demanding more."

Chapter Ten

Florence jerked her head up, catching herself before she fell off the wagon seat. She pulled her wool scarf over her head and wrapped it tight around her shoulders.

"Sorry, sweetheart," murmured Ben. "I know you're tired, but we've got to get home before we stop."

"I understand." She placed her hand on his arm. "You're just as tired. We'll make it together."

She gritted her teeth in the closest thing she could manage to a smile. Luckily, he didn't notice. He faced forward as they pushed on, using the wagon's lamps and the full harvest moon's light to find their way. A wild stagecoach ride had bounced them from Virginia City to Bannack City in one day. Johnny was over the moon with the excitement, but she felt bruised. Last night's hotel room wasn't anything as nice as in Virginia City.

They'd headed out early in a rented wagon, eager for home. When they stopped to change horses in Tanner's Ford, Ben said they'd come back and see the town another day soon. At that point she didn't much care to see anything but a flat surface. That was a few hours ago.

She turned around to check Emma and Johnny. They lay in a nest of blankets in the back, rocked to sleep as if they were still on the train. She grabbed onto the seat and forced her eyes to stay open. They drooped again. She turned her head, hoping the movement would help. A patch of white splotches headed their way. She didn't believe in ghosts, but out here, who knew what went on. The splotches came closer.

"Welcome to the Rocking E, Ben."

The voice was out of a nightmare, like the cawing of a raven. She shivered. Ben grinned and hauled the horses to a stop.

"That you, Trace?"

"Yep. Been a long time I've waited to welcome you home," grated the voice.

"Been a long time I've been wanting to hear it. What happened to your voice?" Ben spoke in weary delight.

"Old news. Can't be fixed."

Florence clamped her lips together. The man obviously didn't want to discuss what must have been a horrific event. Had someone tried to hang him? She straightened her back and pushed back the hair which had escaped hours earlier. Ben wrapped his left arm around her shoulders. She welcomed the warmth.

"Trace, I'd like you to meet my wife, Florence. Our children, Emma and Johnny, are asleep in the back. Florence, this is my oldest brother, Trace. He's the ramrod of the Rocking E. This is where I lived until my parents died."

"Ma'am." Trace touched the brim of his hat with his hand and nodded. "I expect you want to get home, but Beth's got beds set up for you here."

"I'd hoped to get to the ranch tonight." Ben spoke somewhat defensively.

"It's not set up for a wife yet, much less a couple of kids," replied Trace. "The boys have been working on Jessie's place."

Ben scratched his chin. "Be nice to see home again."

"Beth's made a few changes, but not many," said Trace. He turned to Florence. "I can take you up with me, ma'am, if you don't mind. You'll be in the hot bath Beth's got waiting long before Ben gets the wagon up the hill."

"Bath?" She almost moaned the word.

"You'll take my wife and leave me to go on alone?"

Ben sounded like he was joking with Trace, but she didn't know these people, or her husband's relationship with them. After the very surprising visit by Nevin MacDougal, she'd decided to keep her mouth shut. It was difficult, but she could manage.

"You'd rather I bring your pretty wife on *my* lap?" The new voice came from the far side of the wagon. It almost laughed, sounding as if he'd poke fun at anything.

"You touch my wife and I'll have you flat on your back with a broken nose!" blasted Ben.

Florence almost gasped. She hadn't heard him speak so strongly since the brute tried to take Emma. She realized she wasn't so good at keeping quiet. "I assume you're another brother, whoever you are?"

"That's Jackass, the next oldest to me," growled Ben. "He's staying far from you."

The rider came close to the lamp. All she could see was the flash of white teeth in a wolfish smile.

"Good evening, ma'am. Pleased to meet you. I'm Jack, twin to Simon. He's up at the house with Beth. He's got a baby growing in her, and doesn't like to leave her alone."

Ben muttered a curse.

"Shut up," growled Trace.

"What?" Jack replied, all innocence. "It's true. Simon insists Beth's growing his daughter." He turned to Florence. "I've got to wait a bit for my turn, but I don't mind." He winked. "Much."

"Another word and you're sleeping in the barn until Christmas!"

Trace's voice sounded like someone had taken sandpaper to the inside of his throat. Another Elliott mystery. Ben placed his hand on her arm and squeezed gently. She looked away from the enigmatic brother. Ben hadn't said much about his family, other than there were a lot of them.

"Trace is right. I pushed you too hard today, and you deserve a hot bath. Do you want to ride double with him for a few minutes? I'll follow as quickly as I can."

"Please," she groaned, already thinking of the luxury of being clean and warm. She could finally take off the clothing she'd worn since boarding in Philadelphia.

She stood up, creaking a bit from sitting for so long. Ben held her hand until Trace lifted her into his lap. She placed her left arm behind his neck. He wrapped his arm around her and held on her right thigh. His was only the second lap she'd sat on. His hand felt warm, but it didn't excite her. Not the way Ben's touch did.

"I trust Trace with my life, and my wife," said Ben. "But don't listen to a thing Jack says."

Florence closed her eyes and leaned into Trace's chest. He turned his horse and rode almost straight uphill.

"Nevin said you're a widow, that you and Ben just got married," said Trace.

She was too tired to keep track of secrets. Ben said he trusted Trace. So would she.

"I told Ben I was a widow to explain why I had Emma and Johnny with me. They're my children now, but I've never been married before."

They rode on for a few minutes. "Will this hurt Ben when the truth comes out?"

She shook her head, rolling it on his broad chest.

"You plan to tell him any time soon?"

"I won't have to. Once he takes me to bed…"

"Ah, yes. A virgin with two children. But why tell me now?"

"I've learned a bit about Ben in the past week. If he says to trust you with his life, he means it. Secrets can wreck families. I don't want to start with a lie."

Trace seemed very much the responsible older brother. He thought for a while as they rode. "Shouldn't you have told Ben before now?"

"We were never alone. The children and I had to stay in the Bride carriage, while Ben rode with the men. We shared a room in Virginia City and in Bannack, last night. I slept with the children in case they had nightmares. I thought to tell him tonight—"

"I guess tomorrow night before bed is soon enough." He chuckled. "And here I thought having Jessie married off would bring some peace to the valley." She felt his thighs move under her. It sent a signal to the horse, which moved a bit faster up the hill. "What has Ben told you about us?"

"Very little. I think Ben said he has five brothers and a sister, and three cousins. Nevin said Ross was married to Amelia and had an older half brother. He mentioned your sister just got married. That seemed to astound Ben."

"It surprised all of us," said Trace drily.

A few minutes later they rode into a yard lit by a lantern. Two dogs, tails wagging, approached.

"That's Cleo and Tony, Beth's dogs," said Trace. "And here comes Simon."

She was handed over like a sack of potatoes to another tall, smiling man. He waited for Trace to dismount and then handed her back. He nodded to her and silently took the horse into the barn.

"His silence makes up for Jack, I expect?" she said.

"Something like that," replied Trace. "You need the privy before we go in?"

"Yes, please."

Though she insisted she could walk, he carried her to the small building.

"Rest here until I come back with a lantern. You're safe, no snakes or anything. I'll be just a minute."

Florence sank down on the seat and sighed in relief. After days on a train, then wagons and a horse, it was delightful to sit on something still. She did what was necessary, then stepped outside and looked up. The bright moon took up most of the sky. The rest was sprinkled with brilliant stars. She hugged herself and waited as the lantern wobbled toward her.

"You take it. I know the way," Trace said. He handed the lantern over. A door opened and light shone out. A woman waited on the porch.

"There's Beth. You head that way, the path's clear. I figure you gals could use some time together. Beth is twittering like a fool at the thought of another sister in the valley. I'll be in the barn with Simon. We'll bring your children in when Ben arrives."

"Thank you," she whispered, tears choking her throat. "You're a good man."

"That's what Beth says when she's not threatening to hit me over the head with a fry pan. I'm a happy man when she's happy."

He strode off toward the barn. She lifted her skirts with one hand, held the lantern high and stepped forward. She was almost there when she stumbled. Beth hurried toward her.

"Oh, hon, I didn't think. I should have come for the lantern. You must be so tired."

Florence stared. "Elizabeth?" She gulped. "Elizabeth James?"

The other woman grabbed Florence's hand. She lifted it along with the lantern. She blinked at the light.

"Florence? Florence Peabody?"

"I'm Mrs. Benjamin Elliott now. Timothy threw away the letter with your married name and address. I didn't know if I'd ever find you!"

Beth laughed, the sound floating around them. "Good to know my brother is still as thickheaded as before. Oh, what am I doing? You need a hot bath more than anything."

Beth pulled the lantern out of her hand and half-carried her, both of them laughing tears, into the kitchen.

Chapter Eleven

"You touch my wife and I'll kill you." Ben said the words calmly to Jack, stating a fact.

"You mean, if she trips I'm supposed to let her hit the floor?"

"Don't be absurd. You know exactly what I'm talking about."

Jack growled something Ben didn't catch. He leaned over and tugged at the lead horse's reins. The wagon started moving again, slowly rising up the track. Ben said nothing for a few minutes.

He looked at Jack, who carefully kept his face averted. Ben rolled his shoulders. It wasn't Jack's fault Ben was sent to live with The MacDougal. Jack did nothing to cause the beatings the four youngest Elliotts had received over the years. For all Ben knew, Trace, Simon, and Jack had had a hell of a life.

"What happened to Trace?"

"He stopped a couple of thugs who didn't appreciate him saving a lady. They roped him and dragged him through town. Wrecked his voice and damn near killed him. Happened right after you four moved across the valley. He couldn't get out of bed for weeks. The lady nursed him back to health."

Ben winced in the dark. "I never knew. We would have moved back to help."

Jack shrugged. "You know The MacDougal. Sink or swim. Plus, he wanted you working on his ranch." Jack moved his horse away from the wagon and back to avoid a few scrub trees. "I remember him coming over once with Sunbird. I expect she made him take her. He stomped around and complained at the shitty job we were doing. Sunbird unloaded food for us while he pretended not to see." He spat to the side. "Bastard."

"You have no idea," said Ben mildly.

"We're getting one. Ranger and Patrick said nothing, but I heard he took the whip to Jessie once."

Ben grunted. "You seen Ranger's back?"

Jack glanced over. "Come to think of it, Ranger never takes his shirt off to work, like the rest of us."

"Don't make a fuss if you see it."

Jack gave him a speaking glance, asking for detail. Ben cursed himself for starting the conversation, but forced himself to continue. He stared between the horses and kept his voice level. It still gave him nightmares.

"We were stacking hay high in the barn. Fin was mad about something and pushed me out of the loft. I landed so hard I couldn't inhale to scream. Ranger told The MacDougal that Fin pushed me on purpose. Fin and Hugh said it was a lie, that I was fooling around and fell." He glanced at Jack. "Telling a lie and carrying tales are bad, but playing when you should be working is worse. He lashed Ranger to a beam, handed Fin the whip, and walked out."

"What were you doing, reading a book as usual?"

"I was flat on my back with a broken leg!" His chest heaved as he held his voice down because of the sleeping children. "For a long time after I landed I could barely breathe. I tried to move but my whole body was on fire, especially my leg. I had to lie there and listen to Fin and Hugh's laughter as that." He clamped his jaw so he wouldn't swear. "That whip ripped my twin's flesh, again and again, because he spoke up for me."

"He scream?"

Ben snorted. He raised an eyebrow and looked sideways at Jack. "We talking about the same man?"

"Right," said Jack. "I can't see him giving the bastards that satisfaction."

"Patrick ran for Sunbird, and I passed out. Patrick said Sunbird tore the whip out of Fin's hand and chased them out of the barn, swinging it, while Patrick took Ranger down." Ben gritted his teeth and stared straight ahead. "We both ended up on a blanket in a corner of the kitchen. Me on my back, and Ranger on his front. He refused to have her touch him. But she rubbed healing stuff on his back when he was delirious. It would have been even worse, otherwise."

"Shit!" Jack's epithet was low, but intense.

"After the swelling in my leg went down, Sunbird wrapped a green hide around the break and tied it on. It dried tight. I wore that thing all summer, using a crutch to walk. She told The MacDougal I'd never be able to ride again, and even walking without a stick was a maybe. That's when he said I'd be going to school in Virginia, like Ma wanted."

Ben inhaled deeply, and then let it all out. Water under the bridge. "Sunbird lied." He forced a smirk and turned to Jack. "You could blame me being a lawyer on Fin."

"Damn," whispered Jack, serious for once. "If I'd known that, I'd have taken Jessie's whip to him as a wedding present to all of us."

Ben swallowed past the chill in his lungs. He nudged his rifle with his foot to make sure it was near.

"He was here?"

Jack nodded and gave Ben a sour look. "He chased Jessie and her inheritance to Virginia, and then here. Ace and Jessie married, and we thought he was gone. But he came back, with his own wife and a judge from Helena. Tell you about that later, but his wife will keep him in line. Patrick took it upon himself to tell her about the way things are in Texas. She said things would change when she got there, or her husband would be afraid to close his eyes at night."

"Damn. Wish I'd had a chance to put a bullet in him." The thought of nailing Fin's hide to the barn wall helped calm him. He rolled his tight shoulders.

"You considering murder, Mr. Lawyer?" Jack's sarcasm was back.

"I expect at least half this valley would agree it was self-defense."

"Sheriff Chambers might not, and he's still the man with a badge." Jack chuckled. "Fin's wife's almost as big and loud as he is. She'll make him as miserable as she can. As long as Amelia has a son before The MacDougal dies, Fin won't be back."

"Doesn't Gil own the MD Connected?"

Jack shook his head. "Unless one of them has a son before The MacDougal dies, everything goes to Finan Junior, including the MD Connected. Auntie says Amelia's baby is due mid-March. Fin swears he'll sell the MD Connected to miners the moment his father dies."

"We'll tie the matter up in court. They're not going to lose their ranch."

Jack laughed, his usual reaction to anything good, bad, or indifferent. "Damn right. Amelia's going to give Ross a son, Beth will have Simon's daughter, and Jessie will settle down into an obedient wife."

Ben forced a laugh. "The first and second are possible, but Jessie will never settle into a wife. Even when she traipsed around Charlottesville in her dress and bonnet, she was stubborn and independent. She's tiny, but no man will settle her down."

Jack's teeth shone white when he smiled. "No, but three might. You haven't seen how Ace, Sin, and Henry control her."

"Control Jessie? She's better with a pistol, rifle, knife, and whip than most of the men in Montana Territory."

Jack smirked. "You might want to remember I told you this so you can thank me later on." He leaned over and dropped his voice to a whisper. "They control her with sex. It's the only thing the rest of us couldn't do to her."

"Control her with—?" Ben dropped his voice. "How?"

"Ace threatens to make her sleep alone, and Sin mentions spanking. I thought Henry was an easygoing man, but he gets this look on his face, and Jessie quiets right down." Jack chuckled. "Though maybe she's winding up," He shrugged. "In any case, I think

Trace gave them the idea. You might want to think about that."

Ben grunted. How could he think about controlling his wife with sex when he'd never been alone with her except once? From the way she reacted to his mouth on her breast, he figured she'd enjoy the physical aspects of marriage. He sure hoped so, for all their sakes.

Since they hadn't talked about anything personal, he didn't even know if Florence could cook or take care of their home. Ma had come from the same society, arriving when the valley was total wilderness. Unlike Ma, Florence had a home to start in, even if it was just a one-room cabin. She also had Beth and Amelia to guide her. Hopefully, Jessie wouldn't be too much of an influence. He didn't want an angry wife who knew how to throw knives but wasn't as accurate at his sister.

"Nevin said you didn't want your dear wife to know about Ranger. What's that about, huh? Got a secret you don't wanna share?"

Though it had been many years since they'd seen each other, Ben reacted to Jack's taunting as if they were boys.

"That is between my wife and me. And if you say one word more, I will—"

"You'll do what?" taunted Jack. "Talk me to death? You've been sitting on your ass for years reading books while I've been working every damn day. So has every one of your brothers, and cousins. Jessie's husbands haven't been ranching that long, but I'd be careful about taking them on. Their fathers may be lords, but they can scrap with the rest of us. I don't think you're up to even that."

Jack rode off, getting the last word as always. Ben stewed for a moment and then shook his head at his immediate return to the same childish behaviors. Brothers, no longer how many years apart, came back together the same. It was the same with Nevin and Ranger last night.

So was their ability to catch him unaware, pin him down and, if they'd wanted, beat him as flat as a carpet. He stewed for a while as the wagon rolled under the moon.

Jack was right. He could not take anyone on except through the law. So that was how he would pull his weight. One day their descendants would live in this valley, and the land around it. They needed to have laws in place to protect what was theirs.

Ranger knew ranching but had patience for little else. He would think Ben a liability because he wasn't as physically strong. Ben had to immediately establish that all those years of education had practical value. From what he could discover, there were few lawyers in Montana Territory. Those who had any skill were owned by mining corporations or the railroads.

The land held gold, silver, copper, and who knew what else. Those who held the land held power, both openly and under the table. Too many wealthy miners and railroad men were quietly putting laws on the books that could destroy the lives of men who lived on the land. The right to clean water was most important, followed by mineral rights. Mining operations needed to be controlled so they wouldn't poison the land. Damage upstream could destroy the water, and therefore the land, belonging to ranches downstream.

Before he headed west he spent time, and Bonham money, making connections in Virginia, New York, Washington, and Philadelphia. He made sure the men behind the power met him and knew he had a dream.

He felt almost sick when he saw the smoke belching from the steam engines driving the gold-digging equipment at Alder Gulch. The smoke came from trees which used to cover mountainsides. Without the trees, the land would slide, fouling streams and rivers, destroying the trout and stopping water from reaching pastureland.

The buffalo were almost gone thanks to the greed of the white man. He would not have the land, air, and water of his great-grandchildren destroyed through lack of action. Sunbird's people had lived on these lands forever. Their ways were harsh, but they mostly took what they needed, leaving enough to grow back.

It was up to him to go to work, first by cultivating businessmen.

Bannack and Virginia City might fade when the mines played out, but Helena would continue to grow now that they changed its name from Last Chance Gulch. He heard there were even homes with Mansard roofs there. They would be palatial compared to the one-room soddies and cabins most people occupied.

He may not have the muscles or quick reflexes of his brothers and cousins, but he had a brain. He also had a dream and a valley full of family driving him to make that dream work for all of them.

He sighed. It seemed he also had a virgin wife with two children. A wife who thought the height of passion was an intense debate. Once Ranger showed her the more physical side of passion, he would settle her into life on the ranch. He wasn't sure how to ease her into having sex with all three of them, but she was an intelligent woman. The logic of it made sense.

Because of the amount of work required, most ranches had three partners. Since women were scarce, why not share one wife between them? Three men to do the hard ranch work and to raise the children. More parents in case one, or more, died.

If his father had shared the ranch with two others, he and his siblings would not have been separated. Four of them would not have been sent to Texas as unpaid servants of a brutal man. He scratched his chin. He couldn't see Ma sharing Pa with anyone.

But surely Florence would appreciate why three husbands were better than one?

Did he have time before winter set in to convince her she could be happy with her children and a few men to warm her bed? He'd have to make sure she realized the debates she loved were suited to long winter nights when they had the time to linger.

Perhaps the best of both worlds would be to debate under the covers. He could make his arguments more pointedly that way.

As long as she didn't try to discuss her theories with Ranger.

Chapter Twelve

Beth helped Florence through the kitchen and into the bathing room she insisted Trace create off the kitchen. It had two copper tubs which drained from holes in the bottom when a plug was pulled. Beth told her the water went through a pipe into a shallow pond near the garden.

She hung the lantern from a hook over a steaming tub and shut the door. Florence moaned in anticipation and began ripping her clothing off. Beth laughed and helped her old friend. The dress and underthings dropped to the floor.

"These are filthy. I've been wearing them since I left Philadelphia over a week ago."

"Believe me, I understand," replied Beth. "I got married in the dress I wore all the way west and for an additional few days in jail. My bare feet were dirty, and my hair looked like a packrat's nest. Trace arranged for me to have a hot bath before he joined me for our wedding night." She sighed fondly. "He even took the time to pick me a posy of wildflowers. He said a bride should have flowers for her wedding." She blinked rapidly. "Don't mind me. I become so up and down when I'm growing a baby." She wiped her eyes. "That bath helped me cope with everything, so I made sure to have one ready for Ben's wife. You must be exhausted."

She pushed Florence to sit on a stool and helped her remove her boots and stockings.

"What with taking care of Emma and Johnny, I haven't had time to do more than sponge my face every day. I had no idea what I was getting into when I agreed to take the children. But I couldn't leave them to be preyed upon by the worst of the worst."

"That's a story for another day," said Beth, and helped Florence step into the tub. She moaned and sank down, knees to chin. Steaming water rose to cover her shoulders. Beth pulled the stool behind her and began to undo her braid.

"Oh, my. I think I'm going to cry. This is bliss. I cannot thank you enough." She suddenly sat up and faced Beth. Water sloshed but didn't go over the edge. "Oh! Timothy sent your grandmother's inheritance, as promised. He's the reason I came out here." She slumped. "Of course, my parents were delighted to have an excuse to send their unmarriageable daughter far, far away."

"Obviously, you're not unmarriageable," replied Beth. "And I'd half forgotten about that money." She pushed Florence to lie back again. "How is my dear brother?"

"He's a pompous banker married to a harpy with money." Florence pressed her hand over her mouth. "I shouldn't have said that. It's the fatigue talking."

Beth laughed. "Yes, you should say it. We're sisters now, and shouldn't have secrets. Timothy was always a selfish boy. He wanted money, and now he has it. As long as he stays far away, I can be happy for him." She picked up her comb and began at the ends of Florence's hair, working the knots out.

"Don't worry, he will never leave Philadelphia," said Florence. "That's why he was delighted to hear I was going to visit you. Now you have your money, he wants nothing to do with you. I'm sorry that your brother—"

"I don't need him. I've got three husbands, five brothers, and three cousins-in-law, along with two, now three, sisters-in-law, and children. I have friends in Tanner's Ford as well. Sometimes the family who raised you is not worth your energy."

Florence shook her head to clear her ears. "Did you say, three husbands?"

Beth sat back, holding the comb in her hand. She nodded. "I

married Trace, but discovered the next day that Simon and Jack were part of the package." She sighed, a satisfied smile on her face. "And what a package they are. Between them, they keep me fully loved."

Florence wrapped her arms around her nude body. "I don't understand. How can someone have three husbands?"

Beth rubbed her swollen belly. "Trace is my husband in law, but laws can be stretched to suit necessity. I've found that, when there's enough love to share, and more than enough work to get done, three husbands can solve a few problems."

"Don't you mean cause a few problems?" Florence shook her head, frowning. "I've never done more than kiss Ben, though that was very, very nice. I can't imagine what it would be like to share that with another man."

"What did it feel like when Ben kissed you?" She leaned forward. "Has he kissed you anywhere other than your lips?"

Though the bath was warm, Florence felt the rush of heat that rose at her memory of him baring her breast, and then kissing it. He did more than kiss, though. He nibbled and sucked, making her feel all soft and wet and needy between her legs.

"What are you thinking of right now?"

"Um, he kissed my breast," Florence whispered.

"From the look on your face, you enjoyed it."

Florence nodded.

"Imagine that feeling, times three." Beth scrunched up her face and shook her head. "No, times three hundred." She grinned. "If you've never had an orgasm, you can't imagine what one man can do to make you soar, much less three."

"No one but Ben has made me tingle."

Beth winked. "You haven't met Ranger and Patrick yet. Maybe they will make you feel just as good when they kiss your breast."

"Beth! You don't expect me to let them touch me?"

"Let them? I expect you'll be demanding they touch you, kiss you, and every other thing." She leaned closer. "You remember when your older sister, Charity, told us not to believe the horrid things Miss Primula said about marital relations? She was right. I would never have expected what happens when my men touch me. Until you've had an orgasm or three, you won't understand."

Florence settled back in the tub. The luxury of a deep, hot, bath was too great to sacrifice, no matter what they talked about.

"Charity liked to point out what I was missing. But really, is it that good?"

"Sometimes, it's like being in heaven. And then they do something so...so *male*... I want to smack them upside the head and send them to the barn for a week!" Beth laughed.

"Do you love them all?"

"Yes, in different ways, and they love me. Our first night, Trace proved how well we got along in bed. The next day, as soon as we got on Elliott land, Trace had me strip down. We did it right there, in bright sunlight. Trace warned me Simon might be watching, and that made me hot!"

"Was he?"

"Oh, yes. And I was glad I'd put on a bit of a show. When I met them, Simon and Jack looked at me as if I was the only one who could make them whole. Amelia didn't even see her husband, Ross, until the morning, after he pleasured her many times."

Florence swallowed, forcing it past her dry throat. "And you both accept the situation?"

Beth nodded. "We would never have believed it, but we're all very, very happy." She looked down, smiling fondly as she rubbed her belly again. "This is Simon's child. I want to have Jack's next. Jessie's men don't care which one of them fathers her babies. I've only recently met Ranger and Patrick, so I can't answer how they'll feel about it."

"I can't believe we're calmly discussing me sharing my marriage bed with three men, two of whom I've never met."

"Does the thought make you upset, or eager?"

Florence squeezed her thighs together. The spot between them, which had been aching since that first kiss from Ben, was throbbing. Her breasts, though in warm water, were firm, her nipples hard.

"Eager," she whispered.

"That's the attitude! If I wasn't already madly in love with their brothers, I'd be tempted by Ranger and Patrick. Wait until you meet them."

Florence nodded absently. Between the exhaustion, the shock, and the hot water, her brain wasn't functioning very well.

"There are only four married women in this valley now. You, me, Amelia, and Jessie. We have to stick together." Beth went back to attacking Florence's hair. "You don't have enough time to wash this tonight, but I'll tell Ben to buy you a copper tub right away."

Florence turned around. She shook her head, eyes wide. "You mustn't. I can't ask him to spend money on me. I don't know what his finances are, what with a new ranch and all—"

"Hush," she pushed Florence to make her lean back again. "Then it will be a wedding present from Amelia and me. We have our own account with Patsy Tanner at the mercantile. Amelia brought all sorts of fancy dresses with her, ones she'll never wear. She sells them to Patsy, and gets credit in return." She patted Florence's shoulder. "Our men don't have to know anything about what we buy. Here's the soap. I want you finished before the children arrive, so don't fall asleep on me. The other tub's for them."

"What about Ben?"

"He's a man. He can use what's left over, or the creek." Beth laughed when Florence almost giggled at her disgusted expression. "Don't start your marriage by catering to your husbands. They'll get used to it, and when you've got a baby, you'll want to put your attention on your child, not childish men." Beth pointed out the nightgown and wrapper hanging from a nail on the wall. She set a wide flannel on the stool and left the room.

* * * *

Beth smiled at Trace. He relaxed in his corner chair, sock feet toward the fire. Arms slid around her from behind. Simon set his hands on her belly. Though she wasn't showing very much, he liked to touch her there as often as he could. He even spoke to his baby, whispering into her belly and telling stories of the high jinks he got into while growing up.

"What do you think of the newest Mrs. Elliott? You think she'll fit in?"

Beth turned her head and smiled up at the father of her second child. "Once she finds out what good loving is, yes. I'm looking forward to her finding her feet. She is going to stir you men up a fair bit. I don't know Ranger that well, but I can already see sparks flying."

"You can tell this from a few minutes?"

"No, I can tell it from sharing a classroom with her for years."

Simon turned her around to face him. His raised eyebrows begged an answer.

"Florence and I attended Miss Primula's Ladies College together. I've liked her since we were girls. Her father allowed her to use her brain instead of trying to beat the intelligence out of her."

Simon placed his palm on her cheek. "I wish I could thrash him for you."

"I'd much rather you encourage Bridie and Meggie, and any other girls, to be strong, intelligent women."

Simon pulled her close. "My daughter is going to be a sweet, smart, wonderful girl. Just like her momma."

He brushed his lips against hers. His cock rose, pressing against her belly. She returned the kiss, taking Simon's tongue deep in her mouth. Neither paid attention to the opening door.

"Hey, it's my turn to snuggle Beth tonight, not you," groused Jack. "Sy, you'd better come out here and carry Emma. Ben's not strong enough. Ranger said he busted his leg, but I think it's all those years sitting in front of a book instead of doing real work."

"Jack! At least let me meet the man before you insult him," said Beth.

"Ignore him, Beth," said Simon. "He's never got along with Ben for some reason. But it's no excuse to take it out on others."

Simon addressed the last comment to Jack. He grabbed Jack's shoulder and shoved him out the door, Jack still complaining, before Beth could think up a good response. She returned to the bath room to help her sleepy friend dry and dress herself before they were invaded by men carrying children.

* * * *

Ben stopped the horses in the puddle of light that streamed out the kitchen window. Trace took the lead horse to hold it steady. Ben did his best to climb down the side of the wagon rather than fall off. He held on the boards as he walked around to the back. Both kids were still sleeping, curled together like puppies.

"We'd better carry them," called Jack. "You're too weak."

"Shut up, Jack," said Simon. He said it almost automatically, as if it was a common phrase. "Good to see you again, little brother. Welcome home." He held out his hand. When Ben took it, Sy pulled him close. He slapped him on the back a couple of times before releasing him.

"It's grand to be home. Sometimes I never thought I'd make it."

"Poppa?" Emma sat up, pushing hair out of her eyes.

"Right here. We're at your Aunt Beth's home. I lived here when I was your age. This is your Uncle Simon."

"Your mama's got a warm bath ready for you," said Simon quietly. "May I carry you inside while Uncle Jack brings Johnny?"

Emma bit her lip. She looked toward the kitchen and then relaxed. Ben saw Florence in the kitchen window, waving them in with a welcoming smile. Emma tugged on his sleeve.

"Are these the good men you told me about, Poppa?" Her whisper was louder than a spoken question would be.

He leaned close and kissed her forehead. "Some of them. This whole valley is full of your new aunts and uncles and cousins. Every single one of them will protect you and Johnny. You'll be safe here."

She rose to her knees, turned her best blazing smile on Simon, and held out her arms. He curled her into his chest.

"Wait for Johnny," she ordered. "He might get scared if I'm not with him."

Jack gently picked up Johnny, blankets and all, and followed Simon. Ben was too damn tired to fight Jack over the weakness comment. That, and he was right. He could have carried both if he had to, but it was safer for his brothers to help.

"There something I should know about these two?"

Ben winced at Trace's unfamiliar voice. After what Jack told him, he was surprised the man could talk at all. Trace led the horses under a shelter to protect the wagon in case of rain or heavy September frost or dew. They unhooked the animals and led them to the barn.

"Florence had Emma and Johnny when I met her, but I'm fairly certain she didn't give birth to them."

"She lied to you?" Trace asked the question calmly, with no accusation in his voice.

"No." Ben thought a minute before answering. "She hasn't had a chance to say much. We've been married for days, but I've not really been alone with her."

Trace gave a noncommittal grunt.

"She literally fell into my lap, on her way to the dining car the first morning. Emma asked her if I was her fancy man, her protector." Trace looked up for a moment but said nothing. "It seems their '*Maman*' had one. When I replied I must be, as I'd protected her from falling, Emma gave me a practiced smile. Not one a child should understand the need for."

Ben grabbed a brush—it was in the same spot as when he was a child. They worked quietly for a few minutes.

"Florence doesn't know what the child meant?"

Ben shook his head. "I'm not sure how much she knows about their past. We'd barely met when the train stopped at a town and the four of us went walking. A man went after Emma, saying she belonged to him."

"You kill him?"

"No, the sheriff interrupted too soon. I said I was Emma's father, and Florence was my wife."

"Sheriff take your word?"

"No, he wanted a license, which I couldn't produce, of course." Ben looked at Trace over the horse's rump. "There happened to be a preacher waiting at the station," he drawled. "Just in case a bride wished to get married. The sheriff insisted I 'renew' my vows to prove Emma and Johnny were mine. Florence needed a husband, and I was—"

"Convenient."

Ben nodded. "Very. Long story short, I promised to bring a wife home, and I did."

"She got three decent husbands for her children. Convenient for all of you."

"Problem is, she thinks she only has one. I don't know how to tell her the way things are here. What if it drives her away?"

Trace shifted to the other side of his horse. "My wife and yours recognized each other from when they were schoolgirls. They've been alone for awhile in that bath room. I expect Florence knows about Beth's three husbands, and those of the other valley women." Trace pointed the hoof pick to Ben. "If she's well bedded, Florence will get used to it, even be eager to go after you, just like the others. That's something you, Ranger, and Patrick have to solve."

Ben ruminated on that while they worked in comfortable silence, finishing at the same time. Ben followed Trace, both leading their horses, and turned them into the paddock.

"Half an hour after I stepped into a jail with a screeching woman, I said 'I do,' and we've settled in fine," said Trace. "You might have been pushed into it at the time, but you married Florence because you wanted to, just like me and Beth."

"That I did." For many reasons, most of which he'd never tell his brothers.

"Beth's already decided to keep the little ones with us overnight. Your place ain't ready for a family, and Nevin said he wanted to borrow them to keep Daniel company." Ben grunted when Trace, three inches taller and far more muscular, slapped him on the back. Trace grinned down at him through his bushy moustache. "You boys need time alone to show the little woman the way things are, here in the valley."

"Little woman? You ever call Beth that to her face?"

Trace shook his head. His grin reminded Ben of happy days before their parents died. "Not unless I want all my meals burned, my undershorts starched, and a cold bed in the barn. But a wife doesn't have to know everything her husband thinks. That's lesson two on being a husband."

Ben raised an eyebrow. "What's lesson one?"

"No matter how wrong you know she is, your wife is always right. Apologize and then kiss her until her eyes cross."

Ben shook his head as they walked toward the kitchen together. "Taking blame when you're right goes against everything I've been taught as a lawyer."

Trace stopped and turned at the edge of the porch. He smirked like an older brother smartening up a younger.

"You want to be right and sleep in the barn? Or do you want your wife screaming your name as you fill her with your seed?"

"Good point."

Chapter Thirteen

Florence woke to the smell of coffee. She remembered Beth helping her to bathe Emma and Johnny. A quick goodnight to a blur of faces, and she'd tucked them into the spare bedroom. Emma asked her to lie down for a moment and that was the last thing she remembered. She quickly put her wrapper on and went into the large, sunny kitchen. She'd brought extra clothing, but it was still in the wagon.

"I guess you haven't got Beth's morning problem yet," said one of the men when she entered. She'd met them in the dim light last night, but was too tired to match names and faces. He elbowed Ben in the ribs, and the others laughed. Florence realized they meant Beth's queasy morning stomach due to the baby. A rush of heat flowed up her face, causing another series of hearty laughs.

"I'm Jack, the one Ben doesn't trust," said one smiling man. "That's Simon, my twin." He pointed to the one she remembered carrying Emma. "Trace is the one in the moustache you cuddled up to last night." Ben smacked him on the back of the head with his palm. "Ow! I meant cuddled up on his horse!"

"Our Meggie's cooking the ham and eggs, and that's Bridie stirring the porridge," said Trace, sending a quelling glance to Jack.

Florence nodded at the giggling girls. She noticed the men casually passed Beth's seven-month-old son, James, around. Jack suddenly lifted the baby off his lap. Pee dripped off one of the baby's toes. Jack grinned and held him out to Ben, who jumped to his feet to prepare his wife a cup of coffee. He got thanks from her and snickers from his brothers. Jack expertly took the wet diaper off, washed

James down, and nonchalantly set the bare-bottomed boy back on his lap. James chewed his finger and looked up at his uncle.

The door to the bedroom opened, and Emma peered out. When Florence beckoned, she padded into the room hand in hand with Johnny. They hid behind her, peeking from either side at the four men.

"Look, Emma, there's Bridie," said Florence. The girl waved the tip of her red-gold braid at Emma, who smiled shyly but didn't move.

"Your cousin Daniel MacDougal can't wait to meet you, Johnny," said Simon. "He's ten years old. Isn't that how old you are?"

Johnny shook his head and held up four fingers, peeking from behind them. All the men looked up when Beth came down the stairs.

"Better this morning?" Simon greeted her as soon as her feet reached the floor. When she nodded, he gave her a slow kiss, one that had Florence turning her hot face away in embarrassment.

"You men can take your breakfast outside and leave space for the women and children," announced Beth a bit breathlessly. Trace immediately handed out tin plates and spoons. Jack passed James to Beth. By the time she'd put on a dry diaper, the room held only the two women and hungry children, as Bridie and Meggie had left with the men.

"Could you help me tie this old sheet around my neck?" asked Beth. "My darling son makes quite the mess when I feed him oatmeal."

Florence did so and then made sure her children were preoccupied with their own bowls of oatmeal. Beth encouraged them to sprinkle some late blueberries on top.

"How do you make those big men listen to you like that?" asked Florence quietly.

Beth looked up with a wide smile. "They know what's good for them. If they want to share my bed at night, they do what I say during the day." She stirred the bowl of porridge Meggie must have dished out earlier to cool. "Hand James one of those small wooden spoons, please."

James snatched the spoon eagerly, though it went nowhere near his mouth. Florence watched Beth slip in mouthfuls of porridge, distracting her son with his spoon.

"You really do share your bed with Trace, Jack, and Simon?" Florence spoke in little more than a whisper.

Beth nodded. A tinge of pink appeared on her cheeks. "And enjoy it immensely."

"Pardon me for asking, but, one at a time?"

"Yes." Beth looked up. "Or two at a time, or all three. It depends. Each has its pleasures."

James grabbed the spoon Beth held still. He shoved it toward his mouth. Beth managed to help it arrive close to the right place. The sheet saved her dress from a few blobs of oatmeal.

Florence tried to think of what Mary had told her, and put three men in the bed instead of one. She should be horrified, but instead the tingle between her thighs, the ache that had bothered her since she landed in Ben's lap, intensified.

A roar erupted outside, followed by raucous laughter. Emma and Johnny ran to the window to look out. Florence stood up. Ben, flat on his back, scrambled to his feet and went after Jack.

"Ben and Jack are fighting," said Florence, trying to keep her shaking voice calm. Emma hid behind her. Johnny, however, eagerly watched. "I think Jack just punched my husband in the belly." She winced. "But Ben got him in the chin."

"Don't worry, they do this all the time," said Beth. "Emma, they're play fighting, not really trying to hurt each other."

Emma frowned, but came out from behind Florence to watch. Johnny laughing beside her helped her relax even more.

"The new dog just arrived so they have to sort things out between them," said Beth quietly to Florence. "Trace will make sure nothing gets too serious."

"The dogs are watching the men, not fighting," said Florence.

Beth snickered. "I compare the men to a pack of dogs. They always fight to see who's on top, to prove they're better than the others. Trace is always the leader, but now with Ben, Ranger, and Patrick home, the rest have to establish rank." James turned his face away from the spoon and fought to get down. "Wait until there's six Elliotts, Amelia, and the MacDougals, plus Auntie and Daniel, and Jessie and her three. Twelve big men, four wives, Auntie, and our children." She laughed as she wiped her wriggling son's face clean.

"Will twelve of them fight? I don't want the children to see anything upsetting."

"They'd never do anything to scare or hurt any child. But you'll see strutting and posturing, shoving and pushing, staring and daring, and maybe even some wrestling. Ben is at a disadvantage because of his bad leg and his years away from the ranch. He'll have to prove his worth another way or deal with constant sniping." She kissed James. "We can't let on, but Amelia and I look out the window and laugh."

Florence turned away from the window before they noticed her watching. "Anything else I should know about?"

"Did you see how Simon met me at the bottom of the stairs this morning?"

Florence nodded. "That was quite the good morning kiss."

"He did it because I'm carrying his baby. He has to point that out to everyone as often as he can." She rolled her eyes. "Trace was the same when I carried James, and Ross is ever so careful with Amelia. Jessie swears she's not going to have a baby for years, but the way I hear it, every one of her men is determined to get her in the family way as soon as possible. While Amelia's husbands and mine want to know who the father of their children is, those English men don't care who makes her babies."

"How would one know, if they all, um…share with her?"

Beth's cheeks flamed. "Only the father-to-be puts his—" She flicked her eyes at the children. "His you know what, where. The others make do with other fun until the wife is sure she's with child."

"Other fun?" Florence managed to get the question out, though her voice shook a bit. "I'm not sure what happens with one man. What does one do with *three?*"

Beth shook her head. "I won't talk about that before breakfast, especially as you've never even undressed in front of a man. And don't let Ben know we've spoken about this. Men have strange ideas about what women need to know. They think not telling us upsetting things will protect us. In fact, we are far better off if we know in advance. That way, we're prepared for whatever happens."

Beth stood up and handed James to Florence. She held him awkwardly until Beth showed her how to tuck him on her hip. He sat there as if he belonged. When would she have her own baby?

"What about you?" asked Beth. She tilted her head, a smile playing around her mouth.

"Me?"

"Will you share your bed with Ben, Ranger, and Patrick?"

* * * *

Florence waved good-bye until the trail took the wagon out of sight. Bridie held Emma's hand. Johnny stood between Trace's legs. Both children were eager to see their Uncle Nevin again, as well as the promised older cousin, Daniel.

She looked around for a few minutes and then looked forward. It was so quiet after the city, the train, and all Ben's family. But Beth said no one would bother them for a few days, so they could "get better acquainted." Her facial expression made Florence blush, which only made Beth laugh harder.

"Maybe this means I'm not a good mother, but I'm glad we'll be alone for a few days."

"You mean you don't like being asked twenty questions a minute as long as one of them is awake?" Ben turned his head to kiss her cheek.

"Emma looked happy when Beth told her she and Johnny would stay with Nevin, Daniel, and baby Hope. Johnny's fascinated with the idea of being a big brother."

"I thought it was Nev's sword-sized knife that caught his interest?" He shook his head, smiling. "Counting Auntie, there'll be five adults and Daniel to keep them busy. We won't have time to keep an eye on them. From what Trace said, we've got a lot of work to do before the winter if we want to live in any comfort."

"Should I be upset they're happy to stay with Nevin?"

"All the children will visit back and forth between their uncles and aunts. When Beth and Amelia have their babies in the spring, we may have our two back, along with James or Hope. Our children might as well get used to visiting family."

Florence nodded absently. Her children were nothing like Mary's loud and boisterous ones. But, having experienced their constant chatter for just over a week, she really appreciated the quiet morning. She loved them, but knew they were in more experienced, equally loving hands. She wanted to get to know her husband before being overrun with children. She had to meet Ben's brothers, as well. Beth said Patrick was a sweet man and that Ranger, though gruff, would never hurt a woman or child. The protestations made her even more apprehensive about meeting the older brother.

Of course, Beth telling her that they expected her to share her body with all three brothers, only made her worries worse. What if she didn't like them? Worse, what if she liked them as much as, or better than Ben? Would he get jealous?

Beth's neat, well-kept yard and extensive garden soon gave way to a rougher area. The well-worn track from town turned into a bumpy set of ruts heading northwest, farther up the valley. Forested hills swooped above the far side of the valley with high, sharp mountains beyond.

Ben sat tall in the seat, glancing about as if memorizing everything. He had a physical vigor to him that she hadn't noticed on the train. Of course, there wasn't much opportunity to do more than stroll. But there was more to it than how he held himself. Since they awoke in Virginia City, Ben seemed far more relaxed, as if something terrible had been taken from his shoulders.

Perhaps it was because he was home with his family. Some family! As one of only two girls, both of whom were to be seen and not heard, she couldn't imagine growing up with six siblings, with another seven cousins next door. And when Ben's parents died, the MacDougals brought the four youngest Elliotts into their home. That gave them ten boys and two girls to raise. Beth said there was a bunkhouse on the MD Connected where the boys used to live, and where Auntie's older relatives sometimes spent the worst of the winter.

Florence could see Beth taking in another family like that, but she wasn't so sure about herself. Maybe when she'd lived here a year and had a baby like Beth, she'd feel more sure of herself.

Having children meant one first had to get naked with a man. Beth and Mary swore it was absolutely wonderful with the right man, or men in Beth's case. Beth insisted that her men, and Amelia's, were considerate, and she couldn't see Florence's men being any different. She insisted Florence's first experience, and all those that followed, would be wonderful.

Florence had more than enough to worry about with one husband. She and Ben would be alone, so he was the only one she would think about. But, what if Ranger and Patrick made her skin crawl, like some of the men she'd been forced to dance with back home?

No! She would not anticipate anything negative. She would think about how wonderful it felt when Ben touched her. She closed her eyes, remembering the time Mary took the children when they stopped one sunny day. Ben took her behind a building and kissed her senseless. Then he unbuttoned her to the waist and touched her breasts.

Her memories made them tingle almost as much as they had back then. She remembered how his tongue and teeth nipped, licked, and tantalized her until she was ready to explode. She wanted more, but the train's whistle erupted. They rushed to do up her buttons and ran through the town, hand in hand, laughing like children. They'd barely made it onto the train. She let the others think her red face was from running, but Mary gave her a knowing wink.

Florence rubbed her thighs together, but the ache grew instead of easing. She turned to Ben, but he didn't seem to notice. While he couldn't be demonstrative while they were on the train, she had yet to experience a satisfying kiss since they arrived in Virginia City, much less a few caresses.

Beth's men often stood near her, or touched her gently when they passed. They kissed her often, especially Simon. He also liked to kiss her growing belly and speak to the baby right through her skirts. Beth tolerated it, laughing and rolling her eyes at the same time. Florence had the impression that, if she and Ben weren't around, Simon would do a lot more than kiss.

Ben didn't touch her. His brothers must have noticed it, as they gave her a bit of a leer, as if knowing she and Ben had yet to consummate their union. Perhaps Nevin had noted the pillows in Virginia City and spread the word. Florence took a deep breath. She needed time to get comfortable with Ben before tonight. Both of them were good with words, so she started there.

"You and your brothers seem to get along well," she said.

"Is that sarcasm? I saw you and Beth watching me scuffle with Jack in the yard."

"All right, you seem to get along when you're not having fisticuffs, or strutting around like a rooster, or trying to see who's top dog in the pack—"

Ben laughed, deep and loud. He'd undone a few of his shirt buttons. When he tilted his head back she saw the long line of his throat. A few dark hairs peeked from his shirt.

"Don't you know brothers usually fight like Kilkenny cats?" He turned his hazel eyes on her. She found a hint of sea-green in the cognac. "It keeps us in shape so we're ready to fight to protect what's ours."

She bumped him with her shoulder. "I think you fight because you like it."

"I used to," he drawled. "Now that they're all stronger than me, it's not so much fun."

"You'll have to dazzle them with your rhetoric."

"You and Beth may be the only ones around who'll understand all the words." He gave her a serious look. "That sort of talk would rub them the wrong way, and that would really get me thumped. That's especially true with Ranger and Jack. Neither of them got a chance at an education. Jack always wanted to travel, so my opportunity sticks in his craw."

"What about the others?"

"They don't care one way or another. Trace and Simon are homebodies. I expect Ranger and Patrick, now they have a home of their own, will be the same."

"Beth said something about Ranger being gruff. That, no matter how angry he might seem, he wouldn't hurt me or the children."

Ben stared forward for a moment. "When Ma died, something in Ranger broke. We all missed her of course. Still do. But it was different with him." He turned to Florence, frowning. "After Ma died, it was like a piece of his heart was ripped out, and it never healed."

"You haven't seen him for years. Do you think he'll be better now?"

"Nope. Other things happened in Texas that made it worse." He shut his mouth and leaned forward. He slumped, resting his elbows on his knees.

Florence crossed her arms and looked away. The way things were going, Ben was never going to take her in his arms. She let the conversation drift away with the breeze. Part way up the mountains, trees with golden leaves waved her along. She spotted an antelope grazing.

She looked up when a pair of large black birds flew from the south, circling high above. They suddenly dropped, diving straight down.

"Ben, look!"

He sat up, his eyes following her pointing hand. His shoulders relaxed, and he smiled.

At almost the last moment the two birds pulled out of their dive. One rolled onto its back for a moment before righting itself. The other trilled and then made a "quork" noise. They climbed, dove, and rolled for a few minutes.

"Are they flying over to welcome us?" She put a smile in her voice, hoping to change the mood with her silly suggestion.

"Actually, they are," replied Ben. "Ross always has ravens around. They're his totem animal." He caught her eye and winked. "You saw the size of Nevin's beak?" She nodded. "Ross has the same nose. He says Raven granted it to him, and Nev was just lucky to have the same. Amelia hopes their daughters get her small nose."

The ravens swooped lower, chattering. "Do they want something?"

"Didn't Beth put some hard-boiled eggs in that basket of food she sent?" Florence nodded. "Toss one in the air and see what happens."

She opened the basket at her feet, dug in and found one of the eggs, still in its shell. She held it up. Both birds quorked. They wheeled over her head, their noises almost sounding like laughter.

"What are you waiting for?"

She threw the egg straight up as hard as she could. One bird swooped to catch it while the other waited below. The first caught it in its beak without crushing it. It flew away, winging fast to the southwest. The other made a tour around the wagon once, chortling, and followed.

"They're going back to the MD Connected to eat," said Ben. "Ravens are smart to begin with, and the ones Ross raises are even more so. They've seen you with me, and remember people for years." He finally turned to her. "If Ross's ravens see anyone hurting his family, they attack if the person comes near again. Obviously, Fin and Hugh hate the birds. I expect they'll show a few dents in their skulls if they ever lose their hair."

"Those birds are very big, and their beaks look dangerous. Will they hurt the children?"

"No. They love to play with kids, and are great at spotting danger such as rattlesnakes, but they're tricksters." He smiled and shook his head. "I was about eight when Ross moved in with us for a bit. We had a big dog with thick fur. Raven loved to ride on that dog's back. He'd use the dog to sneak up on us and snatch our hats. He'd drop them in the most awkward places, just so we'd play with him. After Ross introduces Emma and Johnny to them, they'll act as another layer of safety."

Since Ben seemed a lot more relaxed, she snuggled up against him and rested her hand on his thigh.

"Does Nevin have a totem?"

"Black bear. He's got four claw marks across his chest from meeting a big one when he was a bit older than Emma."

Florence gasped and sat up. Her heart pounded. "Did the animal attack him?"

"Nevin likes sweets almost as much as Simon, so they both search out trees with beehives in them. Nev says he was after the same honey tree as the bear. They had a discussion about who got what. The bear got the honey, and Nevin got the mark of his totem."

"Oh, my goodness! Is that common around here? The children—"

"Children learn early to watch their way, Florence." He looked at her and spoke solemnly, as if he was one of her teachers providing a lecture. "We're intruders here. Before white men came and ripped up the ground, things were stable. Not perfect, but stable. The strong knocked off the weak to survive and breed stronger young. City life is different. The weak still die, but often they're preyed upon from viciousness, not a need for survival. Life is simple out here. You are strong, or you die. It's something you'll have to get used to."

She thought about his comments for a few minutes. When she set off from home, determined to make a new life for herself, she had no clear knowledge of what she was getting into. But she would never return to the old life. She felt far more alive here than she had in her entire life in the city. She now had an extended family and sisters she'd yet to meet, and children. Even more, she had a home of her own, one she was determined to fill with love.

"What else will I have to get used to?"

Chapter Fourteen

Ben swallowed wrong and choked. She waited while he got himself under control.

"I expect you had a fine house in Philadelphia, with running water, light, and heat," he said. "You had butchers and grocers deliver your food, prepared by a cook and served by a maid. In the evening you sat on a padded chair and read the day's newspaper, or a new book, by the fire."

She nodded. He patted her thigh, just the same as he did the horse.

"Get used to none of that happening any time soon."

She waited, but when he just stared at the horses, she sat up straight. If he wasn't going to start the conversation, she would.

"What do you have to tell me about your brothers?"

Ben turned to her, his eyes were wide and mouth open. He closed it with a snap. "Beth talked to you?"

She nodded. "She's the friend I mentioned, from school. She told me many things about her relationship with your brothers." Ben gulped. "She said you'd want me to share my bed with Ranger and Patrick."

Ben groaned and dropped his head, but only for a moment. He had a lopsided, rueful smile when he turned to her.

"Florence, I knew nothing of this sharing when we got married. It was only when I met with Nevin and Ranger in Virginia City that I found out. Remember that I promised to bring Ranger a wife?"

"Yes, but you didn't start looking until you got on that train."

He winced. "I figured none of the women Aunt Jessamine introduced me to would ever go west of the Missouri River. In any case, I apologized to Ranger and said I'd find him a suitable wife as soon as I could."

"What did he say?"

"Nevin described you to him. Ranger said that, since the valley women share their husbands, you'd do fine. Then they told me about Beth, Amelia, and Jessie."

"I see. And when were you planning to tell me that I was to be, as you call it, 'shared'?"

"Honestly?"

She nodded, sharply.

"After a bit. I wanted to ease you into loving us, one at a time."

"What if I don't like them? Do we get divorced? Really, we only married to save Emma." While it was true at the time, she had few regrets about Ben, until Beth told her about three husbands being the norm. Now, she wasn't so sure.

"If you want to leave, I won't stop you. Divorce is quick and easy in Virginia City. There's lots of fine men eager to marry a widow."

"Since I'm asking for honestly, I'd better tell you I'm not a widow. Emma and Johnny's mother asked me to take them. She was very sick. She worried what would happen to them when she died."

"I figured it was something like that. We'll work things out between us." He scratched the side of his nose. "I don't mean to be harsh, but our home isn't going to be very big. A small cabin is faster to build and takes less wood to heat. I won't apologize for that, but we'll make it better as soon as we can." He nudged her playfully with his elbow. "Three men can build an addition faster than one."

She bit her lip and looked to her left, away from Ben. Beth had explained that the original Elliott home, which she lived in, and Amelia's across the valley, were identical. They were also the largest homes in the valley so far.

The men were almost finished building a large home for Jessie, since the tiny Double Diamond original cabin had chinks big enough to see through. Beth said the Bitterroot Ranch cabin was fine for three brothers, but wasn't the best for children. While they could live there, and many had a lot less, Emma and Johnny were far better off living with their hero, Uncle Nevin. Daniel, age ten, was another incentive for both children.

They rode on for a few minutes.

"You sorry you married me and got hauled all the way out here?"

She placed her hand on Ben's thigh and slightly squeezed. He twitched. "I may not have known what I was getting into when I decided to head west, but I'm very happy to be married to you." She made no promises about anything, or anyone, else.

"According to the church, we're not married. Yet."

The heat in his eyes raised a slow burn from her lower belly, up her chest and face, all the way to her hairline. Here it was. His explanation.

"When will that happen?" she whispered.

He cleared his throat. "Tonight. I think it best we, uh, get to know one another in the dark." Ben shifted in his seat. "Fewer distractions that way. Remember, Nevin said Ross and Amelia met in the dark."

"I expect distractions can be a bother."

That meant he wasn't going to kiss her, or touch her, until after supper? She closed her eyes and clenched her jaw, forcing herself to not say anything more. They rode on for a few minutes before he placed his one of his hands over hers.

"If it helps at all, I'm nervous, too."

"You are? I thought men were usually eager to, um—" She rolled her lips together and covered them with her fingertips to keep from finishing her thought out loud. He chuckled.

"Yes, but a wife is different. We haven't had much time alone." He lifted her hands to his mouth and kissed it. "But we've got the rest of our lives to solve that problem."

She swallowed. He kissed her hand again, this time slowly. He gently kissed each knuckle. A shiver rolled through her. His nervousness seemed to have disappeared. Hers hit with heart palpations and sweaty palms.

"Just a moment," he whispered. He checked that their way was clear and then sat on the reins to free his hands. "Let's do this properly, Mrs. Benjamin Elliott."

Chapter Fifteen

Ben lifted her off the padded seat and onto his lap. She grasped him around the neck with her left arm. His thighs were warm under her bottom. He supported her back with his right arm, leaving his left free. She looked up into his golden hazel eyes. The green was even more pronounced.

"I'm going to kiss you now," he murmured.

She closed her eyes and opened her mouth as his descended. His kissed her forehead, her nose, her cheek. Finally, she felt his lips on hers. She tasted coffee when his tongue slid under her top lip. Tender and sweet. She relaxed against him, giving into his touch.

A blossoming warmth spread through her, spiraling out from the heat of his thighs under her own. She inhaled when he broke the kiss. He followed a line from her mouth to her ear, and then down her throat. She tilted her head back, arching.

He brushed the top of her breast. A zing shot between her legs. She held still, hoping to feel it again. Then his whole hand rested on her breast. Her nipple budded as if cold, but she felt hot. The sensation was amazing. She inhaled, pressing closer to him in silent appeal. He squeezed, catching her nipple between his fingers. She groaned. His hand jerked off.

"Did I hurt you?"

She opened her eyes. She shook her head. "I want more." He exhaled and smiled gently.

"Show me where you want me to touch you."

She looked around, but of course there was no one near. She unbuttoned her top just far enough to reveal the top of her breasts. Her chemise covered the rest. He took it farther, pushing the fabric back to reveal one entire breast beneath the thin white cotton. He leaned over and took her breast into his mouth. The thin fabric, once wet, provided no barrier to his touch.

His tongue swirled around her nipple. She inhaled a gasp, her mouth suddenly dry. He scraped his teeth over her breast, agonizingly slowly. She quivered on his lap, twitching as the pleasure shot between her legs. When he gently nibbled her tip and grinned up at her she groaned out loud. He laughed and replaced his mouth with his hand. He cupped her breast as if weighing it.

The wagon wheel went over a rut, throwing her to the side. He caught her as she flailed on his lap. She scrambled back to her seat as he grabbed the reins and steered the horses back onto the track.

"Did I hurt you that time?" he asked, giving her a wry glance.

She shook her head, unable to meet his eyes. She concentrated on buttoning her top, ashamed that she'd acted like the woman she'd seen from the balcony in Virginia City. Did he think she was eager to fulfill her wifely duties? She groaned to herself, more eager than ever to discover what that meant.

"I'd better pay attention to driving, though I'd much rather kiss you," he said. He cleared his throat and looked around. "This ranch used to be the RB. It belonged to Rowena and Bertram Jones. He died long ago, but she stayed on. I must have been about Johnny's age the first time Ma let me come over with the others to help pick berries for jam. I don't remember if this path even existed back then."

She nodded, clutching the wagon's side with one hand and the seat with the other. She still panted, her body tight with a tension she'd not known before that time in the unknown town. If his mouth on her breast made her feel like floating, what would his mouth do to the rest of her?

She sent a mental prayer to whatever caused the train to jostle her just as she passed Benjamin Elliott, Esquire. As a widow with two young children, she would not likely have had the nerve to approach someone as fine as Ben. She would not have had the time or energy. She would be far too busy learning how to care for Emma and Johnny to look for a husband.

If she'd arrived in Virginia City, alone with two children, what would she have done? Not knowing a soul, with two small children terrified of strangers and crowds, she might very well have found more trouble than she could handle. How would she have found Elizabeth James of Philadelphia, when her friend was now known as Beth Elliott of Tanner's Ford?

They lumbered around another group of scrubby trees. She sat up when Ben pulled the wagon to a stop. At the end of the track waited a small cabin and a large shed. No, it must be a barn. Both listed to one side. She gulped. This was her home.

"I see why Beth insisted they keep Emma and Johnny for a while," said Ben wryly. He sighed. "Far from the Taj Mahal, but it's ours."

"That's all that matters," she replied, holding back a shudder.

He tapped the horses and they continued plodding. As they approached, the decrepit state of the cabin became clear. Light streamed between the logs as the sun went in one side and out the other. So would the wind, dust, insects, and small animals. And snakes. She shuddered.

A tall, lean man stepped out the front door, startling her. He had to duck to get through the low door. Ben pulled the horses to a stop beside him. The man lifted his hat. His hair was a bit darker than Ben's, and he had brown eyes, but there was a family resemblance. He looked younger than Ben. Was this Patrick?

His eyes flashed as he chuckled. He winked at her flush and dropped his gaze to her breasts. They tingled and swelled. Her nipples hardened. Did he know what Ben did with her on the trail?

His wicked smile reached his eyes. She shuddered. This man would have done what Ben did with her on the trail. His eyes said he would have stopped the wagon and continued with her until they were finished. Another zing shot through her. Though she'd barely met the man, her body was reacting, eager to experience his touch. Was this what Beth meant about wanting more than one man? If it was so wrong, why did it feel so good when he merely looked at her?

"I'm Patrick, ma'am. Welcome home." He nodded his head at the cabin. "Don't worry, you don't live there. I'm just staying here for a bit to give you two privacy up at the house, bein' just married and all."

"Goodness, Patrick, you've grown like the proverbial weed," said Ben, smiling wide. "Florence, in case Beth didn't tell you, Patrick is the youngest of us. Last time I saw him he was considerably shorter."

"Don't know that type of weed," said Patrick. "There's the house up yonder."

Florence looked where he pointed. Tucked into the natural curve of a hill was a two-story home. The unpainted boards had yet to weather to the cabin's silver gray. The hill, now brown with autumn, snuggled close on the north and west. It would protect them from the bitter winter winds. She almost groaned in relief. A much different type of groan than Ben had made her produce a few minutes earlier.

"Let me help you down, ma'am."

She absently nodded and stood up. Patrick grasped her waist. Tingles radiated from his hands. Startled, she placed her palms on his forearms and looked into his brown eyes. He set her on the ground but didn't let go. She looked up at him, unsure of what to do.

"Ma always demanded a welcome home kiss," he murmured.

Before she could react he pressed his lips against hers. It wasn't the peck she would have expected from a brother. Instead, he opened his mouth and kissed her slowly and thoroughly. Her hands slipped around his waist. One of his hands strayed across her breast. When his calluses grazed her erect nipple she found herself pressing into his hand. She was still gasping for air when Ben came up behind them. Patrick let go as Ben turned her around.

After Ben's attention, Patrick's arousing kiss made her mind spin.

She stared at Ben, mouth open. He winked and pulled her to his chest, wrapping his arms around her shoulders. She rested her head on his chest and savored his warmth. Another warm body pressed against her back and bottom. She stiffened. Patrick rested his chin on her head, his hands on her hips. She felt a certain hard length just above her buttocks.

Patrick sighed, deeply and thoroughly. She tingled, back and front. Beth was right—Ben's brother made her want the same things Ben's touch provoked.

When Trace carried her the night before, she'd felt nothing but his warm arms. Same when each new brother-in-law had given her a welcome peck on the cheek that morning. Patrick's touch made her feel light-headed and needy. Though she felt relief at enjoying Patrick's touch, she wasn't sure what to do about it. What did he expect? What did *Ben* expect?

"Welcome home, Florence," said Ben. He pulled her forward, away from Patrick's disturbing touch, and swooped her into his arms. "This may not be our final home, but it will do for now." He turned sideways and carried her into the cabin. A quick kiss to the forehead, and he let her stand. "This is how many women live. Lots of miners would consider themselves lucky to live as well."

She caught her breath and her balance and concentrated on the dust motes drifting in the sunbeams. One corner held a cot with a couple of neatly folded blankets. Beside it was an apple box with a tin plate. A tallow candle was stuck to the plate by dripped wax. An extra shirt and pants hung from a couple of nails. A few more blankets filled a box which, by the picture on its side, used to contain canned peaches.

"Just think, all of this could have been ours," joked Ben.

"If you told us you were bringing a wife, we would have fixed things up better," said Patrick, following them in.

"You're staying here?" asked Ben. He peered through a large crack at Patrick's horse. The gaps between the logs were so wide

Patrick had tied the reins around one of the logs.

Patrick tilted his head, considering his answer. "That depends on how good a cook your wife is. Trace's barn ain't too bad and Beth's cooking is great. Don't know about Florence here."

"Cooking wasn't something we had a chance to discuss before we got married."

Patrick groaned. "None of you ask the most important questions before saying 'I do.' Trace lucked out with Beth, but Ross needs Auntie at home if he wants decent food. Jessie's third man, Henry, can cook." He turned to Florence. "Our sister will do darn near anything to get out of the kitchen." He looked at her with a hopeful expression, as did Ben.

"I hear divorces are easy to obtain in Virginia City," said Florence to Ben. Beth had told her of her options, in case things didn't work out. "Will you divorce me if I can't cook?"

"Nope," said Patrick, butting in. "There's no other woman to take your place. I asked Ross and Ace about it. They said there's other duties a wife can do to make up for being no good with the stove."

His knowing look sent a rush of heat to flood Florence's face, faster and more intense than she could ever remember. She couldn't read Patrick's expression. Ben's was also blank. They looked like her instructors when they expected her to fail, like the men who rejected her because of her brain and lack of beauty. She clasped her hands together and answered the safest way she knew.

"I expect to perform my duties with competence. I have numerous texts, but I do not believe book learning provides an adequate education. Therefore, whenever possible, I follow up my research with hands-on experience."

Ben coughed and turned away. She thought she saw him hide a smile. Was he laughing at her? Her hands trembled as Patrick frowned and blinked at her.

"There's a powerful lot of big words in whatever you said, ma'am, but I still don't know if you can cook."

"I can do many things, but will have to adapt my methods and become familiar with your equipment before I can perform adequately."

Patrick looked at Ben. There was definitely laughter in Ben's eyes, and his lip twitched. "Florence says she can cook, but it may take her some time to get settled and at ease with the stove and oven. We shouldn't expect miracles, but we'll be well fed, and she'll improve over time."

Patrick's whole face blossomed in a huge smile. He whooped, grabbed her around the waist and lifted her up. He kissed her on the lips, set her down, and whooped again.

"No more burned biscuits and porridge glue! I'll bring the wagon up to the house." He almost banged his head rushing through the low door in his eagerness.

Florence wrapped her arms around herself and looked at the interior of the cabin once more. Her eyes saw, but she didn't take it in, too busy chastising herself for responding to Patrick's simple question as if she was in elocution class. Ben was the only Elliott male to have an education beyond what his parents provided. She had to learn to use words that these men wouldn't require a dictionary to understand.

"I'm not sure which answer I wanted you to give," said Ben. He came up behind her and rested his hands on her shoulders. "Would I prefer good food in my belly, or a warm woman in my bed?"

He nuzzled her neck. The tingling returned. It increased when he slid his hands from her shoulders to her breasts. He gently squeezed. She leaned her head back. At five foot five she was eight inches shorter, her head the perfect height to rest on his chest. He caught her nipples between his fingers. A jolt shot from them to the ache between her legs.

"Why not both?" she said, daring to be wicked.

"Why not, indeed." Ben rubbed his hips against her bottom. Once more, she felt the hardness that she'd been promised would make all the work of caring for a man worthwhile. But she had to apologize first.

"I saw you laugh when I spoke with Patrick just now. I tend to use precise language when I'm nervous. I should apologize to Patrick."

"I laughed because your words could apply to more than cooking." He rolled her nipples between his thumb and fingers. She gasped, losing her concentration.

"What do you mean? I don't remember the exact words." She rubbed her bottom against him.

"You expect to perform your duties with competence. That means, Mrs. Elliott, that you need lots of practice. You also said you like doing hands-on research."

He brought her hand around until it covered the bulge in his pants. Her palm pressed his hard rod against his belly. It was hot, even through his pants.

"And then," he said, moving her hand up and down his shaft, "you said you need to become familiar with our equipment. Want to see my equipment now, Mrs. Elliott?"

She grasped him, feeling the hot, thick rod for the first time. He groaned and rubbed against her.

"You can come on up to the house now," called Patrick from the doorway. "I emptied the wagon for you."

Ben groaned and dropped his head forward. He chuckled. "And we thought we'd be all alone here. We'll continue that tonight." He kissed her neck and stepped back. Her palm felt cool after his heat, though she burned from her thighs to her neck.

"Is that a promise?"

"I expect your screams of release will echo through the valley."

She turned to him and bit her lip. "I'm not quite sure what that means." Her nipples hardened further at his wolfish smile.

"Trust me, Mrs. Elliott will be very happy by morning."

Chapter Sixteen

"I'll finish here. You get ready for bed," said Ben. "Turn out the lamp when you're ready for me to come up."

His wife wiped her palms on her skirt once more. A flush erupted from the lace around her throat. He read a mixture of eagerness and worry. He gave Patrick a speaking look, but his brother chose not to understand. Patrick was a born flirt. He didn't have Ranger's hard, dangerous edge. Instead, he had an adventurous spirit which made him push all his boundaries. And, too often, those of his brothers. The kiss he gave Florence on arrival proved he was eager to push hers as well. At least she had reacted well to his attentions.

Ben cleared his throat and jerked his head toward the door. Patrick looked at Florence, and then back to Ben. His eyes brightened.

"That's right. You two want to start your honeymoon." Patrick pushed his stool back and stood. His grin was as wide as a hound dog's. "Don't worry about makin' noise, ma'am. I'm a deep sleeper. So's Ranger. We had to be, the way this one snores." He jerked his thumb at Ben and ambled closer to Florence.

"I do not snore," said Ben. The other two ignored him. Florence wiped her hands on her skirts again, and swallowed hard.

"I take it your mother also insisted on a bedtime kiss?" Though her cheeks flushed pink, she did not back away in horror.

"Yes, ma'am. Pucker up."

Ben had to admire his younger brother's technique. He took his time to explore Florence, both her lips and, with his hands, her bottom. When he finished, they were both breathing hard. Patrick winced as he carefully walked toward the door.

Ben didn't move, didn't even breathe, until Patrick's saucy whistle faded. He turned to Florence.

"You enjoyed that, didn't you?"

Though her face, and other parts, flamed with heat, she nodded her agreement.

"Patrick would like to do a lot more than kiss you. Ranger as well. Would you like more than Patrick's kiss?"

"How can I answer that when I haven't ever shared my bed?"

Ben put his hands on her shoulders and spoke softly. "Do you want to feel even better than when Patrick kissed you?"

She nodded, biting her lip. "I've got a terrible ache, right here."

She placed her hand over her pussy. His cock throbbed, eager to solve her problem. If he was her first, would she let his brothers touch her?

"Any one of us could take care of that ache for you. That kiss from Patrick shows how much he wants to be the one going upstairs to you tonight."

He moved her hand aside and placed his over her pussy. He gently rubbed his fingers in a circle. She put her hand on his, directing him to press harder. He ran the tips of his fingers slightly between her legs, looking for her clit.

"Ranger thinks he should be your first because he's the oldest."

"Just because someone's older, doesn't mean they're any better." She spread her legs a bit, asking for more.

"He also says he's better. He's certainly got a lot more experience than I do."

"Experience is good," she whispered. "But, I can't believe this is happening."

"Do you want it to happen? Would you like to find out what it means to scream with joy for the first time?" He brushed his other hand over her taut nipples.

"I want more." She groaned.

"We'll make sure you get everything you need."

"We?"

He felt her heart pounding. It went so fast that she had to pant.

"Patrick, me, and Ranger. Is that what you want? To be kissed, and touched, and loved until you scream?" He lightly pinched her nipples through her dress. "You want us to show you how?"

"Oh, yes please."

"I opened a celebratory bottle of wine. It's on the apple box beside the bed. Why don't you have a glass while you get ready? I'll check the barn."

She bit her lip and nodded. He admired the way her bottom swayed as she climbed the stairs set into the back wall. His cock was so hard and eager, he wished he had the confidence to be her first. But too much was riding on the outcome. If it was only going to be the two of them, he would make slow, sensuous love to her all night long. But she needed immediate explosions to make her crave more.

He pushed thoughts of bedding his wife out of his mind and headed for the barn in the dusk. The days were getting shorter. By Christmas they'd be getting up in the dark, doing what they could in the few short hours the sun peeped above the horizon, then heading to bed early.

They used to gather around the fire after dinner. Ma would read something, and they'd work on small projects. Ranger would whittle, and the others would mend leather, sharpen knives, or repair the clothes they'd ripped, since Ma refused to fix a problem they caused. It didn't matter what they did, as long as they shared the end of the day.

That was the life he wanted for his family. Not huddling around a meager fire in the dark, an uneasy silence broken only by yells and threats. He'd had enough of that in Texas, though he escaped to flourish in Virginia while Ranger and Patrick were forced to stay. He owed them for the four years he lived in a decent house with clean sheets and hot, plentiful food. His stomach tensed in remembrance of his Texas life.

"She ready yet?" Ranger's voice drifted through the dark maw of the barn. Ben shook off bad memories. Tonight was the start of a new life. A far better one, for all of them.

"She's more than ready. What about you?"

"You have to ask?"

Ranger set a shoulder against one side of the doorway. Ben leaned against the other. He grunted at Ranger's close shave and chopped hair. It wasn't neat, but it would do.

"She know who's going to be upstairs with her?"

Ben winced. "Not exactly. She knows all three of us want her, and I never said it would be me the first time."

"I'll tell her." He snorted a laugh. "After all, I want her to know who's the best man in this family."

"We'll see about that come Christmas."

They both looked up at the light flowing from the upstairs window. A shape moved across the room.

"That flash of white must mean she has her dress off," said Ranger. He coughed and cleared his throat.

"Are we watching the show from here?" Both turned at Patrick's eager question. He approached from behind them.

"There won't be a show," said Ben. "When Florence turns out the light, we won't see anything."

"You'll hear a fair bit, though," said Ranger. He gave a smug smile. "Moans, groans, cries, and a shout or two, I expect."

Patrick licked his lips. "She's a wild one, all right."

"How do you know from a peck on the cheek?" scoffed Ranger.

"I didn't peck no cheek," protested Patrick. "I lifted her down from that wagon and kissed her the same way you did those ladies in Texas. And when I touched her breast, it stood out hard against my hand." He nudged Ranger with his shoulder. "I listened when you told Nev how to tell if a woman liked it." He nodded, grinning like a child with a treat. "Florence liked it all right. She stood there, gasping for air, waiting for another. She did the same thing just now, when I kissed her good night. Damn, I wish I was you tonight."

Ranger nodded thoughtfully. "Ain't that something. Seems your educated wife might not be as cold in bed as I expected." He pushed himself upright and straightened his shoulders.

"You should know that Beth and Florence know each other from school," said Ben. "Beth told her lots last night, including that all the valley wives share their men. We talked about it on the way here. But she still doesn't know what to expect tonight."

The yard suddenly went dark. Three pairs of eyes shot to the window above them.

"Time for her to find out."

Chapter Seventeen

Ranger shut the kitchen door behind him. He leaned a hip against the table edge to take off his boots and socks.

"Someday soon we'll be enjoying our woman on this table," he murmured, promising himself something that he'd dreamed about for years.

All the time Ben was in Virginia, he'd prayed his twin would bring back a wife as promised, though he didn't get his hopes up. Few things worked out the way he wanted, so it was best not to anticipate pleasure. Far better to expect the worst, and be surprised.

He was rarely surprised.

Of course, Ben would choose a woman with a brain just like his brother. Unless she had good housekeeping skills, a female egghead would be almost as useless on the ranch as Ben. How many times had he heard Finan Senior complaining about educating females? Sunbird suited the old man perfectly as she said little, just worked from before sunup until after sundown. Just like her husband.

Finan said only the Clan leader and his closest men needed to think. The rest of them must follow orders, using their bodies however the Clan needed. According to The MacDougal, men were to labor outside the castle and wage war while women must labor inside and give peace. Both must give themselves physically to the Clan. Men were rewarded with women. Women were rewarded with the children that came from such unions, whether they wanted the partners or not.

Ranger had a real problem with that. He believed women should choose who they wanted touching them. In the Clan system, children obeyed everyone. Women followed their own hierarchy and obeyed the men. Everyone obeyed the Clan Chief, The MacDougal.

Everyone except Ranger Elliott. He followed the orders of his range boss, treating him with respect, but he refused to be subservient. His scars proved how much it infuriated The MacDougal.

But, thanks to the Bonham inheritance, the three of them were free of The MacDougal and his brutal ways. They owned the Bitterroot Ranch outright, as well as the Texas longhorns he and Patrick spent five brutal months pushing north over the Western Trail, right through Dodge City.

They had a decent home and a few chunks of gold nuggets buried here and there. They shared the valley with their ever-increasing family. It was everything Ma and Pa had wanted when they followed Sunbird, pushing into the wilderness.

And now it was their turn. He, Ben, and Patrick. He wanted what his brothers had with Beth, what the MacDougals had with Amelia. Laughter, loving, and sensual promise. A warm woman to turn to when the world seemed too harsh to face. Children who looked like him, laughing and calling him Pa. A lamp shining in the window on damn cold winter days, welcoming him home.

And it all started tonight.

Florence didn't yet know who'd be climbing those stairs. But a lie was not the way to start, whether it was a ranch partnership or a marriage. He'd give her a few minutes to figure it out. If she didn't, then he'd tell her.

Of course, there was nothing stopping him from making sure she was hot and bothered before he explained it wasn't Ben making her pussy clench in need.

He bent over, careful of the hard cock straining to get free, and picked up his boots. He set them on the far side of the door, out of the way. He unbuckled his belt. He thought a moment before deciding to keep it on.

If he followed instructions for once, Patrick had filled the rose-patterned basin and ewer with warm water. A cake of fresh rose-scented soap and a couple of clean, soft flannels should be waiting as well.

Ranger's lip twitched. He'd have to find a shorter name for her. If she had so much book learning, he expected she was uppity. One way to take her down a peg or two would be to call her Fanny. But not tonight. At least, not out loud.

He unbuttoned his shirt as he padded across the kitchen. Should he treat her as a widow, or virgin? He put his foot on the bottom step with a thump. A gasp, quickly stifled, erupted above his head. His lip twitched.

Virgin.

He would be her first. As the fourth of six boys, he'd never been first for anything. He would be the one to raise her passion and show her about loving. The hard, hollow pit in his gut softened a bit.

Their Ma made sure none of them would ever think of a female as a possession, no matter what the law declared. But in his mind, Florence would always be his woman.

He took his time, making sure she heard each time he set his foot down. Three more steps, and his eyes breached the floorboards. She waited, her back to him, in front of the window. As expected, she wore a white nightgown which covered her from neck to wrists to ankles. A line ran from her head to her ass. Her braid.

Her breath hitched every time his foot hit a step. Was the damn woman terrified? He strolled across the room until he was right behind her. She wrapped her arms around herself and ducked her head.

The women he'd bedded were well experienced. With nothing to lose, he'd asked them to show him what they liked best. The main thing he learned was that each woman was different. Worse, she was different each and every time. From that, he learned to take it easy and slow.

"I don't know what to do," she blurted. "I've never done this before. Beth says it's wonderful, but…"

She rushed the words past her lips so fast it took him a minute to catch up. She sniffled. He tilted his head far enough to see glistening trails down her cheeks.

Shit.

Crying before bedding was never good. He screwed up his face in a grimace. How was he going to make her scream a couple of orgasms when she was already crying? Worse, he knew Patrick and Ben were listening. Judging. What would Ben want him to do? She shivered and hugged herself tighter. He gave up thinking and just let things flow.

He walked around her, putting his back to the window. She kept her head down. He sighed and tugged her against him. She kept her arms tight, still crossed as if to protect herself.

"Shh," he murmured. "No talking. Tonight is for touching." She snuffled against his chest. "You got sharp elbows," he said.

He found her fists and pulled her arms open. She resisted a bit, but she was too puny to stop him. He set them over his hips, released her hands and pulled her body close. Having pushed her, he retreated, holding his hands loosely on her shoulder blades.

It took a moment, but she slid her hands around him, under his shirt. She sighed and dropped her face against his bare chest. He inhaled her fragrance for the first time. Rose soap along with cinnamon, lemon, and apple from the pies she'd baked. Patrick had managed to sneak some supper, including a piece of pie, to him in the barn while she was in the privy.

The woman could cook, all right.

"You smell good, like apple pie," he whispered.

"Did you decide to choose food, me, or both?"

Ranger didn't know what Florence was talking about, but he knew his answer. "Both."

He felt her lips move over his chest as she smiled. "I knew you were a smart man." She inhaled. "You smell like leather and"—again she moved her head—"I don't know what, but I like it."

He dropped his right hand, sliding it over her back and down to cup her right ass cheek. It fit his hand like it belonged there. She gulped and breathed faster. He shifted his hand lower. He gathered up some fabric and moved his thumb between her cheeks. Her breath caught. He shifted his hand to her left cheek so his fingers could investigate that groove. She shivered.

He held still except for his right hand, running up and down, rubbing her thick cotton nightgown over her asshole and slightly between her legs.

"You like that."

"Yes." She shifted her feet, moving them farther apart.

"Then let's get rid of this."

He knelt at her feet and lifted her hem, just enough to rest his hands around her ankles. It put his face just above her belly. The cotton bunched over his arms as his hands trailed up her calves, over her knees, to her lower thighs.

She gasped and seemed to lose her balance. She grabbed his head with both hands and spread her feet apart even further. He smiled in the dark and ducked his head, flipping the cotton over his back. She squealed when he rested his face against her belly and held onto the back of her thighs, just below where they joined her pussy. He inhaled her natural fragrance.

One time, when Ben was in Virginia and Patrick asleep in the hay, he watched two women who'd come back to the ranch, pleasure each other this way. They did things to each other in ways he'd never thought about. When they saw him watching they demanded he use his fingers on them. They made him work until they'd each come a couple of times.

He'd never wanted to touch his tongue to a woman before. But Florence was fresh, clean, and virginal. Anything he did would be her first time. He wanted to make her enjoy it so much that she wanted to do it again and again. With him, with Ben, and with Patrick.

He kissed her curly mound.

"What are you doing?" She squealed when he flicked his tongue over her clit.

"Pleasuring you."

"But—"

"You want me to stop?" He gritted his teeth, face screwed up, waiting for her answer.

"Um, no, but I can't see what you're doing."

She wanted to watch? So much the better. He lifted her nightgown to her waist and stood up, taking the rest of it with him. He kept on going, turning it inside out. Because of the tight neck and sleeves, her head and hands were caught inside.

"I'm stuck!"

"You sure are," he replied. He held the cotton over her head in one fist. He took his time admiring her body as she struggled and complained with her arms over her head.

Height, half way between Beth and Jessie. Nice ankles and calves, and sturdy thighs. Her unlined belly proved she'd never grown a child. Wide hips for big-headed sons and daughters. A small waist that would soon thicken with a child of her own. And breasts large enough to satisfy any child or husband.

He walked around and checked out her back end. Yep, her ass cheeks were nice and full. They pressed against each other snug enough to slide his cock back and forth between them. Her breasts were big enough to do the same.

"Let me go!"

She called out, but he heard no fear. She kicked back and out like a cow. Her heel connected with his knee. He swatted her rump. She squealed. He laughed, enjoying himself more than he could remember. She stopped moving.

"Do you think this is funny, Mr. Elliott?"

"Maybe this'll learn you not to wear nightgowns to bed, Mrs. Elliott."

He released her and grabbed her under the knees and around the back before she could react. He carried her to the bed, careful not to drop her as she scrambled to get her head free. He debated tossing her down, but she might get away. He sat down, keeping her in his lap. He yanked off her wrist buttons, and then grasped her collar.

"No!"

He stopped. "No?" He gritted his teeth, praying she didn't mean what he dreaded.

"Please don't ruin this gown. Beth lent it to me. I'll undo it if you let go."

He waited until she'd finished unbuttoning and then pulled it up. This time it came off easily and sailed to the floor. He had her on her back, his body on hers, before she could speak. He kissed her mouth, slowly and sensuously, until her muscles relaxed.

He cupped her breast, flicking her nipple with his thumb, and looked down. She pressed her breast against his hand, silently asking for more.

"I like you naked," he whispered. "It makes it easier to do this."

He drifted his callused fingers lightly down her ribs to her belly. He slowed, noting every place where she gasped or quivered. When he had them all memorized, he parted her lips with his middle finger. He kept his hand high, his finger barely touching her. She moaned and moved her thighs apart an inch.

"If you want more, spread your legs for me."

Her breath hitched, and then she moved. Her fragrance floated up, stronger than before. As promised, he pressed down, circling her clit without touching it.

He wanted to shuck his pants and slam into the sweet pussy right under his hand. But he'd wanted to do a lot of things over the years that never happened. He promised Ben she'd scream, and dammit, he never broke a promise.

"You like me doing this, Mrs. Elliott?"

"Oh, yes," she whispered.

He kissed his way down her neck to her breast. When he pulled her nipple into his mouth, she groaned, arching up. "Ben and Patrick said you would."

"Ben and Patrick?"

When she stiffened, he lifted his head and met her eyes.

"You're Ben's brother, Ranger?"

"Yep. You taste good." When she didn't reply or relax, he flicked her clit with his finger. She gasped and arched. "You want me to stop and get Ben? Or should I just keep going?" He touched her clit again. She whimpered as he rubbed his knuckles either side.

"Don't stop!"

"Ben said you were a smart woman."

He kissed his way down her neck to her breast. When he pulled her nipple into his mouth, she groaned, arching up once more. He circled her nipple with his tongue, feeling all the tiny bumps. Another day, he'd investigate the color. Pink? Rose? Salmon? But tonight was all about touch. The quick nip he gave her nipple made her whole body tremble.

He smiled his kisses down her ribs and belly. Someday, an edge of pain might be what she needed to explode. Tonight, she needed a long, slow arousal. He knelt on the floor at the edge of the bed and pulled her hips toward him. He caught her by surprise and, by the time she gripped the sheets to stop him moving her, she was in position.

Chapter Eighteen

Florence grabbed the sheets, but Ranger already had her where he wanted her. She felt out of control, her senses far beyond anything she could ever imagine. The glass of wine she'd consumed while pacing back and forth had gone to her head.

No, it went to her entire body.

"What are you going to—"

"Shh," he whispered. "Don't think. Feel."

"I don't know how."

His deep chuckle made her shiver. She could see the shape of his body between her legs. Was he going to put himself in her now? It was supposed to hurt, but—

Something smooth and warm flicked the center of her being. She gasped, every part of her mind concentrating on that spot just above the juncture of her legs.

"That's your clit. Feels good?"

"Oh, yes!" She hated to beg, but... "Can you do it again?"

She dropped her head against the mattress and used her heels to lift herself closer to his busy tongue. She wanted the tingling he caused. Nothing could be better than this. If only it could go on and on.

He slid a finger inside her and pressed up.

She was wrong. This was ecstasy.

He continued with his tongue and finger. No, fingers. She couldn't think, couldn't move, could do nothing but feel her body. Nothing existed but his mouth on her clit, his fingers inside her. A tension coiled around her, binding her tight. Someone begged and cried, demanding more. She writhed, sobbing. A new sensation, this one against her bottom, intruded. She wanted it gone, wanted to only feel the other. The finger pressed into her and twisted.

She exploded, shattering into pieces, scattered into stars in the night sky.

She hauled air into her lungs, sure she would never feel anything so intense again.

But he started once more. He rolled her over and pulled her knees until her head was on the mattress and her bottom high. His hands pressed back her flesh and his tongue began again. This time, his tongue concentrated on the place between her opening and her bottom. His fingers probed inside her, pressing against her barrier, stretching her wider.

She whimpered when he stopped, but then something new started.

He moved her knees together. Something long and hard slid between her legs, against her swollen flesh, finally rubbing against her clit. Then it was gone, backing up until—yes!—once more it pushed forward.

His hands held her hips, holding her down.

"You like my cock, don't you?"

She nodded, her face moving against the crisp sheets.

"My cock wants your sweet pussy and clit. This is your pussy."

Something larger than his fingers entered her. It stretched her deliciously, in and out. A little farther each time, bouncing against her barrier.

She wanted more, but he pulled back and released her.

The bed dipped. He lay down and easily lifted her. She squawked, falling forward until her hands hit his chest and her legs straddled his. Her breasts dragged across his face. He chuckled, released her waist and took a breast in each hand.

Her pussy and clit throbbed, begging for more, but his hands felt so good where they were. He tugged her breast, sucking it into his mouth. Hot flesh surrounded her. His tongue pressed her nipple against the roof of his mouth. He released her, letting his teeth scrape on the way out. She groaned and shoved her other breast in his mouth. He did the same to it, making her pussy throb.

"Sit up a bit," he said.

She did, willing to do whatever he wanted as every moment seemed more wonderful. He grasped her hips and lifted, shifting her back.

"Catch my cock with your hand and guide me under your pussy," he said, panting the words.

She reached down, eager to touch the instrument of so much pleasure. She found it and was barely able to circle the hot, firm flesh with her fingers. She released him when he set her down on the length of his cock.

"Your turn to work. Rub back and forth on my cock. Let it scrape your clit."

His strength was such that he easily pulled her forward and back with his hands on her hips. She leaned over, arching her back to press down. He released her, and she took over.

No more was she at his mercy. She ground down against him, moving as she needed. Forward until her clit touched his belly, then back.

A tension curled within her. Same, but different. She sped up, needing more. He stopped her, holding her hips still. She struggled. She was too far back on his hips to feel anything. She grasped the cock rising before her belly.

"If you want more, lift up and put me in you."

She nodded, unable to speak. He helped to lift her, and she guided him to her open pussy. He gently let her down. She caught herself on her knees, his cock barely entering her. She slowly bounced, not letting him in very far, or out.

It wasn't enough. She wiggled, pressing down, but her barrier stopped her.

"You want help? It'll hurt, but just for a minute. And never again," he said.

She tried, but couldn't get enough momentum to break through. Instead of answering, she found his hands and guided them to her hips. He held her steady while she spread her knees wide. He teased her for a moment, putting his cock in and out, in and out. Just enough to make her want more. She opened her mouth to complain, and he pulled her down.

She gasped at the sharp pain. His fingers played with her clit, turning her attention forward of the fading pain. Soon, all she felt was his fingers on her clit. She hesitantly moved. Her pussy ached, but with need. She lifted up, and a heavy fullness moved with her. It stretched her pussy wide.

He tugged at her shoulders, and she remembered what she'd done before. She leaned forward. His hand waited for her clit. She dragged herself across his knuckles. His cock dragged along her sides as it slid out of her pussy.

She hummed in contentment, moving back and forth, pussy and clit, as the tension wound higher. She was in control. She could move when she wanted. Hard, fast, and high, lifting herself up, or slow and low, dragging her clit against his cock. His free hand grasped her breast, ramping up her sensations. She arched to drag her clit against his hand, speeding up as the tension mounted.

He rested his hands on her bottom, letting her move as she needed. She leaned so far forward that her clit rubbed against him. Faster and faster, feeling every inch of him as she slammed back, then rubbed against him.

He rubbed a finger in the sensitive skin past his cock. She growled, demanding whatever he could give. He growled back, panting as hard as she. She whimpered, needing more, desperate to feel the wonderful shattering of everything. His fingers crept over her back hole, scratching against it. She clenched him inside, shivering in need.

His cock swelled inside her, his finger plunged deep, and she exploded, screaming her joy. He shouted, grabbed her hips and shoved up, lifting and slamming her down. His wildness made her laugh. He erupted into her. Again, she shattered, clenching him as he pumped her up and down, slower and slower. Finally, his hands released her hips, and she slumped onto his chest, sobbing. He held her so tight she shook along with him.

A long time later, when she could breathe, she coughed and wiped her eyes.

"You okay?" he whispered. His voice was deeper than Ben's.

She laughed and pushed herself to sit up. "I'm better than okay. I feel wonderful."

She bounced on his chest as he joined her in laughter. "Yeah, I'd agree with that. Come'ere."

He pulled her down and kissed her. She grabbed his ears and kissed him back, demanding more of the wildness she'd just experienced. When she sat up, lungs hauling air deep inside, he snorted a laugh.

"Damn, you're a fast learner."

He rubbed his hands up and down her back and over her bottom.

"I learn quickly, but I need lots of practice to get it right. Can we do that again?"

"Ah, sweets, you've got some learning to do about men."

"You going to teach me now?" She leaned forward, dangling her breasts over his mouth.

"A man needs time to recharge." He lifted her off his hips and set her down beside him. "Don't worry, I'll be good as new in a few hours."

"A few hours? But I want more now!"

"Then it's a damn good thing you came to this valley, sweets." He groaned and rolled off the bed.

"Where are you going?"

He didn't answer, but she heard water splashing.

"Damn, it's not warm anymore." He laughed. "You're so hot, it won't matter."

He padded back to the bed and gently cleaned her from waist to knees. The cool water felt good on her overheated skin. He got another cloth and used it to wipe off her face and breasts. By the time he was finished, she was sleepy. He tucked her in and kissed her forehead.

"Go to sleep."

He traced a finger around her nipple under the sheet. It rose in response.

"When can we do that again?" she murmured sleepily.

"By morning. You might be sore since this was your first time. It was also pretty wild." He kissed her hard nipple. "Slow and gentle can be just as good. Now go to sleep. We've got a lot of work to do tomorrow."

She was asleep before his footsteps faded.

Chapter Nineteen

"Holy, Jesus, Ben! Where did you find that firecracker?"

Ranger paced back and forth in front of Patrick's tiny cabin like a mountain lion. If he had a tail, it would be slapping back and forth in agitation. He'd stomped into his boots, shoved his arms into his sleeves and done up a couple of buttons on his pants before storming out of the house.

When Ranger continued to pace without saying more, Ben slammed his fist against the bare chest. "Hold up a minute. You told her who you were?"

Ranger nodded. "Yeah, but I waited until she was well on the way." He pushed Ben's hand away and continued, though he slowed his pacing a bit. "I had her sit on me, to make it easier for her."

"What did you do to her that's got you like this?"

"Do to *her*?" Ranger finally stopped. He glared at Ben. "She damn near wore me out, and then demanded more!"

"Are you speaking about Florence, the intellectual, educated woman you swore wouldn't want one man in her bed, much less three?" Ben spat the quote back at his twin.

"Damn good thing I didn't take a bet on it." He snorted a laugh and pulled at his hair, still pacing. "She's gonna wear out all three of us!"

"What a way to go," sighed Patrick.

"Hah! Wait until Ben stumbles downstairs with his eyes crossed and knees shaking."

Ben stepped in front of Ranger. "What do you mean by that?"

"I told her your cock might be ready by morning. But I also said that maybe slow and easy might work as well as fast and hard." Ranger shook his head. He sighed. "Damn, but she loves it fast and hard."

Ben looked at Patrick. They both looked at Ranger.

"You look like someone just cleaned your clock," said Patrick.

Ben could understand the touch of envy in his expression. He couldn't really complain as Ranger had done as he'd asked. He'd made sure Florence knew who had thoroughly bedded her. He just wished it was he who had made her scream like that. Ranger might have been her first, but he would be her best. The most important thing was that Florence was happy.

"Yeah, well, my hour hand won't be pointing to twelve for a while," replied Ranger.

"Did my twin just make a joke?" Ben gaped in pretend awe at Patrick, who did the same.

Ranger swatted Patrick on the back of the head. Patrick snorted a laugh. Ben did the same. Ranger looked at them and scowled. It made both of them break out into laughter. Ranger finally managed to chuckle a bit. They quickly hushed so that it wouldn't wake Florence.

"Damn, I don't remember ever seeing you laugh," said Patrick quietly.

"Yeah, well, we ain't had much to laugh at since Ma died," replied Ranger.

Ben leaned his head back, stared at the stars and chuckled. "Just before I left for Virginia, you told me to bring you a wife like Ma. Well, how'd I do?"

"She can cook," said Patrick. "Them pies was as good as Beth's."

"I heard Ma and Pa make some of the noises that came out the window just now," said Ben.

"Don't tell me that," complained Patrick, covering his ears.

Ben and Ranger looked up at the stars, something they did most clear nights with their father while he told them stories of the constellations. Castor and Pollux, the Roman twins, was their favorite, of course.

"Imagine what life would have been like if we'd had three fathers instead of one?" Ben asked the Big Dipper the question.

"We wouldn't have had to leave the ranch," said Ranger.

"Maybe one of our fathers would have found another wife," said Patrick.

Ben looked up at the house where his wife, their wife, slept.

"We've got a pretty good argument for sharing our wives. Men die of accidents, and their wives are left with nothing. They become prey to the strongest man who wants to take over her and her ranch. Four parents spread the work a lot better. Trace took in two orphans, Gil another. Between us four families, we've got lots of room for more."

They stood a moment in silence. Ranger yawned. He patted the flat front of his pants. "Good luck on satisfying Fanny before breakfast. I'm ready to sleep." He ducked into the cabin.

"I get the cot," called out Patrick, following him. "You get the blankets on the floor."

"Too late," said Ranger.

Ben trudged back uphill, smiling. He hadn't realized how much he'd missed hearing his brothers squabbling. He shucked his boots in the kitchen and undressed before climbing the stairs, clothes in his hand. The moonlight was at the wrong angle to show his wife's naked body, but at least he didn't stub his foot on the way to bed.

He lifted the sheet and slid into bed. Florence's soft snores didn't change. He lay there for a minute, enjoying the feeling of lying beside her while he decided what to do. His cock was as hard as the bedpost. Listening to his wife's demanding cries had made him almost come in his pants. Ranger did say she wanted more. He rolled over, cuddling against her back.

"Ben?" she murmured.

"That's me. How are you feeling?"

"Wonderful. Is it morning yet?"

"No, why?"

She rolled onto her back and grasped his cock. He choked. She laughed softly.

"Oh, good," she said. "You're ready. Let's try it slow and easy this time."

He checked to see if she was ready. His finger slid easily into her pussy. He played with her clit for a few moments, fighting not to come just from her soft cries. Finally, he settled himself on top of her. She opened her legs and sighed.

He slid into her hot pussy for the first time. Though Ranger's cock was the first to enter her, Ben was the first to settle between her legs, face to face. She wriggled, moaning. He lifted himself up and worked her, in and out, fighting for control. He tried to last, but she moaned and tightened herself around his cock. He pumped a few more times, grimacing at the strain.

She cried out, and her pussy gripped him like a vice. He exploded, slamming against her again and again before he collapsed on his elbows. He panted, fighting to breathe, his chest pillowed by her breasts. He heard a squeak in his brain, as if his blood pumped so hard it almost escaped out his ears.

"Mmmm, maybe try it slow later," she murmured.

He looked down. She softly snored underneath him. Out like a match and he hadn't even pulled out. He rolled onto his back, gasping for air and laughing at the same time.

Ranger was right. It would take all three of them to keep Florence happy.

After he used the last clean flannel to tidy her up, he hauled her across his chest. He marveled at her soft skin, sliding his hands up and down her back for a few minutes. They were now well and truly married.

Life was good. His twin was happy, his wife was happy, and he'd never felt so marvelous. He fell asleep with a smile, one palm cupping her bottom cheek.

Chapter Twenty

"Mmmm, that smells like coffee."

Florence inhaled deeply as she fought to open one eye. She closed it again when the tall man beside her bed waved a mug of something delicious past her nose. Still half asleep, she rewarded him with a lazy smile of welcome. She rolled onto her back and stretched under the sheet. Pleasant aches reminded her of places she hadn't known existed the previous morning. They tingled, demanding attention.

A finger traced around her nipple. It rose in response. She arched her back, silently asking for more. She heard the thud of a mug being set on the floor. He tugged the sheet and exposed her breast to the September morning cool.

His mouth was so warm. His tongue slipped around her nipple, and then he engulfed as much of her breast as he could. His other hand slipped under the sheet and worked its way over her trembling belly and between her legs.

"Oh, yes," she murmured. She spread her legs, silently begging for more. His fingers entered her pussy, pulsing and rubbing. His thumb rubbed against her clit. She gasped, lifting herself with one heel to press into his hand. He pushed her nipple against the roof of his mouth, rolling it with just enough pressure to make her shiver.

"You coming down to breakfast, wife?" The voice floated up the stairs.

She froze.

"Ben?"

"He's the one made your coffee," said the man now running his fingers through the curls between her legs.

She gasped and pushed herself backward. She fell off the bed in a tangle of sheets, shrieking. She hauled them around her and peeked over the mattress. Her bottom hurt where she landed, but she was too mortified to care. She could barely catch her breath.

It was one thing to be seduced by Ranger in the dark. Waking up to Patrick's mouth and fingers was quite different.

"Morning, ma'am. Ben said you like lots of cream and sugar, so I put in two spoonfuls." He bent over and picked up something from the floor.

"Patrick?" Her voice squeaked.

"Yes'm?"

"What are you doing here?"

"I brought you coffee." He held up the mug as proof. His smug smile proved he knew exactly what she was asking, but he chose not to answer.

"I mean, in my bedroom. Ben's and mine. "

"But, it's not just your bedroom. It's mine, and Ranger's, too. See, all our clothes are here." He pointed to a line of nails against the slanted wall. Men's clothing. Lots of it.

"You sleep here?"

"Yep. Ranger, too. And now Ben and you. You want me to leave your coffee? I've got chores to do."

"Please," she whispered, unable to speak any louder.

Patrick winked, set the mug on the floor, and ambled down the stairs, whistling. She huddled on the chilly floor and tried to bring her heart back into the right place. From pounding in arousal, to fear, to embarrassment. All in less than a minute.

She remembered exactly what happened the previous night, with Ranger's body arousing her rather than her husband's. But it felt so good, she didn't want him to stop. She dropped her head in her hands. The scream she'd heard must have been her own. And then again, with Ben. How could she show her face in front of them ever again? And now Patrick...

She heard the murmur of male voices and then a door closing. She gasped and ducked behind the bed when heavy footsteps came up the stairs.

"Come out, come out, wherever you are," called Ben. At least, she thought it was Ben.

"Who is it?" Her shrill voice echoed around the room.

"Your husband. Who do you think?"

"You can ask that after what happened last night and this morning?"

She peeked over the mattress. His head appeared above the floor.

"Where are you, sweetheart?" He spotted her. "Aw, did Patrick surprise you?"

"Your brother attacked me!"

"Hmm, that's not what he said."

"What!"

"He said he came over to give you coffee, but you stretched out and smiled. When you pushed your breasts up like that at him, he figured you wanted him to touch you. He just did what you wanted, sweetheart. After all, you enjoyed what both Ranger and I shared with you last night. He missed out."

Though the thought mortified her, he was right. She had enjoyed both Ranger's wild action and Ben's loving. If she was honest with herself, she'd have to admit she knew it was Patrick touching her. But she didn't want to be honest. Embarrassment and desire mingled to produce anger.

"I never opened my eyes because I expected you to be the one touching me!"

He ambled across the floor toward the bed and picked up her mug. He walked around and sat down where she huddled behind the mattress. She glared, but took the coffee when he held it out. She sipped, and then swallowed. It was good coffee, made the way she liked it. He lifted the mug from her hands and set it just out of reach.

"I think you enjoyed it when Patrick touched you," he said softly.

Florence gulped. Her nipples rose, hard and demanding. Ben pulled her into his lap, sheets and all. She sighed and lay against his chest. His hand found a way through to her breast. She was chilled, and his warm hand felt so good. He didn't move, just held her snug.

"Did Beth tell you who's the father of her new baby?" asked Ben.

"Yes, Simon."

"And Amelia?"

"She's having Ross's baby. But the next one might have red hair, like Gillis."

His hand barely moved on her breast. But the tiny friction made her quiver.

"You cold?"

She shook her head. It rolled under his chin.

"I told you that, when we married, I knew nothing of this sharing," said Ben quietly. "Except for what Jessie told me when she came out from Texas over two years ago, I hadn't heard from my family for years. Jessie didn't say much, except to remind me of my promise to bring Ranger a wife. I realized after I got to Virginia that I wouldn't marry."

"Then why did you marry me, if you didn't want to?"

He squeezed her breast. "When I decided not to marry, my decision was more to do with the fact that, as a practicing lawyer, I would have to leave my wife alone for weeks at a time. I didn't know I'd meet a strong, independent woman like you." He kissed her nose. "Even if that sheriff hadn't pushed us to marry, by the time we got to Virginia City, I expect I wouldn't have been able to let you, or your children, go."

He leaned over and picked up her coffee. She took a deep drink. She held it in both hands, savoring the warmth. He wiggled his hand back to cover her breast. He weighed it, heaving a great sigh. He held her for a few minutes, gently squeezing her, keeping up the friction. She had to concentrate to listen to his quiet words when he began again.

"If my father had ranch partners, like I do Ranger and Patrick, even if he and my mother died, we'd still have two uncles to give us a home. We wouldn't have been forced to leave. Just as you will have Ranger and Patrick's company when I'm away."

"Is that why you sent Ranger to me last night and gave Patrick my coffee, even though you knew I wasn't dressed?"

She could understand his reasons for wanting her to share herself with his brothers. Having never been loved, a part of her craved the thought of three strong, handsome men loving her. Even though Beth said it could happen, she never expected to feel the same tingling with Ranger and Patrick's kisses, as she felt with Ben.

"If Trace dies, Jack and Simon will still be there for Beth. She won't lie alone in bed crying, fearing for her safety and that of her children. Under the law, a man owns his wife and children. If a big brute like the one who wants Emma, married Beth, he could steal her ranch, her body, and her children, just because he forced her to marry. That's why Trace married Beth, to protect her from Joe Sheldrake. If we have a town bully, that's him."

Ben waited, just holding her and letting her think. If Beth, Amelia, and Jessie did it, she would be the odd one out. She enjoyed Patrick's laugh, though she hadn't yet met Ranger, not really. Would it be so bad, loving more than one person?

"It's not just out here that a woman alone, especially one with children, is at risk," she said. "Emma and Johnny's mother had no one to protect her."

"Ah, yes," he said. "You ready to tell me all about that?"

"I went to the station, eager for my journey." Florence spoke slowly and quietly. "A pale woman wearing a clean, mended, but good-quality cloak approached. She asked me if I was going on the train. When I nodded, she asked if I would take her daughter with me."

Florence remembered how the woman's eyes shone with tears which did not fall. She had no pride left, just love for her children.

She also looked very ill, as if she could barely stand or support the weight of her cloak.

"I could tell she was a woman of education, fallen on hard times, like so many others. I asked her why she had to let her daughter go when she obviously loved her so much. She told me her name, Evangeline Leduc, and that her husband died. She could not find honest work. Because she had beauty, she did what she had to in order to feed her children."

"Why did she choose you?"

"She said I looked like a strong woman with a backbone. She admitted it would be more difficult for me to find a husband with a child, but she was dying. Her face was yellow, her hair listless. She had a hollow look, as if she kept herself alive only for her children. She told me she did not want her daughter to be forced into such a life."

Tears gathered in Florence's eyes. She sniffed, pressing her lips together as she fought to speak. "She was worried someone would make offers for Emma."

Ben's heart suddenly pounded against her back. "Emma would have no protection when her mother died."

"My last letter to the newspaper was against poor women going to jail while the men who used and profited from them stayed free. How could I not take the child with me?"

"And Johnny?"

"Emma asked, in French, about her little brother. She pointed to a small shape huddled by the wall. Her mother explained in the same language that he should be safe." She bit her lip and sniffed. "I saw a small boy sitting on a carpetbag, staring at us. He didn't move. Before I could think, I called out in French for him to come with his sister." She stopped to wipe her eyes and sniff back tears. "Johnny grabbed his bag and ran over. They hugged and smiled up at me."

"You couldn't leave him behind."

She shook her head. Tears leaked out. "Ben, I wrote letters. Lots of them, trying to change things. As far as I could tell, my writing helped no one. Freeing two children from such a terrible future was something real. Madame Leduc thanked me, but I told her I did this for myself, as well. I'd wanted a husband and children to love for years. No one wanted me, as I'm too educated and opinionated, and I refuse to obey a man simply because he is one. But as a widow with two young children, I no longer needed a husband."

Florence turned her tear-stained face up to Ben.

"Only after she turned her back on her own children, did I see the tears running down her face. But she smiled as she walked away, Ben." Florence burst into tears. "Knowing her children were safe, she smiled!"

Ben rocked her back and forth as she cried. She cried for Emma trying so hard to take care of the brother that was less than eighteen months younger. She cried for the little girls and boys who did not have someone like her to rescue them. And she cried because she had strong, warm, loving arms around her. Arms that would also comfort their children.

She finally subsided into sniffles and hiccups. Ben helped her drink her coffee so she wouldn't spill it due to her shaking hands. She let out a shuddering breath and leaned against his chest again.

"You don't need to tell me it's better to have three husbands," she said. "Emma and Johnny will always have a home, even if something happens to us." She tilted her eyes to meet Ben's. "Can you promise me that?"

"I can, and will promise that, and so will Patrick, and Ranger."

Ben kissed the top of her head. "Thank you for telling me about our children. Their mother is a very strong person. Do you know anything about their father?"

"Madame Leduc gave me a letter. She was from New Orleans. Her husband came to visit the city and they met. They married quickly, very much in love. His father did not approve. He said she was common and insisted he divorce Evangeline, or never return."

"That sounds like what happened to my parents."

"She was with child when he died, Emma only a year old. After Johnny's birth she came north to try and find her in-laws. But with a small child and a tiny baby, right after the war, it was difficult. She was pretty and was bothered by men. She decided it was either find a man to care for her, or have one take her anyway."

"She found a protector, or fancy man."

Florence blinked, suddenly understanding. "Oh! That's what Emma said when I fell in your lap." Ben nodded. "You knew! Why didn't you say something?"

"I suspected, but you intrigued me." He chucked her under the chin. "You obviously didn't know much about how to care for children because you let them be themselves. I found it wonderful that you let Johnny kneel on the seat and look out the train window."

"But, how else would he see out? The windows are high."

"Proper young gentlemen do not gawk out the window. Nor do young ladies eat breakfast with their hair ribbon askew. Nor," he drawled, his lip twitching, "do women arrive in the dining car with wisps of hair trailing over their ears." He tucked a few strands back from her face. "I, however, do not follow the dictates of Eastern society. I found you wonderfully fresh, witty, and a puzzle. As a lawyer, I have a desperate need to figure out puzzles."

"Oh."

"I assume Madame Leduc's place of work declined as her health worsened?"

Florence nodded. "Two days before the Bride Train left, she discovered someone had arranged to buy Emma. That's why that man went after her. Mrs. Leduc knew the greed of the brothel owners. They would kill her to sell her daughter. She heard rumors another man wanted Johnny."

"Did you keep the letter?"

Florence shook her head. "I plan to write another for the children, with only the important details. The names of their mother and father, where they came from, and that their mother and father loved them very, very much."

"One of the first things I will do is to apply to the courts in Helena," said Ben. "Emma and Johnny will legally become our children. I expect I'll do the same for Daniel. Bridie and Meggie Redmond will marry in a few years and start their own families. But if they wish to be adopted by Trace, I will help them as well."

Florence sipped her coffee. Ben accepted her and two children. He liked her, even though other men had said loudly that she should be burned at the stake for her blasphemous views.

She could love him just for his easy acceptance of her and her children. What would his brothers think, when they found out? Would they think she'd tricked Ben into marrying her? Not only was he convenient, as a lawyer he was a man of substance. He was also a very caring man who would be a good father and husband. She wasn't sure about Ranger and Patrick accepting her children, however.

"You ready to start cooking breakfast now, wife? The rest of us have done our morning chores, and time's a-wasting."

He moved his hand from her breast, dropping it to her belly. His finger trailed in her curls, near her clit. A surge of need shot through her.

"Are you planning to finish what you're starting?" She opened her thighs in invitation.

He took her mug of cold coffee and put it aside. He stood up and dropped her on the bed. "Nope," he said cheerfully. "I'm hungry for food. You, I will have later."

He winked and sauntered from the room, finishing her coffee. Just before his head disappeared down the stairs, he turned back.

"Patrick left a haunch of fresh venison on the table. A few pies would do for dinner. And another three of apple."

The only thing she could reach was a pillow. She threw it at him. It didn't go far, but he got the point. He continued down the stairs, chuckling.

She unrolled herself from the sheet and dropped it on the floor. A pink stain blemished the middle of the white bottom sheet. Evidence of her married status. She flushed at how she'd screamed, demanding more, that first time.

With Ranger, not Ben.

How could she face the man? Would he laugh at her, or smirk? If she pretended it had never happened, would he do the same? That way, they could get to know each other better first. Perhaps then she could be in the same room with him without dying of mortification.

She dropped onto the bed. She'd gotten to know Patrick by his kiss right off, and that hadn't changed the way the younger man felt about her. But Ranger seemed to be a far more complex man.

She dressed, thinking hard. She wanted more of their loving, but without embarrassment. She also wanted to get to know them better. She hadn't even seen Ranger properly yet.

First, she would make them apple pies, and venison, too. But she would demand some treats in return. And she wasn't going to wait until after supper!

Chapter Twenty-One

Ranger worked quietly in the barn, sorting nails. Ben's new wife should be busy turning the house upside down to put her stamp on it. That's what Beth said every woman did when she got a new home. Florence had no reason to go near the barn, and he had a tricky bit of blacksmithing coming up, so he should be safe from interfering females. He needed to gather all his supplies, and today was the time to finish the job.

Though she had told him to continue last night, he felt a twinge of unease that she might have regretted it afterward. He was as honest as he could be in the circumstances. It was a well known fact that a hard cock has no morals, but he was not a man who deceived women.

Unless they wanted to be deceived. A number of widows over the years had wanted to pretend he was their husband and they were innocently enjoying his attention. The fact he heated their blood in ways their dead husband never had, was also never mentioned.

But Fanny was no widow eager for temporary fun. She was Ben's wife, the only one on the Bitterroot Ranch. He'd let her show the way. Hell, he hadn't even seen her, not really. But he certainly knew his way around her body.

The woman was wild and demanding, though she was new at this. He had a lot to teach her. His cock rose at the thought of continuing what they'd started the previous night. But she was Ben's new wife, and he would not go after her. If she wanted more of him, she'd have to start it. He would be the one to finish it, though.

Decision made, he went back to work. It was another glorious September afternoon. The sun shone so bright he enjoyed the barn's dimness. Any day now the weather would change, bringing cold winds and wet snow. Ten years in Texas, and he hadn't forgotten the bone-chilling Montana winters. But those winters killed all the poisonous spiders, scorpions, and every other damn critter that made Texas the hell it could be.

He picked up a handful of horseshoe nails and absently set them on the rail. He missed, and they fell to the dirt floor. He cursed and bent over. If he didn't get them all up, a horse might step on them and get a puncture. Injuries that seemed like nothing could kill a man, a child, or a horse.

"I was hoping to find you here."

Fanny.

Ranger's cock hardened even more at the challenge in her voice. He put his fingers on the last nail, sifting it out of the dirt. A hand slid over his ass. He jerked upright.

"You got time to play, big boy?"

"Thought you had pies to bake," he growled.

"All done. Bread in the oven, biscuits ready to mix. All I need is this."

She ran her hands around his waist. One went to his chest, the other to his crotch. She caressed him through his pants. He gulped. Damn! Her hand on his cock felt good. The barn was dark, and he had his back to her. Did she know who she was messing with? He doubted she knew what she was asking for, either. One night of marriage did not prepare a woman for all a man could do.

"You know whose cock you're demanding, woman?"

She faltered for a moment then grasped him again. His blood surged to respond.

"Ben's not here. I want more of what I got from you last night."

He'd give her what she wanted, but she'd get it his way.

"You want to play with me, little lady?"

"Yes, I want to play with you, big man. Ben and Patrick left me aching this morning."

"My cock, my rules."

He felt her shudder against his back. She licked her lips. Her heart pounded against his back as her breathing sped up.

"What rules?"

He put his hands on hers to stop them moving. "You do what I say, or I don't play."

"Um, what do you want to play?"

He used his hand to rub hers on his cock. Up and down, showing her the pressure he liked.

"We're going to play stallion and mare." Her breath caught. She panted against his shoulder. "You ever see a stallion mount a mare, little lady?"

"No," she whispered. "I don't think ladies are supposed to watch those things."

"Why not?"

"I expect it would make them feel hot."

He mulled that over, still using her hand to please himself.

"You like feeling hot?"

"Oh, yes."

"You hot now?"

She nodded against his back.

"Then you'd better strip down to your boots."

She gasped and tried to pull away. "Here?"

"No, out in the sun where I can see better."

"Are…are you going to watch?"

"Damn right. But you're not going to see me doing it. Don't move."

He twisted her around so she faced the bright doorway. He found a clean flannel cloth, one of Patrick's old shirts that they'd ripped up for rags. He tied it just tight enough to cover her eyes. He wanted her to concentrate on his touch, but be able to see if she needed to.

Holding her shoulders, he encouraged her to walk to the door and out into the sun. He moved her to where he wanted and released her.

He backed up and set his hip on the work table he'd earlier moved into the sun.

"I'm ready any time," he said. "Get them buttons undone, or I'll have to pull them off like last night."

She flicked her sleeve buttons first, then the ones holding the lace tight around her neck. Why did women wear such tight clothes? Sunbird wore a loose dress, summer and winter. When it was cool, she put a long-sleeved shirt underneath. Nothing else but moccasins.

Come summer, he wanted Fanny to wear nothing but a thin cotton dress and boots. That's what Beth wore, with a collar dipping low enough to let her get lots of air. Even better, Jack told him, was that it left room for a man's hands to get a quick feel. No petticoats, either. He wanted to see his woman's body when the sun was behind her.

She peeled off her blouse, leaving only her shift between her skin and the sun. Her breasts, topped with large nipples, pressed against the fabric. She held her blouse out, uncertain. He moseyed over and took it from her hand.

"That's one, but there's lots more to come off," he said. He patted her bottom, just hard enough to get her attention, and sat down again. Carefully.

She fiddled at her waist, and a petticoat dropped to the ground, though she kept her skirt on. She let it lie there and repeated the movement. Another fell.

"Anytime you want me to pick those up, sweets, you let me know," he said.

She held out her hand. "Hold me while I step out of them."

He took her hand and did as she asked, and then tossed her petticoats on the table. "Need any help?" He went after her skirt buttons. She smacked his hand. He laughed and moved back.

She unbuttoned her skirt. Expecting more petticoats, he choked when it fell. She wore nothing but boots, stockings, and her shift. A thin shift that the sun shone through.

"Well?"

Her voice broke his concentration. She waited, hand out, for him to help her step out of her skirt. He held her trembling fingers as she carefully lifted her foot. Because she didn't know how high to lift, he caught a flash of dark hair between her legs. His cock jerked. She leaned on his hand and lifted her other foot. He tossed her skirt toward the table one-handed, holding her still.

"That's far enough for now," he said. Something wasn't right. "Your hair. It has to come down."

"I need to wash it."

"I'll fill the reservoir for you." He'd do any damn thing to have this vision in his yard, and in his hands.

"Don't lose my pins, please."

He grunted agreement, dropping them in his pocket as he removed them. He unwrapped her braid from around her head. Finally, he ran his fingers through it, unweaving her braid. When free, her hair damn near reached her ass. She sighed and shook her head. The breeze caught the ends, making them flutter. Not today, but soon she'd ride his cock, dangling that hair over his belly and chest.

Suddenly, he wanted her naked. He reached around, grabbed the loose front of her shift in his fists and yanked. It ripped all the way to her belly. She squeaked and covered her breasts.

"Stop! What are you doing?"

He calmly ripped the rest until it dropped to her feet.

"Hands at your sides," he demanded.

"But—"

"This make you hot, Mrs. Elliott?"

She bit her lip and forced her hands down. "Yes," she whispered. Her fingers curled into fists, but she held them at her hips, not covering up his view of her.

He stalked around her in a slow circle. She knew what he did and shook her head, rippling her hair down her back. She raised her chin and glared. He knew the glare was there, even though she had a blindfold over her eyes.

Damn, she was something. He liked what he felt last night, but seeing her standing like this, the sun showing every crinkled bump around her nipples… He leaned closer. Pink, not coral. Pink, and hard.

He rubbed his knuckles over them. She quivered and pressed her shoulders back, raising her proud breasts. One day, an Elliott child would suckle there. Today, it was his turn.

He supported her breasts and bent over. He scraped his teeth over a nipple. He blew on it, and then took it into his mouth. He trailed his other hand lightly down her belly. She quivered when he touched the spots he'd noted last night. One finger between her wet lower lips proved she enjoyed this just as much as he.

He backed away and walked behind her. Damn, she had a fine ass. He moved her hair over one shoulder, admiring the long line of her back. Her ass curved out with two little dimples above the full cheeks. He knelt behind her and placed his hands on those cheeks, pressing gently. She reset her feet so he didn't push her forward.

He separated her cheeks with his thumbs. A sweet little brown asshole beckoned. She liked him playing with it last night. He used one hand to keep her cheeks apart and stroked a finger up and down, deep between them. He drew his finger down. Down to where her fluid seeped from her pussy into the space between that and her asshole. When his finger was wet he scraped against the tight brown iris. A tiny ring of pink appeared for a moment. He chuckled.

"What are you laughing about?"

"You like this." He did it again, pressing just enough against it for the very tip of his finger to rub against the pink circle. She clenched her cheeks, catching him.

"Damn, I want you now," he growled.

He stood up and, since no one was around, pulled off his shirt. He kicked off his boots, cursing when the left wouldn't come off quickly. He kicked it aside and shoved off his pants. His cockstand stood proud, hard, and throbbing.

He walked up behind Florence. He stopped when his cock tucked against her lower back. He held both of her breasts, squeezing and kneading. She panted, her shoulders moving with every breath. He nipped a cord in her neck and then kissed it better.

"You know what I'm going to do with you now?"

She shook her head, fast and eager.

"I'm going to walk you over to that table by the barn. I'm going to bend you over until your pussy points right at my cock. I'll use your dress to pad the edge. Because then I'm going to ram my cock in your pussy so hard your hips will slam against the table."

She moaned. He nudged her boots apart with his foot. Farther, until he had easy access to her pussy. He dropped a hand to her thigh. It was slippery with her juices.

"Feel this?" He ran his right hand up her thigh until his hand hit her pussy lips. "You're wet and eager. This means you want my cock. Right. Here."

He cupped his hand over her public bone and inserted two fingers. He curled them forward, pressing against her spongy spot. She trembled.

"You want me to mount you like a stallion?"

"Yes!"

He helped her move forward. When she was close to the table, he stopped her. He lifted her clothing and swept everything off the table with one sweep of his arm. He laid one petticoat on the table and folded the rest into a barrier. He set it against the edge and urged her forward until her hips held the fabric in place.

He placed her palms on the table, spread her legs and bent her over. He stepped back. A woman with long brown hair waited for his cock. She bit her full lips on one side, mouth open as she panted. Her ass tilted up at him. One day he'd take her there, and she'd enjoy every damn minute of it.

The sun glinted on the fluid that eased out of her pussy. He slid a finger between her legs, gathered her juice and licked his finger. His woman or theirs. It didn't matter.

"Are you just going to look at me, or are you going to do something!"

He swatted her ass, just enough to sting. She jerked upright, shrieked and turned around. But she didn't try to take off her blindfold. She liked what he did to master her.

"I am doing something," he replied. "I'm watching my handprint turn pink. Right here." He placed his palm over the pink. Of course, it fit perfectly. "Back in position," he ordered.

She delayed just enough to purposefully annoy him, but not get another swat. Then she angled her ass, spreading her legs wide and tilting her pussy at him.

Red flag to a bull.

He stepped up behind her, inserted his cock, and surged in two inches. She groaned and wiggled against him. He filled her, his wide cock straining her near-virgin pussy. He backed up and made sure he didn't go more than an inch more each time. But he held her hips with both hands and made a big show of surging forward, grunting hard.

When he skewered her all the way, he pulled her back against his chest with his left arm, both of hers caged. He played with her clit with his other hand, making slow circles around it. She muttered and twisted, trying to make him move where she wanted.

But he was in charge. He felt the tension building and plucked her clit. She shuddered, clenching him inside as her own explosion neared. He set her hands back on the table and lifted her hips. The first stroke was slow, but he sped up, slamming her hips back against him, using her pussy as he had his fist too often over the years.

But this was nothing like it. He held a warm woman in his hands. A woman whose weeping pussy clenched him. She moved her feet together, tightening her grip even more. She wanted him. Wanted this.

She gasped, straining and begging wordlessly for more. His balls hardened, ready to release. She keened, begging him *please, oh, please.*

Eyes closed, he pounded hard, taking her as a stallion, hard from behind. She suddenly gasped. Her pussy clamped down on him, just in time. The coil of tension running from his ass through his balls and to the end of his cock suddenly released. He pumped, again and again, sending his seed deep inside her.

He fell forward against her back, lungs heaving. Only then did he feel the sweat dripping down his temples. He opened his eyes. Patrick stood beside him, cock in hand, pleading silently. He slid out and moved over.

"More?" she moaned hopefully. "Please, tell me there's more!"

"You want to finish what we started this morning? You left me in pretty bad shape."

"Patrick?"

"Yes, ma'am!"

"Oh, yes!"

Patrick turned her onto her back and lifted her legs wide. Her moans turned to groans when he surged into her. He lifted her legs and tucked them over his forearms, grasped her hips, and went home.

Ranger moved her hands to her nipples. She took over, pinching and stretching them as Patrick warmed her up again. Ranger went back to work on her clit. Patrick labored above, changing angles to make her gasp.

Ranger pinched her clit, now that she was well warmed up. A flush covered her from pussy curls to the top of her forehead. Suddenly she screamed and arched her back so high only her head touched the table. Patrick supported her hips as he pounded. Her orgasm hit him hard. He roared like a bear, slamming her onto his cock. The two of them gasped, covered in sweat.

Patrick, gasping like a fish out of water, turned to him with the biggest shit-eating grin he'd ever seen. He released her legs, bent over and kissed her on the lips. She hauled her arms around him and returned it just as wildly. When Patrick finally broke away, he staggered to the barn and leaned both arms against it, fighting to breathe.

Ranger gathered Florence into his arms, catching her dress and petticoats from under her. She rested her head, her eyes still covered, on his chest. He nodded to Patrick to lead the way and open any doors. He pulled their wife to his chest and carried her into the house and up the stairs. He set her down in the middle of the too-small bed, her petticoats and dress still under her.

"Rest now," he whispered.

"But—"

"But you're all tired out. Have a nap and you'll feel better."

He pulled on a shirt and gently cleaned her. He tugged her clothing free so she lay naked on the sheet. He removed the blindfold and kissed her forehead before covering her with a sheet and blanket. She never opened her eyes, just sighed and smiled contentedly. He removed her boots and stockings and watched her for a moment, his heart pounding.

They'd never spoken to each other, except during sex. Would she care about him as Ranger Elliott, or did she only want him for how he made her body feel? Too many women over the years had been the same. They'd call him when they needed servicing, but didn't want him in their parlors. He was only good enough for the barn and the bedroom.

He bet she was the same. A rich, Eastern woman used to servants. Well, he wasn't going to put up with that. Too hell with her. He didn't want an uppity, cantankerous, high-brow woman spouting drivel from the books she wanted to read all the time.

All he wanted from her was hot, tasty meals, clean clothes, and damn good sex. If she could manage that, they'd get along fine.

He tossed her clothing toward the chair in the corner. Soft snores filled his ears before he'd gone six steps.

Chapter Twenty-Two

"So much for a big welcome home," said Ben to himself. No one else was there to listen.

Right after breakfast he rode out to check the borders of the Bitterroot Ranch. Trace and the Rocking E lay to the east, the division marked by a creek coming down from the mountains. Gillis and the MD Connected were to the south, across the narrow river. Mountain ranges climbed to the north and west. No miner would foul his water or steal his cattle.

He hadn't bothered to return for dinner, and it was getting on toward suppertime. His stomach, used to regular meals, growled like one of Nevin's totems.

As he rode the last few miles home, he imagined Florence running out of the house, throwing herself at him and demanding hot sex. After all, he'd left her hot and bothered that morning on purpose.

Instead, silence greeted him. They needed a dog or two. As the last ranch in the valley, no one had a reason to pass by. But a man on a horse could make it over the ridge without anyone seeing him. That was one of the things he'd checked that day. Deer trails could also bring horses, in and out. He couldn't count on Ross's ravens to warn them of danger.

He took his time in the barn caring for his horse and trudged to the house. Nine out of ten said his dear wife was snoozing. She hadn't had much sleep since taking on the children, so he didn't blame her. As her husband, he had a legal right to wake her with a kiss and go on from there.

He left his boots by the back door and slung his hat over the rack of elk antlers. He padded up the stairs in sock feet. Sure enough, there was a lump in the bed. His cock swelled against his buttons. He undid them before things got too uncomfortable.

Florence must have been hot because she'd stripped down to nothing for her nap. He stopped, checking out the scene. Something didn't add up.

Her dusty skirt and petticoats were jumbled up, tossed over the chair in the corner. A woman who had to heat water to wash her clothes, then used a sad iron on them, did not toss clothing aside. She hung it up to keep it clean and reduce wrinkles. A man in a hurry, however, wouldn't much care about those details.

Her boots, stockings tucked in them, sat neatly by the bed. Small clots of dirt stuck to her heels. She would never come into the house without wiping her boots, as she would be the one cleaning the floor. He hunkered down and looked along the floor from the stairs to the bed. No sign of dirt.

"When the facts do not fit your hypothesis," he murmured, "change your hypothesis. Facts do not lie."

Petticoats would get dusty when dropped in the yard. So would a skirt. He didn't see her blouse or shift. Dirt clung to her boots, yet there were no tracks across the floor. That meant someone carried her. The same someone might have tossed her clothes aside, all jumbled because she was not wearing them at the time. The boots came off after she got in the bed. All evidence pointed to his new bride stripping down to her boots in the yard and getting carried upstairs.

"Well, well," he said to himself as he stood. He looked at the basin in the corner. It was dry that morning, but a flannel floated in it. Florence sighed and rolled onto her back. She pulled the sheets with her, exposing one breast. As he watched, the nipple rose in the cool room. He unbuttoned his shirt and let it slide off. Belt and pants followed, and then socks.

His cock bounced as he stalked forward. As he approached the bed he inhaled the unmistakable aroma of sex. He'd left his dear wife wanting that morning on purpose. She must have demanded sex. But was it with Ranger, or Patrick? Or both?

He lifted the sheet and settled beside her on his side. He wanted to see her face.

"Hmm, Ben?"

"That's me."

"I like that game," she murmured, eyes still closed.

"Which one?"

"Stallion and mare. Can we play it again another day?"

Ben imagined the view of her ass and pussy when taking her from behind as a stallion would a mare. His hips moved involuntarily, as if he was doing the same.

"Sweetheart, I haven't seen you since this morning, right after breakfast. I've been riding the boundaries. But anytime you want to play, I'm ready." He captured her breast with his palm. "So are Ranger and Patrick. Which one did you go after? Or was it both?"

Her eyes flashed open. The pulse at her throat jumped. She clutched the covers. He winked and smiled. She stared at him, mouth open. She licked her lips and swallowed.

"You like what you saw of my twin brother?"

"Twin?"

"Ranger and I used to look identical. Our faces are still much the same, but not our bodies. If you hugged him, surely you noticed how much broader his chest is compared to mine?"

She shook her head, but he wasn't sure if it was in agreement, denial, or lust. He looked at her nipples. Tight and hard on rapidly swelling breasts. The answer was lust. He reached for the cloth that had covered her eyes. He held it up.

"You knew it was Ranger, but you didn't see him, right?"

She nodded.

"Good. I'm pleased you went after what you wanted. How was it?"

The pink on her face darkened. She tried to roll over and turn her back to him, but he moved on top of her, supporting himself by elbows and toes. He settled between her legs, though a sheet kept them apart. He tilted his hips, rubbing his cock against her clit.

"I can't think when you do that," she gasped.

"Did Patrick help, too? You left him mighty frustrated this morning."

She opened her eyes and glared up at him. Their noses were inches apart.

"He started it, not me!"

"You teased him, and he responded. He's randy as all get-out but with little experience and big needs." He kissed her nose. "He came near with your coffee and saw you sleeping with nothing but a sheet covering you. Yet he didn't rip the sheet off, spread your legs, and take what he was desperate for. You smiled at him and stretched. When he touched your nipple like this," he put his weight on one elbow and traced around her hard nipple with a finger, "you arched your back, begging for more, right?"

She bit her lip, face flaming, but nodded in agreement.

"Do you know how much self-control it took for him to just touch your clit and breasts, making you feel good, but driving himself crazy?"

She shook her head. Her chin quivered as if holding back tears. He kissed her lips. She pressed them tight for a moment before relaxing.

"Remember last night, just before you came for the first time?"

She nodded.

"What if you felt like that and found Ranger lying on his back, cock hard and ready? What if you ran your finger around the tip of his cock, like Patrick did around your nipple? Ranger would moan and lift his hips, his cock leaking the fluid that proved he wanted you. Would you be able to touch his cock and nipples, pleasuring him, without climbing on that hard cock and riding it until you exploded? That's what you asked Patrick to do this morning. To have you begging, and not take what he needed."

"I didn't know—"

"We know you didn't. But then you went after Ranger when I was nowhere around. He wouldn't touch you unless you knew who you held. You demanded sex, and he gave it to you."

He ran his hand over her breast. She arched her back into his palm and nodded.

"He bound my eyes and made me strip. Standing in the yard."

"I figured that when I found your dusty skirt and petticoats on the chair. Where's your blouse and chemise?"

Her eyes blazed. "He ripped my chemise in half! Just grabbed it in his fists and tore it in two!"

"And you loved it."

She jammed her eyes shut. He nibbled her ear, smiling. This was the type of loving he liked. Slow and sensuous. Of course Ranger would demand things of her before giving her rough sex. He needed to have that power, especially over a woman whose education would make him feel less of a man.

"He finished, but I asked for more, and Patrick…"

He waited, but she said nothing more. Behind closed lids her eyes darted all around.

"And?" he prompted.

"I don't want to say it."

"And then Patrick gave you another orgasm."

She groaned and turned her head away.

"That's three for three, isn't it, sweetheart?" His heart swelled along with his cock. "You enjoy all of us. And we enjoy you."

"Why aren't you angry at your brothers touching your wife?"

When he didn't answer, she glared up at him. He rolled onto his back, taking her with him. She squirmed, pulling the wrinkled sheet from under her and pushing it aside. They ended up with her legs straddling one of his. Now it was Florence looking accusingly at him. He was the one with the secret to tell. She cleared her throat and stared down at him like a sexy schoolmarm demanding an answer.

"I'm not angry because, if you weren't happy sharing us, then Ranger and Patrick would have to go without. That wouldn't be right." He closed his eyes. "And I want us to have more children than just Emma and Johnny."

She frowned. "Ben, I can only have one child at a time, no matter who the father is. Twins do not run in my family, thank goodness. Doing…that with Ranger and Patrick won't change the number of children I have."

"I don't know," he said, fingering her hair. "I'd love to have a set of little girls who look just like you."

"Are you trying to tell me something?"

He nodded. He knew her secret, and now he must tell his. "I can't make children. If Ranger and Ben don't share you, we won't have any more."

"How do you know this? It's up to God to say—"

"God's had his say. Soon after I arrived in Virginia, a storm of mumps swept through the city. Every part of my body swelled up, especially between my legs." He winced, remembering the excruciating pain. "My fever was high for many days. I was so weak I could barely walk for weeks. The doctor said I was lucky to be alive, but would likely never be a father. That's when I decided not to marry. It wouldn't be fair to my wife."

He almost laughed at the relief in telling her. No one else needed to know about his failure as a man.

"Is that why you agreed to marry me, because I had two children?"

"Saving Emma was the only thing on my mind at that moment." He caressed her cheek. "But yes, after we got back on the train I realized how relieved I was to have found a woman whose company I enjoyed, and had a family I could share."

"You really didn't know about your brothers sharing wives?"

He shook his head. "Not until Virginia City. Ranger and Nev

explained about Beth, Amelia, and Jessie sharing three men each."

She laid her head on his chest, perhaps avoiding his eyes. He hugged her.

"What did you decide to do if I refused to stay with all three of you?" She spoke into his chest.

He replied in the same quiet manner. "I would ask if you wanted a divorce. If you did, I'd set you up with a home and business wherever you wished. We can still do that, if you don't want us."

They lay there while she thought. He rested one hand on her curving bottom cheek and trailed the other up and down her back. He tried to appear calm, but every pound of his heart screamed *No!*

He wanted this woman. Not just for bedding, or for the other duties of a wife. He wanted her courage, her companionship, her ability to laugh, and to make him laugh.

But if she wanted to go, he would release her. Because, even if she could like him, he didn't know if she could tolerate Ranger. Patrick was a born flirt, so easygoing he could fit into whatever mold was wanted.

Ranger was demanding, both in personality and because he was the Bitterroot Ranch's ramrod. Where the ranch was concerned, he made the final decisions. Florence was equally hardheaded. Unless someone backed off, their two personalities would mix like black powder and a match. Ka-boom!

"I don't think I want a divorce."

His chest muscles relaxed enough that he could breathe again. He sucked air deep.

"Emma and Johnny have a family now," she said. "I can't destroy that."

She drew circles on his belly with a finger. Now he understood how difficult it was to concentrate with a finger driving one crazy.

"What about us?" he croaked.

"Us?"

"Florence, Ben, Ranger, and Patrick."

"I don't know. I haven't seen Ranger, just, um," she fluttered her fingers instead of speaking bluntly. "Much less discussed this with him. Or Patrick. I want to get to know them with my clothes on before deciding anything." She glared at him. "But I want a few concessions for choosing to stay."

"I can understand that. Have you got a list yet?" He wasn't surprised when she nodded.

"I want my own room, like Beth has. Just a small place with a narrow cot, where I can be alone. If the door is closed, I am not to be disturbed."

"That might take until next summer. We're trying to finish Jessie's house first, so she doesn't freeze during the winter. Ranger said the gaps between her cabin logs are so wide he didn't have to look in the window to see Jessie cuddled up to Ace. That's when he told Trace she was compromised and they had to marry."

"I think I can wait until summer. Someday, I'd like a bathing room like Beth's."

"Sweetheart, someday we'll build a wonderful big house for all of us. Maybe we'll need a bunkhouse like the one at the MD Connected because of all the children we have."

She jerked her head up, eyes wide. "How many children?"

"All the orphans we find who need a home."

Her eyes suddenly shone with tears. "You mean that? What about Ranger and Patrick? Will they agree?"

"If we can save children like Emma and Johnny, or Daniel, Bridie, and Meggie, we will. Any of us Elliotts or MacDougals. Children are our future."

"Oh, Ben!"

She pulled herself up his body until she could reach his lips. His cock sprang free. She needed leverage to move so opened her legs, kneeling on either side of his hips. She kissed him, eyes open, gently.

"You are a very good man, Benjamin Elliott."

"Good enough to keep as a husband?"

She waggled her bottom so it rubbed against his erect cock. "Husbands do provide a few advantages to a woman."

"Aren't you sore? If Ranger played the stallion, I expect he pounded into you a fair bit."

She shrugged but her face, and breasts, pinked up. "Not enough to give up pleasure."

"Lift up and let me out." He slipped out from under her when she lifted her left arm and leg. "Now scoot forward and hold onto the headboard."

She frowned, but settled on her knees. She held onto the iron headboard with both hands. He moved her knees apart, lay on his back and settled. He grasped her hips and pulled her toward his face.

"What are you doing—oh!"

One lick of his tongue on her wet pussy and she went silent. He'd have to remember that during arguments. If he didn't like where the conversation was going, distract her with arousal. She relaxed and pressed her clit against his nose.

She didn't stay silent for long.

Chapter Twenty-Three

Florence refused to meet Ranger's eyes when Ben introduced him at supper. She also avoided Patrick, though he snickered at her for doing so. Since they worked on the ranch all day and slept in the drafty cabin, she could pretend they didn't exist except during meals.

She couldn't face them, knowing how she'd behaved. It wasn't that she was ashamed or anything. She was just a bit uncomfortable with how much they knew about each other's bodies, without knowing anything about them as people.

The situation continued for the next few days. Ranger's knowing wink when she accidentally caught his eye made her temperature climb, even through September's chill. They never spoke, other than, "pass the peas," so of course they hadn't discussed her first time or the afternoon when he made her scream, followed by Patrick.

She took quick looks at Ranger when he didn't know she was watching. Ranger and Ben's faces were alike, but their bodies no longer looked like twins to her. Ranger's skin was roughened from working outdoors, and his body was far more massive. His callused hands had small scars and cuts on them. Ben, working alongside, had new cuts every day. His fingers bled as he hadn't yet developed calluses.

Ben never, ever swore. Ranger did it all the time. Ben used words with more than one syllable. Ranger preferred grunts. Ranger was wild and demanding, while Ben's loving was always sweet. He took his time, doing things that made her beg him to take her. He would shake his head, smile, and continue licking, sucking, probing, and doing everything but making her scream her orgasm. She felt wicked when she had to demand he take her. Only then would he give her release.

Patrick was always pleasant, though a devilish flirt. His hand or parts of his body would "accidentally" touch her every time he was near. Every morning and evening he asked for a kiss. So far, she'd said no. He'd pout and complain that she was chicken.

There wasn't that much difference in their ages, just a few years. She sensed his growing frustration. He was a far more capable rancher than Ben, yet Ranger treated him as if he was merely a hired hand. From what she'd learned about life in Texas, it was no wonder Patrick kept his head down and mouth shut.

But the Bitterroot was his ranch, as well as Ben's and Ranger's. He should have a greater say in how things were done. She couldn't talk with Ben about it because she needed privacy. The only time they had time alone was in bed, but the last few nights they collapsed and barely moved until morning. With winter's blast approaching, there was far too much work to be done to ensure they'd survive until spring.

How would she get through a long, cold, dark winter if her precious books never made it from Virginia City? Even if they did arrive before the snow closed the passes, she had nowhere to put them!

Florence ruminated on where she could safety store her books as she lifted the dry clothes from the bare bushes where she'd placed them hours earlier. She'd done loads and loads of wash because, after cloudy damp days, today was warm and sunny. Her arms, legs, and back ached from hauling water and heavy clothing. She had no idea what to make for supper. Nor did she care. They could all eat burned biscuits and glue porridge, as Patrick said the first time they met.

She smiled when Ben approached. He began lifting the men's heavier pants from the sturdier branches. She continued working, her heart lighter. Just having his company made the work go faster. If he had time to come home this early, perhaps they could make use of the bed for more than sleeping tonight.

"I'll be leaving soon," he said as if discussing the weather. "Should be back in a week, maybe ten days depending on the weather."

Her hand, about to pick up a pillowcase, stopped. Moving slowly, she placed her armful of sheets into the willow basket. She turned her back and started on the wool socks.

"I assume from your words that I am not accompanying you," she said. He was playing it cool, and so would she.

"No, we'll be riding cross-country, to Helena and back. That would be me, Nevin, and Jack."

She heard relief in his voice. Had he expected her to turn on him and scream like a fishwife just because he was traveling without her? All she knew of Helena was that it was a long way north of Virginia City, the end of the line for the train. It was a big, bustling city, and some very rich and powerful people lived there. She could get books there. And a bath tub. Soft towels instead of strips of flannel from someone's worn winter sheets. But not if they had to carry it on horseback.

"You're traveling with Jack? I thought you two didn't get along particularly well."

"Trace says it's time we learned how. One of Jack's complaints is that he's never been anywhere. He won't be able to say it after this."

"And Nevin is going because…?"

"Because he's almost as fast as Ross with a knife or his fists."

She stopped cursing Ben in her mind and turned. His half smile looked sheepish. "What has that got to do with it?"

Ben shrugged like a little boy caught with cherry pie on his face and a piece missing from the dish. "The brothers figure Nevin will make sure Jack and I don't kill each other."

She whirled away from him, stomped over to her basket, and stuffed the socks in it.

"Florence, I knew you would be upset at the news. I'm not happy about having to leave you like this. But one of the reasons I'm going to Helena is to file the adoption papers for Emma and Johnny, and Daniel. I also need to meet the men who will be shaping the Territory into a State. All of this must be done before the snow closes the passes, and that could be any week now."

She realized Ben had to go, but that wasn't what bothered her. It was being left without a buffer. How would she be able to stand being around Ranger, and even Patrick, without Ben?

Ranger irritated her just by the way he walked, talked, and carried himself. She was sure he grunted on purpose instead of saying please and thank you. After supper, if she caught his eye he would send amused glances that set her smoldering. At least Ben wasn't aware of her unease.

"Don't worry that my brothers will try to climb into your bed. Unless you ask, they'll wait until I'm back to sort things out with you. Mind you, if you ask, they'll make sure you're satisfied."

Florence curled her fingers into fists. If she was a violent woman, which she hadn't thought possible until marrying into a family of so many thoroughly frustrating men, she would hit something. Instead she took five deep breaths, as taught by Miss Primula. *Ladies do not show excitement of any kind, at any time. They are demure and silent.* Florence failed, repeatedly, the classes related to acting like a lady. She knew how, but chose not to.

"In fact," said Ben, almost laughing, "Ranger said the only time he'd touch you is if you know it's him, and beg for what he will give you. That's a direct quote, by the way."

"Ranger said...!"

If the man was in front of her right now, one of her fists would already be deep in his belly. Her boot would be kicking his shin. Hard! She didn't want him anywhere near her. In fact, the mere sight of him made her nauseous!

"That may happen if pigs learn to fly," she growled. "Backward and upside down!"

"Hmm, sounds like someone is riled up. Ranger got you all fidgety, wife?" Ben slid his arms around her waist and kissed her neck. She resisted giving in.

"I am merely surprised that you decided to go without discussing it with that wife you seem to have forgotten about lately."

He kissed her again. One of his hands automatically rose to cup her breast. "You're right. *Mea culpa.* I should have mentioned it. And I've not forgotten about you, though we've barely had time to say more than a mumbled 'good morning' the last few days. I think about you all the time while I'm riding or working."

"If you are so busy, how did you find the time to interrupt my laundry?"

"I came home to pack." He squeezed her breast and rubbed his groin against her backside. He was hard and, despite her pique, she was eager. "Want to help me?"

She leaned over for a kiss.

"Dammit, Ben! If you've got time to bend her over and lift her skirts, you've got time to help me put this bloody gate on."

Florence pulled back. Of course, Ranger had to mention what they'd done, what she had demanded. Her face flamed at how she'd screamed her release as he pounded into her. She quivered at the memory. It was days since she'd last experienced a release. Ben's were soft and lovely, but nowhere as explosive as those Ranger had caused. She could use some fireworks about now. Unfortunately, it was more likely to happen with all their clothes on.

Ben sighed. He gave her one more caress and released her.

"I see your mouth matches the size of your muscles," Florence said to Ranger haughtily.

She forced herself to turn and face him. Immediately, she wished she hadn't. He stared her in the eye. He pushed his hat back with one thick finger, a finger that had done wonderful things to her. And he knew she remembered. She could tell by the way his eyes crinkled. She looked at his lips to avoid his eyes, but they pulled into a smirk.

He also knew she remembered what his lips had done. As her breasts filled, she moved her gaze to his shoulder. That part of his body should be safe to look at.

"I'd like to see the size of your mouth, Florence Elliott," Ranger said, his voice purring. "Maybe while Ben's gone we can find out if it fits me. But you'll have to beg me."

"I'll never—!"

As soon as he caught her glare he flicked his tongue like a snake. Her pussy flooded in memory of that tongue. He rubbed his knuckles over his pants buttons, and she realized what he meant. Put her mouth there? She gasped, dropping her jaw.

"Looks like it'd fit, all right," drawled Ranger. He winked and turned to Ben, suddenly all business. "Let's get that gate done. I don't want children to fall in the pigsty and get chomped on." He strolled toward the barn, his long legs eating up the distance.

"He…that…what…oh!"

Ben patted her bottom and chuckled. "Ranger sure has a way of winding you up. Maybe if you see more of him, it'll wear off."

"I highly doubt it!"

"Anytime you want to open your mouth for me, I'm ready and waiting," he murmured. He placed her hand on his bulging buttons.

"I swear," she grumbled, "if that gate wasn't to help my children, I'd undo your buttons and try it right here, right now, just to spite that man!"

Ben groaned, ending with a chuckle. "That thought is going to keep me hard all the way to Helena and back. And that is not a good thing while riding a horse." He gave her a quick kiss and hurried off to the pigsty.

Florence barely held herself back from stamping her foot. If it wasn't for Ranger, she wouldn't be hot and needy, with no one to help relieve her ache. She loaded the rest of the dry clothes into her basket, a gift made by Gillis's Auntie, and stomped into the house to slam some pots and pans around.

Chapter Twenty-Four

Even after the pigsty gate was fixed and Ben rode off, Florence banged around in the house. Ranger, putting away his tools, laughed that he'd twisted her tail so well. He also laughed when Ben told him what she'd said in anger. He wouldn't mind at all if she took his cock in her mouth, for any reason. He loved to make her squawk.

Did Ben not understand that leaving a horny wife alone with two equally horny brothers was not a good idea, even without saying what she wanted to do with his cock? Or did the man say it on purpose, wanting them to fill her uppity mouth with one cock, while the other took her pussy? Fanny had a fine edge between anger and lust. Get her in a temper and then touch her, and she'd go off like black powder.

That thought made his pain worse. He gave up, unbuttoning himself enough to relieve the pressure. Maybe he should buy a pair of loose pants lined with flannelette. His cock would have room to grow, and it wouldn't be rubbed raw every time he took a step.

His hand dropped, slowly rubbing himself as he thought of Florence kneeling in front of him. She'd look up at him with all that hair hiding her body. Her nipples would poke out between the brown strands. She'd hold his cock in her hands and rub it against her breasts. No, between her breasts. He'd slide between them, back and forth. Her tongue would touch his tip with every forward stroke. Then she'd open her mouth and take him—

"You gonna stand there all day jacking off, or do some work?"

Fuck. Patrick. It was the same phrase that The MacDougal would use. Only they would have put in six hours of work and had stopped to eat sandwiches and have a drink of water. That man would squeeze blood from a stone, then boil the stone and serve it for dinner.

"She stood in the yard and offered to take Ben in her mouth, just to get my goat," said Ranger.

Patrick snorted. "If she'll do that for me, I'll buy her a dozen goats."

Ranger lifted an eyebrow at his youngest brother. "By damn, you made a joke."

Patrick stood straight, his jaw tight. Ranger realized he was only an inch taller than his younger brother. Patrick's muscles weren't as big, but they were more than Ben had. Yet Ben was two years older. Who knew what Patrick would be like when he finished growing? Ranger took a good look at his littlest brother, the first in a long time.

"You've grown up pretty damn good."

"'Bout time you noticed."

Ranger shook his head. "I noticed, but I didn't *see*."

He winced at his behavior since they left Texas all those months ago. Patrick had ridden the same hot, dusty Western Trail. He stayed with the cattle when they passed Dodge, so Ranger could have a whiskey in town. Not once had Patrick complained.

Even before, when they were both under The MacDougal's yoke, Patrick hadn't complained. He'd cowboy up and move on, just like Ranger. They worked the same hours and did almost as much work.

"If I was Ben, I might apologize," said Ranger.

"Good thing you're not, because I'd have to punch your lights out."

A slow smile played around one side of Ranger's lip. "Damn good answer, partner."

They looked at each other for a moment before both nodded and turned away. Patrick grabbed the broom and began sweeping. Neither of them could stand still for long, in case they got a beating. Ranger figured it would be years before ghosts of The MacDougal faded.

"Where's Ben gone? I saw him riding out with full saddlebags."

"Helena, with Jack and Nev. Said he'd be gone a week or so."

Patrick looked up. "Did he say what we're to do with his wife?"

Ranger turned his back, hiding his reaction at the reminder. "He didn't have to. The little woman can take care of herself."

"Not if we take all the carrots, parsnips, and cucumbers."

Ranger, caught swallowing, choked. He turned his head. Patrick gestured with his finger.

"Shit, Patty, I didn't know you had a funny bone."

"Funny bone, hell. I've got a boner so big and hard—"

"—that I could use it as a pickax," finished Ranger. Both groaned.

"Since we're all in the same shape," said Patrick, "let's get her so riled up that she doesn't know if she's coming or going."

"You mean 'accidently' touch her until she heats up, and then stop?"

Patrick nodded. "I'm already doing that. But what if she turns the tables on us?"

"How?"

"Oh, I don't know." Patrick thought for a moment, then grinned eagerly. "What if she strips to her boots and struts around the yard chewing a carrot?"

"We'll haul out our cocks, take a seat, and watch the show. But we don't touch her unless she begs for it. I want her to know exactly who's between her legs from now on."

The clang of a dinner triangle rang out.

"We might be hornier than we were before she came, but at least the food's better," said Patrick, rubbing his growling stomach.

Ranger nudged him to go first and the two of them headed to the kitchen for supper. When they left the barn, Fanny pushed her shoulders back and glared at them. Lips pursed, she twirled, skirt swinging, and stomped back inside.

"View's better, too," added Ranger. "And we know how the tits and ass under that dress look and feel."

"Shit," muttered Patrick. "Now I won't be able to sit down to eat without my pants cutting my cock in half."

Ranger nudged him with his elbow. "We said we won't touch her. Nothing says we have to stay covered up all the time. If you feel tight, undo a couple of buttons."

Patrick tilted his head back and laughed. Ranger joined him, clapping him on the shoulder. Patrick punched back. Ranger bent him over in a headlock and rubbed his knuckles over his scalp. Patrick swept out his foot, sending Ranger on his ass in the dirt. He pulled a knife and lunged, landing on his gut when Ranger rolled out of the way and to his feet. Patrick rolled as well, avoiding the boot aiming for his gut. He grabbed the boot and twisted, sending Ranger back down.

They looked at each other, both on their asses in the dirt, and broke into laughter again.

"Damn, it feels good to be home," said Ranger.

"Supper's getting cold. Are you two coming, or not?"

They looked at Florence, then each other, and howled once more. Florence whirled around and stomped back inside, slamming the door behind her.

"I've got an idea," said Ranger. "You know that surprise party the wives are planning? Since we don't have a bathtub, and Fanny wants to wash all that hair of hers, what if we show her Jessie's hot spring?"

He hauled himself to his feet and held his hand out to Patrick. Both knew it was far more than a hand up he was offering. Patrick took his hand and rolled to his feet. They turned as one toward the kitchen.

"I wash her back," said Patrick. "You can do her hair."

Chapter Twenty-Five

"A bath?"

Florence looked from Patrick's too-innocent face to Ranger's smirking one. A bath meant taking all her clothes off. That would be fine if she was in Beth's bathing room, with the door locked. Otherwise, she didn't trust either of them.

No, she didn't trust herself. The ache she'd been blissfully ignorant about until that first night at the ranch, intensified each night Ben snored beside her. And now he was gone, for up to ten lonely nights.

"Where? Beth has a bathing room—"

"That's too small," said Patrick. "We thought you'd want to rinse your hair in something bigger."

She narrowed her eyes. "There aren't any bathtubs bigger than Beth's west of the Missouri River."

"Did we mention a tub?"

Ranger had an evil glint in his eye. Either evil or lustful, it mattered not. Both led to the same thing. She pressed her thighs together under the table where they couldn't see. Ranger leaned toward her on one forearm. He smelled of horse, leather, and musk.

"We're talking about a rock pool hot spring. You could wade out as deep as you like. Move around until the water's just right."

She swallowed, thinking of the luxury, and the cost. "And afterward?"

"We visit Jessie. Everyone will be there, including Emma and Johnny."

Oh, evil indeed. A bath, and a chance to visit her children.

"No one goes near me," she demanded.

"Ace says there's no soap allowed in the water," said Patrick, "so you have to get wet, soap down, and then splash buckets of water over yourself where the soapy water will run downhill away from the spring. And then you can go in the water and soak for as long as you want."

He gave her a sweet little boy smile that she didn't trust for an instant.

"And you'll be there ready and willing to bring hot water for me," she said, eyes narrow. "You'll even pour it over my hair, just because you are a kind, thoughtful man."

"You got me confused with Ben, ma'am," said Patrick. "I intend to help you because I want to see you naked again. You are one fine-lookin' woman!"

"At least you're honest about it." She turned to Ranger. "I expect you want to help me out of the goodness of your heart."

"Nope. It's the hardness of my cock I'm wanting to help. I don't give a damn about anyone's heart."

"You will not touch me!" She slammed her palm on the table, shooting daggers at his eyes.

"Damn right I won't!" He stared back and slammed his fist down even harder, making the tin plates bounce.

"Well, then!" She couldn't think of anything else to say, but had to say something.

He moved his head even closer. His eyes shifted from hazel to golden. Ben's went sea-green when he looked at her so intensely. He only did it when he was lying on top of her, plunging deep into her pussy, or wanting to. She gulped.

"I'm gonna watch you parade around with your tits and ass hanging out. My hand will be on my cock, enjoying every minute of your free show. I don't need to touch you to have a damn good time." He raised a supercilious eyebrow at her and leaned back.

"I'll help you with the buckets of water," said Patrick. "I won't touch you, much, but I'm gonna look all I want."

Florence trembled under their scrutiny. They looked at her as if they could see through her dress, right to her skin. With Ben gone, she was going to wear a shift, a corset, drawers and at least three petticoats! Thank goodness it was cool enough to do so.

"The party's for supper tomorrow," said Ranger. "We're going, and we'll take you if you want. But if you want to get really clean before meeting the whole valley…"

In other words, if she didn't want to smell like a privy, she would have to trust them. She'd meet everyone and… She thought for a moment. There was no reason she had to go home with Ranger and Patrick afterward. She could visit someone else and let Ben's two partners stew in their own juices until her legal husband returned.

"What's goin' through yer educated mind, Miz Elliott?" drawled Ranger. "I can darn near see those wheels a'turnin'. The smoke's gettin' thick 'cause yer wheels ain't been greased in too long."

"My thoughts are my own," she replied primly. She stood up. Patrick jumped to his feet, giving a hint of the manners someone had drilled into him. Ranger tilted his head and looked up at her. He dared her with his insolence. "I want a long soak," she said, "and my hair has to dry. When do we leave?"

"After breakfast, so why don't you put together somethin' to take for our dinner. We'll have you clean as a whistle and dressed before we eat. By the time we finish eatin', all that hair of yours should be dry. Then we'll head on to Jessie and the Double Diamond ranch."

"What should I bring for supper?"

"Nothin'," said Ranger.

"Nonsense," she replied. "I'll bring these two apple pies."

"That's tonight's dessert!"

"Not anymore," she said sweetly. "You wouldn't want to tell Jessie that you ate my present to her, would you?"

Ranger snorted like a bull and stormed out. Patrick sighed dramatically at the pies but followed without touching them.

They'd thrown down the gauntlet, and she'd picked it up. They might make the rules, but she knew how to play a few games of her own. Taunting Ranger would be suitable payment for his insistence on watching her. She was sure Patrick would 'accidentally' brush against a few times while pouring water over her. Let Ranger stew in his own juices!

Already her body tingled, demanding rough hands. But she would never, ever beg that arrogant, demanding, overwhelming, tantalizing man to touch her! No matter how much she wanted him to stroke her pussy, nibble her nipples, and do that wonderful thing with his tongue on her clit.

She looked out the window, making sure the men couldn't see her. She rubbed her breasts, pinching them right through the fabric. The tops of her thighs were wet, and if she sat down, her dress would be as well.

But no matter how needy, how desperate she got, she would not beg! Instead, she would make them crazy with need. She rubbed her pussy through her dress. She wanted release, but her clothing was such a nuisance.

An idea struck and she snickered. Ranger threatened to watch her bathe, his hand on his cock, and satisfy himself. What if she touched herself at the hot springs? She could rub herself and watch his face as he saw what he wanted to do, but it was her hands doing it!

* * * *

Ranger cursed the stupid idea, his hard cock, and the way Fanny purposefully egged him on. No way could he call that woman 'Florence.' Not when she moved like one of Miss Lily's finest gals, all the while pretending she was virgin, pure and innocent.

She knelt on a sandy patch where the water would drain away from the rock pool. She faced him, naked as the day she was born, her soapy hair piled high on her head. She raised her arms, lifting her breasts, and washed her hair. Soapy water flowed down her neck, around her collarbone and over her breasts. He stared at a bubble stuck right above her nipple. It would pop. It had to pop. There!

Patrick, just as naked, helped. Her hair kept falling down, and he'd have to catch it and bring it back up, rubbing the strands together to get it clean. That wasn't all he rubbed. Ranger groaned quietly and gripped his cock.

"I'm ready to rinse," she called.

She stood up and tilted her head back. She squeezed her hair from her head on down, forcing the water out. Patrick warned her before pouring the first bucket over her head. She turned her back to Ranger with the second bucket. He swore when she bent over, put her hands on her head and rubbed to get more soap out. Her ass jiggled, as did her breasts.

He took some of the pre-cum from his cock and used it to help slide his hand up and down. Two more buckets, and she was done. His hand slowed as he waited for her next move.

She wrapped all that hair up and tucked it up somehow with a flannel.

Good. She'd get in the water and—*shit!*

She stood up and faced him, this time with her eyes open. Her wet body glistened in the sun. Even without the slight breeze, her nipples would be damn hard. But not as hard as the cock in his right fist.

She held the bar of soap in her palm, stared him in the eye and rubbed it over her breasts. She circled them a few times before dropping her hand to her belly. A couple more circles there and she rubbed her thighs.

"Patrick, could you wash my back, please? I just can't reach."

The witch said all that while daring Ranger to speak, to breathe!

Patrick, cock at full mast, took the soap. He ran it over her shoulders and down her back. She stood still, taunting Ranger with every inch of skin. Patrick, seeing her attention was elsewhere, continued down her back to her ass. He used both hands to massage her ass cheeks.

"Thank you, Patrick. May I have the soap back, please?" Her voice was much higher than before.

Patrick ran the soap up her back, around her ribs and over her breasts before Fanny slapped his hand. He laughed and held his palm open. She took the soap and he backed away, still laughing and looking his fill.

She soaped up her hands, put the bar down and rubbed her skin. She ran her hands over her breasts, pinching her nipples. Her nostrils flared wide. She opened her mouth, panting. All the time, she stared at him.

His hand kept pace with her slow circles, though he went only up and down.

She turned her back and placed her hands on her back cheeks, doing more circles. She bent over, feet wide, and slid one hand over her ass toward her pussy. With the other hand she—*shit!*—used her fingers on her clit and between her lips.

She moaned and inserted her fingers in her pussy. Her cheeks moved as she clenched. He sped up, eyes straining on the pink lips between her legs. She turned around again, watching his hand on his cock. He knew she watched because her fingers moved at the same speed as his, following his hand as if it was his cock in there.

He was close, his balls tightening. She dared him to come. Dared him to prove that he wanted her so much she could make him jack off while she watched. If he came, he'd spurt half way across the damn pond. He'd jerk and moan because it felt so good.

And she'd laugh at him.

No. Damn. Way.

He pushed his need back. No woman would laugh at Ranger Elliott. Especially the woman who refused to admit she wanted him to throw her to her knees and slam his hard cock into her.

She said she wouldn't beg? Ha! He'd gone without sex for many, many years. She'd been without for, what, four days?

She gasped when Patrick poured a bucket of water over her shoulder. From her reaction, Ranger figured it was on the cold side. He admired how Patrick poured the water so it washed her front and her back. Of course, he had to stand so close that his cock rubbed her hip. Repeatedly. Ranger stood up and stretched.

"Nice show. Time for a swim and then dinner."

She trembled, glaring at him like the icicles he had to imagine to stop his balls from exploding. That was one thing memories of Montana winters were good for. Think of being naked in a blizzard and your cock shrunk. He looked down. He'd have to work on the shrinking. His cock was still raring to go.

He walked past her, aiming for the colder side of the pool. He pretended to ignore her as he lolled in the chilly water. She waded in, released her hair and ducked under the warm water. She stayed close to shore. Likely she'd never learned to swim.

He lay on the warm rocks to dry before putting on clean clothes. He watched her out of the corner of his eye as she finally strolled out. She bent over again to wring her hair out. He yawned when she glanced his way.

One of these days he'd have her begging for more of what made her scream so loud. He'd wait until then. And then he'd show her as much action as a whore on nickel night.

And she'd scream *his* name.

Chapter Twenty-Six

Florence sat demurely between Patrick and Ranger in the buggy, stewing. All three of them were clean, in fresh clothing, and aching for release.

Patrick knew he pushed the boundaries while helping her wash, but she had expected that. Ranger, however, had done the unexpected. She knew she almost had him exploding while he watched her touch herself. She saw how fast his hand moved, how set his jaw and intense his stare. Yet he suddenly pulled back before erupting. His look said he believed he had won a battle against her. Maybe he had, as she was far more frustrated now than before touching herself to make him squirm.

Ranger guided the wagon around a clump of trees and suddenly, they were there.

"Goodness, why are there so many people?"

"Everyone wants to meet Ben's wife and kids," said Ranger. "Even though Ben's away, you're still an excuse for a party. Happy wedding, and all."

She stared at the crowd of strangers. "You didn't tell me that!"

He shrugged. "Figgered you'd just get upset."

"Upset!"

At least twenty people turned and waved.

"Mama!"

Emma rushed forward, her hair flowing behind her like a cape. Trace lifted Florence down, and she immediately knelt to hug Emma. Johnny pushed past a forest of Elliott legs and demanded the same.

"My, you look wonderful. I'm sure you've grown an inch,

Johnny."

"Come help me cut the wedding cake," said Beth, holding her hands out to the children. They squealed and danced around her to the large home under the trees.

Trace held up his hand. A few people stopped talking, but the area still buzzed.

"Hobble yer lips!" bellowed a huge man in a kilt. Red hair sprouted from his head, face, arms, and bare legs. A baby with matching hair, thankfully only on her head, cuddled against his chest. Silence descended. He grinned and nodded a welcome at her. He could only be Gillis MacDougal, with his daughter, Hope.

"Elizabeth James and Florence Peabody were friends in Philadelphia," said Trace in his now-familiar croak. He carried James, his hefty son, in the crook of one arm. "Now they're both Elliotts."

Cheers erupted, as well as comments from the single men as to the unfairness of the Elliotts and MacDougals getting all the women.

"Ben's not here, but our wives planned this party before he left for Helena with Nevin and Jack, and they'd be very upset if we put it off. You've already met Emma and Johnny. Now it's time to get to know Florence, Mrs. Benjamin Elliott." He held up his hand before everyone surged forward. "I want a line. Double Diamond first, since they're hosting, then the MacDougals, Circle C, and the rest."

Good-natured complaints and jostling went on until Trace was satisfied.

"One kiss each, boys."

"What!" Florence turned to Trace, face hot.

"It's the custom to give a bride a wedding kiss. Since you didn't hold a wedding in the valley, this party replaces it."

"There's no groom!" called someone from the back.

"She doesn't need one," said Trace to the heckler. "She's got Ranger and Patrick."

"I don't need them, either!" she called out. The men laughed, thinking she was joking.

"Don't worry about remembering names," said Trace quietly. "Double Diamond, step forward. Ace, Sin, and Henry. They talk funny, but we like them anyway. Good thing, since they married our sister, Jessie."

A tall, brown-haired man stepped forward, followed by a striking blond giant and an exuberant shorter man. These were the English aristocrats.

"Your children are adorable," said Ace. He kissed her cheek. Sin and Henry both winked before doing the same. A petite woman dressed like a boy shook her hand.

"I'm Jessie. Let me know when you want to learn how to ride or defend yourself with a knife or two. Since we women are outnumbered, we have to help each other."

"Don't be giving her ideas, Jessie," yelled Ranger. "She's got enough of her own."

"She'll need them if she has to share a house with you," replied Jessie loudly.

Trace nudged his sister aside. "You met Nevin, so you'll recognize Ross MacDougal. The bellowing bull is their half brother, Gillis, with his daughter, Hope. Amelia's inside with Beth and the children."

Ross kissed her hand like a courtier. Gillis let the baby give a wet kiss before moving back.

"The Circle C is on the other side of the Rocking E, so you might see these galoots now and then," said Trace as the next trio stepped forward. "Luke Frost is the ramrod. He says he's the best-looking."

A man with a horrid scar across his right cheek and nose approached. He was even taller than Trace. He sighed dramatically and took her hand.

"Yet another fair maiden comes to our valley, already spoken for. This is not right. The only women to grace our valley are snapped up by this lot!" He glared majestically at the Elliotts and MacDougals, who laughed at him. He bowed and brought her hand to his lips.

"*Enchanté*, Madame. If you would like to experience true appreciation, visit the Circle C at any time. We will be delighted to entertain you."

"Luke should go on the stage with that act," said Trace with a snort. "Gabriel Downey, I'd like you to meet Florence Elliott."

Florence looked up. The man was a whole foot taller than she and twice as wide. He moved like a bear but his dark brown eyes crinkled when he smiled shyly. He bent way over to kiss her cheek gently and stepped back.

"I'm Oscar Cutler, ma'am. Call me Oz."

This man, thankfully, was much shorter. He also had a black patch over his right eye. He took her hand and stepped very close. He checked that Ranger was watching, and winked with his good eye.

"If you can cook, we'd appreciate an invitation to dinner of a Sunday. Or we can come get you any time—"

"Back away from the lady before you get squashed even shorter," yelled Ranger.

Just to spite Ranger, Florence raised herself on her toes to kiss the man's cheek. At the last moment he turned his head. She caught him on the corner of his mouth. It was a quick peck, but he held her close, his back to Ranger to hide the fact they weren't still kissing.

"Only fair to twist his tail if he gets to look at such a pretty lady all the time," said Oz quietly. He released her and stepped away as Ranger pushed his way toward them.

"That's enough kissing," bellowed Ranger. "Her husband isn't here to stop you, so I will." He pointed to the next six men in line.

"Wave to Florence when I call you out, as she's itching to get back to her children. The Flying X is east of the Circle C. Byron Ashcroft, Cole Taylor, and Don Stevens are all polite Southern boys. The J Bar C, with Jed Abrams, Riley Jansen and Clint Fortune, is east of here. Their mothers were sisters, but you can't tell since the cousins don't look alike. Wave to the nice *married* lady, boys."

She saw a jumble of faces, all tall, before Trace took her from

Ranger's protection and swept her away. He pushed her into Jessie's home and shut the door behind her, with him on the outside.

The woman dressed as a man looked Florence up and down, and then held out her hand. Florence, pleased to be accepted, shook hard. Jessie scrunched up her nose. "Anything you want to know about keeping my brothers in line, just ask. Knives, rope, whip—"

"Blindfold, tie-down straps, spanking," whispered Beth.

Jessie's face flushed. Florence felt the same heat rising from her own.

"Did you tell her about the watchers?" asked Jessie.

Beth shook her head. "I was hoping to keep her from learning about that for a bit."

"A woman can't protect herself from things she knows nothing about," said Jessie, scowling. She turned to Florence. "There's two reasons why this house is built here. One is so it's close to the road and the river. The other is because the trees block the view from the hills. The first few weeks I was here, I found that someone was staying up above for a long time, watching."

"That's not all you found," said Beth.

"I also found the remains of the family that used to live here. They'd been murdered, and their daughter stolen. But we'll tell you about that another time."

"Were the people caught?" Florence winced when the women shook their heads.

"Someone doesn't like the Elliotts and the MacDougals," said Beth. "We have our suspicions, but—"

"It's that bloody Frederick Smythe!" Jessie slammed her right fist into her open left palm. "If I could tie him to a tree and get my whip out—"

"Hush," interrupted a new voice. "This is a celebration of Florence's wedding. Not the time for all the ugliness to be brought out to air." The petite woman turned to Florence. "I'm Amelia, Ross's wife." Her belly was bigger than Beth's. "My first," she said, seeing where Florence was looking.

"I won't be having babies for a while," said Jessie with a growl.

"From the satisfied looks on your husbands' faces, I don't think you have a choice," drawled Beth. "The more you play with men, the faster the babies come."

"That's the darndest thing," complained Jessie. "If you want to have fun, sooner or later your belly swells up, and you can't ride a horse anymore!"

"You can tell we like our fun," laughed Amelia. She winced and sank into a chair, rubbing her belly.

"Are you all right?"

"By summer, she be fine," said a soft voice. Florence turned to find a small Indian woman, the oldest person she'd yet seen. Her strong nose reminded her of Nevin and Ross. She pointed to herself. "Auntie. I birth good babies."

"She certainly does," said Beth. "James might have died if Auntie hadn't known how to turn him before he was born."

"That relieves my mind," said Florence.

Auntie knelt and touched her hands to Amelia's swollen belly. "You tell Ross yet?" She frowned when Amelia shook her head. "He find out soon anyway."

Amelia groaned. "Once Ross and the rest of those overbearing men find out, I'll never get a moment's peace!"

"Find out what, 'Melia?" Beth knelt beside her, a concerned look on her face. "Something wrong?"

Amelia sighed. "Almost everyone's here. I might as well tell."

"You tell your man first. I get him."

Auntie slipped silently out the door. A moment later Ross burst into the room. He strode over to Amelia. Beth moved away so he could take her place.

"Auntie said you wanted to tell me something. Is it about the baby?" He looked scared, as if his world might crash around him.

"That's just it," Amelia said with a sigh. "We're not having *a* baby. Auntie says I'm carrying twins."

Ross's face turned ashen. He blinked. Then he jumped to his feet and gave a yell that near shattered Florence's ears. He gently lifted Amelia into his arms and spun around, still whooping. The door smashed open and Gillis pushed through the crowd. When he saw Ross's wide grin, he sagged against the doorframe. He shook himself and scowled.

"Are ye daft, laddie? Ye scared ten years off me life with that war whoop!"

"Twins!" yelled Ross. "We're having twins!"

Florence covered her ears in time to save them from the burly Scotsman's war cry. He turned and bellowed the news over everyone's heads. Cheers erupted. He roared something about whiskey and closed the door behind him. Ross sat on a bench, Amelia in his lap. He whispered in her ear, and a flush rose up her neck.

"If Amelia doesn't have a son before Gil's father dies, they could all lose the ranch," said Beth quietly in Florence's ear. "Two babies double the chance they'll have a boy."

"What if they have twin daughters?"

"If the babies are healthy, Ross will still be the happiest man in the valley. He loves children so much, he won't mind. Children are wonderful, no matter where they come from. Plus, Ben said he'd make sure The MacDougal's will wouldn't stand up in court."

"Ben said he wanted lots of children," said Florence to Beth, "and he didn't mind from where. He expects we'll have others join our family because they need a home."

"We all feel that way," said Beth. "Look at Daniel, playing with Johnny like they've always been brothers. No one thinks about who provided the seed or birthed them. All that matters is that they're ours now. Daniel's a help to Amelia, and I don't know what I'd do without Meggie and Bridie."

"No wonder Ben was so willing to marry me to save Emma, if his whole family likes to take in children."

"Ben told a few of us about your children's past," said Beth. "Only so we would understand why they may act in certain ways. All anyone else needs to know is that their mother was dying and asked you to give her children a better home."

"Thank you." Florence relaxed a tension she hadn't been aware she was carrying. "I worried about Emma saying something and being judged badly by it."

"Daniel's father was the town drunk who tried to beat the devil out of the boy."

Florence looked at the happy boy playing with Johnny. They both had their backs to her. "Why would he do that?"

"Daniel was born with a hare lip. He couldn't close his mouth. His father told him he killed his mother by being born, and the devil punished him with a mouth that would never kiss."

"Oh, Beth, the poor boy! Can anything be done? I heard about surgery—"

"Already done. He's been adopted into the MacDougal Clan, but having younger cousins to look up to him will do wonders for him."

"I don't think Emma and Johnny saw many children. It may take a while for them to learn how to play."

"By next summer, you'll never know they'd never lived here."

"I hear you and Ben brought a few crates of books with you," said Beth, changing the subject as the door opened and others moved near.

Florence nodded. "I don't know where we'll put them all. I want to keep my favorites with me, but Ben mentioned Amelia had a bunkhouse. Maybe I can store them there."

Beth pointed to the wall opposite the door, lined with narrow shelves. The ones near the bottom were deeper.

"Bookshelves?"

Beth nodded. "Jessie's husbands come from homes with huge libraries. They had to leave almost everything behind, but that's not stopping them from starting over. Ace has vowed to fill these shelves with books. I don't think he cares what's in them. He said if no one reads them, they'll still serve as insulation. That's why they're on the north wall."

"We could store our books here, out of the weather," said Florence, thinking. "It would be wonderful if someone even read them now and then."

"Now and then?" Beth rolled her eyes. "Reading is what helps us get through the long, cold, dark evenings before going to bed. I hope Jessie likes company, because this room is going to be filled with people all winter. Anyone who has books is popular. From what Ben said about the number arriving, this may be the largest library south of Helena."

"Ben sent his law books by train from Virginia, and many of mine are nonfiction and reference. But I did bring my favorites."

"Any penny dreadfuls?" Beth looked hopeful.

Florence opened her eyes and gasped, holding her arm up as if holding off a blow, mimicking a pose used on many of the covers. "Of course, but don't tell Ben I read such things."

Beth laughed, nodding her agreement to keep the secret. "Time to give out the wedding cake. I'll carry the tray and you give a piece to everyone who wants one. They'll expect a kiss in return."

"More kisses?"

Beth laughed at her complaint. "Something tells me that you're not getting enough loving. Ben's only been gone one night."

"Yes, but we were too tired to do anything but sleep for the three before that," muttered Florence.

"Aren't there two other men eager to prove their worth?"

Florence scowled. She looked down and straightened her apron. "Two men, too eager. And I don't want them in my bed!"

"Ooh," said Beth, her eyes sparkling. "Sounds intriguing. Good thing the children are all staying here until Ben gets back."

"Good. I'll stay as well."

Beth shook her head. "I gave Bridie and Meggie the responsibility of taking care of Daniel and your two, as well as Jessie and her men.

They want to prove they can run a home. It's something young girls have to do, to show they're ready to marry."

"Marry? How old are they?"

"Meggie's sixteen and Bridie's fourteen. We're not letting them marry until they're eighteen, but there's already a line of men eager to offer for Meggie. Since everyone knows Jessie hates housework and, though Henry is a good cook, he'll be out working with the men, the girls will be able to prove themselves."

"Goodness. I doubt I could do all that at sixteen, especially without running water or anything else."

"So you see why I have to send you home with Ranger and Patrick tonight," said Beth. She sighed and made her chin quiver as if near tears. "To that cold, lonely bed on the second floor while they sleep in the drafty cabin. It may freeze tonight, or rain. Maybe even snow. The wind will howl over them—"

Florence glowered as Beth burst into laughter.

"They don't want to be inside with me. In fact, Ranger said he wouldn't touch me unless I begged him, and Patrick is following his game. I don't care how much I want it, I will not beg them. Ever."

Beth laughed so hard she had to sit down.

"You should see your face! Oh, I can't wait to hear what happens."

Florence stuck her chin out and spoke through gritted teeth. "What do you think will happen, dear friend?"

"If you're smart you'll get them to come to your bed. Wait!" she added before Florence could burst in. "You let them think that you gave in, when all along, you planned it that way."

Florence blinked. She tilted her head. "Beat them at their own game?"

"No, let them win their game. You, however, will win the war."

"What are you saying?"

Beth flicked her eyes around to make sure no one was close enough to hear.

"What if you pretended to get so drunk you didn't know what you were doing? If you behaved outrageously, making Ranger crazy by touching him, maybe stripping off your clothes because you feel hot, he might break. I expect he'll decide you'll not remember a thing in the morning. To his mind, anything the two of you did, or said, would never have happened."

"I get what I want, a hot night of sex, and Ranger thinks he's still winning because I won't remember that he gave me what I wanted without begging."

Beth nodded. "If he does find out, he won't hurt you, even if you make him wild."

Florence tapped her chin for a moment. The tension which had stalked her, day and night, flared high. Tantalizing Ranger at the hot spring had left her with a greater need than she'd thought possible. The possibility of having that need met, set her body flaming.

"It's not like I'd be deceiving him. I'd demand hot sex, and he could give it, or not. Demanding is not begging. We both get what we want, without me having to beg."

"And he'll think you don't remember it. He'll be on his toes, wondering. And the more he wonders, the more he'll think about you." She shrugged. "You can probably only do it once, and you may still go without until Ben gets back, but you'll get one night of what you need."

"Tell me what drives your men wild. I need a few ideas."

Chapter Twenty-Seven

"So tired," mumbled Fanny as Ranger carried her from the buggy.

The small woman had slept on the seat while he helped Patrick put the horse away. Patrick had passed out in the straw right after, snoring. It was just the two of them now. It was far too dangerous to lose control in Texas, so they didn't drink much. This was Patrick's first opportunity to get stinking drunk, and he'd taken to it as if he was born a Scot.

"You're not just tired, you're sauced," Ranger muttered. Fanny was cute, in a drunken kitten type of way. When she wasn't on her high horse, she was the type of woman he enjoyed. Soft, cuddly, and agreeable.

"More punch."

"No." Or, not so agreeable.

"Want punch!"

She opened her eyes and pouted up at him. He held back a grin at how sexy her mouth looked. How his cock would look sliding past those plump lips.

"You already had about six too many, sweets."

Her pout changed from sexy kitten to alluring siren. She ran her fingers between his shirt buttons, tickling his skin. She inhaled and snuffled her face between his arm and chest.

"Mmmm, you smell good."

"So do you, sweets."

She opened her mouth as if to yawn. A sharp pain struck his arm.

"Ouch! You bit me!"

"Want punch!"

He managed to open the kitchen door, carry her through and push it shut again without dropping her.

"Pee!"

He stopped, dropped his head, and sighed.

"Why couldn't you say that before I got through the door?" She struggled to get loose. "Okay, we'll go to the privy."

Of course, once they got there she needed help. Her legs wouldn't hold her up long enough for him to lift all those damn petticoats and skirt. He finally unbuttoned her petticoats and skirt at her waist and pushed everything down to her ankles. Her drawers came next and she sat with a sigh. She leaned her head back, thunking it against the wall, and let loose. She certainly did have to pee. He snorted a chuckle and pulled everything off her bottom half. Since he'd have to do it later anyway to get her into bed, he took off her boots and stockings as well.

Since she was empty now, he laid her skirts over his left shoulder, picked up her boots and slung her stomach over her clothes. She squealed and kicked, so he smacked the bare bottom pointing to the sky. He laughed when she squealed even louder. He had to keep his hand on her hot ass to keep her from sliding off. He finally curled his fingers around her thigh, just below her ass cheek, to hold on.

His fingers brushed against warm, wet curls. She stopped struggling. He almost stopped breathing.

"More," she whispered.

"No." He swallowed hard, and forced his fingers to stay still. He could smell her arousal. How could he miss it, when her bare ass was right in front of his shoulder?

"More!" She opened her legs as far as she could and wiggled. When he changed grip, his knuckles touched her pussy. "Yesss," she sighed, echoing his groan.

"I said, no." He bit the words out through gritted teeth.

All night, she chatted with other men, almost flirting sometimes. She knew he watched, and sometimes stuck her tongue out at him, daring him to interfere. She wanted it, bad. Every time she went back to that spiked punch, half of him cursed and half cheered.

He had a sneaking suspicion Ben left them alone with her so they could take his place in the bed. But Ranger wasn't going to touch her unless she knew who he was, and begged him for it.

She knew who he was tonight, all right. And she'd been taunting him sexually all night. Even now, she tried to rub herself against his hand. On the way home she'd slumped against him. Her hand accidentally landed in his lap. He couldn't move it away because he needed both hands to hold the buggy's reins.

No, he wanted her soft hand right on his hard cock. Every time the buggy went over a bump, her hand rubbed him. He tortured himself, knowing he wanted her, but it was only chance that her hand was there. Now that she was awake, sort of, she was horny as hell. But he wouldn't give her satisfaction unless she begged him, drunk or not!

It was easier to get her through the door this time, since he had one hand free. He walked through the kitchen and stopped at the bottom of the stairs. His cock was so hard it would hurt like the dickens to climb the stairs. It would rub against his pants with each step.

She pulled up the back of his shirt. Next thing he knew, her fingers had walked past his belt and played with his ass. A jolt of lust shot right to his cock. He could not climb the stairs like this! He opened his buttons and released his cock, groaning in relief. She slid her finger up and down between his ass cheeks, just as he wanted to do between hers with his cock.

"Stop that!"

"No," she said, pouting.

"Fanny, if you don't stop playing around, I'm going to—"

"Spank?"

He imagined the flat of his hand landing on her ass. She deserved it!

"Yes, dammit, I'll spank you."

"Spank, spank, spank!" She sang the words, over and over.

He snorted a laugh and started up the stairs, following his cock. She pushed her fingers far enough to touch his asshole. Every step he took rubbed her finger into him. Every step shot to his balls like the two were connected.

When she wasn't being the Eastern lady, she was a lot of fun. The woman he'd seen tonight, laughing and friendly, was one he'd like to know better. He also wanted to get closer to the bundle of hot sex lying on his shoulder.

In spite of himself, he liked her more than any other woman he'd met. It wasn't just her body, though that was an advantage. No, she stood up to him as few did, her eyes sparking and daring him to challenge her. Her education was a problem, but he could do nothing about that.

He hadn't realized how much he liked making her do what he wanted. It was a game they both liked to play. Was she playing a game with him now?

He reached the top of the stairs and put her down. She clung to him, giggling. She started to slip so he grabbed her around the waist and pulled her against him. She rubbed her naked ass against his released cock. He groaned. Game or not, he wanted her tonight.

"You're asking for trouble, Fanny."

"Want trouble!" She reached her hands around and found his cock.

He groaned again, fighting for sanity as she squeezed. He wouldn't take advantage of a drunk woman, but she was not so drunk that she was out of her mind. She knew who he was, and was as close to begging for him as could be without the words being said.

Ben made it clear he wanted them to enjoy each other. She obviously wanted him, and every part of his body wanted to give her everything he could. He held her hips still, pulling her ass hard against him. It was sweet torture.

"If you want trouble, sweets, you'll have to beg me for it."

She stopped for a second, and then giggled. He let her pull away, both relieved and disappointed. But instead of leaving, she sank to her knees. She got there without falling over, mainly because she clung to his legs. He stood still, waiting. He was a strong man, in every way, but there was only so much he could take. If she touched him…

"Want trouble," she said, breathing the hot words over the head of his cock. The way her hand was wrapped around him, it almost felt like her mouth. But no, that would never happen. No decent woman would do that to a man like him.

* * * *

Florence held Ranger's thick cock in her hand. Beth was right. Ranger was too stubborn and had too much honor to take advantage of Ben being away, unless she flat out begged him for sex. That was not something she was going to do. After all, the man taunted her, making her hot every time he looked at her. This was the only way she could meet her craving without backing down.

If he really wanted her to stop, he would have tossed her in the bed and stomped downstairs by now. Instead, she had his cock in her hand.

She'd only drunk one glass of punch. The rest of the time her glass contained plain grape juice. She'd give him a taste of fun, and then tell him she was sober and wanted more. By then he would be just as wild as she was that first night.

He'd teased her until she could barely think straight, and then told her who he was. She'd do the same to him. Surely he wouldn't mind that she'd lured him into bed. After all, he was a man, and Beth said men wanted as much sex as they could get!

He rested his hand gently on her head. She sucked his cock right into her mouth. He clamped his hands on either side of her head.

"Jeezus!"

He tasted of salty musk. She rolled her tongue around the head while he used curse words she had never heard before. She found his balls and rolled them between her fingers.

"Oh, fuck. I'm gonna come. Sweets, if you don't stop that I'm gonna—"

She raked him lightly with her teeth and then sucked hard while squeezing his balls, just like Beth told her. His cock jerked in her mouth. She pulled back, holding both fists over him to stop him going too deep, again following Beth's suggestion, and sucked again.

"Fuck!"

Salty fluid sprayed into her mouth. She pumped him with her fists, and he kept going, cursing the whole time. She swallowed him deep then pulled back as he shuddered. Finally, gasping as if he'd run all the way home, he sagged. He gently pulled out of her mouth and sank down beside her on the bare floor. He pulled her into his arms and kissed her, slow and deep.

She let herself go, giving and taking as their tongues fought. He finally released her and leaned his forehead against hers.

"Oh, Fanny, what you do to me."

She snuggled against his chest, her hand "accidentally" brushing his cock again. It strained to rise, not quite inert.

"If you weren't drunk, you'd never touch me like that. I want to pleasure you all night. You are one hell of a woman, and I want you so bad. But in the morning, you won't remember a thing. You don't really give a damn about me. And that hurts, sweets." He whispered the last three words so softly she barely caught them.

"You made me crazy that first night, knowing everything was new to you. It was me who showed you how your body could shiver when my fingers touched you. My finger was the first thing inside you. I made you explode with my tongue on your clit and my fingers in your pussy and ass. The way you looked at me, like I'd shown you heaven, well, nobody's ever looked at me like that before. I was so damn happy. I thought I'd forgotten what it was like to feel that good." He sighed and kissed her forehead.

She stayed there, pretending to be half-asleep while she thought what to do. He would never speak to her this way if he thought she wasn't drunk. This was the man Ranger hid away from the world. He was a good man. Even though she pushed him beyond his boundaries, he still he held her gently.

She could learn to love this man. But he might never let her see this side of him again if she told him the truth tonight. She couldn't do that, to either of them. She squirmed, rubbing his cock. He laughed gently. The puffs of air tickled her skin when they blew her hair against her neck.

"But you're an egghead like my brother, all schooled up with fancy manners like Beth. You've read books full of stuff about things I've never even heard about." He rested his chin on her forehead. His heart pounded against her breast. "Dammit, sweets, I'm just a stupid cowboy who thinks he can run a ranch. I don't know much, but I can make your body sing."

Who told him he was stupid? The man acted like he knew exactly what he was doing every moment. Trace told her that no one knew how he got all those longhorns from Texas to Montana without a thousand things going wrong. They were proud of him, but he couldn't see it.

"After getting this drunk, your head will pound, and your mouth will feel like the floor of a hundred-year-old saloon. You'll swear never to drink again." He sighed and touched her forehead with his lips. "You won't remember a thing about my loving, sweets. And I'll never tell a god-damned soul."

She pressed her lips together, fighting tears. Why didn't Ranger let her see this thoughtful, caring side? He must have been badly hurt to be so terrified about letting his feelings out. Could he ever heal enough to let her see even a glimpse of this wonderful man again?

He caught her nipple between his knuckles, and her mind froze. She moved to give him easier access. He chuckled. "Someone's not passed out quite yet. You want more of this?" He pinched her harder.

She gasped when the pain shot to her clit. "I thought you'd like a bit of the edge. Let's see what we can do to make this a night you'll never remember."

He rose to his feet, easily lifting her body as he stood. He carried her to the bed and laid her on her back. She let her body fall where it will, as if she wasn't in control. He surprised her, taking his time unbuttoning her jacket and her blouse. He eased her arms out and pulled the clothing away, leaving her sprawled and naked.

"Don't move. I'll be right back."

He returned in a few minutes with a lantern and a tin plate. He set the lantern on the apple box and the plate on the floor. He quickly stripped down as she watched from under lowered lashes. His body was beautiful, and he moved like a cat, with no effort wasted. He picked up her clothing, and his, and laid them over the stool.

He sauntered back and looked down at her. His cock rose, thickening as the tip pulled out of its sheath. She stretched and opened her eyes as if just waking. She gave him a lazy, welcoming smile.

"You still want trouble, sweets? Because I'm ready to give you more than you can handle."

"Oh yes, want trouble," she purred. She moved her hand between her legs as she had at the pool. He shook his head, nostrils flaring.

"No more of that teasing. I'm going to make you so hot you'll beg me to take your ass—damn." He grimaced. "You'd feel it in the morning if my cock went there. I won't do that tonight, but I can use my finger to warm you up. I think you'll like that just fine."

She ran her fingers through her lower curls. He leaned over, grasped her hips and hauled her to the edge of the bed. He pushed her knees up to her shoulders and knelt on the floor. She blinked at him in confusion. He nuzzled her mound with his chin. She squirmed. He inhaled, closing his eyes and breathing deep.

"Ah, Fanny, you smell so good."

He pressed her lips wide with his thumbs and blew warm air on her exposed pussy. She clenched her inner muscles in reaction. He dropped his head, flicked his tongue and she arched, gasping.

"You taste as good as you smell." He tickled her clit with his tongue, making her squirm. "After that long soak, there's no one's scent on you but mine. You already swallowed me deep, and by morning, I'll have entered every part of you. My cock in your mouth and pussy, and my fingers in your ass."

Chapter Twenty-Eight

Ranger lifted Fanny's legs, spreading her so he could lick her from ass to clit. She was limp in his arms, but awake. She purred, squirming and squeaking as he made sure to lick every inch. She was drunk enough to relax and enjoy what he did, but not so much that she would pass out.

Best of all, she didn't talk. None of those big-brain words tonight.

She tasted like spring, fresh and clean, with a touch of musk. He wanted to lick her for hours, until she screamed and begged for him to sink his cock in her, but he had a few things to do tonight, and she might pass out at any time. He pulled back and, tilting her so the light shone between her legs, looked closely.

Her swollen clit lifted its red head from under its hood. Her pussy lips were small, making it easy to see his prize. He pressed a finger in her, watching how she clenched around him. He smiled to himself. She was so damned fascinating, he could study her for years. He'd memorize every freckle, wrinkle, line and scar under the sun so he could count them every month, touching them with his tongue.

That tight little asshole made his cock jump. He wanted to look down and see his cock entering her ass as she kneeled before him. Someday she'd slam back against him, forcing his cock deeper as she found her pleasure. He dipped his finger in her pussy and then pressed into her ass. It went in far easier than that first night.

Yeah, spiked punch had its uses, and calming women into letting themselves go was one of the best.

He twisted his finger. She caught him, clenching her ass muscles to hold him tight. "Soon," he whispered. He pulled out and kissed the spot, licking and flicking his tongue. She shivered and tried to close her legs. But he was having none of that. Not tonight. Tonight, he was in control.

He grabbed her thighs, lifted her pussy to his mouth and went to work. It took only a few minutes of heaven before she shuddered and whimpered, dripping with need.

He set the tin plate with its spoonful of lard on the bed. He lifted her and lay down. She flopped on him, belly to belly.

"Time to do some work, sweets," he said.

"Work?" she mumbled.

He guided his cock between her legs, setting it just inside her pussy. Then he pushed her hips so she slid down his body. Her nipples dragged over his chest as she took his cock into her.

"Very nice."

"You want more, you sit up and work it," he said.

She pouted. After a moment, when he didn't help, she pressed her palms on his chest and pushed herself up. It must have rubbed her clit against his groin because she suddenly perked up. She leaned forward and ground herself against him. She clenched his cock inside, slowly shafting him with her pussy.

He let her amuse herself while he played with her breasts.

She sat up and arched her back while wiggling her ass and pulsing up and down. It felt damn good. Her eyes glazed and she panted, so it must have been good for her as well. She sped up until she slammed down on him, her breasts bouncing.

He caught her nipples and pinched until she gasped. She shivered and moaned. The tension built higher, compressing his balls, but there was something he had to do before either of them came. He took a pinch of lard and rubbed it over his fingers, one-handed. With the other he pressed on her back, making her lean over. She followed along, still rubbing her clit against him.

He rubbed his larded fingers between the cheeks of her ass. They slid easily. He gathered more and pressed it into her asshole. It warmed on his fingers, letting them easily slip just inside her. He took more and this time pressed his longest finger in.

She gasped and shivered, clenching his cock and his finger.

He probed deeper, past his first joint. He twisted then pulled out. She whimpered, slowing.

"There's more, sweet Fanny," he promised as he got more lard. This time, when he entered her, he went in as far as he could. He felt his cock through the thin layer separating them. The extra touch on his cock ramped him up. She needed to come soon, or he wouldn't be able to hold off.

He used his finger like his cock, with the same rhythm. Only he added something new, curling his finger forward and scratching her from the inside of her ass.

She slammed down, head bowed and hair falling over him like a curtain. She moaned, trembling. He went back to pumping his finger and found her breast under the curtain of hair. He pinched her nipple, and she shuddered. Her pussy channel began to clench around him as if she was almost ready to come.

He shafted her ass with his finger, in and out and twisting and curling, and then pinched her nipple again. She lifted up, threw her head back and gasped, unmoving. A moment later and she exploded above him, crying and pounding on him, her pussy clamping his cock.

He felt the hot wire sear from his balls through his cock and out, exploding into her. He pulled his finger out and clamped his hands on her hips, shoving her down as he slammed up. Again, and again, and again, until a hot white light exploded between his eyes and she collapsed on his chest, sobbing.

He pulled her close with one arm, fighting the same tears.

He couldn't fight them forever. He let his tears fall, dripping silently down the sides of his face. A sob escaped. Just one, but it felt like an ax to his heart.

He clamped down, shutting off feeling again. Feeling led to hurt, and he'd had enough hurt to last the rest of his life.

But because of that moment, he could understand love.

And knew it wasn't for him.

Chapter Twenty-Nine

Florence woke up smiling. She stretched. A few aches made her remember what she'd done. She groaned and pulled her pillow over her head.

She'd seduced Ranger and gotten more than what she bargained for. All she wanted was a night of hot sex. She planned to tell him that she'd enjoyed every minute of it.

But along with hot sex, he gave her part of his heart. He would be hurt, and therefore furious, if he found out that she knew he was a caring and gentle man. Typical male, to get embarrassed and upset for speaking from his heart.

Beth said she must pretend to have a hangover today. Since Beth never had one, she could only say what it was like for the person who watched. Luckily, Ranger had described it so well for her. Sore head, rotten stomach, and sore eyes, especially in the sun. Oh, and her mouth would be dry.

She really felt wonderful. After last night, she expected Ranger would stay far away from her. Until she worked out her reaction to all he said, it was for the best.

"You want ham and eggs for breakfast? We've got lots of lard to fry them in." Ranger stood at the bottom of the stairs and yelled. Someone groaned and ran from the kitchen, slamming the door behind. It must be Patrick, suffering from the real symptoms of a hangover.

"Just coffee, thanks," she called back.

Her voice creaked, which made Ranger laugh. She quickly dressed in her extra shift, drawers, and gray work dress. She was starting on her sleeve buttons when she heard footsteps coming up the stairs. She slumped on the bed and blinked at her wrists, as if her head hurt and she couldn't even concentrate on something so simple.

"Had a bit too much to drink, sweets?" he called as he climbed the stairs.

"I don't know," she moaned. "I don't remember."

Ranger looked, and sounded, far too cheerful. "That's too bad. It was a great party. Anything else hurt, other than your head?"

She chewed on her knuckles as she shook her head. What they'd done together didn't make her sore. It was more like her body hummed in memory of his touch. He'd never know that, of course.

"I remember the party. Amelia's having twins," she said slowly. "The children are staying with Jessie, and there's something else." She stared at her knees. "Oh, the punch was good." She blinked up at him, squinting in the morning light. "I have to ask Beth for the recipe. Some sort of fruit juice, I think."

"I think there was a bit of sour mash in there as well," he said under his breath. "I brought you coffee." He held out a mug.

She managed to hold it in both shaking hands. He held on while she sipped.

"Ugh!" she cried. "That tastes terrible!" She screwed up her face. "There's no sugar or milk in it."

"That's the way I like my coffee. Thick and black."

"Well, I don't!"

"Then you'd better head into the kitchen and get to work." He set the mug beside the basin. "I'd better do those buttons up or you'll never get anything done."

She continued to slump while he attacked the four buttons on each of her sleeves. He must have had a splash in the creek because he smelled wonderful. She watched his thick, blunt fingers fight the small buttons. She remembered what they'd done, and shivered.

"Patrick's in worse shape than you, but he knows that's no excuse not to get work done." Ranger raised his head from his task to give her a speaking glance in rebuke. "I'm heading to the Double Diamond to check those steers. Once Ben gets back, we'll drive them to Virginia City. We'll get a lot more gold there than in Bannack."

"What are steers?"

"Don't know everything, Florence?" The corners of his eyes proved how much he enjoyed taunting her.

"Of course not."

"You make a steer by castrating a bull calf."

She wrinkled her nose. "Doesn't that hurt?"

"Most things in life hurt. But Jessie's careful so they barely feel it. After that and branding, the calves jump to their feet and trot over to their mothers."

"Jessie does things like that?" She couldn't help her voice rising.

Ranger nodded, his smile wicked. "And she made sure her men know just how good she is. But don't you get any ideas. You know nothing about knives, except in the kitchen." He finished his self-appointed chore and picked up the mug. "And I aim to keep it that way." As he walked away, she watched his bottom cheeks in the snug pants, remembering the feel of them naked.

"You like my cooking!" she called out. He stopped at the top of the stairs, but didn't turn around.

"That, too," he said after a moment. He raked her body suggestively with his eyes and continued down the stairs.

She waited until the kitchen door closed behind him. Then she looked out the window from the side, so he couldn't see her. "When he doesn't know anyone can hear, he's a loving, gentle man," she said to herself. When he rode away, he waved at the window as if he knew she watched.

"But the rest of the time, he's so arrogant!"

She went to make the bed but noticed his scent on the sheets. She pulled them off the bed and carried them downstairs to wash. She needed no reminders of the previous night!

She made herself a cup of proper coffee and ate bread and cheese and tidied up the kitchen, though she had to admit that Ranger had left it very neat. It irked her even more.

She boiled the sheets to remove all memories of Ranger and hung them out to dry. She filled the water reservoir once more, letting it heat as she cleaned the house. Once it was hot, she found the biggest galvanized tub she could find and set it in the kitchen. She washed every inch of her body, removing his scent.

Unfortunately, she couldn't remove her memories of his touch or the soft words he spoke from his heart. How the way she looked at him after that first time made him happy. How he was a just stupid cowboy and she was an egghead.

She remembered everything.

But if he found out she had heard his gentle words, he'd think she did it to humiliate him. Only God knew what he'd do at that point.

* * * *

Florence stewed all day, thinking about Ben, and Ranger, and Patrick. Her memories of Ranger's attitude grew with each hour. She listed out loud all his faults. His arrogance. The way he treated Patrick. How he taunted Ben for not being as strong, while insulting him for learning so much. How much he disliked the fact she was an educated female who not only had an opinion but had the bad taste to express it!

She was so caught up in her stewing that she didn't see the weather approach. She rushed outside as the first droplets fell, and pulled her sheets off the bushes. The wind slammed the door shut behind her. The storm came so quickly she watched as the mountains disappeared behind sheets of grey.

Ranger was clear over to the Double Diamond, almost as far as Tanner's Ford. Patrick was also out in the rain, but she knew he had a slicker on his horse. She didn't see one behind Ranger when he rode out. He would be very, very wet if he came home. Either that, or he'd stay overnight.

It was likely sinful to feel so good about another's misfortune. After the last few weeks, she'd come to the realization that everything had to be looked at in perspective, including sin.

It was a sin to kill in cold blood, but not to do so to protect innocent children from evil.

If someone threatened her children, or any child, she would do whatever necessary. If neither Ben nor the sheriff had shown up when that brute wanted Emma, she would have clawed his eyes out, bit his nose off—anything to stop him.

She carefully folded her sheets so they wouldn't wrinkle, and set them over chairs and tables to finish drying. She wanted a warm, dry bed to sleep in tonight. Alone. She hadn't shared a bed since before Charity was married, and relished the ability to stretch out without touching anyone.

That was the only advantage, however. Now that she knew what else other than sleep could happen in a bed, she wanted company. With Ben gone, and no one to replace him, the bed seemed so empty.

That added another sin to her list. It was a sin to have relations with a man to whom one was not wed in holy matrimony, and an even greater sin to enjoy it. But Beth, Amelia, and Jessie had no problem loving three men. The sheriff, the doctor, or much of the town didn't care. They insisted it was nobody's business as long as everyone benefitted. With so few wives available, sharing a household with three male ranch partners was good news. That allowed more men to settle into a family instead of haunting the saloons and gambling joints.

She enjoyed Ben's loving. He was gentle with her, while Ranger brought a rough edge of excitement. She loved it both ways. She knew Ranger had a soft side, but would likely never see it again. As for Patrick, she didn't really know him well enough to judge.

Beth said stealing a horse in Montana Territory would get you hanged, but sharing a wife in a bonded life of togetherness just brought looks of jealousy, from both women and men.

The church, from what she'd seen out East, didn't care about truth.

The men who thundered from the pulpit about hell and damnation did nothing to help women like Evangeline Leduc. They called hail and brimstone down when a woman fed her children the only way she could. Not one penny of what those unctuous preachers put in their pockets went to help those in need.

She put another few sticks in the stove and moved the stewpot to the back to simmer. Since she couldn't make her bed, she might as well get the biscuits started. Patrick would be hungry when he got home, and he deserved a decent meal. After all, he didn't pretend to be someone he wasn't.

Ranger, should he make it home tonight, could eat whatever was left.

She pulled the lid off the lard tin. She stared at a hole left by a gouging finger. She clenched her buttocks, remembering where that lard had gone, and with which finger. Face flaming and heart pounding, she used a tin cup to scoop out what she needed. She mixed it with flour and baking powder, adding a pinch of salt along the way.

How could she have ever guessed that Ranger putting his finger, um…there, would make her shiver just thinking about it? Though she strained to explode at the time, she still heard his quiet words about what he wanted to use instead of his finger.

Goodness, would it fit?

If it hadn't been dark that first night, and she'd seen his cock, she wouldn't have thought it would fit in her pussy, either. But it had. And it felt very, very good.

Beth said that, when she wanted to make a baby with Trace, and then with Simon, she had taken care of their needs in other ways. One was her mouth, which Florence enjoyed that time with Ranger. The other must be her bottom. Beth even hinted that sometimes she took all three men in her body, at once. Her mouth, her pussy, and her bottom.

That would never happen to her, since Ranger wasn't going anywhere near her bed again. Nor was she going to accost him in the barn. But maybe she, Patrick, and Ben could try a few things.

The door crashed open and then slammed. She jumped, hand over her breast.

"Man, that sleet is nasty." Patrick looked at Florence, realized he'd frightened her, and gave her a sheepish look. "All those years in Texas and as soon as that cold rain hits, I remember the one thing I liked about it. I was never this cold in Texas."

He shrugged out of his slicker and hung it on the peg by the door to dry. His boots went beside it, his hat above. These were not things she had to teach them. It was an ingrained habit.

"Patrick, I appreciate you taking your boots off and hanging your slicker up."

"Sunbird always made us do it," he replied. "Ross and Nevin's ma. She was the only good thing about Texas once Fin and Hugh arrived."

"What was she like?"

Florence put her head down and went back to working the lard and flour between her fingers to make light biscuits. Patrick poured himself a cup of coffee, straddled a chair and sighed.

"At first, when it was just us Elliotts near, she'd sing around the kitchen. Ranger would make her laugh sometimes." A quick glance showed his lips curved up in a sweet smile. "He carved these little animals. He had some that looked so real you would swear they could walk away."

"Did he bring them with him?"

When Patrick didn't answer, she looked up. He shook his head, all traces of good humor gone.

"Ben lay on the floor in the kitchen for weeks while his busted leg healed," he said into his cup. "For the first week or two, Ranger lay beside him on his stomach. Sunbird would sing and rub in her medicine, calming his fever nightmares."

"What was the matter with him?"

"He got whipped, and his back got infected. He's a bit touchy about it. That's why he keeps his shirt on. Anyway, The MacDougal caught Sunbird helping Ranger when he expected her to be working. Ben pretended to sleep. She jumped up right away and went back to work. The old man didn't say anything, but that night he cursed Ranger for being too lazy to work. He went after him the only way he knew he would hurt."

"How?"

"Ben said he picked up one carving, then another, watching to see when Ranger tensed up because he might break a favorite. When The MacDougal saw which one made Ranger the most upset with him touching it, he tossed it in the fire."

"Oh, my godfathers." She stared at Patrick. Was this why Ranger was afraid to show that he cared? He'd lost his parents, his older brothers, and then this vicious man gleefully destroyed what he'd created from love.

"Ranger turned his face to the wall and didn't say a word as it burned. The next night we got another lecture about nothing mattering but the Clan. The shelf that used to hold the carvings, was emptied while Ben and Ranger slept. We figure The MacDougal threw them in the fire like they were kindling." Patrick sipped his coffee.

"And Ranger hasn't carved anything since."

"Nope. He hauled himself off the floor the next morning and went back to work, even though he could barely walk. From that day until we started our trail drive, he never spoke an extra word to any of them. Just Sunbird if he found her alone."

"How does she stay married to a man like that?"

Patrick shook his head. "You don't understand. She was raised the same way, with total obedience to the Chief. Unless something changes, she won't leave until he dies."

"And then what will happen to her?"

"Louisa's husband, Señor Montoya, has a ranch nearby. He'll make sure Sunbird arrives safely back here." He finished his coffee and stood up."She's Auntie's sister. Amelia writes to her. I expect she'll sing for a few days when she finds they're expecting twins." He set the cup beside her. "You'll say nothing about the carving."

She nodded. "Thank you for telling me. It helps explain why he's so afraid."

Patrick snorted. "Ranger? Afraid? You've got the wrong man." His stood tall, his jaw thrust out. He looked every inch the man. "Ranger's afraid of nothing. Not one damn thing!"

"I believe you," she said, mostly to calm him down.

"I'm not sleeping in that cabin tonight. I brung up the blankets this morning and made myself a bed in the parlor. I'm going to have a lie down. Call me for supper."

Florence waited until she heard Patrick's snores.

"Ranger's afraid, all right," she said to the flour and lard mixture. "He's afraid of his heart breaking. He thinks if he doesn't love anyone, or care about anything, he won't get hurt. But he does care, though he hides it from everyone."

She put the bowl aside. She'd spent so long listening to Patrick that she'd made the mixture too fine for biscuits. It might work as a shortbread base, though. She let her concerns about Ranger fade. Soon she was humming as she worked out how to create something wonderful from damaged goods.

"Ouch, dammit! One more of those and I'll wring your scrawny neck!"

Ranger's roar sent her running to the door. She hauled it open just in time. He barreled through, scowling like he was about to explode. Thin lines of red streaked one cheek. He was totally soaked, from hair to toes, just as she expected.

"Quick!" He leaned over and bent his head toward her. "Grab that little beggar before he goes down my back."

Chapter Thirty

"What are you talking about?"

"Find the tail and you'll find the beast," yelled Ranger. "Shit! Get your claws outta me!"

A large lump moved between Ranger's back and his soaking wet shirt. Florence cautiously reached in past his collar. She touched fur. Then she heard the faint meow.

"A kitten? You've got a kitten climbing down your back?"

"Yes, dammit, now get the little beggar out before he claws me to death!"

She bit back a laugh at his thunderous expression and coaxed the ball of fluff out. She held the marmalade-colored vicious beast in both hands. It curled up and mewed, damp fur making it look pitiful. Ranger stood up, wincing. He unbuttoned his shirt and reached inside the front.

"Come on, sweetie," he murmured. "Don't be scared." The second kitten, this one gray and white, blinked as he held it up to his eyes. It mewed, far more weakly than the marmalade. "Good, you made it." He nodded in satisfaction and looked at Florence. He scowled. "What?"

She bit her lip to hold back, but it didn't work. A laugh burst out.

He frowned. "What's so damned funny?"

"The ferocious beast which has the mighty Ranger Elliott swearing and complaining about its ruthless claws, is a kitten?"

"Don't you dare laugh. That tomcat's name is Vicious."

"I'm not calling a tiny kitten that!" She crooned to him, purring in her hands. "He's Caramel, for his color." She stroked the soft fur with a finger. "What are you calling yours?"

A flush colored his cheeks. "They're not mine. They're yours. This one's the runt of the litter. She needs extra care. Beth didn't want to name her in case she died."

"Beth gave you these kittens?"

He nodded as if resigned to putting up with females. "Beth hauled me into the house and shoved these two at me. She said you needed something soft to cuddle at night, since Ben's gone."

He flicked his thumb at the gray one in his hand. It grabbed with both paws and chomped. Its tiny teeth didn't even break through his callus. A ghost of a smile flickered over his face as he watched.

"You can't give them back," he grumped. "Beth doesn't want the wild one because of James, and doesn't have time to care for..." He coughed. "For this one."

"I'll bake you a pie if you tell me what you named her." She used a singsong voice to wheedle it out of him.

His lip twitched. "Won't work."

His kitten curled up in his huge hand while hers tried to escape. She set Caramel on the floor. He immediately set out exploring, his spike tail straight up. She'd have to move very carefully not to step on him. The other one just lay there and purred in Ranger's hand.

"She's like a fluffy ball of dust," said Florence.

"Fine, we'll call her Dusty," he growled.

"Your face is scratched."

"Vicious Caramel didn't want to sleep in my shirt. I was almost home when he decided to climb out. He almost escaped out the collar of my shirt." He touched the tiny red marks with a finger. "Damn cat thinks he's a mountain climber. If I still had my beard, I wouldn't have these scratches." He glared as if it was her fault.

"Did Ben tell you to shave off your beard?"

"Dusty needs some milk," said Ranger, ignoring her question. "Beth said to soak the corner of a flannel and let her suck it."

Ranger, avoiding her eyes, made sure Caramel wasn't under his feet as he stepped around the kitchen. He found the bowl of milk Florence had in the cool room. He dipped the corner of the cloth in the milk and encouraged the tiny kitten to eat. Caramel returned and attacked Ranger's boot, climbing onto his toe to chew and suck the wet leather laces. Florence had to turn her back so Ranger wouldn't see her face.

Beth might have given the kittens to Florence so she wouldn't sleep alone in bed. She got the point loud and clear that Beth thought she should be sharing her bed with a couple of men instead. But Ranger had carried the little ones home. Though he cursed and swore about Caramel scratching him from waist to nose, he hadn't done anything to stop the kitten.

A man who would do that still had inside him the little boy who carved animals. He cared, so much that it made him uncomfortable. There was hope for Ranger, after all. She pressed the shortbread crust into a pie pan while Ranger fed Dusty. He cleared his throat after about ten minutes. She brought the pan over and set it on the table.

"We're not sleeping in the cabin anymore." Ranger glared as if expecting her to shriek.

"Of course not," she replied calmly. "It wouldn't be safe for Dusty. You have to feed her every few hours, and you couldn't do it with that wind howling between the logs. She'd be too cold."

"Right," he said. The stool creaked when he shifted his weight.

"Patrick set up a bedroll in the parlor. He's been asleep for a while."

Ranger grunted and stood up, still carrying Dusty. He looked down, frowned, and then picked up Caramel as well. The much larger kitten purred and settled against his chest.

"He's not bad when he's asleep," he muttered, and strode out of the room to find Patrick.

"Neither are a few men I know," she replied, too quietly for him to hear.

Chapter Thirty-One

"Nobody can read that many books in their whole lives," said Patrick the next evening. He used a small piece of hard maple to help push a needle through the leather, repairing a bridle. The plate in front of him held the last crumbs from the peach shortbread pie. Caramel purred contentedly in his lap.

"Most of the books I shipped are from my own library," Florence replied.

Ranger, quietly rubbing his saddle in the far corner, said nothing. Dusty, tucked into his shirt, purred against his belly. Florence and Patrick had started nattering with each other about her teaching Patty to read better. If Ranger had somewhere else to go, he'd already be there. He didn't want to move in case they realized they weren't alone. He both wanted to hear what Florence would say, and disappear so he could pretend it never happened.

"Where are you going to put five crates of books?"

Patrick asked the same question Ranger would have. He couldn't imagine what a pile of books from one crate would look like. The thought of having them in the house made his skin crawl.

"Mr. Langford of the Double Diamond wants them for his library."

"Ace? Is that what all those empty shelves are for on the north wall?"

She nodded. "It seems all three of them grew up with large libraries. They want to have the same here."

"Did you know Ace's older brother is the Earl of Denby?" Patrick shook his head in awe. "He grew up in a palace."

"His older brother might be the Earl," replied Florence, "but I hear all three are younger sons. In England, the eldest inherits everything. The fathers produce extra sons in case the first one dies, but they are extra once he marries and has sons of his own to inherit. They have to make their own way. Unless they marry a rich heiress, they have to join the church, or the army."

"Or come to Montana and win a ranch playing poker, with three aces," crowed Patrick.

"Since you're the youngest of six brothers, where would that leave you?"

Patrick groaned. "Working on someone else's ranch. Just like I've done since Ma and Pa died."

"But sons of aristocrats don't know how to do anything more than drink, gamble, race horses, do ridiculous stunts and swordplay, carouse with their mistresses, and ruin young women," said Florence. She curled her lip as if it was an insult.

"That sounds pretty good to me," said Patrick. Florence thought he was joking, and laughed.

Ranger gave the boy points for making her laugh.

"But they can all read," she said again. "Every gentleman is sent to school, or has a tutor, from the time they're about seven. They learn how to conduct themselves properly. Everything is based on who your father and mother are, how much money you have, and how well you conduct yourselves. Most men go on to college."

"What do they do there?"

"Unfortunately, most of them drink, gamble, et cetera," she said, rolling her eyes. "But they also debate, study under professors, and learn to read and write Classical Latin and Greek. Those are ancient languages used hundreds of years ago. People read books in those languages, but few speak it anymore."

"Why?"

"Why doesn't anyone speak Latin?"

"Why would you waste time learning to speak a language nobody uses?"

Two more points for Patrick.

"Learning is never wasted. When you can read, the whole world opens up."

Ranger held back a snort. Florence talked like one of those traveling gospel thumpers, as if she had the key to eternal salvation. She was just as much a fake as they were.

"When you open a book you can travel to distant places, see marvelous things, learn about science, and history!"

"So what? I'm doin' fine right here," continued Patrick.

Ranger nodded in agreement.

"Oh, Patrick, you have no idea what you're missing! A man who has knowledge held out to him and refuses to grasp it, who shuns the printed page in ignorance, that man is beneath contempt!"

Ranger held so still he could almost hear Dusty's heart beating.

"That's crazy," said Patrick. "Reading's not everything."

"It is to me." She sat up straight and pounded her finger into the table. "A male who refuses to read, who cannot value knowledge found in books, is not a man. He's an animal, toiling in the fields like a mule, never lifting his head to see the sun. I would want nothing to do with such a beast."

Ranger's breath caught. His lungs refused to work. *Damn her to hell and back again. I'm a man, not an animal!*

Echoes rippled through Ranger's memory. Jack only said it once, but Ranger never forgot. Even though Ma thrashed Jack and washed his mouth out with soap, it didn't change a damn thing. Ma kept trying to help, but she died a year later.

Ranger closed his ears to the talk and made slow circles on the leather with his polishing cloth. Damn her! She can say this after he went to Beth and begged her for the worst two kittens so Ben's wife would have company? When Florence laughed and helped him haul the vicious kitten from under his shirt, he thought she understood.

He was stupid, all right. At least where Florence was concerned.

Well, never again.

He couldn't kick Ben's wife off their ranch, so he'd have to learn to live with her. He could live without a woman, but Ben needed someone to use his high-falutin' words with. When Ben was away, Patrick could keep her warm.

Yep. Come spring he'd build himself a cabin in the woods. About a half mile uphill was a nice little bench of land just the perfect size. Florence would still feed him and take care of his clothes, but he'd treat her as a servant.

If that's what she thought of him after all he'd done for her, well, she didn't need him. She was Ben's wife, and he'd keep his hands off.

He laughed inside his mind, taunting himself. There was only one female who understood him, and she slept with him all the time now. She liked to curl up between his neck and shoulder, purring in his ear. Dusty gave him more comfort than any female, ever. Ma was too busy with a home, seven kids, and a husband, to pay much attention to any of them.

Dusty needed him. If he didn't feed her and keep her warm, she'd die.

As soon as Ben's wife went upstairs and Patrick headed to the privy, Ranger went to bed. He set the saddle in the parlor where he and Patrick now slept. Yeah, the damn woman slept in their bed, all alone, while he and his brother lay on a couple of blankets on the hard, cold floor.

He lay still when Patrick returned. He heard his brother's quiet curse and understood the reason. Patrick wondered if Ranger had heard what Ben's wife said. He had enough pride that he'd never let on.

"You sleepin'?"

Ranger, flat on his back, didn't move.

"Range?"

Patrick swore again. He kicked his blankets across the room with his sock-clad toe. "Might as well work since I cain't sleep now," he muttered. He stomped back to the kitchen and his leatherwork.

Ranger lay there a long time, unable to either sleep or get up, as he'd have to pass his brother. Patrick finally came in, hauled his blankets out, and settled in the kitchen. He was gone before Ranger got up the next morning. Ranger left before Florence started stirring upstairs.

Chapter Thirty-Two

Patrick looked at Ranger sideways the next time they met, at dinner. Ranger ignored him and dug into the mashed potatoes. He ate silently, grunted his thanks for the meal, and went back out.

The Bitterroot herd didn't have a lot of cattle for the size of it, so he helped Trace since Jack was away. He slept in the barn with Dusty that night. She travelled with him in a sling pouch that Beth created. She'd laughed while she sewed it for him. At the time, he enjoyed her laughter. Not now.

When Trace told him to go home, Ranger went to help Ross and Gil. After all, Nevin was off to Helena with Ben and Jack. Since he helped one brother, he'd help the cousins as well.

He dropped by Jessie's place every day to make sure Meggie had someone to fuss over. She did a bang-up job as housekeeper, and Bridie was coming along well. Both girls stood a bit straighter with the responsibility.

Emma, Johnny, and Daniel were always happy to see him and Dusty. That morning, Emma's eyes pleaded silently when she handed Dusty back. He recognized the look and told her Dusty was getting too big to carry along. The kitten needed someone else to take care of her. Was Emma up to the responsibility? She nodded, taking in every word as he explained how to care for the beast.

He told himself he had something in his eye when he rode away. He'd miss that damn cat, but he knew he had to get rid of her. Any more time together and losing her would rip an even bigger hole out of him.

That was the problem with females. Claw a spot into your heart, settle in, and then rip it out as they leave.

He decided to spend the night with Gillis and Ross. Jessie said the two men were making Amelia crazy because they wanted to wrap her up and keep her safe. Ranger spent some time working around the ranch the next morning so Ross could get some riding in. Ross insisted someone must always be within calling distance in case Amelia needed help.

Chopping wood was hot work, especially since the woodpile was behind the house where there wasn't much breeze. He chanced taking his shirt off and got into a rhythm.

Female laughter and a buggy's wheels had him scrambling into his shirt. He finished buttoning it as Beth and the woman he could only think of as Ben's wife rode into the yard.

"We're here, sister dear!" called Beth.

"Damn, Beth shouldn't be traipsing around in her condition," he muttered. Did Trace know his wife took the buggy out? She was farther along than Amelia, but only carrying one baby. Two, if you counted James, which Ben's wife held awkwardly.

Ranger watched as Beth carefully climbed down and then took James. Ben's wife managed to get off without falling as well. The two women walked into the kitchen, destroying the peace of his day.

With all those women around, Amelia didn't need him hanging about. He saddled up and rode off. When his stomach started growling, he headed for the Double Diamond. One good thing about having lots of family around was that there was always a place to cadge a meal in the kitchen, or a hay bed in the barn.

He rode into the yard and dismounted. No kids ran out demanding hugs and, in Johnny's case, to be tossed in the air. He watered his horse and left it with some hay. He washed his hands and opened the kitchen door.

"What have you got cooking today, Miss Redmond?" He closed the door and bowed to her, as he did every time he stopped by.

Meggie curtsied. "I have bread and apple butter, a thick soup, and apple pie for dessert. Do you want to start with pie?"

He rubbed his stomach and moaned as if starving. "You're my kind of woman, Miss Redmond."

She served him a piece, complete with sharp cheese. She waited, hands clutching her apron, until he took a bite.

"Cinnamon and cloves with a touch of lemon peel," he said. She beamed at him getting it right. "I do believe that is the best apple pie I've had today."

She laughed, half-child and half-woman. "You always say that."

"And it's always true." He picked up the slice in his hands and bit in. She was good with pastry, though Beth did a better job. By the time she found a man who suited her, or a couple of them, Meggie'd be a damn fine catch.

"Where's everyone else?"

"Emma and Johnny went with their new aunt and uncle, and Bridie's helping Daniel with kindling for the fire box."

Ranger put the pie down. His mind whipped over everything Ben had said, including that the children had no living relatives. That meant the "aunt and uncle" weren't. He didn't put it past a woman to steal children, but why come to their valley when there were orphans in every city?

"On their ma or pa's side?"

"Their pa's. They said they wanted to show Emma and Johnny photograph albums of their family." She spoke as if the albums were made of gold. "They showed us a photograph that looks just like Johnny, only in old-fashioned fancy duds. They said it was his pa!"

Ranger let himself breathe. Whatever they wanted, it wasn't selling his children to be brutalized for some rich man's entertainment.

"Do you remember their names?"

"They talked really fast, so it was hard to understand. I think they said Pinton or something." She brightened. "But they left a letter addressed to Uncle Ben."

Meggie went to the fireplace mantle and took an envelope out of the silver tin that Sin brought with him from England. She handed it to him with a flourish.

"See! Isn't that fancy writing?" She pointed to the first line and ran her finger under it. She read the words slowly. "Mr. Benjamin Elliott, Esquire. What's an esquire?" She looked at him with complete trust, as if he could answer any question, solve any problem. At least he knew this answer.

"Ben says it's a fancy word for lawyer." He took the envelope, making sure it was right side up. He looked at the slanted writing. "Yep, those letters sure are fancy with all them curls. Emma didn't mind going with them?" He kept his tone light.

"Johnny wanted to stay, until he heard they had toys from their Grandma. Emma was so excited she jumped up and down. She kept laughing about finding her family." Meggie turned away, her face crumpling.

Ranger stuck the letter in his pocket and pulled the sixteen-year-old to his chest. She sniffled against his shirt.

"I know, honey. You miss your ma and pa."

"Don't tell," she said, voice choking. "Mr. and Mrs. Elliott are wonderful to us, but—"

"But you'd rather be with your own ma and pa."

"Does the hurt ever go away?"

"I won't lie to you, Megs. The hurt gets smaller, but you always wonder how things would be different, if they didn't die."

He held Meggie close, letting her cling to him. Trace and Sheriff Chambers were pretty sure her father's accident was more of a dry gulching. A mining claim with good color, and two motherless girls ripe for early marriage, added more suspicion. In almost his last breath, their father begged for Trace and Beth to take his girls and keep them safe.

Ranger let Meggie cry even though he wanted to haul his ass after whoever had stolen his children. After a few minutes she pulled away, sniffling.

"I'll have to wash my eyes so Bridie doesn't see I've been crying."

She dipped a flannel in the pail by the back door and held it to her eyes. He looked at his pie. How could he eat it when his stomach felt like it was full of boulders? He couldn't let Meggie read the letter. There might be something in it that would frighten her.

"You look angry that they're gone." Meggie squeezed the flannel in her fist. Water dripped onto her boot.

"Jessie says I look angry most of the time, but usually I'm just thinking. You did no different than Jessie would have, if she'd been here."

He spoke the truth, and Meggie knew it. Only a few adults knew why Florence brought the children with her. Of course the kids would want to see an aunt and uncle, and pictures of their lost family. But where did the imposters get those photos? He pushed himself to his feet and held out his arms. Meggie gave him another hug. He kissed her wrinkled forehead.

"I'll stop by as soon as I can. Say hello to Daniel and Bridie for me."

Meggie waved as he rode off, though she didn't look very happy. He trotted down the road, back the way he'd just come.

"Where the hell could they be?"

He finally took the letter out of his pocket. He snarled at the envelope. It only took a moment to slice it open with his smallest knife and pull out the single sheet of paper.

EMMA was printed right at the bottom in bold letters. He bet her tongue stuck out at the side while she proudly printed her name.

Whoever the couple was, they had his children. His gut didn't tell him they were in danger, but the itching between his shoulder blades wouldn't go away. He crumpled the letter in his fist.

"Stupid, stupid, stupid!"

All he got back was echoes. He shoved the paper in his pocket and trotted back to Amelia's. Ben's wife would hate him even more, but he had no choice. He could put up with her disgust. His pride was nothing compared to the lives of his children. Ben and Florence might have adopted them in law, but they were his as well. Maybe the only ones he'd ever have, especially after Florence discovered his secret.

Would she laugh in his face and eagerly tell everyone? Curl her lip and call him a dumb animal?

For once, his rage wouldn't build. He always figured one day his secret would escape. He would live with the shame but hold his head up anyway. He'd done that for years. The MacDougal called him every ugly name he could, in English and Gaelic. The man found the tiniest weakness and worked at it, ripping with sharp claws until there was a gaping hole.

But he was no longer a boy. He was the boss of the Bitterroot Ranch. And his brother was married to an uppity city woman who was about to rip him to shreds.

To hell with it. All he wanted was to make sure Emma and Johnny were safe. Then he'd take them home to the Bitterroot.

Home? He sighed. He couldn't take them away from their cousins. They needed to laugh with other children, surrounded by love and warmth. Even when Ben returned, the tension between the four of them would hurt a sensitive child like Emma.

He'd ask Ben to make sure Florence got to visit Emma and Johnny every few days. Once the cattle were gone, they'd be returning to Amelia's until the babies were near. That was just across the river. Having Florence away visiting her children a couple times a week would give him a chance to relax.

He snorted a laugh. At least he now had something to look forward to. Every few days he and Patrick could have their home to themselves for a few hours.

Ranger slowed as he approached Amelia's yard. He didn't want to upset the women in their condition. Ross and his brothers would have his balls in a sling if anything happened to their wives or babies.

He'd have a quiet word with Florence, find out what was going on, and then leave. His pistols were loaded, and he had his knives. Depending on what the letter said, he'd borrow a shotgun from Ross. If he knew how to use Gil's damn claymore, he'd take that, too!

He rode into the yard calm and cool. He dismounted and watered his horse. He tied it to the hitching post and went into the kitchen. Florence, flour to her elbows, rolled out pastry while Auntie chopped meat. Florence gave him a quick glance, and then stared.

"What happened to the children?"

As Ben said, the woman was smart. He held up his hands. "They're safe. But we have a bit of a situation."

She reached to her back, pulled on the bow and took off her apron. She folded it and placed it on the counter, every movement precise. The old woman looked at him shrewdly.

"Safe, but not safe?"

He nodded. No one could ever lie to Auntie, so they didn't bother.

"Beth and Amelia?" he asked Auntie.

"They sleep to grow babies. You go." She shooed them away.

He escorted Florence outside. She kept quiet all the way to the barn, though she walked so fast she almost dragged him behind her. Then she whirled around and stabbed him in the chest.

"Where are my children, Ranger Elliott? I will pay, or do, anything to get them back!"

"A man and woman came to Jessie's. They said they were an aunt and uncle. They took Emma and Johnny."

Chapter Thirty-Three

"They don't have any—"

"They brought a photograph and promised more."

She shut her mouth. Gulped. "Of who?"

"A young boy who looks just like Johnny, only wearing clothes from twenty-some years back."

Florence swayed. He reached out to hold her, but she grabbed the pole beside her instead. He stepped back, bile curdling in his stomach. He'd forgotten what she thought of him. Of course, she wouldn't want to touch an *animal*.

"What do they want? Where did they take my children?" She glared at him, as if accusing him of stealing her babies.

"They're mine, too." He stared her down. "I visit them every day, sometimes twice. When did *you* see them last?"

Her face turned white. She flashed from anguish to fury in a second. She stepped forward, face raging, and reached to slap his face. He grabbed her wrist and held it. Though she fought, he easily held her arm still.

"Don't ever try that again," he warned.

She ignored his cold fury. "How dare you accuse me of not wanting to see them! You have no idea what it's like. You're a man. You can ride a horse, go where you want. Since I'm a woman, you men say I can't go anywhere alone. And then you head off on your horse so I can't even ask you to take me to visit them!"

She wrenched her arm and, this time, he let her go. She gritted her teeth, her eyes flashing. Her face almost looked like the time she rode his cock. Passion was passion, whether fury or orgasm. He almost laughed. She must have seen it because she pounded his chest with both fists. This time he did laugh. She couldn't hurt him with her puny fists. It was her words that killed him.

"I swear, Ranger Elliott, as soon as I get my children back, I'm going to learn how to ride. I'm going to get pants like Jessie's, climb on a horse, and go where I want to, when I want to! Not you, or anyone else is going to tell me different!"

Now he understood why Trace got Beth all stirred up. Having a woman this angry at him made him want to tame her with his cock. But that would be Ben's job, and maybe Patrick's.

"You do that, sweets. But you're stuck with me for now."

She hauled her emotion back. She stood still and white, like a marble statue. He suddenly realized she really was scared.

"I'm fairly sure they're not hurt. I just don't know where they are," he said.

She sagged for a moment, and then squared her shoulders. "The men aren't far. They can spread out to cover more ground. We've got hours before dark, and—"

"They left a letter. Meggie said it's for Ben."

"Why didn't you say so?" She poked him in the chest. "Tell me what it says."

He grabbed her finger. His hand shook. *Think of the children.*

"I don't know what's in the letter. Emma wrote her name on the bottom." He pulled the crumpled paper out of his pocket and held it in his fist.

"Well, read it to me!"

He swallowed, fighting past his dry throat. "I can't."

"Why, do you need spectacles?"

He found enough air to speak her words back to her. He did so, slowly. "I am beneath contempt. An animal in the field. A beast, and not a man."

She flicked her eyes over his face, frowning.

"What are you saying?"

"I. Can't. Read."

He closed his eyes and let his breath out. There. He'd admitted it. Saying it out loud, repeating her words back to her, took some of the pain away. They were just words, he realized. He could refuse to believe them. It was different with a broken leg or severe beating. That you had no choice about. You died, or lived, thanks to the ones who took care of you.

But words were nothing but hot air, or scratches on paper. Unless he gave them power, they couldn't hurt him. And he refused to bow to the power of another man's, or woman's, words anymore.

"You can't read?"

He stared at her frown. "Nope. I'm just a dumb animal." He said it almost cheerfully, glad to throw her words back in her face.

"A what? Oh!" Her face turned white, then red. She swallowed. "You heard me talking with Patrick the other night."

He nodded. "Every damn word. You sure said them loud enough."

"But, Ben said your mother taught you to read. She taught all of you."

He shrugged his shoulders, surprised at how easily they moved without that weight. "Maybe, if she'd lived, I might have learned. I can read big blocks, like the way Emma writes her name. But anything else moves around on the page and I can't catch the words."

"The words move?"

He nodded. "Ma said if I kept at it, I'd find a way to rope them and tie them down. Once I knew how to stop them, I'd be reading in no time. But she died."

"And the man who took you in did not value books," she said hollowly.

"Oh, books have value," said Ranger. He gave a sardonic laugh. "You rip the pages out to start a fire. Shakespeare, Milton, he didn't care." He saw her start of surprise. "Just because I can't read doesn't mean I don't like someone else doing it. Ma read damn near every night. She read every play in that Shakespeare book, except *The*

Taming of the Shrew. Pa read that one out because it riled Ma so much."

A ghost of a smile flashed across her face.

"Ranger, are you afraid to read?"

He shook his head. "Nope."

"Do you refuse to read? Believe books are worthless?"

"Of course not. There's a lot of good learning in books."

"If you can tie the words down."

This time she did smile. It wasn't the sneering attack he expected. This wasn't happening at all like he expected. Ma used to say that it was better to get something unpleasant done straight off, rather than worry at it all day and make yourself sick. He'd worried about this most of his life. A fear of his secret, that of being so stupid he couldn't even read a primer, making people think he was worthless.

No more.

"This winter'll be the first time I'll have a chance to read since Ma died."

He heard his mouth saying something he hadn't wanted to admit to himself. He blinked. It was true. Now that his secret was out, he could sit at the kitchen table right by the lamp to wrestle the words into place. That was far better than hiding in the barn. He'd be one hell of a lot warmer.

She poked him again. "If you *want* to read, then I was not talking about you! Are we clear on that?" Another poke.

He held her hand still. This time she trembled. "Clear."

"Then hand me the damn letter so we can find our children!"

She yanked her hand away and snatched the letter from his grasp. She eagerly pulled the page out. She smoothed it against her thigh and looked at it.

"Oh, my, this script is hard to decipher. I need more light." She hurried out of the barn and held the letter close to her face.

"*Dear Mr. Elliott. We are representatives of the Pinkerton Agency. We were hired by Emma and Johnny's grandmother to find them. Mrs. Johnston was unable to search for them until recently.*"

"Pinkertons? They cost money." Ranger scowled. "She'd better have a darn good reason why she waited so long."

"Shush and let me read. *If you would be so kind as to bring your dear wife, Florence, to the Tanner's Ford Hotel, we will explain all. You will wish to see the photographs. Yours, squiggle and splotch.*"

"Squiggle and splotch?"

Florence waved the letter at him and frowned. "I told you, I can't read their script very well." She sniffed. "Miss Ashburton would have rapped their knuckles for having such bad handwriting."

Silence fell for a moment. The paper trembled in her hand. His secret was out, and he didn't feel ashamed. The children were fine. And Ben's wife made him as hot as ever. He almost hugged her, but caught himself in time.

"Oh, Ranger, they're at the hotel. I know Mrs. McLeod wouldn't let anything happen to them." Tears ran down her cheek. She sniffed and wiped them away. "I don't care that Mrs. Johnston is their grandmother. She can't use the Pinkertons to take our children away!"

"No one's taking Emma and Johnny anywhere but home. Don't worry, we'll have them back home before supper. I'll just saddle up and—"

"Oh, no you don't." Florence grabbed his shirt. He tugged, but she'd wrapped the cloth in her fist. "You are not going to that hotel without me." She narrowed her eyes at him like Ben used to do to Jack just before they had a tussle.

He already knew the woman was stubborn. Ornery was another good word for her. He looked at his horse, thinking about trying for it. She tightened her grip and stepped closer. She might even have growled, unless that was his stomach.

Her breasts rubbed against his chest. His cock reminded him that this woman loved to play. There was no way she didn't feel the ridge rising against her belly. He looked down. A flush rose from her throat to cover her face.

She'd undone a few of her shirt buttons, likely while working in the heat of the kitchen with Auntie. He watched her breasts rise and fall as she panted. Two little nubbins pressed against his ribs. He moved his chest from side to side, just an inch or two. She inhaled a gasp as his shirt rasped against her. He pulled at the *vee* of her blouse to increase his view. Her breasts swelled. So did his cock. She poked him, this time in the belly. Hard. He winced.

"Ranger Elliott, if you get on that horse without me, I will—"

He leaned over until his mouth was right by her ear.

"The next time you ride double with me, sweets, you'll sit in my lap with your ankles wrapped around my back." He stroked her erect nipple, enjoying her gasped response. "You'll ride my cock, your clit bumping against me as my horse walks just right. I'll hold your bare ass in my hands and move you however I want. I'll keep you just off the boil until I'm damn good and ready to let you come."

She pulled away from him. Her swollen breasts heaved as she panted. There was no way he'd ride a horse with his cock this hard unless it was buried in her soft, wet sheath. But there was something more comfortable which suited both of them.

"You want that right now, sweets, or do we borrow Beth's buggy?"

Chapter Thirty-Four

Florence clenched her fists, her fingernails biting into her palms, as the buggy rolled toward town. She knew Ranger was right when he insisted Emma and Johnny were fine and she should relax, but the shock of hearing they were gone hadn't faded. Worse, she was mortified that Ranger heard her horribly unkind words and thought she meant him. She remembered being frustrated that evening. She'd enjoyed her time with Ranger, but felt badly that the wonderful way he made her feel was because he thought she would never remember his caring words.

She was even more frustrated now.

His touch on her breasts, and his promises, had set her on fire. She'd gone days and days without the release she'd never known, but now craved with desperation. Instead of concentrating on rescuing her children, she was thinking of doing wicked things with the man sitting beside her. She squeezed her fists harder, focusing on the pain of her nails digging into her palms.

Ranger took her hand and pried her fist open.

"This won't do anything to help the children. What will they think if your hands are bleeding by the time we get there?"

She opened both hands. Four red crescents arched across the mound of each hand.

"How did you know?"

He chuckled. "I know you, Mrs. Elliott." He laughed and brought her hand to his mouth. Instead of the kiss she expected, he drew his tongue over the sore part of her hand. He nipped, and she shivered. His touch raised her hope for more. The thrum of need in her pussy and breasts increased. If he would only—

"If I put my hand between your legs right now, I'd find your drawers sopping."

"Excuse me?" She gave him a look of scorn to cover up the embarrassment of him being right.

"That's exactly what I mean. You huff and puff in your corset and starched garters—"

"One does not starch garters."

"—but underneath that starch is a hot woman eager for the touch that will make her scream as she explodes. My touch."

She squirmed on the seat. "That is not a suitable topic of conversation. We should think of Emma and Johnny."

"We can't change what's happening to the children until we get there. Talking about what we want to do with you gives you something else to think about."

"What *we* want to do with me?" Though she replied in a haughty manner, she clenched her inner muscles to ease the throbbing between her thighs.

"We. Me, Patrick, and Ben. One at a time, in pairs, or all together."

She forced away the images that shot to her mind. She waited until she could swallow through the lump in her throat before replying.

"And what makes you think I want anything to do with that?"

"Because, Mrs. Elliott," he said, almost growling, "you love it when we touch you." He glanced over, his eyes hungry. "You want us to lick your sweet pussy. You want to swallow our cocks, and our seed. You want those cocks in your pussy and," he dropped his voice, "in your ass. Don't you?"

She trembled, and only part of it was from the buggy rolling along the road. He snorted a laugh when she didn't answer. They both knew he was right. Up ahead she saw the lane that led to Jessie's home. She pretended to look hard for someone as they drove past, but could barely see past the raw urge. They were silent until Tanner's Ford was just ahead.

"If I wasn't afraid of being thought stupid," he mused, "I could have asked Meggie to read that letter for me." He cleared his throat. "Then I wouldn't have had to drag you along," he added gruffly.

Florence had never been told she was stupid, but she'd heard it used on others. Often the person didn't understand the cryptic directions, or hadn't been trained properly. As far as she was concerned, those types of curses showed far more about the person talking, than the one being belittled.

"If I ever see that horrid MacDougal man, I will take your pistol and shoot him."

Ranger leaned forward. He might have pretended to see better, but she figured he was avoiding looking at her.

"Don't blame The MacDougal. He did what he thought was best for the Clan."

"How can you defend him after everything he did to you?"

"He came from the Scottish Highlands. Thanks to the English, life was pretty bad there for a long, long time. There was little food, and the only thing that mattered was survival of the Clan. Just like with Ross's Indian kin. The weak die in bad times because the strong can't care for them without dying as well. The most important thing is keeping the tribe alive. One person isn't important."

"Do you really believe that?"

"I've lived it most of my life, since we were taken in by The MacDougal. I don't have a Clan or Tribe, but if anyone tries to harm my family, they will die. No matter how far they run, they will never escape. Emma and Johnny are part of my family now."

Florence wasn't going to ask if she was included. She also wasn't going to say anything about someone taking the children from an Elliott home, right in the valley. From what she'd learned about men, Ranger's anger was also directed at himself for not making sure the situation never developed.

"Finan MacDougal is an ignorant man who does what he can to make his people strong," said Ranger. "I can't really fault the man, because he made me who I am. But Fin Junior is a weakling who preys on others to make up for his own failings. I could easily kill him like a rabid dog."

"Did they call you stupid?"

"Naw, it was Jack. He caught me stumbling over a book that Patrick read the year before. He danced around the kitchen taunting me."

"Children can be cruel."

"So can mothers." He chuckled. "Ma whipped Jack's butt six times with her willow wand and washed his mouth out with soap. I got his dessert for a month. Ma was serious about learning."

She imagined his tiny mother switching Jack's backside for shaming Ranger.

"I think I would have liked your mother."

"I'm not surprised," he drawled. "I told Ben to bring home a wife like Ma."

"Ben didn't plan to marry me. He only did it to save Emma."

"Ben only does what he wants, so he must have wanted you. After all, the two of you like to talk, talk, talk, all the time." He concentrated as he brought the buggy around a rough spot. "I bet he didn't meet another woman in all those years who suited him half as well as you." He chuckled to himself. "There he was, all torn up because he promised to bring me a wife and married you instead. And all the time, he didn't know that Patrick and I planned to share any wife that one of us married. And wasn't that a surprise to you, Fanny?"

"I wish you wouldn't call me by that horrid name again. You make me sound like a dance hall girl."

Ranger slowed the horses. He turned to her, his body stiff.

"When have I ever called you that name?"

She frowned. "I don't remember, but you used it a few times."

He stopped the horses completely. He stared between their ears. His teeth were clenched, as were his fists.

"The only time I called you Fanny was the night you were too drunk to remember anything." He turned to her, his face ferocious. His chest heaved as he glared. She shuffled her bottom toward the outside of the seat. "Were you drunk, Florence? Or were you playing me like a fool?"

"Everything you did that night, you wanted to do." She clasped her hands in her lap, fighting for a calmness she couldn't feel. "I wanted to as well. And no, I wasn't drunk."

He ground his teeth for a moment. "I asked you two questions."

"You were up on your high horse about making me beg for you to touch me. Well, Mister Ranger Elliott, I helped you get what you wanted." She pointed her finger at him, but was too far away to poke him. "I wasn't playing you, I wanted you to touch me and that's the only way you would. I was going to tell you, until you started talking. And yes, I would touch you the same way again. After all, I was sober that first time as well. I wanted your cock in my mouth. I wanted to suck you dry, knowing that I had that bit of power over a man who could kill me with one blow with the back of his hand."

"If I was going to hit you, Florence, you'd be in the dirt right now."

She saw how he flexed his fists and ground his teeth. He was telling the truth. He was angry enough, or hurt, to attack her. But he was not that kind of man.

"Beth encouraged me to pretend to be drunk, to help let us both enjoy ourselves. I didn't know you would say wonderful things to me, things that you didn't want me to hear." She dropped her head to flick a beetle off her skirt. "Lovely words you don't want anyone to hear."

He growled under his breath.

"You are not a stupid cowboy, Ranger Elliott. You are a smart, honorable, kind man who is afraid to show love in case you get hurt. And I'm not an egghead who cares for nothing but books."

He must have heard her. There was nothing but a couple of feet of air between them. But he stared forward for a long time.

"And Ranger? I do want you to put your cock where your finger went."

He jerked in his seat. He growled something and slapped the reins. She held on, bouncing on the seat, as the horses ran far too quickly for the road.

She said nothing more, as she'd said enough. Or was it not enough?

Chapter Thirty-Five

Emma and Johnny, having finished dishes of ice cream, sat by the window and carefully turned pages in a photograph album. The four adults spoke quietly on the far side of the room. Because the children looked so happy, neither Ranger nor Florence could show their anger or unease. What happened in the buggy hung over them like a shroud, adding to the tense situation.

The agents watched them closely, seeming to pick up on every gesture or quavering word. They refused to give their names, saying it was confidential and wasn't important in any case.

"Mrs. Johnston could do nothing while her husband was alive. He was against the marriage from the start. When John Johnston and Evangeline Leduc married, Mr. Johnston said he was no longer a member of their family. As soon as Mrs. Johnston buried her husband and received access to his funds, she hired the Pinkerton Agency to find her son, his wife, and any children they might have," said the female agent quietly. "She was most distraught, and not because she lost her husband."

"Another arrogant, angry old man throwing his children's life away," said Florence bitterly. "Rich men think they can pretend their child never existed, just because they married someone of a different class."

"Your aunt, Miss Jessamine Bonham, sends her regards," said the male agent to Ranger. "She expressed irritation that she did not receive an announcement of her namesake's marriage. However, the fact he is the son of the Earl of Denby mollified the old woman."

Ranger scratched his chin. He hadn't looked at, touched, or

spoken to Florence since he helped her down from the buggy in front of the hotel. "You talked to my aunt in Virginia?"

"The Pinkerton Agency leaves no stone unturned," said the man, as if quoting a slogan. "Evangeline Johnston, may she rest in peace, managed to give us Florence Peabody's name."

The female agent turned to Florence. "We found Evangeline, and got her a doctor. She told us about you, and insisted we thank you for saving her children. She also told us about a very unsavory character who wished to do Emma harm. I held her hand while she passed. She was still smiling, ma'am."

Florence covered her mouth, choking back tears so the children didn't hear.

The male agent cleared his throat and continued. "Sheriff Barstow sent us to a Benjamin Elliott of Tanner's Ford. The sheriff was very helpful, and in return asked that we put him in touch with a certain widow named Mary Douglas. We did so. He mentioned visiting in the spring with his new wife and children."

Florence smiled through her tears. "Imagine, the two witnesses at our hasty wedding, getting married themselves. I do hope they visit."

The female agent took over. "From the description Sheriff Barstow provided, we believe the man Evangeline told us about, and the one who encouraged your marriage, is the same man. He has since died in an unfortunate altercation."

"You have anything to do with that?" asked Ranger.

"Perhaps. We inadvertently provided his identity to the individual who wished to purchase Emma. He was not pleased his payment had not been returned," said the female agent.

"So one nasty creature killed the other. Maybe that will help to stop Emma's nightmares," said Florence.

"We have found the two Johnston children," said the male agent. "We need to know your plans for them."

"They are Elliotts now, not Johnston," said Ranger. "They'll live here in Tanner's Ford, surrounded by relatives and people who care about them."

His words were mild, but the experienced agents didn't miss the threat. The much-shorter male agent didn't seem bothered by Ranger's size or deep growl.

"Their grandmother is eager to see them. Mrs. Johnston has no one else in the world."

"Then tell the old woman to visit," replied Ranger. "Come in the spring. Mrs. McLeod can arrange for a suite here at the hotel."

"I don't think that's what she had in mind. She is extremely wealthy."

"Someone already tried to buy Emma," said Florence. She grabbed her skirts in tight fists and leaned slightly forward. "My children are not for sale. Not to anyone."

"But Mrs. Johnston is their grandmother. A blood relative."

"My husband is a lawyer," said Florence. "He is in Helena, filing papers to formally adopt our children. By now they are Emma and Johnny Elliott. Our children. And they will remain with us."

The agents looked at each other. A silent message passed.

"Would it be possible to have photographs taken of the children? Mrs. Johnston would appreciate evidence that her grandchildren are well. She can then decide what she chooses to do next."

"Good idea," said Ranger. "We can get ones of the whole family at the same time. There's a newspaperman in town who takes pictures. Buford Hames could take some after Ben and the others get back. He's an interfering busybody, so the picture could end up in his newspaper if there's no news to report."

Florence nodded her agreement and stood up. Ranger followed.

"Time to bring our children home," she said.

The Pinkerton agents stood as well. They nodded, eyeing her with the same shrewdness she'd seen during the whole meeting.

"We'll wait in town for your husband to return. You may borrow the photograph albums. I expect the children will enjoy showing them to the rest of your family."

Chapter Thirty-Six

Florence crossed her arms and muttered ladylike curses as Ranger took the buggy back to the Rocking E. If it wouldn't have been noticed by everyone watching in town, he wouldn't have touched her to help her in and out of the buggy. The closeness she'd felt as they rushed to save their children had evaporated as if it never existed.

Men! She heard him say caring words, so he was all in a lather. Now that he knew she'd heard him speak those things, he would say nothing that wasn't absolutely necessary to her.

He hadn't replied when she told him that she'd spoken to the female Pinkerton agent. She and the agent had a quiet word while Ranger held the children in his lap and looked at the albums with them. The woman had promised the grandmother wanted what was best for her grandchildren. She would not take them from a happy home, but they should not be surprised if the Mrs. Johnston arrived in Tanner's Ford once the snow cleared in the spring. The two agents would quietly leave Tanner's Ford as soon as they received the Elliott family portraits.

If she was forced to leave the valley, Florence would insist on receiving a copy of every portrait. It might be all she would have to remember them with. Ranger's reaction was so strong she might have to leave. She doubted he'd speak with her ever again unless forced to.

They settled the oblivious children with Beth. He pointed out to Beth that he was looking forward to her cooking when he returned the buggy. He rushed to the Bitterroot to dump her off, and was gone again. The whole time he looked straight forward, as if she wasn't there.

Since she was gone most of the day, first at Beth's, then with him to rescue the children, she hadn't had time to prepare anything for supper. Patrick was due home, and he would certainly be hungry.

That wonderful night with Ranger had left her wanting more. Even though he was so furious she was surprised he didn't burst into flames, she still craved his touch. The fool man would cut off his nose to spite his face!

Still grumbling, she went inside, lit a lamp, and looked at supper possibilities. Ranger wouldn't be home. Patrick would. She hadn't had a chance to get to know Patrick well. Would he ease her throbbing need with Ranger out of the way?

She tried to ignore how her nipples tingled, pressing her swollen breasts against her chemise. She removed her damp drawers and set them to dry by the fire. It deepened her ache as every time she took a step, her pussy lips stroked against each other.

She should have gone after Ranger about the kittens when he was in a jolly mood. When she thanked Beth for the thoughtful, though lively gift of Caramel and Dusty, her friend expressed surprise. It turned out that Ranger had demanded Beth hand over a couple of kittens because Florence needed something soft to cuddle.

After discussing his behavior, she and Beth agreed it was Ranger who needed the cuddling. He'd used Florence as a reason to get the kittens. Once Dusty was well enough, though Ranger obviously enjoyed her company, he didn't have an excuse to keep her, so gave her to a very appreciative Emma. Caramel, meanwhile, was always underfoot.

She pulled a Mason jar of sausages from the pantry, one of pickled beets, and some leftover potatoes, and onions. The sausages went into the cast iron fry pan to heat. She turned the beets upside down in an inch of warm water to loosen the seal.

She soon had sliced potatoes and caramelized onions in one pan, sausages in the other, and a side dish of beets with cloves and cinnamon. Whoever had put up the beets had a most excellent recipe.

She would have to ask Beth so she could repeat it next summer.

If she was still in the valley next summer.

She looked around the room. It was far smaller than her father's home, but it was hers. Nothing fancy—no sterling silver tea service to polish or pretty tea cups to put away so big male hands wouldn't accidentally break them.

Her mother had lost many lovely things by her father's carelessness. He didn't drink tea, but his hand, or shoulder, or something else would just happen to brush one of her mother's treasures and send it to the floor. It usually happened when he had a setback in his plans. For some reason, making his wife bite her lip so she wouldn't cry made him feel powerful.

Quite the contrast to Ranger, who cherished a wild, tiny kitten so much that he would let it scratch his face rather than harm it. She'd seen him holding James and Hope the same way. He wasn't quite as comfortable with them as their fathers were, but he'd had little experience with children until a few weeks ago.

If she and Ben divorced, would she move to a big city and live in an elegant house? If she did, she could put out all the beautiful things she'd shipped west. No man would enter her home and cause breakage. Not to her dishes, or her heart.

"Smells good."

Florence startled at Patrick's voice. He took off his boots, set his things in the usual place, and looked over. He looked different tonight. Taller, more sure of himself. Caramel ran over to investigate the smells around the bottom of his pants. He scooped the cat up. The contented kitten settled on Patrick's shoulder, purring and looking down at Florence as if he was king.

"I met Ranger driving the buggy back to Beth's. He told me all about the ruckus with the little ones. Good thing everything worked out."

The reminder sent a shaft of cold through her heart. She hugged herself. "It scared me, Patrick. No one is going to take my children away. I know I haven't seen them often, but I love them."

Patrick set the kitten on the floor and took her into his arms. She melted into his chest, needing his calm protective embrace. Ranger was bigger and stronger, but she wasn't quite comfortable with him, even before this afternoon's blowup. Ben could think his way out of any situation, but in a physical fight was at a disadvantage compared to his brothers and cousins. Patrick, however, was just right. Smart and thoughtful, strong and...desirable. Her heart sped up. His scent, of leather, horse, and man, was slightly different from Ranger, but just as enticing. But Patrick might care for her, whereas Ranger was too full of himself to allow space for another in his heart.

"They're our children, Florence," Patrick said quietly. "They belong to me, you, Ben, and Ranger, and the rest of the family. Once Ben gets back with the papers showing they are Elliotts in law, no one will ever be able to take them away from us."

Including herself.

She was under no illusions. If she left, the family would never let her take Emma and Johnny. After all, what life could she offer them that was anything as good as they had in the valley? Four sets of relatives eager and willing to care for them. Cousins and aunts and uncles and more. She was not that selfish. A shudder went through her. She would be alone again, only it would be worse because she would know what she was missing. At least she would know the children were safe, with family that loved them.

Unless she could work things out with Ranger, it was a matter of when, not if, she left. She couldn't live here and drive a wedge between brothers, or force Ben to choose between her and his family.

Ben was better than the best friend she ever had. Not only smart and funny, but he loved her sweet and long. They could talk about anything as they cuddled after, both glowing with completion.

Patrick was kind and thoughtful. He sat back and watched without intruding. When she was working and needed something, often he had it ready to hand to her. She hadn't been with him intimately, other than a few moments when she wasn't aware of much other than her need. Flushing in remembered embarrassment, she released him, pulling away from his warmth. He kissed the top of her head and walked over to wash up. She went to the stove to dish up supper.

And Ranger? The man exasperated her! Worse, he made her feel things that sent her out of control. She remembered pleading with him for more, unable to imagine living without it. Only after it was over did she regret how her body took over her mind. His insistence that he wouldn't touch her again unless she begged, brought humiliation.

Even sitting beside her in the buggy that afternoon, he seemed overpowering. Her instinct was to protect herself, which meant hitting back. The only way she knew was with words. Few women other than Jessie knew how to fight back with anything else. Any woman who did strike a man was taking a chance of being beaten, perhaps until death.

Even before this day, she knew Ranger would never do that. But his continual anger at her would hurt Ben. The twins had shared every moment from the instant of their creation, except for the few years while Ben studied law. They were together again, and she would not drive them apart.

But neither Ben nor Ranger was here tonight. Patrick was.

He sauntered over to her in stocking feet. There was a suggestive light in his eyes that she hadn't seen before.

Patrick knew they would be alone, because Ranger told him. A thrum of need made her grab the back of the chair to steady her legs. Patrick brushed past, his elbow grazing her breast. She inhaled a gasp at the touch.

"I've been thinking of supper for hours."

He looked into her eyes. She had thought his brown eyes and hair were boring compared to the twins' hazel. But she was wrong. Those brown eyes had a depth to them which pulled her in. Hours of Ranger's arousing presence, along with too many nights alone, made her shiver in need.

"Are you ready, Florence?" He murmured the words, his eyes suggesting he was asking about far more than supper.

How could she make a decision about staying—or leaving—unless she had sampled everything the Bitterroot Ranch had to offer? Ben's loving was sweet. Ranger's was wild and forceful. Would Patrick be in the middle, or something far different?

She bit her lip. "Yes," she said, panting slightly. His eyes closed for a moment. He exhaled and his tense shoulders eased. "How many sausages? I'll only eat one and—"

He barked a laugh and looked down. His pants bulged. She flushed at the unintended double meaning.

"Damn right you'll only eat one tonight, Florence," he said with a gentle laugh. "But let's fill our stomachs before we faint from hunger. There'll be lots of time for everything."

She put four fat sausages on his plate along with almost all the potatoes and onions. He waited until she served herself before taking that plate from her as well. She set the dish of beets on the table. He set her plate down, and his, and then stood behind her chair.

She wiped her hands on her apron, hung it on the hook and let him seat her. He leaned over, lifting her chair right off the ground before setting it so her stomach was a few inches from the table. He waited a moment, inhaling deep breaths by her ear, and then her hair.

"I'm looking forward to getting to know you better, Florence. Caramel is spending the night in his blanket-lined apple box. Nothing's going to distract us."

Chapter Thirty-Seven

Patrick watched the trembling woman across from him as he ate the delicious supper. Ranger might stomp and complain, but he liked Florence as a wife just fine. She could cook, worked hard, and had a passion that flared to life whenever any of them looked at her. His need matched hers, which would make this night all the more special.

Tonight, she was his bride. Only his. Whatever happened before this meal did not exist. Tomorrow did not exist.

The only way she would leave the valley was if Ranger drove her out. But he was damned if she would leave. Not when he finally found a woman who made him feel like a man. Cooped up on The MacDougal's ranch, he'd seen few women. The only ones around were Sunbird, Jessie, Louisa MacDougal, now Montoya, and her servants. Ranger was usually able to find a decent yet willing woman in town, which he shared. That was it for feminine company.

One year there was a widow whose eyes widened and smile beckoned when they rode into town. They met with her twice, a couple of months apart, before she was gone again. Though she hadn't stayed long, they'd used her time wisely, to mutual benefit. He even spent an hour or so talking with her over coffee while Ranger snored upstairs. He learned a few ways from that very merry widow to seduce a woman, things his brothers wouldn't think of. Tonight was the first time he had an opportunity to try them.

Florence was smart, and had a smart mouth as well. That was part of her charm—the way she could stare in his brother's faces and tell them what was what. Amelia kept the MacDougals in line as well, but she did it gently. Beth was more open about it.

All his life, Patrick had seen Jessie tell big men off. She did it as easily as breathing. The situation was a mite different now. He stopped a snicker from escaping. He loved to watch how Ace, Sin, and even Henry, controlled his maverick sister. She was a wild one, but one raised eyebrow from Ace, or a slight head shake from Sin, would set her back on her ass. Not all the time because they knew when to fight and when to let things flow. They hadn't tamed her. Instead, they encouraged her with rewards.

Ranger wouldn't admit it, but he liked Florence's sass. It gave him a reason to conquer her, and his brother needed to be in charge to feel he mattered. But why conquer, when he could seduce?

Florence, for all her bravado, wanted to belong, just like Jessie. And, like Jessie, she had to fight to prove her worth. Only when she realized her men would protect her, by not allowing her to injure herself or others, would she give up the reins.

He was ready for tonight, but his woman had no idea what the night would bring. She thought Ben was the brains and Ranger the brawn. He, however, had some of both along with a sense of adventure that wanted to drive her wild.

He stabbed his last piece of pickled beet as a topping for his last slice of sausage. The sweet spice of the beets cut the grease and peppercorns of the sausage meat. Onions and potatoes went with anything. He finished chewing and sat back in his chair. Since he'd eaten so quickly, having gone without food for most of the day, she was just finishing her smaller portion.

"That sure tasted good. You got any dessert?" He winked. "Or maybe you're my dessert."

Florence's face turned almost as red as the sunset. She jumped to her feet and began cleaning up. He patted her bottom on his way past, enjoying the memory of her startled squeak as he did the last chores in the barn.

When he returned with two buckets of water, Florence was upstairs. He dipped out a basin of warm water before filling the stove's reservoir with the cold. He washed up well as Caramel finished his dish of milk. He put the kitten on an old blanket in his apple box, took a generous helping of lard in a cup, and headed up to bed.

No more sleeping on the parlor floor.

Florence, wearing a thick white nightgown that covered her from neck to wrists to toes, stood by the window, brushing her hair. One small lamp sat beside the ewer of water. He lit the big one and, without speaking, hung it from a hook in the rafters on the near side of the bed. He was going to watch this woman. Every special spot that made her catch her breath, every twitch and wiggle, he'd see. He wanted a good look at her pussy and, if she let him, her ass.

And when he finally let her come, he would watch her explode.

He set the cup on the floor under the bed. He walked up behind her, slid his hands around her waist and pulled her snug against his chest. He stood there, just feeling how wonderful it was to hold his woman before bed.

It wasn't sexual. Oh, he had a hard-on like a ten-penny iron nail, but that was separate from the feeling in his chest. She felt welcoming, and warm, and her scent rose around him like a blanket, comforting him.

He took her hairbrush and stepped back far enough to take over the job. He took long strokes, from her forehead almost to her ass. All that thick brown hair that soon would drag across his chest.

"I don't remember the last time someone brushed my hair for me," she said softly. "I wasn't pampered."

"You'd better get used to it. I'm the type of man who likes to pamper his woman."

He let the soft-bristled brush go past her hair and over the curve of her ass. She shivered but said nothing, so he added it to the long strokes. Every time he reached the end of her hair, he spent more time massaging the round cheeks which flared out from the small of her back.

"Am I your woman?" she whispered.

He turned her around. The lamplight shone on her forehead. He used a finger to tilt her face up. He hadn't had a chance to look at her so closely before. Broad forehead, strong nose and blue eyes. A full mouth he had to taste. The first kiss was gentle and sweet, a hint of things to come. When she sighed and opened to him, he pressed his arm against her back and kissed her fully.

"That answer your question?" Patrick held her shoulders with his hands, putting space between them. He panted, his chest heaving from a pounding heart and a long kiss. "Or do you need more persuading?"

She tilted her head to one side. Her lips twitched. Only an inch separated his chest from the hard nubs of her nipples. The cotton nightgown was thick, but two peaks still pushed the fabric from her body. Her nostrils flared and the lamplight caught the sparkle in her eye.

"What did you have in mind?"

"Feet."

She shut her mouth and blinked up at him. She frowned. "What about my feet?"

* * * *

Instead of answering her, Patrick handed her the hairbrush and swept her into his arms. He made no comment about her size, but carried her as if she was as tiny as Jessie. She ended up on her back on the bed with her knees bent. He removed a small glass bottle from his pocket, sat on the bed, and put her feet in his lap. She handed over the brush when he held out his hand for it.

He uncorked the bottle and poured a shiny liquid into his palm. He picked up her left foot and spread oil from ankle to toes. An aroma of citrus spread through the room. He corked the bottle and put it aside. His grin was infectious.

"Ever had your feet massaged?"

She shook her head. At first it tickled a bit as he wiggled her toes. She moaned when he pressed his thumb under the ball of her foot. She hadn't realized how much her feet hurt until he took the pain away. She closed her eyes and relaxed, letting him do whatever he wanted.

Neither of them spoke, though she could feel his presence like a warm quilt. He didn't dominate the room just by being there, like Ranger. He wasn't like Ben, either. If Ben was in the room, they were usually talking about something. With Patrick the silence, and his touch, was enough.

He worked his way up both her legs to the knees, pushing her nightgown as he went. She just lay there, enjoying his quiet touch. It wasn't sexual, yet as his hands rose higher on her legs, her pussy lips and breasts swelled. He slowed when he passed her knees. His fingers no longer dug into her muscles. Instead, they swept over her flesh.

"Time for this to come off," he said quietly. "Keep your eyes closed and let me do the work."

He followed his words with a soft kiss to her inner mid-thigh. She inhaled a breath. He chuckled and shifted to lift her hand. Four buttons, then a kiss on her exposed inner wrist. The same thing with her other hand. He lay them on the bed beside her hips and tugged on the ribbon holding her chest placket closed. Instead of just spreading the cotton, he pulled the ribbon out of the holes, slowly exposing her skin. He gave her another slow, gentle kiss, this one between her breasts.

"Lift your bottom and help me." She did as he asked. He removed her nightgown and moved off the bed. "You want to watch?"

She heard the challenge in his voice, and opened her eyes. He'd hung her nightgown up. His feet were bare, his shirt unbuttoned. She curled around onto her left side. He let his shirt slide off his shoulders. Though a bit smaller than Ranger, Patrick was still more muscular than Ben. He turned in a circle, arms up, wearing a cocky grin.

"You ready to see the rest?"

She faked a yawn. "Beth says if you've seen one man, you've seen them all."

Patrick scratched his chest. She watched his hand slowly descend to his trousers. He opened the buttons one by one. She clenched her thighs together, trying to hide her eagerness. He winked, proving how closely he watched her.

He carefully lifted out his cock and let his pants drop to the floor. His cock rose from a dark nest of curls. She watched as a drop formed at the tip, glistening in the bright lamp over her shoulder. Eager to feel him in her, she clenched her internal muscles.

"Beth might be right about seeing," he drawled. "But the doing is a whole 'nother thing."

His cock stood out, proud as a divining rod, as he approached the bed. He stopped with his thighs just inches from the edge of the mattress. His cock, aimed right at her, throbbed along with the vein in his neck.

A large drop of liquid shone on his tip. As she watched, it grew. She reached out her finger and caught it. She looked up at him and sucked her finger into her mouth. She pressed it in and out, just as she had Ranger's cock the night she pretended to be drunk.

Patrick's eyes widened. His nostrils flared as he inhaled. He stepped forward until his thighs pressed against the mattress.

"You want more than a finger to suck, or are you just teasing?"

Once again, he dared her. The bed was low, so she rolled onto her bottom and sat on the edge of the bed. He backed up enough to give her space. She caught his cock in her hands. It jerked, and another drop emerged. She bent her head and flicked it off with her tongue. His sweet musk enticed her so she slid her mouth over his large mushroom head. He cursed, and then grabbed her face and pushed her back gently.

"Glad to see you're not a tease. But another few minutes of that, and I'll be too far gone to stop."

He caught her legs under her knees and lifted, flipping her onto her back as he knelt. She slammed her arms down to catch herself, but he hauled her back toward himself.

"Now that's a pretty sight. Your pussy lips are all red and juicy." He winked. "Looks like you want me as much as I want you."

She opened her mouth to say something, but he kissed her swollen lower lips. All she could do was gasp. He started out gentle, his tongue skimming her flesh. He ignored her clit, concentrating on the lips.

After a few minutes, he moved to the tender area between there and her bottom. He flicked his way across it, ending up at her back hole. Ranger had put his fingers in there, driving her wild by twisting and bending them with his cock already in her. He switched from tongue to finger, gently pressing against her. She relaxed, remembering how good Ranger's finger had felt.

"Hmm, seems like someone's finger already been in here?" He looked at her from between her legs. "Or has it been more than a finger?"

She shook her head. "Just a finger," she squirmed when he twisted it, "but his cock was in my pussy as well."

"This when Ranger thought you were drunk?"

She nodded.

"You want me there tonight?"

Before she could answer he took her clit in his mouth and made his tongue dance over it. She shuddered at the intense jolt.

"Oh, yessss," she moaned.

He lifted his head, panting as hard as she. His brown eyes glittered above the wide, toothy smile that shone on her.

"Roll over, and let's get going."

He placed a blanket on the floor and helped her to roll over. He set her so she knelt but her upper half, to her hips, lay on the bed. He moved her hair to the side, pulling it from her face.

"You comfortable?"

She nodded. He moved until she could see his face. He looked solemn and eager.

"If you hurt, you tell me, and I'll back off. Anytime you want, you tell me to stop, and I will. You trust me?"

Ben wasn't a man to push her, and Ranger wanted to push her too fast. But Patrick seemed to know, and understand, her needs. She wanted to be pushed, but only so far and so fast.

"I trust you not to hurt me," she said.

He kissed her temple and turned to one side. He lifted a cup from the floor and set it on the mattress beside her hip.

"This lard will ease my way. Remember, if it hurts, tell me and I'll back off. We've got all night."

Chapter Thirty-Eight

Patrick's heart slammed into his chest so hard he thought it might explode. Florence lay on the bed, the right side of her face on the sheet, her long brown hair to the side. He had a perfect view of her back. Her shoulders slanted down to her waist before curving out into the finest butt he had ever seen. Not that he'd seen more than a handful of females, but even if there was a better one somewhere in the world, it didn't matter.

She was his, and she trusted him. Ben and Ranger had awakened her passion, showing her the joys of their mouths on her pussy, their cocks in it.

But it would be his cock that entered her ass and gave her pleasure for the first time.

Ranger was sometimes too eager, used to experienced women. But after he eased his cock into Florence and used his fingers on her clit to make her buck under him, she would be ready for Ranger and Ben.

He spread her thighs and slid his fingers into her slick folds. She tilted her ass up to encourage him while her pussy clenched his hand. She wanted more, all right. He played with her, making her think only about what he was doing now, and not what was to come.

One day, he would watch her riding Ben's cock. She'd lean forward to take him in her mouth. Ranger would knee behind and slowly shaft her ass. They'd keep her at a knife's edge until she couldn't take it anymore and exploded around them.

His cock throbbed, eager to plunge deep. But he wouldn't rush it. No, she needed to be frantic with need before he entered her there.

Patrick kept teasing her pussy, taking her near the edge and then backing off. His cock dripped with eagerness, but he held back. Finally, he scooped up some lard and pressed his finger into her ass for the first time. Though she relaxed and let him in, her virgin ass pressed tight against him. She moaned and pressed back against him as he gently stretched her. In and out, adding another finger, then another. By the time he could easily fit all four fingers in her, they were both sweating, panting, and shaking.

"This is the next step," he gasped.

He guided his cock into her eager pussy. He fought the demons of hell to not slam deep, again and again until he came in a blaze of glory. Instead, he settled himself in her and, once more, put a couple of finger in her ass. They went in easily.

She trembled, and he pulled out completely. She used words he didn't understand, but he figured were ladylike curses. Considering how close he was to the edge, and how long he'd been there, she was nowhere near as frustrated as he. But he was a man with a mission. He would not fail her.

"You ready?"

"I've been ready for hours!"

He spread lard on his cock and placed more at her brown dot. Shaking with effort, he pulled her cheeks apart and pressed the tip of his cock against the ring of pink that appeared.

"That's it. Push me out to let me in."

Her groan sounded as if it came from her toes. His was about the same.

The tight walls of her ass grabbed his cock. They put a sweet pressure on him that he'd never felt before. He grimaced, gritting his teeth to hold back from taking her. Instead, he stayed still and let her push herself onto him.

Damn, Ranger was going to owe him so much!

Inch by slow inch he settled into her. She gripped the sheets with her fists and slowly impaled herself until his balls tapped against her pussy. He fell forward, resting his elbows on the bed on either side of her back as he fought to breathe.

She wiggled under him, and he knelt up. He eased himself almost out, and then in again. Every pleasure point in his cock was on high alert, ready to blow. But she wasn't ready yet. He sped up, giving her an extra jolt when he hit home so his balls would slap against her. They slapped lightly, as he wouldn't put his cock all the way in. She wasn't ready for that.

He kept his eyes closed, knowing the sight of his cock sliding in and out of her round ass would send him over the edge.

"You like this, Mrs. Elliott?" He could only manage one word per breath.

"More!" she growled.

He reached under her with his clean hand and squeezed her breast. After a moment, he dropped his hand to her clit. He drew circles around it, his finger jerking. He could feel the orgasm building, his balls tightening in a way that he knew he could never hold back. He held onto her right hip with one hand, pulling and pushing her as he slid in and out.

He used his left hand directly on her clit, pressing down and wiggling it. She cried out and went crazy, slamming herself back against him. He finally let himself see. Her back was flushed. Her hair tossed all over as she shook her head. His tanned hands held her hips.

And, between her white cheeks, his dark cock slid in and out like a piston.

His cock. In her ass. And she wanted him there.

He grabbed his cock, holding two fingers around it so he wouldn't go too deep. He found her clit with his other hand. She gasped as another orgasm hit her.

Energy gathered from the toes he braced on the floor, up his legs, though his thighs, and out his cock. He threw his head back and roared as his balls exploded.

Chapter Thirty-Nine

Florence sprawled over Patrick's chest. He'd cleaned them up, brought her a drink of cool water, and then climbed into bed. Her head was still spinning from the multiple orgasms. No doubt about it, Patrick's abilities to make her shatter were no less than Ranger or Ben's

"I hope that's not the last time we do that," he said quietly.

Her breath caught. How could she live without this? It wasn't just the sex. That was unbelievable and fantastic.

No, it was the way Patrick cared for her, before, during, and after. How he cuddled her now, slowly stroking her back as he stared at the ceiling.

"I don't want to lose you, either. It's just that—"

"It's just that Ranger has a chip on his shoulder the size of Texas." Patrick kissed her bare shoulder.

"I didn't know he couldn't read. But that has nothing to do with intelligence. I was thinking we could cut a hole out of a piece of paper so he only sees one word at a time. That should stop them moving around on the page. He might be able to read that way."

"Reading's just part of it," said Patrick. "I didn't realize how much he and Ben protected me from Fin and Hugh. Ross and Nevin went north after a couple of years, and the other two came to Texas. They wanted to grind us into the dirt. Fin damn near killed Ranger with that whip, but he could get over a physical hurt. But he was never the same after The MacDougal burned all his carvings."

"I swear, if I get within a hundred miles of those people, I would take a whip to them myself," said Florence. "Though, from what I've heard, Jessie would be at the front, riding Nightwind, whip in hand."

"No, she wouldn't. The horse is growing a colt." Patrick winked.
"And if Jessie isn't yet, she'll be growing her own baby pretty soon. It
will be Sin, riding that huge black Friesen of his, who'll head straight
for them at a gallop. Gillis, wearing his kilt, shirt and bonnet, will
brandish his claymore and bellow in Gaelic like a berserker. Ross and
Nevin will race their horses, silent and fast like their knives, and the
rest of us will be somewhere in between."

She laughed at the thought of seeing Gillis in full Highland rage,
as long as it was aimed at someone who deserved it.

"If anyone tries to hurt anyone in the family, I expect the same
thing will happen."

"Damn right," said Patrick. He reached a hand down and cupped
her bottom. "Nobody's gonna hurt what belongs to us, including our
women and children."

"I don't belong to you."

"Nope. By law you're the property of one Benjamin Elliott. But
since he'll be off lawyering a lot of the time, me and Ranger will have
to keep you in line."

She tried to sit up, but he easily held her down with his arm. He
moved his hand so that his fingers slid between her legs. In spite of
her irritation at his remark, a twinge of want struck. He moved his
arm to her breast, and she managed to push him away and sit up. She
scrambled off the bed before he could catch her.

"You think you can keep me in line, do you?"

"Yep."

Patrick stretched out. He yawned and crossed his arms behind his
head. She narrowed her eyes at his knowing smirk.

"And how to do intend to do that?"

He looked down. His cock swelled and began to rise.

"I think there's something about me that you can't get enough of,
Mrs. Elliott."

She crossed her arms under her breasts, purposely raising them and drawing his attention. His cock bobbed. She shook out her hair. When she was sure he watched, she raised her arms and ran her fingers through it. She let it fall so that it covered her front. The ends dangled above her pussy curls. Patrick's chest rose and fell quickly, proving he was not as relaxed as he pretended to be.

"I don't need you. I've got two other men eager to please me."

"Ben is somewhere between here and Helena, and Ranger's sleeping in Ross or Trace's barn. But I'm here, and ready to go again. You up for it, pretty lady?"

Chapter Forty

"If it isn't some of the Tanner's Ford boys. Good evening, gentlemen."

The annoying English accent slid over Ben's shoulder like a water snake over wet grass. It was just as welcome. Nevin, looking over Ben's shoulder, had his stoic Indian face on. Jack, to his left, looked like he'd eaten a dead skunk and his belly suddenly realized it.

Ben stood up and turned around. A man about his size wearing an Eastern suit nodded. He had slicked-down, dark hair parted in the middle, a narrow moustache, and a politician's practiced smile.

"I don't believe we've met," said Ben. He settled his shoulders, letting his right hand drop to his side. His coat was always open for easy access.

"You must be the missing Elliott. Benjamin, I believe it is." The man nodded. "I hear you're a lawyer. We need men like you." He waved a hand around the saloon. "Are you enjoying your evening? The Nugget is one of my establishments."

"Girls look good, but the whiskey's got too much snake juice for my liking," replied Jack.

He slowly got to his feet, hands loose and jaw set. Nevin did the same, quietly backing them up. The three of them had fought over who got to sit facing the room. Three men who wanted their back to a wall had a hard time sitting around a table. Ben lost out that night.

"Ben, this here is Mister Frederick Smythe," said Jack. "He's building that two-story house beside the mercantile. Smythe's already met our cousin, Nevin MacDougal."

Ben nodded politely. Nevin didn't. This was the man who lost the

Double Diamond to Jessie's husband, Ace. He'd threatened to make Ace pay for the insult, as well as the loss. He was also rumored to have arranged for the killing of the family who had owned the ranch previously. The disappearance of Molly, the pretty, fifteen-year-old daughter, and her subsequent discovery and rescue from an unsavory brothel down the street, was also linked to the man.

Ben didn't let any of that show. He believed in innocent until proven guilty in a court of law. Accusations were proof of nothing. However, the man irritated him just by being in the same room.

"Care to join us?" Ben warned Jack to be quiet with an eyebrow twitch. "Nevin and I don't often drink whiskey, so perhaps you could suggest something that we would find more palatable."

Without looking away, Smythe lifted his hand and snapped his fingers. A very pretty, very young woman in a low-cut dress approached carrying a tray. She set a bottle and four glasses on the table and scurried away. Smythe's eyes finally left Ben's to linger on her ass. Ben figured she might be sixteen. Maybe.

"Perhaps this bottle will suit you better." Smythe turned his attention to Jack, still ignoring Nevin.

No matter how much Jack might hate the man, he had power. They weren't afraid of that power. They wanted to harness it. To do that, they had to build bridges. Ben had drummed the point into Jack's head during their time in Helena. As part of the trip, they'd all met with Judge Ambrose Thatcher, who Nevin had met a few weeks earlier.

Finan MacDougal Junior had paid for the judge to come from Helena to Tanner's Ford to rule on Ross and Nevin's legitimacy. Since Beth found the wedding certificate for Finan MacDougal and Sunbird, the judge ruled they were fully entitled to inherit. Their children would be as well. A furious Finan and his new bride left town early the next morning, heading for Texas. Judge Thatcher stayed in town a few days, though his scribe and assistant, a lawyer, hurried home to his wife. Thatcher seemed to enjoy his stay in

Tanner's Ford. Trace said something about the judge and Miss Lily having met years ago, before she started her business.

Smythe opened the bottle and poured four glasses. Many white men wouldn't enter a saloon if an Indian was inside, much less pour him a drink. He picked up his shot glass, motioning the others to do the same.

"May I propose a toast to prosperity?"

Ben took a glass, as did Jack and Nevin. It was a test, and all knew it.

"Prosperity," Ben said, and tossed it down.

The others followed. Nevin, still stoic, slammed his empty glass upside down on the table. Ben waited for his throat to recover before inhaling then wished he hadn't. He held back from coughing and choking, though it was close.

"That's a better grade of whiskey, for sure," said Jack. He smacked his lips and gestured for them to sit. Ben also put his glass upside down. A beer appeared at his elbow. He nodded his thanks to the girl, who averted her eyes and served Nevin the same. He also nodded his thanks, receiving a ghost of a smile in return.

"You can have her for the night if you like," said Smythe, watching them closely. "She's new, not quite broken to harness yet. Maybe you three could show her a few things to settle her down. I hear you boys like sharing your women."

"We are all married men, Mr. Smythe," said Ben. "I, myself, have been married only a few weeks. We each made promises to our wives before God, and Elliotts keep their promises."

"An admirable trait," said Smythe. "I don't believe marriage has to curtail a man's pleasure, but suit yourself." He poured another shot for Jack and himself. Ben tried his beer, which was from a tap much better than anything he'd had in Bannack City before. He still wouldn't recommend Smythe's establishment.

"Perhaps you gentlemen could send a message for me." Smythe leaned back, sipping his whiskey. "Ever since that unfortunate incident with Mrs. Ross MacDougal, when our meeting was interrupted, we've been unable to continue our discussions."

Ben looked at Jack, who explained. "Amelia was kidnapped. Ross's ravens tracked us down in town and interrupted our meeting. We figured that was more important than talking about the cattle that Smythe wanted to buy." He turned to Smythe. "You ever get your cattle?"

"I arranged to purchase some from the J Bar C. Mayor Rivers is holding them on his land for me. But we were also discussing buying railroad land, and there is that matter of water rights to sort out. Mr. Jennet, Tanner's Ford's banker, is still interested in being part of our discussions. We'd like to meet further on the subject. As you're a lawyer, you would be very welcome to attend," he added to Ben. "I'd appreciate the MacDougals attending as well." He finally looked at Nevin, who gave a barely perceptual nod.

"I'll pass the word to Trace," said Jack. "But nothing's going to happen until we sell those yearlings."

Smythe nodded. His eyes continually roved the room, as if not sure if someone was going to steal from him or stab him. Likely both.

"I will be leaving for the East in a few weeks. I have meetings in Washington over the winter. Having initial plans in place beforehand would be to everyone's advantage."

"What about that fine home you're building?" asked Ben. "I hear you haven't been in town for some time."

"I have fingers in many pies, Mr. Elliott," he replied smugly. "But rest assured, I fully intend to have a comfortable home in Tanner's Ford. In fact, one of my duties this winter will be to purchase furniture. It should arrive in the spring. By the time I return in June, everything should be ready for me."

"How you going to set it up when you're not around? Not too many housekeepers available out here." Jack pointed out the obvious, which was an insult in itself.

"Too true," replied Smythe with a tight smile. "Therefore, I intend to send one out with my furniture."

"Better bring a couple of housekeepers with you," said Jack. "Single women have a tendency to quit and get married. There's still three sets of bachelors ranching in the valley, along with a passel of miners and all."

"Quite," said Smythe. "I shall keep that in mind." He glanced around the room. "How are the two young ladies that you gentlemen rescued? Have they been able to identify the brutes that attacked them?"

Ben caught the sudden increase in tension in the set of Smythe's shoulders and the way his jaw muscles bunched. It wasn't proof of his involvement in the crimes, but the man was certainly interested in discovering if there was a trail. Ben would give him the truth, but as little of it as possible. The men who attacked Molly Sinclair and Sarah Unsworth would kill them if they thought the young women could identify them.

"Miss Sinclair said she had to wear a mask that covered her eyes whenever the man holding her was in the room. A second man, far more brutal than the first, also made sure she couldn't identify his face. Miss Unsworth said the same."

"It would be a shame if the perpetrators were not brought to justice," said Smythe, finally meeting Ben's eyes. His shoulders and jaw were now relaxed, another tidbit to add to growing evidence of the man's guilt.

While the women did not see the men who attacked them, they did have other senses. They would have heard voices, smelled, touched, and, God forbid, tasted. Sheriff Chambers had not questioned them on it yet. They were still too fragile from the attacks to be pushed into remembering them again. Over time, a body of evidence would emerge.

Ben had learned that Ross was cheated of killing two members of the gang who attacked and killed his young cousin so many years ago. Someone snuck into the jail and shot Josephus and Octavius Browne before they could spill the name of the last gang member.

The decent men of Tanner's Ford were just as eager to ensure whoever did this to Molly and Sarah died slowly and painfully. They now understood why Ross wished to use his skinning knives on the men, taking weeks for the process to be complete before stabbing them in the heart as a final act.

"Let me know if there is anything I can do to help," said Smythe with another crocodile smile. He rose to his feet when a commotion broke out by the bar. "Enjoy the rest of the bottle, gentlemen. I look forward to that meeting."

As soon as he left, Jack finished his glass and recorked the bottle. He stood up, carrying his prize. The others followed. They waited until they were back in their hotel room, one not owned by Smythe, before speaking again. Jack rolled the bottle in a shirt and set it in his saddlebag.

"This is going to Ace, to replace the one he sacrificed that night he decided to get hitched to Jessie."

"You going to tell him where it came from?" asked Nevin.

"Yep. Knowing I took it from Smythe will make the whiskey go down even easier." Jack yawned and started unbuttoning his shirt.

"Smythe was too interested in finding out if the girls knew anything," said Nevin.

Ben nodded his agreement. "And I want to know what kind of game he's playing with railroad land, and why he wants us involved."

"Not tonight," said Jack. "Tomorrow we've got a long day in the saddle, and then we'll be home with our wives."

"Wonder how big Amelia is now?" mused Nevin. "Her belly is growing faster than Beth's."

"Twins don't run in your family, do they?"

Nevin snorted a laugh and shook his head. "We're not like you Elliotts. One perfect baby at a time is better than two half-assed ones."

"I'm too tired to thump you tonight for that insult," said Jack.

"Enjoy this time, between morning sickness and too-big-to-breathe. Beth was randy as hell with James, and she's no different now." He then rubbed his palms, grinning widely. "I can't wait to show her how much I've missed her."

Ben listened to the two happy men talk. He missed Florence, but it was her personality and intelligence he missed more than her delectable body. She was his legal wife, but neither Jack nor Nevin were legally married. Did it bother them? Would it bother Ranger and Patrick?

"Neither of you are legally married to the women you consider wives," he blurted.

Nevin gave Jack a speaking glance. They both turned to Ben, but Jack spoke. "What's that got to do with anything?"

"I promised Ranger I'd bring him a wife, but I didn't find one who met his list." He paced across the room and back, three steps each way. "It was my fault, as I didn't even look for one until it was too late. That's why I took the train from Philadelphia instead of Charleston."

"You heard there was a Bride Train, so you hopped on board, figuring that's all it would take to find Ranger a wife?" Jack crossed his arms and leaned a shoulder against the wall. His expression showed how unimpressed he was.

"Something like that. By that point I wasn't thinking straight. Just wanted to get home. Then Florence fell in my lap and—"

"Whoa!" Nevin held up his hand. His dark eyes glittered. "You telling us you didn't even go looking for a wife? That a woman just fell into your lap, so you married her?"

"The train went around a bend just as Florence entered the carriage. She had Johnny in one hand and Emma in the other. She went sideways and I caught her and hauled her into my lap before she could fall on the floor. She was most grateful."

"You two sound like a couple of cackling hens," groused Ben a moment later, when the other two still hadn't stopped laughing.

"Wait until the others find this out," said Jack. "Mr. Big Bug Lawyer's life is so easy that women fall into his lap."

"Yes, but we all know Florence is the last woman Ranger would choose to spend the rest of his life with." Ben scratched his head as if he had a sudden, ferocious, itch. "Does it bother you that Trace and Ross are legal husbands, that any children belong to them?"

"Why should it?" asked Jack. He shrugged. "We all know the truth. It was only chance that sent Trace to town the night he got married to Beth. The sheriff needed someone, other than that bastard Joe Sheldrake, to marry her. Anyone in the valley would have suited Beth better than that sadist."

"Trace says Beth loves you all, and you love her back," said Ben.

"Sometimes my big brother has a big mouth," groused Jack. A faint tinge of pink appeared on his cheek.

"If you could see your face!" Nevin broke out in a laugh, making Jack scowl all the more. "There's nothing wrong with loving your wife with all your heart, as she loves you." Nevin sat on the bed and pulled off his boots. "I was supposed to marry Amelia. She signed the marriage contract thinking it was me, packed up her life and headed west. But Gillis forged Ross's signature on the papers. He knew no one would marry the MacDougal Devil once they met him. Turns out Amelia likes Ross just fine, and she loves Gillis because he makes her laugh."

Why does Amelia love you?" challenged Jack.

"Because I'm such a talented lover, of course," Nevin replied, as if everyone should easily recognize the fact.

"Same with me," said Jack. "Ain't our wives lucky to have us?"

"You don't want to marry someone else?"

"Hell, no! I've already got a wife I love." Nevin sobered and gave Ben direct, honest look. "I don't know how Gil got over losing Prudence, if he loved her as deeply as I do Amelia. I think it was only Hope, and then Amelia, that gave him a reason to live. And now he's back the way he ever was, except now and then when he thinks of

Prue."

"What's this all about, Ben?" demanded Jack. "You're burning sleep time."

Ben gave up trying to think of an easier way to state his problem. "Florence isn't sure about sharing. She and Ranger get along like black powder and a spark."

"That's the best type of wife to have," said Jack. His grin was back. "The spark is what keeps life interesting. Tell her to try it, and she'll realize she likes it. Three men, all wanting to please her. What more can a woman want?"

"Sleep. Chocolate. Hot baths. Flowers. Her feet and back rubbed. Someone else making supper," said Nevin quietly, counting on his fingers. The other two ignored him.

"Florence has been with all three of us and enjoyed it. The only thing is, she and Ranger..." He scratched the back of his neck. "I asked Ranger to bed her that first time."

"You gave up your wife's first night to your twin?" Jack's eyebrows almost reached his hairline. "There's no way on God's green earth that I'd do that for Simon."

"I made a promise to Ranger long ago. I said I'd bring a wife home for him." Ben shoved his fists in his pockets and kicked at the bed frame with the toe of his boot, unable to look them in the eye. "He also has a lot more experience with women. I wanted Florence to really enjoy her first time."

"Did she know it was Ranger?" Nevin couldn't keep the smirk from lifting one end of his mouth. "Any woman with experience who wrapped her arms around you would know the minute she did it to Ranger that he was someone different. He's got muscles from working the ranch. You've been riding a chair for too long."

"Ranger took a few moments to get her gasping before he told her. He was ready to stop, but she told him to keep going. Beth had already told her about the sharing. In any case, he soon had her screaming. She fell asleep, and I slid in beside her. She was ready for more. I left her wanting in the morning, so she went after Ranger in the barn. She was so demanding he went along with it, blindfolding her. Patrick gave her another orgasm when she demanded more and Ranger was out of ammunition. When I came home from a day on the ranch, she was sheepish about what she did."

"This all happened, and then you rode out with us?"

"I thought it was for the best. Florence said she had to get to know Ranger and Patrick with her clothes on. They avoided each other for a few days, using me as a buffer. I decided I would get out of the way and let them settle it between them. After all, I had to get this business done before winter set in."

"Going away might not have been a good idea," said Nevin. "If she's angry—"

"She's angry, all right, and Ranger says he won't touch her unless she begs him to."

"Damn, that poor boy," said Jack sarcastically. He and Nevin shared a grin. "If she's stubborn like Beth, that ain't gonna happen. She'll get her knickers in a twist rather than give in." He pounded Ben on the back in a brotherly imitation of a hug, though his grin was evil with delight. "Brother, you are up the flume."

"I wanted her to learn to care about all three of us."

"Our wives love each of us," said Nevin. "How much depends on who she's got a mad on with, but the love is deep." His lip twitched. "Sounds like you're still at the heavy lust and light caring stage. It takes a while before you realize what the real feeling is."

"What feeling?" asked Ben.

"I don't know about anyone else, but there's something here," Nevin tapped his breastbone, "that hurts when Amelia's unhappy. I want to do anything to help make her happy again. Massage her sore feet, rub her back, cook supper, or take her to bed. And when we lie down, just holding her close while she sleeps can do more for me than the wildest sex."

"Speak for yourself." Jack looked down at his tented pants. "Just talking about it makes me so horny I want to bury myself inside Beth for a week. A bout of wild sex suits me fine, anytime."

"Maybe they've worked it out by now." Ben said the words with more hope than he felt inside. "Being away like this might have pushed Ranger and Florence into bed."

"Maybe, if Florence is like Beth," said Jack. "My wife can't go more than a couple of days without at least one of us giving her release." He sighed and rubbed his rising cock with his knuckles.

"If they're that contrary with each other, I expect they won't admit they want to rip each other's clothes off," said Nevin.

"I suppose Patrick could help her with that," said Ben.

Jack yawned and stretched. He dropped his pants, leaving him in red flannel and a hard-on, and climbed into bed. "There's nothing you can do tonight, and I'm tired. Worse, I'm not sleeping with Beth tonight."

"If she won't accept Ranger and Patrick fully, we have to divorce," said Ben, ignoring his brother. He sighed from the depths of his lungs. "Considering how common that is in Virginia City, she might not blink at the thought. She's got some money, and the Elliott name will protect her until she finds another husband. If, that is, she wants one."

"Did she enjoy what Ranger showed her?" Nevin looked solemn, but Ben caught the glint of humor.

"That's the thing," replied Ben. "She enjoyed it so much she attacked Ranger in the barn the next day and demanded he service her right there!"

"Then she won't want to go without for long, now she knows about good sex." Jack chimed in with his two cents worth.

"I thought you were going to sleep."

"How, when you two are talking about hot sex? That, and good cooking, is what a man wants in a wife."

Ben scowled. "I want more than that. I want a woman who will talk with me, who'll welcome me home with a smile and open arms."

He scratched his head with both hands. "But I won't share a bed with her while my twin and little brother sleep on a hard floor."

"Then you'd better have a good talk with her when you return. Once the snow hits, she'll be stuck in the cabin for the winter," said Nevin, nodding solemnly. "Maybe you've forgotten how deep the snow falls in those passes. You've been gone, what, eight years?"

Jack sniggered. Nevin caught Jack's thought and the corner of one lip curled up. Ben looked from one to the other and finally understood.

"You're right. Florence doesn't know about winter here." They shook their heads at him finally catching on, their smiles growing with his. "If I can keep her on the Bitterroot until the passes close, she won't be going anywhere until spring. That will give me at least five months to convince her."

"Or start a baby. Women change their minds about things once they've got a little one growing in them. They settle into their nest a bit deeper," said Jack.

To do that, Ben would have to make sure one of his brothers spent a few nights a month with Florence. Was it possible? But what did he have to lose?

"For all you know, your dear wife has jumped both of your brother's bones while you've been away," said Jack. "She might be planning a foursome as soon as you get home."

"I guess I'll be finding that out tomorrow."

"If she stays, Jessie has a book. It's got lots of ideas," said Nevin.

"Florence has crates and crates of books. Why would I want one more?"

The other two exchanged a look. They both broke into shit-eating grins.

"This is a picture book. It has drawings of about every damn way one, two, or three men can satisfy a woman, as well as themselves," explained Jack.

"Page eight is my favorite," said Nevin. He sighed and closed his eyes. A wide smile appeared. "She rides one man, leaning forward so her breasts are near. She takes the second man in her mouth. The third one kneels behind and takes her ass."

Ben choked. "How many pages are there in that book?"

Jack smirked. "Enough to get all four of you through a cold Montana winter."

Chapter Forty-One

"There's Patrick and Ranger by the hotel," said Ben. "If they're both here, Florence can't be far. You two go catch up with your own wives."

Nevin and Jack waved as they rode past the hotel. As soon as they passed Doc Henley's place they sped up, racing to get home. Ben walked his tired horse over to the hotel.

"Who's buying?" He looked from one brother to the other. "I've been eating Jack's dust for the last ten miles. I need something to drink."

"We can't go into Baldy's Saloon," said Patrick. "Ranger's in such a foul mood that he'd end up getting us in a fight, and I've got other plans for the evening."

"If Ben's home, maybe you're not sharing his wife's bed again tonight," snarled Ranger.

"Since you haven't been home in days, you wouldn't know that all we've done is cuddle."

"Since when?" growled Ranger.

"Since after that first night, when you stormed off to Trace's. I've been working hard while you're out traipsing around the valley."

"Boys, can we continue this discussion somewhere other than the main street?" Ben slowly dismounted. He wasn't sure if it was leather he heard creaking, or if it was his body. He took his saddlebags off and placed them over his shoulder.

"Miss Lily might sell us a few beers," said Patrick. "We could sit out behind her place."

Ben tossed a nickel to Billy O'Keefe, who grinned and nodded.

The boy took the reins from Ben and brought his horse to the water trough. Ben hobbled a couple of steps before his legs stretched out again. The three of them cut across the yellowing grass behind Mrs. Dawes' home, heading for Rosa's kitchen door.

"The reason we only cuddled is because Florence is all worked up about leaving the children behind," said Patrick. "She knows they'd be better off here in the valley, so won't take 'em with her. But I'm trying to make her see she doesn't have to leave."

"I hoped you'd work things out while I was away," Ben said to Ranger. "You seemed to enjoy bedding Florence. Can't you get along with her the rest of the time?" When Ranger just stared, his face like stone, Ben sighed and rubbed his sore forehead. "Does she want a divorce?"

"No, she wants the blockhead here to grow up," said Patrick, nodding at Ranger. "If he would just—"

"What the hell?"

Ben ignored Ranger's yell. Instead, he stopped and looked at Patrick. His youngest brother stared back, jaw set in the best Elliott tradition. The glint in his eye dared Ben to make a comment.

"You want to explain that?" asked Ben quietly.

"Florence is my woman, as well as yours and Ranger's," Patrick said to Ben. "I like her smarts, her book learning, and the way she can laugh, in bed and out. I want her to stay, but she won't make you choose. If Ranger doesn't get off his high horse and start acting like the man he says he is, she'll be gone, and we'll be worse off than before."

"How can we be worse off?" Ranger glared murderously at Patrick.

"Because when she leaves she'll rip another hole in our hearts. We'll be lonely for something that we didn't used to know existed."

"Speak for yourself," scoffed Ranger. "I won't miss her."

"I know you miss that damned kitten, so how can you say that about Florence?"

"She lied to me!"

Patrick stood belly to belly with Ranger. "And what do you call taking her husband's place on her wedding night?" He almost growled the words.

"That was different, and she knew it was me. But she pretended she was drunk just so I'd take her to bed!"

"Gee, Range," replied Patrick with heavy sarcasm, "and you only got mad when you found out she knew exactly what she was doing with you, and enjoyed every bit of it when you thought she wouldn't remember anything? Sounds to me like the two of you are even now."

Ben hadn't seen Patrick stand up to Ranger like this way before. Nor had Ranger acted so defensive. An awful lot must have happened while he was in Helena. Patrick was all grown up, and Ranger was hurting so bad Ben could almost see him bleed. He kept his mouth shut and let them argue, since it seemed his twin was actually listening for once.

"I want Florence, Ben wants her, and you want her, even if you're too stubborn to admit it. She hurt you? Well, dammit, grow up and join the rest of us. Sometimes, love hurts." Patrick dropped the attitude and sighed. "All of us lost Ma, Range. Not just you. People die." He shrugged. "Maybe Florence will die like Prudence. Gillis lost the woman he loved, but is he dead? Nope. He's still hurting, but he loves Amelia and Hope, and life goes on. They're going to have twins in a few months. New life to celebrate the future rather than complaining about the past. I may be the youngest in this family, but at least I can see things and accept them. I want Florence to swell with our children. All of ours."

"Amelia's having twins?"

Patrick stared at Ranger for a moment, both of them ignoring Ben, before finally Patrick looked over.

"Auntie says twins, and Doc agrees. Ross damn near carries her everywhere, even to the privy. Poor woman can't wait to have it over with." He dropped his head for a moment and then looked Ben in the eyes. "If Ranger can get his head out of his ass and act like a man, maybe Florence will realize he's worth having around."

"You seem awful full of yourself all of a sudden," said Ranger to Patrick in a dangerously low voice.

"Since you've been away from the ranch, my ego's had a chance to inflate. Usually there's no room for it, because yours takes over," replied Patrick. He sighed when Ranger's face turned even redder. "That was a joke, Range. Dammit, you're so wrapped up in this thing that you're like a wolf with a muzzle full of porcupine quills."

They stared at each other, Patrick with rapidly decreasing patience and Ranger with a stoic mask of indifference that Ben saw on him all those years in Texas. Ben put a hand on each brother's shoulder.

"Do you feel like there's a hole ripped in your heart that only one woman can fill? Because I do. I didn't know what it was until Nev told me last night. He says that need is called love. When Florence isn't near, the hole opens so big it's like to swallow me." Ben looked down and kicked a dry weed. "You're my twin, Range. I never said I loved you because you were always there, part of me. Please don't make me choose between having a wife, or a brother." He met Ranger's tortured eyes. "I'm selfish. I want you both."

Ranger stared back for a few moments and then swore. Quiet, slow and vicious. Ben and Patrick waited for him to finish. It took a while, and he never repeated himself once, in English or Gaelic. He finally exhaled, shook his head and rolled his shoulders. "Damn. I thought that hollow feeling was hunger, and the pain was from a bad piece of meat."

Ben quirked an eyebrow. "Was that a joke? If so, it's not a very good one."

"Yeah, well, I'm out of practice," he growled. "But this thing with Florence isn't over. She's too damn uppity, shoving my face in things that are none of her business. I ain't going nowhere near the Bitterroot."

"Fine. Act like a mule," said Patrick. "At least come to town tomorrow for those photographs that Trace wants done."

Ranger grunted a grudging agreement.

"You coming home, Ben?"

"Not yet, Patty. I've got some business to attend to with Miss Sarah Unsworth."

Chapter Forty-Two

Ben waved off his brothers and turned toward Rosa's kitchen. The last few uncomfortable minutes might be a piece of cake compared to what he had to do next. He knocked on Rosa's door and waited.

"Well, look what the cat dragged in. What you want, Mr. Bigshot Lawyer?"

"Afternoon, Miss Rosa. Would Miss Sarah Unsworth be here? I have something which might be hers, as well as some news."

Rosa scowled at him. "Sarah's been doing better, and I won't have you upsetting her."

"I'm sorry, this may be upsetting. But it's necessary, and I think she'll want to hear it. May I come in?"

Rosa reluctantly backed away and let him in. He inhaled cinnamon, vanilla, and other spices. The aroma of rich, dark coffee floated over the rest.

"I suppose you want some of my good coffee and a piece of Sarah's pie," Rosa automatically grumbled, but didn't wait for an answer before reaching for a plate.

"If you've been teaching her to bake, I expect that pie will be better than anything I've had in Helena."

"That gal has a knack. Starting tomorrow, she's got a job with Sophie, baking for the hotel. Just Fridays and weekends until we're snowed in, but she's well enough to work now."

Ben's tight shoulders dropped a couple of inches. "That's wonderful news. Is she with Sophie now?"

"No, she's next door at Mrs. Dawes's with Molly."

"How's Molly doing?"

Rosa turned her back to get a knife. Ben knew they were kept as sharp as the ones Ross carried. She knew how to use them, as well.

"Molly's young enough that she's getting over it pretty quick. Luckily she just had that one bad time. The men in the whorehouse who wanted a virgin treated her fairly well, and there was only a few of them."

"She say anything more about the man who took her from her parents, or the one who hurt her?"

Rosa shook her head and cut a piece of pie. "You know she had to wear a mask whenever he was around?"

Ben nodded. "Did she say anything yet to identify him?"

"She said he smoked cigars, but so do a lot of men." Rosa looked at Ben. "She said he kept her locked up in a very nice room until her sixteenth birthday. He treated her like a lover that night, and for a couple more. Then he let another man into her room. That one hurt her bad all night. But she got her woman's time the next day and that sickened him, thank goodness. He hauled her to Bannack City and sold her to that whorehouse. She was there another three days before they could sell her the first time."

Rosa gripped the knife so tightly that her fist turned white. She looked over Ben's head, her eyes wild.

"He deserves to be stuck with a hot poker and then skinned. Make it last a week or so to give him a taste of what pain is like."

Ben had a good idea it was another man, or likely men, that Rosa had in mind. She had survived far worse than Molly or Sarah. Thanks to Doc, and helping the girls heal, she might someday allow Doc to kiss her cheek. Doc Henley was known to be a patient man.

"We're not giving up until both men are found, Rosa, and anyone else involved." Ben sat quietly until Rosa finally nodded. She turned her back to him, leaned on the counter, and took a couple of deep breaths.

"What's Miss Sarah doing at Mrs. Dawes's? Buying another hat?"

"Nope. She's moving over there to live. Molly's helping her

settle." Rosa set a piece of peach pie and a mug of black coffee on the table.

"Molly's staying here with me for now, though Doc figures it's time for her to find a more permanent place. I'll miss her, but she needs to be part of a family again." Rosa turned to tidy up a clean counter. "We've taken her for visits to the Double Diamond. She and those miner girls, Meggie and Bridie, get along well. Doc says Trace and Beth want to bring her home with them for the winter. With all the babies coming, an extra pair of young hands will be more useful there than here."

"You're going to miss her, aren't you?"

Rosa shrugged, still with her back to him. "No matter. The girl needs to move on. Just like Sarah."

Rosa cleared her throat and faced Ben. Though she blinked more than usual, no tears fell. Ben figured she'd learned long ago that tears, and screams of protest, didn't make one whit of difference to what happened to a woman.

"Mrs. Dawes found out she's a widow woman. Her husband's partner sent her a note and money from California. She turned her upstairs into a ladies boardinghouse, and Sarah's her first guest. When she's not working at the hotel, she'll help Mrs. Dawes with her millinery work. She's got a good eye, and can help women figure out what looks good on them."

"Did you get a courting hat, Miss Rosa?" Ben was pleased to see a hint of a blush rise from her collar.

"Doc said I couldn't go riding in his buggy without something on my head. Said he didn't want me to get a sunburn." She glared when he winked. "Eat that pie, Benjamin Elliott, or I'll throw it out!"

Ben obediently dug into the pie. In addition to peach he tasted a hint of spice. There was something in the crust as well. Lemon peel? The coffee was just as good, burning down his throat.

"How's Sarah going to handle seeing all those strange men coming into the hotel? Even if she stays in the kitchen, she has to get to work and back. It's starting to get dark earlier now with winter coming."

Rosa made a rude sound with her lips. "You sound like Gabe Downey. That man is so careful of Sarah that he asked about a job at the hotel."

Ben almost snorted coffee out his nose. "Gabe, working in town?"

"No one's gonna bother Miss Sarah if he's anywhere near."

Ben nodded his agreement. "Did he get the job?"

"Nope. But she might want someone to keep order once the word passes that a pretty, unmarried, lady is working at the Tanner's Ford Hotel. Finish your coffee while I get Sarah."

Ben obediently sipped his excellent coffee while he waited. Every minute or so he laughed and shook his head. Gabe was about Sin's height at six and a half feet, but far broader. The man resembled a grizzly on his hind legs, only less hairy. He tensed when the door behind him opened, but didn't turn around.

"Rosa said you wanted to see me, Mr. Elliott."

Ben stood and nodded politely. Rosa came in behind Sarah and quietly closed the door. She stood with her back to it. While Sarah looked nervous, at least she met his eyes this time. Her hair was starting to grow out. Terrified after being held captive for a few brutal weeks, she thought ugly meant safe. Cutting her long hair was her first step.

Doc explained that, because the young woman had absolutely no control over her life during that time, such an act was necessary. A woman's hair was her crowning glory, and Sarah believed her life, and all its potential glory, had been destroyed. Doc hoped she would heal as her hair grew. Moving out was a big step.

"I believe you know the rest of my family, Miss Unsworth. I'm Benjamin, Ranger's twin."

"You're the lawyer."

"Yes, ma'am. I've got something that may belong to you. It's in my saddlebags."

He moved slowly, knowing she still expected to be attacked. After even two weeks of beatings, it could take years before she would stop flinching when a man raised his hand. He removed a carpetbag and held it up.

"The Helena sheriff found this. Your name was inside." He placed it on the table and sat at the end farthest from her.

Sarah stared at it for a moment before opening it. She looked inside. Tears began to flow down her thin cheeks. She didn't bother to wipe them off. She brought out a thick black book. Her fingers traced the name inside the cover.

"My grandmother's Bible," she whispered. She bit her lip and reached in again. She closed her eyes and felt around the bottom. A cry burst from her. "And her pearls!" She withdrew the necklace with trembling fingers. She sat on the bench as if her legs gave out from under her. Only then did she wipe her eyes. Rosa stood behind her, resting her work-worn hands on Sarah's shaking shoulders.

Ben concentrated on sipping his coffee while she composed herself. When she seemed to be breathing halfway normal, he cleared his throat.

"The sheriff also sent some gold. It's your portion of the reward money."

The sheriff had insisted that Ben make it very clear the gold had nothing to do with what the young woman had been forced to endure for at least eight nights. This was not gold for whoring, or for being sold for the purpose, although it was found in the possession of the man guilty of selling her.

"Reward?" She didn't look up from the watch.

"You gave such an excellent description of the man who duped you that he was spotted in Helena."

"Did he treat another woman the same?"

"Yes, more than one, but he finally chose the wrong woman," said Ben with satisfaction. Sarah turned to him. "He tried to pull the same trick with a seemingly naïve young woman arriving by train from the

East. He didn't know that the woman, who called herself Betsy, was there to work with her sister, Big Nose Tess. Tess runs a whorehouse, with willing women. She is not a woman to be trifled with."

"What happened?"

"The man, calling himself Mr. Tierson, drugged Betsy and tried to sell her. The woman he took Betsy to knew she was Tess's sister as she'd seen a photograph. The owner went along, paying Mr. Tierson an enormous amount of gold for this seemingly innocent young woman. But her men followed him back to his hotel and confronted him. He denied it, but there was enough evidence in the room to prove his guilt."

"Was he arrested?"

Ben shook his head. "No, they brought him back to Big Nose Tess's establishment, along with the gold. Betsy confirmed his identity, and he ran into the street. Tess ran after him and somehow he ended up with a bullet in his gut. Of course, no one saw who did it."

Sarah smiled, just a little. She bit her lip. "Did he take a long time to die?"

Ben nodded. "I understand it was very painful for him." Sarah sat up, her head high.

"Serves him right!"

Ben dug into his saddlebag and pulled out two heavy deerhide bags. They clinked when he moved them.

"These are for you and Molly. The sheriff said that an equal amount would be given to any of the women they could find and release. There were a couple of other carpetbags in Mr. Tierson's room with identifying personal items."

"What happens next?" asked Rosa.

Ben looked at Sarah as he answered. "As far as anyone else is concerned, you arrived from out East and traveled to Tanner's Ford, where you met with friends. You found a job baking at the hotel and another working in a millinery shop. You live in a proper ladies' boardinghouse. At this point, your life is your own. There should be enough gold in that bag to take you anywhere you want, and let you be almost anything you wish. You could marry, set up a shop, or return East to your family."

Sarah clenched the pearl necklace. She looked down. "I have no family left."

Rosa squeezed Sarah's shoulders. "You have family here. Molly is your sister. I'm your aunt, as is Miss Lily. Doc is your uncle. And I suppose Mr. Elliott, here, could be your cousin or something."

"Family doesn't have to be related by blood," said Ben quietly. "After all, look at Gillis MacDougal. He's like my cousin, but thank goodness I don't look like him!" He managed to make Sarah produce a slight smile. "Anything you need, anytime, we'll be there for you, Miss Unsworth. You won't be alone ever again. People here care about you."

Tears filled Sarah's eyes. She blinked rapidly.

Rosa sniffed. "And some care more than others, like those Circle C men." She winked at Ben. "Gabriel Downey is quite taken with our Sarah, and Luke and Oz aren't far behind."

Sarah blushed and looked down. Ben and Rosa's eyes met across the table. Both knew that blush meant Sarah Unsworth was well on the way to healing.

"If you'll excuse me," said Ben. "Thanks very much for the pie and coffee. I wanted to stop by here first, but I'm eager to get home." He chuckled and stood up. "I haven't seen my wife in over a week, and I think she needs a kiss or two to remember who I am."

Chapter Forty-Three

Ben lay on his back with Florence sprawled across his chest. He drew slow ovals on her back with his fingers, running from her neck to under her cheeks and back up. She twitched when he ran over sensitive spots, so he made sure he kept doing it. He loved the way her breasts rubbed against him when she twitched.

Ranger made it clear he wouldn't come near, and Patrick was smart enough to stay away for a while. They were totally alone on the ranch for the first time.

"You were eager to see me, wife," said Ben. "Missed me some?"

"Your brothers tell you what happened while you were away?"

"Patrick said you're thinking of what might happen if you left, and that he didn't want you to go." He kissed the top of her head, marveling again at her wealth of thick hair. It was a pity that Sarah had lost hers, but better that than her life. "He also said you want my blockhead brother to grow up, get over whatever it was happened while I was away, and admit he doesn't want to live without you."

She lifted her head to look at him. "Patrick said that?"

Ben nodded. "I replied I was a selfish man because I want both you and Ranger with me."

Her smile faded to a scowl. "I can't believe you and that pompous, arrogant…man are twins! He makes me want to kick his backside and smack his sneering face at the same time."

Ben pulled her back onto his chest. "That's physically impossible, sweetheart. But I know what you mean. Ranger has that effect on a lot of people."

He went back to caressing her with slow loops, calming both of them.

"Patrick told him off for getting angry when he found out you seduced him. From what I heard, he was quite willing."

She groaned and pressed her face into his chest. "He told you what I did?"

Ben chuckled. "I wish I was here to see you catch Ranger like that. I bet he was easy to snare."

"Actually, I had to push him a lot. Beth told me how to do it, and—"

"Beth told you?"

"Well, Ranger was being an ass, refusing to touch me, so Patrick wouldn't, either."

"My hot little wife tricked Ranger into giving her orgasms?" Her head moved on his chest when he laughed. "I'll have to pen a letter to the railroad, thanking them for making that Bride Train pull around the corner at the moment you walked past me."

She again pushed up, this time glaring at him. "It's your fault I had to attack Ranger!"

"Mine?"

"You're the one who married me and showed me those wonderful feelings that I need!"

"You like what Ranger gives you as well, sweetheart." He grabbed her arms when she tried to roll off him, and the bed. "Face the truth. He does something for you that you very much enjoy. Something different from what I do."

She sank back against his chest. He wrapped his arms around her tense body.

"Is Patrick different again, or is he like me or Ranger?" asked Ben.

It took a few minutes, but she finally sighed and relaxed.

"Ranger is wild. You're sweet. Patrick is…Patrick."

He watched a flush rise from her belly all the way to her hairline. Her nipples rose, poking against him. When her breasts turned pink, they began to firm.

"What did Patrick do that made you blush like that, sweetheart?"

She groaned and covered her face with her free hand.

"Did he do something that neither I nor Ranger have done with you so far?"

She nodded. He trailed his hand under her cheeks and, this time, explored her pussy. His fingers came out wet. He touched one to her anus. She twitched, gasping. He pressed his wet finger into her. It slipped in far more easily than before. Her color deepened and her breathing increased. His cock swelled against her thigh.

"Did Patrick put his cock in here?"

She nodded her head, rubbing it against his chest. He pressed his finger in a bit more. She arched back to force it in even farther.

"And did you like it very much when he filled your ass with his cock?"

Another nod. He rewarded her with another finger, pulsing them in and out. His own cock, now fully recovered from their earlier session, throbbed with need.

"I want to watch my brothers make you scream as they show how much they love you. I want to watch you suck my cock while you ride Patrick, and Ranger takes your ass. Do you understand that sharing you shares our love?"

"You don't love me. None of you. You just want me for chores, and this."

"I like you for your ability to talk, and argue, with me on so many subjects. I like you taking care of us. Yes, I really enjoy sharing our bodies. But I love it when your eyes light up when you see me. I love it when I take you in my arms and you relax and sigh. I love coming home to a lamp in the window, supper in the warming oven, and your arms welcoming me to bed."

"I haven't put any lamps in the window for you, or supper in the warming oven," she grumbled.

"Not yet, but you will." He gave her a squeeze. "When I rode into the yard, you came running out with your arms wide open and the biggest smile I've ever seen."

"Yes, well, I was lonely and you happened to be home first. It doesn't mean anything. I'm happy to see Caramel, also."

Ben had locked the cat outside before carrying Florence upstairs. He only wanted one pussy in his bed, and it wasn't a flea-bitten cat.

"Yes, Florence, it means a lot, to both of us." He tilted her head, patiently waiting until she showed him shining blue eyes. "Your tears prove it, love."

"Love?"

"Nevin helped me to understand this feeling I have when I'm away from you. The whole time I was gone, I felt like there was a hole in my heart. It hurt, right here." He placed her palm on his rapidly beating heart. "But when I saw you running to meet me, that hole just up and disappeared."

He blinked hard. Florence's tears escaped down her cheeks, and he gave up the fight.

"You're crying," she whispered.

"I love you so damn much, Florence Elliott. I don't know how I can live without you."

"Benjamin Elliott! You used a swear word. You never swear!"

"If it helps prove how much I love you, then I'll do it again. Dammit, love, don't go away and leave us."

"I love you, but I won't take your brother away from you."

Ben stared at the woman who filled his dreams, day and night.

"You love me?"

"I loved you when you pulled your guns to protect Emma."

"You love me just because I protected your children?" He tried to keep the disappointment out of his voice, but found himself frowning.

"No, but the fact that you will protect us with your life adds to it." She rolled her eyes and sighed. "It took a while for me to realize it, but I fell in love with you when I told you what I wanted in a husband. When you smiled as if you understood that I needed to be treated as a whole person, with a brain and personality all my own, I was lost."

"I do understand what you mean."

"How? You're a man."

"Yes, but in Texas we were treated as many men treat their women. We were workhorses, bound to do whatever we were told without comment or complaint, or we'd be beaten. The MacDougal would feed us what he wanted, when and if he wanted. We had no say in what we wore or ate, where we slept, or what we were ordered to do."

"He did not touch you against your will."

She spoke the words quietly, but they hit deep. Taking a woman against her will was far too common, and accepted, for his liking. That was another set of laws he hoped that would someday be changed. But it would take a long time for men to give up their power over those weaker.

"No, we did not suffer the way Molly and Sarah did."

"Or Emma and Johnny's mother." Florence shuddered. "To think that brute wanted to purchase little Emma, and—"

Ben pulled her close and rocked her. "Shh, love. No one will ever touch one of our women, or children, against their will and live."

They lay there quietly for a long while. Ben thought of the laws, and how he could affect them. It wasn't enough to protect the land, if little girls grew up to be some man's property, to use and abuse as they chose.

As Jessie so eloquently put it, the quality of a person's brain had nothing to do with whether they had a cock hanging between their legs. Except, she would add, a man's brain didn't work when his cock did, whereas a woman's brain worked all the time. He expected Jessie would now agree that a woman's brain didn't work well during orgasm, either.

"How many children do you want?" she asked.

"Children? Where did that come from?"

"It came from what we were just doing. It might be silly, but the other wives insist sex tends to make one's belly round," she said with just enough sarcasm.

"You won't get round from me, love." She rolled back to look at him, but he'd learned to hide his hurt years ago. "I can't give you a baby, but Ranger and Patrick will give you as many as you want."

"Ben, what if that doctor was wrong? Didn't he say it was *unlikely* that you could make a child? That doesn't mean never. The way you and your brothers look, my babies could have any of you as a father. We'd never know." She wrinkled her nose. "At least, they'd be either yours or Patrick's, unless Ranger comes home again."

Ben's heart, which had almost stopped at her words, sped up as his brain raced through the possibilities.

"I could have a child," he whispered. He met her twinkling eyes. "Oh, sweetheart, you have no idea what that means to me."

"Since I was facing a lonely life without husband or children, yes, I think I do understand."

He placed his hand on her flat belly. "Our baby could be growing in there right now."

She gulped. "Maybe not quite yet. If Ranger doesn't want me, I'll have to leave—"

"You won't be going anyway, love. Ranger isn't that stubborn. It will take him a while, but he'll realize this is his home and we all want him here."

"I suppose I will see him tomorrow, when we go to town for those photographs," she said, dragging the words out.

"And right after is the cattle drive to Virginia City."

"Who's going?"

"Ranger, Patrick, and the Double Diamond four. Maybe Trace, since he hasn't been there in a long time."

"You're staying home?"

Ben nodded. His cock rose at the smile which played around her lips. She dropped her eyes and traced a pattern on his chest with her finger.

"So, we'll be alone for days?"

"Days, and nights, and more days. Perhaps even a couple of weeks."

"I can wait for that." She gave him an impish smile. She ran her palm over his cock. "But I can't wait for this." She pulled out of his arms, knelt, and engulfed him in her heat. "Mmmm, that's what I've been missing," she said.

She rose and fell on his cock, gripping him with her inner muscles. He set his hands lightly on her waist. She pouted and moved them to her breasts.

"What the lady wants, the lady gets," he said.

"The lady wants you to put your mouth to better use!"

Ben lifted his head and guided her breast, suckling her and nibbling her nipple. Though he'd just come, his need for her drove him to perform. She took what she wanted from him, grinding her clit against his pubic bone. She sat up again, gasping for breath and frantic for more. He took her breast in one hand and went after her clit with the other. Her orgasm hit, clamping on his cock. He grabbed her hips and slammed up, again and again, until he roared his eruption.

Chapter Forty-Four

Virginia City, one week later

"Have your man-to-man talk. I'm going to play faro," said Jessie to Ace. She poked him hard in the belly with her finger and gave Ranger a sisterly glare. "Be my coffin keeper, Patrick?"

Ace grunted and rubbed the spot as Patrick and Jessie headed to the card table. Henry nodded solemnly at his partners and followed. He pulled out the chair for Jessie to sit opposite the tobacco-spitting dealer. The man continued putting cards down. Patrick settled in the chair beside her and slid the red and white markers into place. The bored-looking dealer glanced up, stared at Jessie, frowned, and then spoke. Jessie slammed her poke down on the table with her left hand, leaving her right ready to pull her pistol. The dealer looked at Patrick and Henry, shrugged, and then shuffled the cards.

"You gonna let your wife gamble your gold away?"

"First," said Ace, using his one-inch advantage to look down his nose at Ranger, "I don't 'let' my wife do anything. She does as she pleases. Second, that's her gold, from selling her portion of our cattle. And third, she's been my wife for less than a month. Any bad habits of hers, you helped create." He gave his belly one last rub. "She ever poke you like that?"

Ranger snorted a laugh. "All the time. At first she used to hit us in the shoulder. As we grew and she didn't, her finger kept getting lower. Be grateful she doesn't poke you below the belt."

"Who says she doesn't?"

Ranger jerked his head back and grimaced. "Jeez—that's my

sister you're talking about."

"Yeah, but I married her."

"*We* married her," interrupted Sin. He handed each a whiskey. "You said 'I do' for Henry and me, but she's our woman."

"And now it's your turn," said Ace to Ranger. "A toast to your leg shackles." He and Sin lifted their shot glasses. Ranger's hand didn't move.

"Who says I'm getting married?"

His two brothers-in-law turned to him. While both Ace and Sin had muscles, neither had Ranger's strength. Ranger idly wondered if this was the time he'd find out if he could take both of them at once.

"You're not *getting* married, my boy, you *are* married," drawled Ace. "You just haven't accepted it yet." The two men held their shot glasses in their left hands, keeping their right hands loose and ready for action. Jessie would never forgive them if anyone got killed. Fighting, on the other hand, was a natural part of life.

Ranger flexed his hand.

"Don't."

Trace's hoarse rasp came over Ranger's right shoulder. He nonchalantly transferred his whiskey to his right hand and gulped it down. It burned all the way.

"Listen to Ace and Sin," said Trace. "Maybe they can pound some sense into that thick skull of yours." He waved his hand. A redhead wearing a dress that barely covered her assets, north and south, sashayed over.

"You boys look lonely. Need anything I can help you with?"

"Just a bottle of whiskey. The good stuff," said Trace.

She batted her eyes and licked her lips as she looked from one man to the other. "You boys celebratin' or something?"

"Yep," said Trace. He pointed to Ranger. "My brother just got married."

She gave a practiced pout. "Pity." Her hips swayed even more as she returned to the bar to get their whiskey.

Ranger watched his brothers-in-law admire the view. "Jessie don't mind you checking out other women?"

They all looked toward Jessie. She was oblivious to everything but the cards and pile of chips in front of her. Her back was toward them, but the dealer's red face said it all.

"She's more than enough to keep all three of us happy," said Sin quietly. He smiled when she jumped in the chair and cheered herself with enthusiasm. "But we're here to talk about your wife. Grab a chair."

He nodded his thanks for the bottle of whiskey and joined Ace at the table. Trace went over to stand between Patrick and Jessie, his looming presence helping to prove that Patrick and the shockingly dressed woman were not bumpkins to be fleeced.

Ace and Sin settled, leaving the chair facing the room free. Sin pulled the cork and poured two glasses. He waited, bottle tipped, for Ranger to join them. Ranger scowled at the grinning pair and took the empty chair. He slammed his empty glass down. Sin filled it and set the bottle on the table.

"Let's try that toast again, brother," said Ace. He lifted his glass, along with one aristocratic eyebrow. "A toast to your marriage, and your wife. To Florence Elliott."

"Florence, and wedded bliss," said Sin, and tossed the whiskey down. He grimaced and sucked air through his teeth.

"Florence," muttered Ranger. He tossed the drink back. This one burned as bad as the first whiskey, but the taste that lingered in his mouth was better.

Ace slammed his empty glass down. He shivered, grimacing like the others. "That's enough to kick a man into next week." He quickly refilled their glasses.

"What the hell is this all about?" Ranger leaned back, cradling his full glass. He balanced the chair on its back two legs and glowered at them.

"You, my friend, are making a grave mistake," said Ace. He

sprawled in his chair, seeming at ease, but his eyes were intense.

"It's mine to make."

"Not when it tears your brothers apart."

Ranger shot his body forward. The chair's front feet slammed onto the floor. Ace didn't as much as twitch. "Ben put you up to this? I swear, I'll—"

"You'll do what?" Sin jumped into the discussion with both feet. "Kick him out of your life because he gives a damn about your scarred hide?"

Their looks of disgust set Ranger's stomach churning. He felt bad enough without having two damn-near strangers rubbing in the fact he was keeping the others apart. He fought the urge to jump up and smash their faces into pulp. But using fists on someone else because you were angry with yourself was something Fin MacDougal would do. From the comment about his scarred back, they knew what else Fin liked to do. He settled on glaring at them.

Sin lifted the bottle. Ranger tossed down the contents in his glass and held it out for more. Sin refilled all three.

"Do you know how much Ace and I would give to have family that wants you? I'm not talking about parents and brothers who don't sneer or insult you the few times you see them. I mean someone who will stand up for you, no questions asked, just because you're his brother?"

"We gave up everything we knew, except each other, to come here," said Ace. He looked over to the faro table. Jessie's pile of chips had grown, as had the scowl on the dealer's face. He smiled fondly and turned back to the table.

"You had two parents who loved you, and still have five brothers, a sister, and three cousins. I have two, much older brothers. My parents hated each other, and the only reason my mother had me was to fulfill the contract of three sons so she could get the promised money and freedom. As soon as I was born and she was well enough to leave, she did. I expect I saw my father a handful of times, but I don't remember any of them."

"You're here. That's all that matters," Ranger grumbled into his glass.

Ace sipped his whiskey. He shrugged. "I finally realized the only reason my brothers tolerated me was to pay off their markers. There's a family history of gambling. Unfortunately, they don't know when to stop. I do."

"I have one brother, eight years older," said Sin, taking over for Ace. "I was the insurance policy. My mother is fair, like me. My brother resembles my father's side of the family. My father's family is shorter, and dark. Our blacksmith was tall, muscular, and blond. His cousin, the farrier, was the same. The kindest thing I can say of my mother, is that she was a flirt. She also loves dogs. Small, ankle-biting ones. Sons, she has no use for."

Ranger grunted. "Father was jealous?"

"Very. She was beautiful, and he kept her close until my brother was well on the way. After he was born, she had a lot more freedom, which she used. All my life I was accused of being the by-blow of one of those men." He picked up his glass and stared at it as if it held the answers he needed. "I wanted to believe it because my father was a violent wastrel who hated everything about me. The blacksmith and farrier were kind men, married to loving women. Until I went to school, I spent most of my free time with one or the other of them."

"Are you their son?"

Sin shook his head at Ranger's question. "They would not even raise their eyes to Lady Statham. I never met my mother's relatives, but just before we sailed, I saw a portrait of my maternal grandfather. Looking at the painting was like looking in a mirror. My mother slept with a lot of men, but I'm not a bastard."

"Is there a point to these sob stories?" Ranger spoke in a bored monotone, but his heart pounded hard.

"I hear you had a tough life after your parents died, not that it was anything as bad as what Ross MacDougal went through."

Ranger shrugged at Ace's comment. Ross was sent to his mother's people when he was five years old to stop his half brothers from "accidentally" killing him. He spent the next five years learning to be a warrior. It was not an easy process. Those skills were part of the reason he was called the MacDougal Devil.

"And now you're using your past as an excuse to destroy your future," said Sin. His lip pushed out in an exaggerated pout. "Poor, wee Ranger. Mummy and Daddy died and left him with big, bad MacDougals. Boo, hoo. He's never going to take a chance at happiness because he might lose it again. Boo, hoo, hoo." Sin's voice dripped with condescension and false pity.

Ranger's guts churned harder. "What's your point?"

"It's about time you counted your blessings instead of your hurts. You have problems reading. Big deal. You're a bloody good rancher and a natural leader. Put the past behind you. Reach out for something good instead of clutching your pain like a blanket."

"In other words," said Ace, "stop beating the devil around the stump and get in the game."

Ranger stared at Ace as if bored out of his mind. Sin slammed his fist on the table and he jumped.

"Act like a man instead of a sniveling child!" Sin blasted the words so loud a few men glanced over. Ace glared at them, and they quickly looked away.

"Why the hell do you care?"

Ace held up his hand. Sin, about to speak, fell back in his chair. He crossed his arms, stretched his legs out and glared at Ranger. If looks could set a man on fire, Ranger would be flaming like a torch. In contrast, Ace calmly looked Ranger in the eye and spoke quietly.

"You brought all those cattle from Texas with only a couple of men. No one guided you, but you did it in only five months, without anyone getting killed. You used Jessie to help us without our pride getting in the way." He swung his eyes to Jessie and back. "And by doing so, set us up to marry the sweetest, orneriest woman in

Christendom. You're now part of my family. I am not going to let you destroy what you and your brothers have spent your lives working to create."

"And what is that?" Ranger put as much sarcasm into the question as he could.

"The future your parents came all the way from Virginia to create. The Elliott family filling the valley with their children and grandchildren." Ace tapped on the table with his forefinger the way Jessie poked his belly. "What they gave up, including their lives, should not be thrown away because inside you're a frightened child."

Ranger shoved the chair back and jumped to his feet before the words settled on the table. "Nothin' scares me! Not one damned thing!"

Chapter Forty-Five

Ace leaned back to look up at Ranger. He lifted his hat, scratched his head, and settled it again. He sighed. "Nothing physical, no. But you're so broken inside that you couldn't even keep a kitten in case you got too attached to it."

"Somebody's done a whole lotta talkin' out of turn."

Ranger growled the words. His heart pounded so fast he thought it might jump out of his chest. He was ready to take them on, take on the whole damn room!

"Yeah, and they did it because they love you. Right now I can't think why." Sin sighed and tossed his hat on the table. "And doesn't that scare the shit right out of you? Because if they love you, then they'll be hurt if you leave." He waited a moment for his words to sink in. "You really want your family weeping and wailing because you're not man enough to belly up to the bar and speak the truth?" He shoved his chair back and stood up. "I'm finished here." Sin grabbed his hat, and the bottle, and stomped toward the faro game.

Ranger stood there, quivering with rage, or something else he didn't want to think about. He hauled air into his lungs. The room spun in a swirl of color and noise. When he was able to blink and clear his throat, he found Ace still in the same place, sipping the bottom half of his drink.

"It would be a bloody shame if you turned out to be as much of an old croaker as the ones we left behind," said Ace quietly. He gestured for Ranger to sit. Since he couldn't think of anything else to do— couldn't think at all—he dropped back into the chair.

"Death is part of life," said Ace. "So are pain, blizzards, floods, and drought. But life also can bring passion, and love, and children."

"They teach you that poetry crap in university?"

Ace ignored the comment. "I can't wait until Jessie gives us a cute little daughter with Sin's blonde hair, Jessie's big brown eyes, and an attitude as big as both of them."

They sat there for a while. Ranger stewed and grumbled while Ace stared into the distance, a small smile playing around one corner of his lips.

"Don't you want a son?"

Ace chuckled. "We want a dozen of each, but Jessie thinks differently." He shrugged. "We'll take whatever the good Lord brings us. From any source." He nodded to where Jessie sat, now surrounded by rough-looking men. "I want that woman to have the best time of her life. We'll be staying on a few days to give her that."

"Because you have money now?"

He shook his head. "No, because once she's big with our first child, she won't be able to do what she wants. No more galloping Nightwind just for the feeling of freedom it gives her. No riding the range day after day, dressing and acting however she likes."

"You going to tie her up?"

"Won't have to once her belly swells."

"She said she doesn't want to have a baby for a while."

Ace's eyes gleamed. "Your sister enjoys spending her nights with three men who are doing everything they can to give her a baby. It's going to happen, sooner rather than later."

Ranger winced and turned away. "Jeeze, I don't want to hear about that."

"I bet Florence is already carrying your child."

Ranger whipped his head back. "*My* child? Why not Ben's? Or Patrick's?" He swallowed, wishing he had a beer for his dry mouth.

"You'll never know. But you were her first and, from what Patrick tells me, she screams the loudest with you."

Ranger cursed to himself. He hadn't felt his ears burning this hot since Ma saw him at the creek with his pants down, thinking about the peddler's much older daughter. His hand pumped a cock harder than he'd known was possible. His mother had sweetly said something about being glad to know it was good for more than pissing up a tree, and she expected him to use it someday to make grandchildren for her.

He hadn't thought of that in years. Hadn't had time or inclination to think back to the good life before Ma and Pa died. Before they went to Texas.

Yeah, Ma wanted to fill the valley with grandchildren. He overheard her one evening. He was hiding in the corner, angry at himself for not being able to read what baby Patty could. She told Pa about sitting on the porch of a summer's evening, rocking great-grandchildren to sleep. When she snuffled back tears, Pa gently kissed her and took her to bed.

Damn, if only Ma could see Trace's son James, Gil's Hope, and the other babies on the way. He blinked rapidly, the smoke getting in his eyes. If only he could hand his baby to Ma to rock in that damned squeaky chair. She'd look up at him with a love that he hadn't seen in too damned long.

A love he saw between Beth and his brothers, and between the damned interfering man across from him and his sister. One that he saw hints of between Florence and Ben.

One he wished Florence would give him.

"She does love you," said Ace.

Ranger flicked his eyes over, caught by surprise.

"Florence," continued Ace. "Beth and Amelia saw it at the party, and again at the photograph session." He shrugged as if not understanding women. "They say she has different looks for you, Ben, and Patrick. She wants all three of you. We know you want her, but do you love her enough to tell her?"

Ace stood up. He placed his palms flat on the table and leaned over, forcing Ranger to look up.

"You've sat around many campfires. Sit too close, you get warm, but you may get burned." He stood up. "It's a risk. But it's bloody cold, dark, and lonely away from that fire."

He nodded once and walked away. Ranger sat, his mind blank, but reeling.

"Ready to go?"

"What?" Ranger stared up at Patrick.

"Sooner we get to sleep, the earlier we can head off in the morning. I want to go home to a bed full of Florence."

Ranger slowly stood. He straightened to his full height, making his back crack. He inhaled, and let it out. He lightly punched Patrick's shoulder.

"So do I, brother. So do I."

Chapter Forty-Six

A few flakes of snow began drifting when Ranger and Patrick reached Tanner's Ford. By the time they rode into the Bitterroot Ranch yard, the ground was white and large flakes muffled all sound. Snow fell straight down as if it meant business.

"I was hoping you'd get home before the worst hit," said Ben as they led their snow-covered horses into the barn.

"We stayed on to meet with that damn Smythe," said Ranger. "He served good whiskey but my trigger finger itched the whole damn time."

"What did he want?"

"He's looking for an agreement with our four ranches." Patrick shook snow off his shoulders. "Man didn't like being outnumbered seven to one. Trace let him talk but we didn't agree to much other than that we'd listen to him and his partners come spring."

"Partners?"

"Smythe wants us to meet with Mayor Orville Rivers and that banker, Hugh Jennet, over the winter," said Ranger. "He talked about water rights and buying up any mineral rights the railroad doesn't already own."

"Trace said we wouldn't be talking to anyone until you review the law and we all do some thinking about it."

Ben nodded. "We'll have to talk between us and establish what we want to accomplish here. Perhaps we should join the four ranches into a loose company arrangement of some type."

Ranger held up his hands. "Don't go all lawyer on me. I'm too damn cold and tired to think. All I know is that these horses need something warm inside them."

"I put on some warm mash with molasses in case you arrived home," said Ben. "I'll get it directly."

"We stopped at the hotel and bought some of Sarah's special pies. Instead of making them flat, she rolls them up." Patrick handed over the saddlebags. "They may be frozen, but I'm so hungry I don't care."

"You staying for dinner, Ranger?"

His twin looked up as he wiped snow off his horse. "How long you want me?"

"Forever good enough?"

They looked at each other for a long moment.

"That'll do."

Ranger looked down quickly, but his rough voice gave him away. Patrick's grin and nod silently added his vote.

"Good. It's plenty warm inside. Join us when you're ready."

Ben returned to the kitchen to let Florence know both brothers had arrived. He gave the warm mash to Patrick and headed back to the house. Florence rushed off to the privy. Smiling in anticipation, he completed the preparations for their homecoming.

Caramel was already fed and settled in his apple box near the stove. Ben stoked the stove to keep the upstairs warm for a while. Once they all got into bed, there'd be enough heat shared to keep anyone warm. He brought the food to the bedroom, hung the lamp from the overhead hook, and spread a blanket on the floor for a picnic. He filled an ewer with warm water and set it on the side table with a bar of rose-scented soap and a couple of flannels.

He also set a cup with a generous dollop of lard beside the bed.

Twenty minutes later, the four of them sat on the blanket, finishing supper. They all pretended there had never been problems between Florence and Ranger. However, neither of them would meet the other's eyes. Ben and Patrick tried to keep their laughter inside, but there was a lot of coughing going on.

After the cold outside, the house felt warm, so Patrick and Ranger had both stripped off their shirts. Their pants were wet from the snow, so they steamed near the stove. The men wore an old sheet, which had been ripped in two, around their waists.

Ben, not wanting to stand out, had stripped to his pants. He also wanted to surround Florence with near-naked men. The last three nights, with both his brothers away, he was too exhausted to play the husband. He also knew it would make her wick easier to light.

"These pasties Sarah's idea?" asked Florence. She looked at Patrick for an answer.

"Yep," replied Ranger quietly. "A man can't carry meat pies in his saddlebags. Sarah said her grannie used to make these and send them with her grandpa."

Florence flashed her eyes at Ranger and, just as quickly, dropped them. Even in the lamplight, her flush was easily seen. She'd spent the day baking up a storm. The stove kept the kitchen so hot that, since she was alone with Ben, she'd removed everything under her dress. She hadn't had time to put anything more on. Being surrounded by three half-naked, eager men kept her breasts hard and nipples taut.

Ranger and Patrick sat cross-legged on the blanket, loose sheets around their waists. Underneath, Ben was darn sure they sported erections as big as his own. Only, they were far more comfortable since nothing kept their cocks confined. He tried to shift to make more room, but wasn't successful. Patrick snickered, knowing what was going on.

Ben chewed the last bit of pastry and licked his fingers. "That's one appetite filled," he said. He winked at Florence. "You're dessert, my sweet."

* * * *

Three intense pairs of eyes stared at Florence. A prickle of awareness covered her skin as if a lightning strike landed a foot away from her body. She'd been nervous about Ranger's return for days, but when Ben said he'd come back to stay, she'd panicked. Part of her wanted to run into the storm and never come back. The other part, the one that remembered the extreme orgasms he provided, wanted to rip off her clothes and jump him.

"There's something that has to happen first," said Ben. He looked solemnly at each of them. "Florence has something to say."

"I do?"

Ben nodded. "We talked about love."

"Oh. That." She gulped and looked down. The lust, which just moments ago had risen like a flood, evaporated without a trace.

"You love me, don't you, wife?" She nodded without looking up. "Then tell my brothers that. To their faces."

She gathered her courage and faced them. Patrick grinned, his usual happy-go-lucky expression hiding the intensity he'd shown her. It would be back, but maybe not when others were around. Ranger's face was blank, but she sensed deep undercurrents.

"I love Ben. I know it's not something that I can pretend doesn't exist, because I tried. Patrick grew slowly on me. No." She shook her head. "It wasn't slowly, more like in spurts. That welcoming kiss sent a jolt through me, as did the bedtime kiss. While Ben was away, and Ranger visiting elsewhere"—she let a trace of sarcasm in—"Patrick and I got to know each other better. My love for him is different than that for Ben, but still deep."

When she glanced at Ranger this time, she saw a mixture of hope and fear.

"My love for Ranger is more complicated." She pushed her hair out of her face. "But then, so is the man." She met him head-on. "You've got a lot of love in you, but you've been taught to hide it. It still trickles out here and there, and I saw it when you thought I was drunk." She lowered her eyes, and then raised them again.

"I apologize for that. If I'd known it would be more than an evening of light fun, I would never have done it. But you showed me what I think is the real Ranger Elliott that night. Loving, fun, and very sweet."

"Don't tell anyone, or I won't be able to hold my head up again," he grumbled.

"You'll hold your head up any time you want," she replied. "You are a fine man, and will be a wonderful husband and father."

"You really think so?"

She nodded. "I wouldn't love you otherwise."

"For the record," interrupted Patrick, "I love Florence, too, and not just what's waiting for us under that thin cotton dress." He waggled his eyebrows in emphasis, and then looked straight at her without any joking. "I love the way you laugh, in bed and out. I like learning book things from you, and teaching you other stuff. You're a lady, like Ma was."

A wicked smile appeared. He stared at her swollen breasts so hard she could almost feel his touch.

"But I also love watching my cock disappear in your ass while you fight for breath. I want to see Ranger's cock doing the same thing, and Ben's. Next year, I want to see you put a baby to those gorgeous nipples. And," he continued after licking his lips like the cat sleeping downstairs, "I want to suckle what's left when our baby falls asleep. I want to taste the sweet milk that we made for our baby." He looked at Ranger, and then Ben. "The baby we all made, with the woman we all love."

Florence pressed her lips together, rolling them over her teeth to fight from crying out. Her breasts ached to hold a child there, to feed, and love, a baby.

"I ain't got fancy words," said Ranger gruffly. He hunched his shoulders, picking at the small flakes of pastry that littered the sheet in his lap. He dropped his head back, inhaled, and then let it out. Only then did he meet her eyes.

"It took a bunch of good men to smack my head hard enough to get through this skull. Someday I'll have to thank them." He grimaced. "Or maybe I'll thump them instead." He winced and sighed. "Dammit, Fanny, I love you!" He blew his breath out in relief, and then scrubbed his head with rough fingers. "There. I said it." He nodded, just once. "Don't expect to hear it again."

Though his words were gruff, she knew he would show his love in other ways. He'd care for her, as well as any children or animals that came into his protection. She expected he'd turn up with a dog next, one that someone abandoned. Beaten, bedraggled, and desperate for love.

Just like Ranger.

She sniffed and blinked. Their faces blurred in front of her.

"Oh, shit, Fanny, I didn't make you cry, did I?"

The mixture of love, worry and profanity made her burst out in a laugh. Ranger rolled his eyes.

"Can you make up your mind whether you're going to laugh or cry, woman?" He turned to Ben with a frown. "How do you stand this whole husband thing? Are all women like this, blowing hot and cold from one second to the next?"

"I asked Trace, Simon, Ross, Nevin, and Gillis about women," said Patrick. "They said the tears thing is common, but it gets worse when she's breeding." His eyes lit up. "You got a baby going already?" He turned to Ben. "She been drinking coffee in the mornings?"

Ben tilted his head to the right and down as he thought. "Come to think of it, lately you've only been drinking tea."

"You tired?"

"Patrick," she said patiently, "everyone's tired. We had so much to do before the first snowfall that we've been dropping into bed almost before we finished supper."

"Just in case, I think we'd better keep a pot under the bed. Trace said dry crusts and sips of water before getting out of bed also helps."

"Patrick, I'm not having a baby yet!"

All three men turned to her with expressions that set her heart pumping and pussy throbbing.

"Then we'd better try and rectify that situation," purred Ben.

"That mean we strip her naked and show her how much we love her?" asked Ranger.

"Damn right," hooted Patrick.

"With you two gone, it's been so busy I haven't bedded my wife for days," said Ben. Though he looked at Florence, he spoke to his brothers. "That means I have her first."

"Nope. I haven't been with her for a hell a lot longer than that," said Ranger. He pulled back his lips in a piratical smile. "I'm sure the lady would prefer my attention first."

"That's your own damn fault," said Patrick. He shoved Ranger's shoulder "I know just what the lady wants." He turned his hot leer on her. "And where."

Chapter Forty-Seven

Florence looked away, sure she was going to burst into flames. Embarrassment or lust—which would consume her first?

Patrick stood up and held his hand out. "The lady needs you to give her a riding lesson, Ben. While you were away, Sin gave her lessons using a horse and saddle, but I think it confused her. Maybe if you show her the right position, she'll do better next time."

With Patrick's help, Florence stood on wobbly legs. She looked toward the bed. When she saw the cup on the floor, she turned to Patrick. He winked and nodded. An even greater heat rose up her body. She couldn't talk if she wanted to. Even then she had no idea what to say. Instead, she tried to undo the buttons at her wrist. Her hands shook.

"I'll take care of that," said Patrick.

He took her left hand. Ranger hauled himself upright and gently took her right. She closed her eyes when Ben, grinning like a fool, started on the ones down her front. They took their time, kissing her skin as it appeared.

Her fear diminished and her lust rose as they worked. She remembered Beth telling her the men should satisfy *her*, not the other way around. Her dress dropped to her feet. She heard the sound of other clothing falling. Three men stood before her in a row, lamplight shining on raised cocks.

"Turn around," she said. "I want to see everything about you."

Ben and Patrick flicked their eyes to Ranger. He shrugged and turned his back. The other two then did the same.

She clenched her teeth to stop any show of pity at the sight of

Ranger's back. White lines crisscrossed his back from shoulder to waist. The left side was the worst. She walked up behind him and pressed her naked breasts against the marks. She was too short to reach much higher than his lower back with her nipples, but she raised her hands and traced a few lines.

"After surviving this, you complained about a kitten's tiny claws?"

Ranger turned his head over his shoulder and looked down at her. There was a light in his eyes she hadn't seen since the night he unknowingly opened his heart to her.

"I told you, that cat is a vicious beast. You should call him Killer instead of Caramel."

"Do I want to know about this?" asked Ben of Patrick. Patrick shook his head, rolling his eyes. Ben nodded and turned back to watch Florence.

"No wonder you're so stubborn," she said to Ranger.

"Stubborn?" He snorted. "You're the one suits that name, woman. Finish checking out my ass, because I want you to play with what's on this side of me."

Florence stepped between Ben and Patrick and cupped the cheeks of their behinds. Ben had a nice one, but Patrick, with all his riding, had taut cheeks. She gave in to impulse and smacked their cheeks. Both gasped and turned around, eyes wide. She and Ranger laughed at their expressions until Ben's slow, wicked smile caused her to falter.

"Fair's fair, wife. Turn around."

She shook her head. The three brothers caught each others' eyes. A signal passed, one she didn't understand, but still made her nipples harden.

"Left," said Patrick.

"Right," said Ranger.

"Feet," said Ben.

She turned to run, but a man caught each of her arms and Ben grabbed her ankles. They carried her, kicking and struggling, toward the bed. All three of them laughed at her puny attempts to escape. Her ineffectual struggles heightened her arousal.

She could do whatever she wanted to them, and they would not be hurt. It was a freedom she'd never even known existed, much less that it could feel so wonderful. She screamed and wrestled, fighting every step of the way, exhilarated from the physical release of using her muscles to their full extent.

Patrick and Ranger held her while Ben sat on the bed. They laid her across his lap. His cock nudged her left hip and his knees ended just past her right. Patrick knelt on the floor and held her back down. Ranger did the same for her legs.

She shrieked more from excitement than pain when Ben's hand landed on her bottom. While she struggled, Patrick snuck a hand under her and grasped her breast. Ranger spread her legs and slid a hand between her wet thighs.

She continued to twist, but it was more to increase the feeling than to escape. She got up on her elbows, giving Patrick more room to caress her. Ranger's long fingers curled into her pussy, but didn't go far enough forward to reach her clit.

She stopped moving when Ben put a palm on either side of her crack and spread her cheeks. She looked over her shoulder, twisting to see.

"Look, boys." Ben scratched at her anus. "That ring of pink is a lot thicker than last time I checked. You say she likes it this way?"

"Yep. I kept a couple of fingers in the way so I wouldn't go too deep," replied Patrick. "She slammed back so hard, my balls slapped her pussy."

"Shit, that makes me hard!" The deep groan came from her feet. "Any lard?"

Patrick chuckled. He reached down and picked up a cup. He held it out to Ranger, who took it with a nod.

"You, Mrs. Elliott, are going to get skewered tonight," Ranger growled ominously as he met her eyes. "Keep her open, Ben."

She gulped at the intense look on Ranger's face. He knew how much she loved being pushed beyond what she'd been taught was acceptable. His side of the line had so much more pleasure waiting.

Ranger scooped some lard on his thick finger and pressed into her, just past her tight ring. He leered at her as he played with her pussy with his left hand while his right finger pulsed in her bottom. She couldn't keep back the groan.

"You said something about our wife needing a riding lesson," said Ben.

"I figured she might ride you, while Ranger rides her ass," said Patrick.

"Shit, yeah!"

Florence groaned as Ranger plunged his finger deep in her, twisting it to increase sensation.

Ben turned to Patrick. "What'll you do to keep from being bored?"

"I thought the lady might like to keep her hands and mouth busy with my cock until there's room somewhere else."

"What does the lady think?"

Florence turned her head to answer Ben. He massaged her cheeks as Ranger kept up his delicious in-and-out rhythm.

"The lady thinks it's about time someone met her needs."

Ranger pulled out. Patrick lifted her off Ben. He centered himself on the bed, cock pointing up like the mast of a ship. Patrick set her down astride his hips. His cock rubbed against the crack of her bottom, all slippery from Ranger's finger.

Ben looked up at her with an expression that caught her heart. She saw love and affirmation, encouragement and approval for her acceptance of his brothers. He looked to Patrick and Ranger, and nodded.

"Anytime you're ready, sweetheart, climb on board."

He inhaled a gasp when she gripped his cock. She lifted herself over him, tilted, and guided him inside. The tip of his hard cock slipped into her wet heat like it was made to be there. She closed her eyes and rose on her knees. She raised her chest and, with her hands on her waist, pulsed, dropping just a bit farther with every downward motion.

Her flesh molded around his cock, filling her as if for the first time. Hands held her hips and guided her to rise and fall, slowly and steadily. She opened her eyes and looked down.

"I love you," said Ben. He smiled up at her. "I feel like nothing outside this room exists. It's almost as good as when I hold you in my arms while our hearts begin to slow."

"That's not going to be for a while," she replied.

She leaned forward, setting her palms on either side of his chest. She tilted her bottom high, changing angles to bring her clit into contact with his pubic bone. She groaned and dragged herself over him. The friction felt so good.

She tensed when Ranger settled behind her. His big hands caressed her from waist to knees, paying particular attention to her bottom. She shivered when she caught her clit just right. A sharp nip to her back right cheek made her sit up. Ranger winked and kissed the spot.

Ben took the opportunity to put both hands on her breasts. He fondled her, stroking and kneading with his fingers. He brushed his palms against her nipples, dragging them sideways. He slid his hands around her back and pulled her forward. She went along, bending over to kiss him.

His kiss, as always, was sweet. But this time there was a bit more depth to it. She relaxed into his kiss, letting him set the pace. She clenched his jerking cock in her pussy and ground her nipples against his chest.

When she came up for air, Patrick took over the kiss. Ranger inserted more fingers in her bottom. Though Ben filled her pussy, she was leaning forward enough that she still had room for Ranger's fingers. He pulsed and twisted, adding another finger while she continued her kiss with Patrick.

Ben's cock throbbed inside her, and Ranger's fingers filled her bottom. Patrick moved to the side and offered his cock. She grasped it with her right hand and brought him to her mouth. She licked his saltiness off, but Ranger's hands tugging on her hips made her pull away from Patrick.

"Up on your knees."

Ranger's deep voice was rough. She turned her head to see his eyes were aimed at her bottom, unwavering and eager. She lifted herself up, letting his thick cock slide almost out. She needed sensation. Lots of it.

Three men, all wanting her at the same time, coiled her arousal even higher. She bent forward like a wild vixen, offering Ranger her bottom. He groaned and pulled her even farther back.

A finger rimmed her hole, making her relax, and then Ranger's cock took its place. She pushed out, puffing to open herself for him. Ben's cock was just inside her pussy, there but not in the way, as Ranger relentlessly pulsed his way into her.

"You all right?"

She opened her eyes to find Patrick's concerned ones looking in. She nodded, and pressed back against Ranger's cock. He groaned, even louder, and she suddenly couldn't go any deeper.

"Hold there for a moment and let your body stretch," said Patrick. He reached between her body and Ben's and found her clit. The added contact made her want more. She leaned forward and, as Ranger pulled out, she sank back onto Ben's cock.

It took her a while to get a rhythm, but it soon took over her world. She moved slowly, up and down. At one point she grabbed Patrick's cock and pulled him into her mouth. He moved with her, up and down, forward and back, before pulling out and paying attention to her breasts.

She dropped her head back and let her body take over, demanding what it needed from her men. Ranger suddenly shuddered and filled her with his seed. He gasped and sank back. Ben took advantage of the freedom and encouraged her to speed up until she was slamming herself down on him. She keened as the spiral of need tightened ever more, until suddenly it snapped and she exploded.

THE END

WWW.REECEBUTLER.NET

ABOUT THE AUTHOR

I'm of medium height, medium build, and I sit in an office in front of a computer for my day job. To be honest, I'm rather boring. It's usually the characters in my head who have adventures.

But my writing gives me an excuse to do interesting things as research. To better understand what happens on a cattle ranch, I spent June of 2011 visiting a series of Montana fifth-generation ranches.

During this working ranch vacation I helped gather cattle on horseback for brandings, sorted sheep for market, pushed cattle to new pastures while riding an ATV, and had numerous adventures.

I fell in love with Montana's wide blue skies and wonderful people. I came home with suitcases full of research books, new cowboy boots and hat, a camera full of photos, and ideas to bring to life through my *Bride Train* characters.

If I'm not at my day job, you'll usually find me in front of my keyboard, surrounded by pictures of hunky cowboys, crafting the lives of Tanner's Ford heroes and *Bride Train* heroines.

Also by Reece Butler

Ménage Amour: *Cowboy Sandwich*
Ménage Amour: Sequel to *Cowboy Sandwich*:
Cowboy Double-Decker
Ménage Everlasting: Bride Train 1: *Barefoot Bride for Three*
Ménage Everlasting: Bride Train 2:
A Contract Bride's Triple Surprise
Ménage Everlasting: Bride Train 3: *Compromised Cowgirl*

Available at
BOOKSTRAND.COM

Siren Publishing, Inc.
www.SirenPublishing.com

CPSIA information can be obtained at www.ICGtesting.com
Printed in the USA
LVOW032154231011

251750LV00005B/221/P